I0761841

REALMS

OF

POSSIBILITY

Vol. II

of

THE STEWARD

M.D. IRONZ

Published in the United States of America

Professorial Holdings

professorialholdings@gmail.com

Necromancer

ISBN: 978-1-7337594-3-4

Also by M.D. Ironz

THE STEWARD
Domaine Delafaire
Realms Of Possibility

Standalone
Dire Covenants

CH 1

"MOM! WE'RE HOME!"

Her cat in her arms, Ellen Doyle held the screen door open for the dogs to slip inside.

She motioned for her tired friends to precede her. "Go on in. I'm sure my mom is around somewhere."

They trooped in through the back door and plopped down on the assorted chairs surrounding the kitchen table. The Chow Chows, Max and Sophie, went directly to their dog bowls and began lapping up water. Smokey, the cat, leapt from Ellen's arms to the tabletop and sniffed at its surface.

"I'm in here," answered her mother, Millie, from deep in the pantry. She peered around the pantry door to see Ellen, Hawk, Mark, and *lost and found* Stacy sprawled around the table like happy, yet exhausted, marionettes.

For an instant Millie's breath caught; then she sighed heavily. "Oh, thank goodness y'all are home!"

Ellen could see that relief and gratitude could not quite displace the gulf of worried concern that had haunted her mother through the night. Ellen reached out and pulled her mother into a firm hug.

"It's okay, Mom. We're good; we got Stacy back."

"So I see; come here, you." Millie opened her arms to hug Stacy as well.

Releasing them, Millie nodded to Mark and Hawk.

"Well? Is everyone all right? And just *where* have you people been?" Millie demanded, but then pointed to Smokey. "Ellen, please get your cat off the kitchen table!"

"We're fine, Mom," Ellen assured her mother, grabbing up Smokey and putting him on the floor. "We're just tired, and hungry. Everything is all right. Do you mind if we just rest and have some coffee? That'd be great."

"All right, I'll put on a fresh pot." Her curiosity held temporarily in check, Millie started lining up mugs on the counter. However, she didn't relent.

"You know y'all got some explaining to do. I swear, the next time you stay out all night and don't even bother to call—not that I didn't try to call you, mind you. All I got were recorded messages saying *the cellular customer is outside the coverage area* or some such. No cell coverage? That's not gonna work. I think we'll need to get a landline phone for that cabin, especially if you're going to spend the night there. For all I knew, someone could've been hurt, lying in a ditch or . . . Oh brother, I don't mean to fuss so—don't mind me. I'm just glad everyone's home safe and sound."

"I'm sorry, Mom, but it wasn't possible to call you. Not from where we were, because it wasn't the cabin, remember? Believe me when I say that we are, uh, *very glad* to be back home."

"Oh, you mean that portal thing?" Millie sniffed. "Well, I'm sorry, too. I don't mean to be such a *worrywart;* but I was getting really concerned. If I hadn't heard from you by noon today, I was thinking I might call the sheriff's office—but then what could I say? Nobody there knows about all this stuff, do they?"

"No ma'am," Hawk answered, gently shaking his head. "Nobody else knows. Calling my office could have been a problem for me. I'm glad you didn't."

"Me, too," mumbled Ellen, as she distributed spoons and placed a cream cruet and a sugar bowl on the table.

Millie poured coffee in the mugs and set them on the table. Taking a seat across from her daughter, she wagged a finger. "Okay, young lady, start explaining."

Ellen sipped her coffee. "I'll give you a quick synopsis, and then everyone can help fill in the details, okay?"

Heads around the table bobbed.

"Well, like I told you before we left yesterday afternoon, Stacy was lost—through a portal; although Mark and Hawk had a hard time accepting that, at least until I showed them how it works."

Mark and Hawk shared a glance of chagrin.

"Anyway," Ellen continued, "we went through the portal, too, and tracked Stacy through the Realm of Shadow. We wound up dealing with the Lady Leanan, who's a member of the ruling house of the realm—and a vampire!"

"What—a *vampire?"* Millie echoed incredulously.

Ellen sipped her coffee and nodded. "Yeah, a vampire. I know how that sounds; but it's true! Ask Mark or Hawk."

Mark just nodded sheepishly.

Hawk dropped a hand on Mark's shoulder and said, "Ellen, you left out the part about Mark's encounter with another vampire, Damien. Oh, sorry man, how's that shoulder?"

Mark scowled at the detective and mumbled, "Ah, that's just another story we'll get into later—no big deal."

Ellen spared her cousin a wry smirk. "Yeah, okay, later if you like . . . Anyway, since Lady Leanan was looking for this guy, Salidar, who was apparently with Stacy, we agreed to work together. We stayed overnight in Lady Leanan's castle—yeah, she has a real one."

Hawk added, "Oh yeah, that's where Mark got to deal with another vampire, Lady Sabrina, didn't you?"

Mark winced. "Don't remind me. Her familiar, Gunther, was a problem that you had to deal with, right?"

"A *familiar?* What's that?" Millie asked.

Mark grinned at Hawk. "Something like a vampire's servant, but *obsessed*, right?"

"Uh, yeah." Hawk looked down. "But like you said, that's another story."

"How about you guys let me finish?" Ellen asked.

"Please, go on," Millie urged.

"Right. So, first thing this morning, Lady Leanan's staff told us that a nobleman's patrol had found Stacy near this forest and brought her to the castle; so, we collected her and came home. That's pretty much the headlines."

Millie leaned back in her chair. "So all of you actually were in another realm, or what—another universe? Portals really work? Is this the sort of thing that your doctor's husband, the physicist, was talking about, Ellen?"

Ellen could only shrug. "You mean Zack; and yeah, I think so."

"My word. If that's the headlines, I'm looking forward to the details." Millie looked to Stacy. "What about you, dear, what can you tell us about what happened to you?"

Stacy shook her head. "Not much, I'm afraid. For some reason, there's a lot I can't remember. I mean I remember touching the globe—"

"A transit globe is a portal of sorts," Ellen interjected. "There are different types and sizes. Oh, sorry, go on."

Stacy nodded. "I somehow went through the globe to the Realm of Shadow; but, I didn't know how to get back."

Hand to her throat, Millie asked, "Weren't you scared, being alone and all?"

"Not really, it happened so quickly I didn't have time to be scared; and, I wasn't alone for long. The next thing I knew, Smokey was there. I figured Ellen would come looking for me. I waited; but, it was getting dark. So, I started walking toward this inn I'd seen in the globe. On the way, I met this guy, Salidar, and we walked to the inn. I know we got there; but, I don't remember anything else beyond that, until I was reunited with you guys. I'm sorry."

"Oh, no!" Millie blurted. "He didn't—"

"No, no!" Stacy threw up her hands. "Nothing like that! He was polite—like a gentleman."

"Oh, well then," Millie soothed, "you weren't hurt? This is just some sort of amnesia, do you think?"

"No, I wasn't hurt. Aside from a gap in my memory, I'm fine," Stacy assured them. "However, I'd like to listen to everybody else's details, if the rest of you don't mind."

"Not a problem at all." Mark took her hand in his. "Maybe it'll help you remember."

STACY DID LISTEN TO everything, but remained uncharacteristically quiet. The things attributed to Salidar shocked her; this didn't sound like the man she'd met at all.

He had been responsible for the attack on Ellen? He was a minion of this Lady Diere and may have somehow been involved in Maude's death?

I am so confused. Just what is it that I can't remember?

Mark squeezed her hand, the one he'd been holding below the table. "Hey, are you all right?"

"I'm fine. I-I guess I'm just surprised. I'm gonna need some time to digest all this."

He nodded. "Yeah, I get that. I think we're all going to have to adjust, if you know what I mean."

She did know, or at least she thought she did. But something nagged at her, something important she couldn't remember, at least not at the moment.

AFTER EACH PERSON HAD the opportunity to offer their individual perspective, a contemplative silence settled in the kitchen.

Millie stood, drawing their attention.

"All right, I know we're gonna go over these details some more, but all of you must be hungry," she reasoned. "So, I'm gonna fix you a real breakfast—and there'll be no arguments! Don't worry, we can still talk. Now, go get cleaned up. Breakfast will be ready before you know it."

ELLEN RETURNED TO THE kitchen, enticed by the savory aroma of another pot of freshly brewed coffee.

Mark and Stacy entered together, followed by the young detective.

As Ellen caught his eye, Hawk smiled at her despite the weary sag of his shoulders. In fact, Ellen realized everyone looked more than a little drawn as they took seats at the table.

Well, after all, it had been a long night.

Ellen nudged Millie. "Mom, I'm sure the pets are hungry, too. I'm gonna feed them now."

"Okay, dear. I've set aside some bacon grease; you can add a little to the dry food in the dogs' bowls—oh, a little warm water mixed in wouldn't hurt. You know they like that."

"Yeah, they do. I'll take care of Smokey, too."

"Fine, but keep him off the table."

Ellen prepared the dog food and set the bowls before the Chows. They commenced to wolf their bacon grease enhanced breakfast.

Smokey, apparently impatient to be fed, wound himself around Ellen's ankles while making a guttural *rr-rowwll* sound.

Ellen opened a can of moist cat food, filled his bowl, and placed it on the floor before him.

Of course, Smokey ignored the food and simply stared up at her.

Resigned, Ellen just shrugged. *Now what? Isn't that just like a cat?*

Millie stood with arms akimbo, blew an errant lock of hair from her forehead, and smiled. "What's the matter, Ellen? Did you think he couldn't smell the bacon grease? You'd better put a little on his food, too."

The cat appeared nonplussed, but kept glancing from the women to his bowl.

Ellen rolled her eyes and chuckled. "My mother, the *pets' favorite chef!*"

"Hmm," Millie mused, "I kinda like the sound of that; after all, dogs and cats are people, too."

"Huh?" Ellen blinked. *What? Dogs and cats are people, too—does she mean like the Were?*

"Oh, you know, see?" Millie pointed to Max and Sophie, standing over their now empty bowls, staring up at her and her daughter. "Like little people in fur coats."

Ellen could've sworn the dogs were smiling.

Millie turned to the table, where everyone else was seated. "Okay folks, breakfast is ready; bacon and eggs, and biscuits 'n' gravy on the counter, buffet style. Get a plate and serve yourselves. I know we still have a lot to talk about, but we can do so while we eat. So, dig in."

No one needed to be told twice. Everyone enjoyed the food.

As the telling and re-telling of details wound down, silence settled over the kitchen once more.

Ellen stood and announced, “I’m gonna make some more biscuits. Any takers?”

“Sounds good to me. I’ll make some more coffee,” Mark offered. “You just sit a spell, Aunt Millie. We got this.”

However, Millie couldn’t just *sit a spell* while someone was doing something in her kitchen. She retrieved the cream cruet and refilled it at the counter. As she shut the refrigerator door, a sticky-note fluttered to the floor. She squinted at her own scrawled note.

“Oh Hawk, you need to call your sergeant. He called earlier this morning. Sorry, I forgot; I should’ve told you sooner.”

“Thanks, Miss Millie.” Hawk retrieved his cell phone from his vest. “Whoops, I must’ve turned my phone off. Trey knew I was coming over here to help look for Stacy. I forgot to call him, uh, when I could. So, I guess I’m going to hear it from him, too. Now, if you’d excuse me, I’ll make the call outside.”

Millie leaned over Mark’s shoulder as he prepared to fill the drip coffee filter. “Four scoops are enough for a full carafe; don’t make it too strong. I think all of you are gonna need some sleep, or at least take naps. You didn’t have anything planned for today, did you?”

“Well, I was gonna work on the truck some—”

“Oh, the truck! Mark, that reminds me; Madeline, from the bookstore, is stopping by this afternoon to see me. She’s bringing me a book, and the license plate for the truck, too.”

“Madeline?” Mark asked. “How did she get the plate?”

“Well, the attorney, Mr. Fornier, called late yesterday. He said he’d gotten everything straightened out with the state motor vehicle people. He had the paperwork and the license plate. The truck is now registered to the farm.”

“Oh yeah,” Mark recalled, “that’s what we decided.”

"Right." Millie bobbed her head. "So, Madeline called to tell me she'd found a copy of an out-of-print book on local herbs, and we talked some. Since she was coming to visit anyway, she offered to stop by the lawyer's office to pick up the registration papers and license plate."

"That's great, Aunt Millie." Mark poured cool water into the coffeemaker's reservoir. "I have the truck running pretty well. I'll need to finish up a few little things and then put some miles on it—you know, a kind of *shakedown cruise* to double-check everything."

"Well, Mr. Fornier said that you'll still have to have it inspected, and get that little sticker for the windshield."

"Oh yeah, right," Mark acknowledged.

Hawk returned to the kitchen and pulled Ellen aside.

She dusted some biscuit mix from her hands and wiped her whitened palms on a dish towel as she followed him inquisitively. "What is it, Hawk?"

"I'm gonna have to go in a bit. Trey and I gotta go to New Orleans; it's related to a homicide case."

"Can't you stay for a few minutes, at least? The biscuits will be ready soon."

"Oh, yeah!" He grinned. "I can stay for some more biscuits. In fact, I told Trey that your mom fixed us breakfast; I think he's sorry he wasn't here."

"Well, you could take him some biscuits, you know?" she suggested.

"That's a great idea! Um, and maybe some extras—you know, for the road?"

She offered a wry smile. "Oh, I suppose that could happen."

"Will your mom forgive me if I don't stick around to help with all the dishes?"

"Oh, I think she'll excuse you—just this once," she teased.

The oven buzzer went off; the biscuits were done.

MILLIE HAD LISTENED carefully to everything. There was a lot to digest. She might not show it; but she was almost stunned beyond words.

So much of what she heard was just so unbelievable, but *was it, really?* It was also quite obvious to her that Ellen, Mark, Stacy, and Hawk—*a law enforcement officer, for goodness sakes*—had experienced *something*.

So, until she learned otherwise, Millie decided to believe it—all of it. She intuitively trusted everyone seated at this table, and somehow sensed that there was truth here.

Millie, somewhat prone to sympathetic empathy, watched their faces. She sensed that each person was wrestling with this newly revealed perception of reality. One thing she knew was certain; life as they knew it would be forever viewed differently. She cupped her hands around her coffee mug, its soothing warmth a comfortable reassurance.

Her daughter stood, drawing everyone's attention.

"Listen, I think it would be best," Ellen cautioned, "if we kept this information to ourselves for now. After all, who would believe us?"

Silent nods of mutual agreement confirmed the inherent wisdom of that strategy.

Hawk glanced at his watch and stood.

"Folks, I apologize for having to eat and run, but I have to go to work. Miss Millie, thanks so much for breakfast; it really hit the spot."

"Oh, take some biscuits for the road," Ellen reminded him.

"Yes, take some," Millie echoed. "Ellen made these biscuits, you know. Let me wrap them up for you."

Stacy and Millie smiled at each other as Ellen walked him out.

ON THE FRONT PORCH Hawk paused. "Can I call you when I get back?"

"I'd like that," she smiled.

"Me, too. Listen, be careful. I know you're home now, but be careful anyway."

She continued to smile as she watched him drive away. An unbidden yawn rudely reminded her of just how tired she really was. As she made her way back to the kitchen, she fought another creeping yawn, and lost.

"Mom, I'm really beat," Ellen announced, her energy obviously drained. "Do you mind if I take a nap?"

"No problem, sweetie." Millie looked up from the sink and said soothingly, "In fact, why don't you all lie down for a little while. I'm about done here; I'll just let the dishwasher finish its cycle. Go on now—go take your naps. I have to collect some herbs for Madeline; so, I'll be in the garden if you need me."

Mark led the way upstairs as Ellen and Stacy followed. Mark entered his room and nodded as he closed the door.

At the door to her room, Stacy started to say something to Ellen, but hesitated.

Ellen looked at her confused friend. "What is it?"

"I don't know . . . It's like I have something to tell you; but, I can't remember what. I'm sorry. I know that doesn't make any sense. Maybe I'm just tired." Stacy shook her head in frustration.

Ellen yawned once more. "Well, I know *I'm* tired. Look, just get some sleep; we can talk later. I'm exhausted; I've just got to lie down."

Stacy gave her a sad smile, and went into her room.

Within ten minutes, everyone on the second floor was fast asleep.

HAWK DROVE HOME FOR a shower and change of clothes before going into his office. As fate would have it, the home phone rang just as he stepped out of the shower. He debated letting the answering machine catch the call; but, the possibility that it might be Ellen, and that something could be wrong, sent him running for the phone, a towel hastily wrapped around his waist.

A quick glance at the caller ID indicated that Trey was calling, not Ellen. He was strangely relieved and a little disappointed—an unsettling emotional dichotomy, he realized as he picked up the phone.

"Hello Trey, you know you just got me out of the shower! Now I'm drippin' all over the floor. What's up?"

"Whoa, that's a little too much information there, ol' buddy! Hey, the missing girl, Stacy, you're sure she's all right? No medical attention needed?"

"Yeah, she's okay—long story. I'll tell you later."

"Okay, did you get any sleep?"

"Nah, but I'll be all right. Had a really good breakfast though—too bad you missed it."

"Arrgh! Stop rubbin' it in! Listen, don't bother coming in to the office. I'm on my way to your place to pick you up. I'm riding with Sgt. Melancon in one of the CSI units; we'll be there in about twenty minutes. Pack for two days on the road. We have to be in New Orleans for a case briefing by three o'clock."

"Okay, I'll be ready. Can you give me some idea what's going on?" Hawk's curiosity was growing.

"Not over an unsecured line," cautioned Trey. "Just sit tight. We'll talk on the road."

TRUE TO HIS WORD, WITHIN twenty minutes the unmarked dark blue SUV pulled up before Hawk's home. Trey got out of the back seat and started up the porch steps.

Before the sergeant could reach the door, Hawk stepped out onto the porch, a stuffed gym bag in one hand and holding out a bag of biscuits in the other.

"Here, saved you these from breakfast. Told you I'd be ready. Just let me lock up."

"Oh man, smells good! Let's roll! We've got just enough time to make the briefing. Jim Franklin asked to see us there."

Hawk grunted in response as he secured the door.

CSI Tech Cassie Spenser was at the wheel of the SUV; her boss, Sgt. Melancon, was riding shotgun. Trey and Hawk settled into the back seat as Cassie carefully negotiated the long driveway.

Hawk nudged the CSI sergeant on the shoulder and handed him a sealed plastic evidence bag bearing a case number and some abbreviated notations.

Mel held it up to better see a small glass vial that held a sickly fluid of oily dull colors; a loop of evidence tape secured the cap on the vial. He glanced at the young detective for an explanation.

"Do us a favor, please, Mel; that needs to be analyzed. I suspect we've seen something like this before," Hawk explained. "It resembles the substance we found in the syringe in the Doyle case. I have a hunch it's related."

"No problem," Mel assured him. "I assume this is the Doyle case number? It may have to wait though, until we're through with whatever may have to be processed from this search warrant in New Orleans."

"Where'd you get it, Hawk?" Trey asked, as he offered the bag of biscuits to Mel and Cassie.

"From a *reluctant* source," responded Hawk cryptically. "I'll tell you about it later. For now, just bring me up to speed. What search warrant?"

Trey bit into a biscuit, and made his partner wait until he'd swallowed. "Damn, these are good! Okay, remember Suzi Origami?"

"Yeah, the one homicide victim we identified at the crime scene on the rooftop of the casino garage. We have yet to identify the other victim, who was dismembered on a lower floor." Hawk twisted in his seat. "We still don't have that ID, right?"

"Not yet, she's still a *Jane Doe*," Trey acknowledged. "Regarding Suzi, the FAST squad located her apartment in New Orleans and notified us. It was in the name of a holding company that they knew Papa George had a hidden interest in, a silent partner thing—another link to Papa George. We filed an affidavit for a search warrant. Anyway, that's one of our destinations. Mel and Cassie will drop us off at the Federal Building for our briefing; then, they'll go on to the search site."

"The FAST squad? But how—" Hawk began.

"To make a long story short," Trey interrupted, licking a trace of flour off a finger. "The sheriff called the U.S. Marshal in Shreveport to formally request their assistance in our homicide case, so the FAST unit based in New Orleans could locate and secure Suzi's residence. Pursuant to the search warrant, they made entry and initiated a cursory search, for officer safety of course. Now they hold the scene for us; Mel and Cassie will conduct a more comprehensive search."

"Wait a minute, Sarge," interrupted Cassie. "Mmm, good biscuits, by the way. I grew up in New Orleans, and I know they have a U.S. Marshal there. Why call the one in Shreveport?"

Trey rummaged in the bag for another biscuit. "Jurisdictional protocols—it's a different federal court district, a different U.S. Marshal's primary jurisdiction. Chantilly Parish is in the Western District of Louisiana, and Shreveport is the headquarters office. The New Orleans area is the Eastern District; and the Baton Rouge area is Middle District. Each district has its own federal district courts and judges; each has a U.S. Attorney, and a U.S. Marshal."

"Okay, Sarge, I remember all that; we got it in the academy," Cassie said. "But that doesn't explain why the sheriff called Shreveport instead of New Orleans, or am I missing something?"

Trey grinned. "Yep, the protocol of politics. Look, Suzi Origami's body was found at the casino in Chantilly Parish, so the original homicide case is our jurisdiction, which is within the Western District. The proper protocol is to make the request of *that* U.S. Marshal. Now the Marshals Service has offices all over the place, even overseas, so asking for help from one office opens the doors to *all* of their resources."

"Really, they're that cooperative?" Cassie asked.

"Oh yeah, they're very cooperative, especially when working with state and local departments. See, most of the Deputy U.S. Marshals are former local and state cops, and/or military. So, that's a lot of prior personal experience at municipal, state, and international levels. They can easily understand what we have to deal with, see? So, whenever we ask for help, they never say *no*.

"And that brings me back to my original point; we seek assistance through the Western District of Louisiana and we get it wherever we need it, in this case, within the Eastern or Middle Districts of Louisiana, okay?"

"Yeah, okay," replied Cassie. "So, we're headed to New Orleans, and the way has been smoothed for us. What about the NOPD? Don't they have a pretty good CSI operation as well?"

"Indeed they do," agreed Sgt Melancon, "and they'll be on the scene to assist, but it's *our* search warrant. So, we'll be taking immediate custody of any recovered evidence relating to our homicide. Do you know why?"

"Um, because that would minimize the chain of custody of the evidence, especially since the FAST guys, acting on our behalf, have already initiated the search?" Cassie offered.

"Hmm," observed Trey dryly, "Sgt. Melancon, trained well your apprentice, you have."

“Oh no,” groaned Hawk, “not the *wise old master bit* again!”

When the laughter subsided, Trey continued. “So anyway, when the FAST unit did the initial cursory search, they found computers; a server, a PC, and a laptop. There were lots of removable data storage media, to include flash drives. All appear to be heavily encrypted. At our request, the FAST guys called in their regional IT wizard to have a quick crack at decrypting the drives and storage discs on the scene. They could have sent the stuff to their lab; but this was quicker. Now our CSI team is en route to assume custody and keep the chain to a reasonable minimum.”

“Oh yeah, I get it,” she acknowledged, “the chain of custody, again.”

“Right! So, Cassie, that’s why Hawk and I will attend the briefing this afternoon. We’ll join you and Mel later on the scene of your more comprehensive search of Suzi’s apartment.”

Hawk rubbed his chin and looked askance at Trey. “They found something, didn’t they? Something on the drives or discs? Something time sensitive? That’s why the rush on this briefing, right?”

That sounded more like a statement than a question.

“I would think so,” agreed Trey, “especially since some people from OCDETF have been invited as well. I heard there’s a lead that’s been developed near Lafayette.”

They rode in silence for a moment, and then Cassie asked, “I know that FAST is the Fugitive Apprehension Strike Team, but OCDETF? That’s the Organized Crime Drug Enforcement Task Force, right? What could they have to do with our homicide case?”

Trey shrugged. “We’ll find out for sure at the briefing; for now we can only speculate. See, we’re pretty sure that Suzi did contract *wet work* for George Papadolis, AKA *Papa George*; he’s been an OCDETF target for some time. They’ve been trying to build a RICO case—you know, Racketeer Influenced and Corrupt Organization case, against him and his operations; but, they could never get enough firm evidence for an indictment. There was a cooperating individual who was supposed to roll over on Papa George, but he turned up dead, Fenton Brewster."

Hawk remained quiet and stared out the window.

Cassie suddenly recognized the name. "Oh yeah! The prisoner who committed suicide—jumped from the roof of the jail, right?"

"Suicide?" Trey grunted. "Maybe—it's not conclusive, as far as I know. Jones and Barrows have that case. The last I heard they couldn't find Brewster's last visitor, some attorney named Salidar. I've never heard of him. So, let's just say that some of us have our doubts."

Hawk just looked at Trey and nodded. He and Trey would have to have a long talk at some point; but, this was neither the time nor the place.

As they drove on, other cases became topics of discussion.

However, all the while, gnawing away in his gut was the question that was beginning to haunt Hawk. How could he make Trey understand what he now knew to be the truth?

Papa George had arranged for Brewster to be murdered; and, he used a vampire to do it!

Hell, Lady Leanan had openly confessed to the murder and clearly implicated Papa George.

And what about this character, Salidar?

This was not going to be easy, not at all.

ELLEN ROCKED GENTLY as the cool breeze wafted the scent of jasmine across the broad expanse of the front porch. The colors of the garden seemed more vibrant, more intense, with an almost dreamlike liquidity.

"Indeed . . . Never underestimate the power of dreams, my dear."

Ellen snapped her head to the right and beheld a youthful Maude occupying the other rocking chair. Her great aunt appeared exactly as she'd been depicted in the old photograph, her hair piled artfully upon her head, and attired in a stiff high-necked dress, the height of fashion over a century ago.

Maude smiled as amusement danced in her eyes. The dogs lay asleep at her feet and Smokey lolled lazily in her lap, thoroughly enjoying a belly scratch.

"Aunt Maude? Am I dreaming?" Ellen managed to ask.

"Well, I certainly hope so, my dear," responded Maude wryly, *"because I'm not."*

"But what? How? I mean, uh, why?" Ellen stammered.

Maude put Smokey down upon the planks of the porch and started brushing cat hair from her lap. *"Oh Smokey, will you ever stop shedding? I haven't worn this dress in ages, and just look what you've done to it. Oh well, I guess I shouldn't complain."*

"Aunt Maude, please," Ellen insisted, *"I'd appreciate some answers."*

"Oh, very well, Ellen," Maude teased, *"after all, it is your dream."*

"Uh, right . . . but this is different; it's like we're really speaking, not just thinking at one another. This is like the old photograph, isn't it? So, please tell me what's happening here."

"That's better—take charge," Maude acknowledged. *"See? You've already realized you've dreamt yourself into the photograph. This dream is a product of your subconscious to a great extent, so you have a degree of control—but you must keep your focus. Otherwise, I cannot access your mind on this plane; we'll drift apart. I'm afraid that's the best way I can describe it."*

"I think I understand," Ellen responded. She firmed her concentration. *"Why didn't you tell me before that we can communicate, or seem to really speak, in dreams?"*

Maude pursed her lips, tilted her head to one side, and said simply, *"You weren't strong enough; nor was I allowed to share that knowledge with you then. Remember that I told you there were certain rules? That there were things I wanted to tell you, but I couldn't—even if I tried? Well, that hasn't really changed that much. Basically, I cannot tell you anything that you don't discover or deduce on your own. But once you do, we can discuss it."*

"So, you're still in that place, and still constrained by those rules? But if I can figure something out, like how I learned to use the Grand Portal, then we can openly discuss it?"

"Yes, exactly!" Maude beamed. *"And what else?"*

"Um," stalled Ellen for only a moment, *"we can communicate within dreams, or at least to the extent that I can exercise some sort of control? Which would mean that I don't have to suffer another near-death experience in order to visit with you? Or like in that other place?"*

"Very good! Now you need to listen. You have done very well, so far; but your journey is only beginning. You have used the spectacles and the journal well; however, you haven't fully appreciated the capabilities of the spectacles . . . Damn! I'm afraid that is all I can say in regard to them."

Ellen started to object, but stopped as Maude raised a cautionary finger.

"Please listen. You have not yet begun to record your own chronicle as Steward in the journal; and the instructions were quite clear. Just begin; blank pages will be provided for your use. You have already surmised that the journal is far more than it appears to be. You are correct; but you will have to discover more in that regard on your own. You need to keep reading, as you already know."

Ellen sat in deep thought and then asked, *"May we speak of other things I may have discovered?"*

"Of course," agreed Maude, *"provided you maintain your focus."*

"I have learned of Salidar—I don't know if that's his true name—who may have been involved in your death. He may have actually killed you! We now know he tried to kill me. He's some sort of minion of Lady Diere—an elf? Who may have also been involved in your death? And I have met Lady Leanan—a

vampire? She was your friend, or so she claims. I have found a number of photographs in which the same three women are shown. I think that those three are you, Leanan, and Diere? Which means that, at one time, all three of you were friends? What can you tell me about all of this?"

"My goodness," exclaimed Maude. *"I am impressed. I can tell you a considerable amount of information. Please, let me answer your questions in reverse order."*

"That's fine," Ellen acknowledged. *"Just tell me everything you can."*

"Trust that I will, child." Maude sighed. *"It is true that Diere, Leanan, and I were friends, for a very long time. Some time ago, Diere and I had a rather strong disagreement; I can't go into the details. Suffice to say, it effectively ended our friendship. Leanan and I just sort of drifted apart. She was increasingly called upon to take a more active role in the administration of her realm, and I was busy with the management of my own business interests; some of which you might find, um, interesting, and perhaps even helpful.*

"Now as for Salidar, he can be dangerous, sometimes more so to himself. You are correct that it would be to your advantage to learn his true name. I would be wary of trusting him; he did attempt to do you harm."

Maude paused for a moment as a pained expression drifted across her face.

"In truth, Salidar did not kill me. This is very difficult for me. He was present when I died. I was seriously weakened; and, I willed myself through my passing. In a sense, I took my own life. However, that act has a price—although I felt it was the best option at that moment. I knew the Grand Portal could not be allowed to fall into the wrong hands. As to whether or not Lady Diere had a hand in my debilitation, I do not know for certain."

"This price," Ellen asked softly, *"would that be your confinement to that grey place in which I saw you?"*

"Alas, that is true, child." Maude sighed. *"And there I remain, for some unknown time. I know no more than that."*

"I'm so sorry, Aunt Maude. I wish there was something I could do."

"There is, my dear." Maude smiled. *"You can prepare to wake up. You are about to have a visitor, and a very important conversation."*

"Wait, don't go! I have so many more questions! How will I contact you again? I don't know how to control a dream—I don't even know how I'm doing it now! Uh, I am doing it now, right?"

Maude's bright laugh sparkled on the breeze and drew a pained smile from Ellen.

"Of course you are, sweetheart. You already know how—it's all in your subconscious. Besides, trying too hard to analyze some things often leads to paralysis by analysis; you won't get anything accomplished, other than more convoluted confusion. Don't worry; you'll manage."

Ellen's dream began to lose its cohesion as her focus wavered. Maude's image faded into the blur of diminished colors that swirled in from the periphery of Ellen's mind and dwindled to a softly diffused glow.

ADRIFT BETWEEN MOMENTS, Ellen slipped into that semi-sleepy state where one can almost be aware of the surrounding environment, that comfortable sense of being secure in one's own room, teetering on the cusp of consciousness, but just as likely to slip back into the arms of Morpheus, a pleasant place to float indeed.

However, the muffled tapping on her door would tip the delicate scale of awareness in favor of the afternoon's reality.

Stacy poked her head in the room and called out in a hoarse stage whisper, "Ellen, are you awake? We really have to talk. Can I come in? Are you awake?"

Rolling her face into her pillow, Ellen mumbled, "I am *now*."

She realized that she remembered every aspect of her dream, and her conversation with Maude. Was Stacy her expected visitor? Were the two of them about to have a very important conversation? Ellen rolled over, propped herself up on her elbows, and saw Stacy standing anxiously in the doorway.

"Yeah, I'm awake . . . Come in."

Now resigned to the visit, Ellen tugged at a window shade, admitting the afternoon light.

Stacy closed the door, plopped down on the bed, and tucked her legs under her. Her expression serious, she leaned earnestly forward and just blurted out her news.

"Ellen! I have my memory back—all of it! I have so much to tell you; but I can only tell *you*. So, just bear with me, okay?"

"Uh, okay, fine. What is it?"

"First, I have to tell you I bear the greetings of the Guildmaster of Storm Haven, and that you are cordially invited to visit him in that realm. He asks that you be discreet and selective in whom you might elect to share this information because the very existence of this realm is a closely held secret. He has provided me with a token that you may use, in your capacity as Steward, to find Storm Haven. Only *you* may use it. It will work only once."

Ellen gaped as Stacy held out her hand. Upon her palm a dark green gem flashed in a slanting sunbeam.

Stacy resumed her soliloquy, almost as if it were memorized.

"You are to hold this emerald tightly as you cast a generic transit spell; the summoned globe will take you to Storm Haven. The gem contains an enchantment that is spent upon a single use. You are to bring it with you to Storm Haven."

Ellen realized she was staring open-mouthed at her friend.

"*Whoa!*" exclaimed an awestruck Stacy. "I just heard myself recite all that; but I wasn't thinking any of it. It must have been the spell. Here, take this."

"Spell? What spell?" Ellen asked as she held the emerald up to the sunlight. A splash of reflected green light danced brightly upon the wall.

"The spell the Guildmaster arranged so that I couldn't tell *anyone but you* about Storm Haven, his invitation, or what really happened to me. Don't you remember at that castle when that kind old man—Jalash-el, I think, said I was under a *forget-spell,* and tried to help?"

Ellen did remember; she was already thinking about the implications. Maude had indicated that this was very important; she wanted to know more.

"Yes, I remember. But tell me what happened to *you.*"

"Okay, but please understand that I didn't know anything about Salidar—none of that stuff you all talked about this morning. That was all news to me; and kinda freaked me out. Let me start at the beginning."

Ellen could only nod.

Stacy settled into a more comfortable cross-legged position and straightened her back. Taking a deep breath, she commenced to give Ellen a comprehensive account of her experiences since accidentally transiting into the Realm of Shadow.

Ellen listened carefully and digested the information.

It was evident that Stacy was experiencing some degree of ambivalence in regard to Salidar. She had saved his life, and he hers, or so it appeared. But she had been quite shaken to hear of his involvement in the attempt upon Ellen's life, and the strong suspicion of his involvement in Maude's demise.

Her memories now intact, Stacy explained how the Guildmaster had shed more light on those instances, as he understood them. However, he had made no excuses for Salidar; if anything, he seemed shamed by Salidar's actions.

"By the way, and I think this is important," Stacy said solemnly, "Salidar's *true name* is *Grimrald.* I heard him called that; *and* he used that name when we arrived at Storm Haven. I don't think he was exactly thrilled that he had to do it in front of me. I learned from the Guildmaster that the use of one's true name is required to enter Storm Haven."

"*Grimrald?* Thank you, I have a feeling that I'm better off knowing that." Ellen swung her legs off the bed and stretched. "Mmmph. What else did you learn?"

"Lots!" Stacy grinned. "Just listen!"

The Guildmaster had explained a great deal more to Stacy, to include the very existence and importance of Storm Haven, and perhaps more importantly, how Maude had been involved in its evolution.

The fact that the Guildmaster and Maude had been friends was sufficient for Ellen to decide that this invitation would not be ignored.

"I'm sorry I couldn't tell you all of this sooner," Stacy said as her tale wound to a close. "I realize now that the forget-spell would not allow it until I was alone with you. But now the spell is gone, dissipated or something, and I can remember everything. Oh yeah, the Guildmaster said that, if necessary, you could *'confide in those you must; but only those you trust'*. He was very security conscious. So, are you going to go?"

Ellen smiled at Stacy's eagerness. "I probably will go. I'd certainly like to get some more answers."

"Can I go with you? I asked the Guildmaster, too. He said that it was up to you. So, can I?"

Tongue firmly in cheek, Ellen teased, "Well, I don't know. Hmm, it could be dangerous. On the other hand, I could probably use a guide, someone who has already been there, and knows the right people. Of course, I'm not sure *when* we'd go."

Stacy beamed; but then her face clouded. "Don't wait too long! Your mother and I fly back to Los Angeles on Friday; this is almost Tuesday already!"

"It's only late Monday afternoon, silly!" Ellen teased; but, her expression turned pensive. "You know, I'd almost forgotten that you all would have to go back. I think Mark was planning to leave next Monday. I'll need to talk to him. In fact, I think we should all talk about this. We know we can trust one another, especially after what we've been through."

"Well, we could go to Storm Haven tomorrow, or Thursday at the latest, but I don't think we can change our flight reservations now without incurring a penalty fee."

"No, not tomorrow, but soon," Ellen assured her. "I need to wind down, figure some things out. Don't worry; you and my mom can make your flight on Friday. If we go to Storm Haven, it'll probably be on Thursday. Besides, I'll need to talk to Hawk; he had to go out of town for a couple of days, something to do with a case."

"Well, can't you call him? I mean, he's got his cell phone with him, right? I'm sure you can reach him before we actually go." Stacy bounded up from the bed, stretched her stiff legs, and groaned, "Mmmph, let's go downstairs. I'm hungry again; and I think Madeline is here."

"Okay," agreed Ellen. "That reminds me; I want to go through some of those old photographs again. I think I now know who some of those people are."

THEY FOUND MADELINE and Millie in the kitchen, and a pot of tea brewing. As if by magic, Millie produced a plateful of scones and oatmeal-raisin-chocolate chip cookies. One whiff of the warm cookies and both Ellen and Stacy decided to forgo the tea in lieu of cold milk. Millie and Madeline just chuckled and opted for the tea and scones.

"Where's Mark?" asked Madeline. "I brought that license plate and registration paperwork for him."

"Still in his room, I imagine," Millie offered.

Stacy and Ellen nodded in agreement, each with a mouthful of cookie.

"Let's just let him sleep. We'll wake him for supper," Millie added with finality.

"Oh, I just remembered—I found some pictures y'all should see." Ellen pushed away from the table. "I'll be right back."

She retrieved the old photograph albums and brought them into the kitchen. She began sorting through them. Whenever she found a picture she felt would be of interest, she set it aside, making certain to note where it belonged in which album.

Madeline leaned over her shoulder at one point and remarked casually as she sipped her tea. "Oh, I remember that picture! That's Maude, Dee Dee, and Leigh Ann at Jackson Square. Maude said that they partied all night. It was a jazz festival or something."

Ellen was dumbfounded; she could only stare at Madeline. Shaking off the initial shock, she sputtered a question. "Wh-what? You recognize these women? You know them?"

"Well, of course," Madeline responded, somewhat amused, and pointed to each person in the picture. "This is your Aunt Maude, and these are her friends, Dee Dee and Leigh Ann. Funny, I don't think I ever knew their last names. They—I mean all three of them—used to go to New Orleans a lot; they liked the nightlife, especially some of the jazz clubs. This picture was taken sometime in the late sixties, or maybe the seventies, I'm not certain. But I haven't seen Dee Dee or Leigh Ann in ages, probably since before you were born. They didn't live around here. I don't think I ever really knew where they lived. For some reason, I thought Leigh Ann had a place somewhere up near Shreveport, but I never really knew. Sometimes Maude would bring them by the bookstore in the evenings; they were interested in the really old books. Some nights they'd browse until we closed."

Stacy and Millie had come to stand over Ellen's other shoulder to better view the photograph.

Ellen looked up, and noted Stacy's focused concentration. However, Millie's complexion had gone ashen; her hands began a slight tremor that set her teacup to rattling.

"Mom, are you all right? What's wrong? Do you feel sick?"

As Stacy and Ellen helped her mother into a chair, Madeline locked eyes with Millie.

"Oh my, you can't think . . . Oh, m-my," Madeline stuttered as she sought a chair for herself, never taking her eyes off Millie.

It took Ellen only a moment to discern the meaning of this development. Kneeling before her mother, Ellen gently took the cup and saucer from her trembling hands. Clasping her mother's stiff fingers soothingly, she looked deep into Millie's wide eyes.

"Mom, you told Madeline, didn't you?"

The kitchen grew very quiet.

Millie's shock was fading; her lower lip began to tremble as she nodded guiltily. Ellen reached out and gently stroked her mother's cheek. A sad smile born of disappointment, yet softened by a sense of compassion, stole across Ellen's face.

"Ellen, please don't be angry with your mother," Madeline urged. "I pestered her to tell me what was bothering her. She's just worried for your welfare. It's really my fault; I was very insistent. And in retrospect, it does seem to answer some questions that Maude would always seem to ignore or deflect."

"Madeline, I'm not upset; nor am I angry," Ellen assured her, rising to her feet. "I probably would have eventually told you everything anyway, because we are certainly going to need to do some research and you are the first person who comes to mind. But we must be discreet, as I'm sure you can understand."

"Of course, my dear," said Madeline, visibly relieved. "I have quite extensive resources in the folklore genre; some of those books are centuries old. And of course I network with other booksellers and librarians via the internet. So, I'm happy to be of service."

"Ellen," Millie began, "I'm so sorry; I wasn't thinking. I should have discussed it with you first; I realize that now. But I trust Madeline; and, I'm sure you do, too. I just know she'll be an asset to you in this—*whatever* it is."

"Relax, Mom. Everything is going to be fine. Now let me ask you," Ellen held the photograph before her mother, "did you ever meet this *Dee Dee* or *Leigh Ann*?"

Millie just shook her head. "I'm not really sure, um, not that I remember. But I may have met Dee Dee once. She looks a little familiar, but not Leigh Ann, I don't think. Do you think that these people are really Lady Diere and Lady Leanan?"

Stacy mused aloud, "So, Dee Dee is really *Diere—a Dark Elf,* and Leigh Ann is really *Leanan—a vampire*?"

"Well," offered Ellen, "it does fit phonetically; and, I—or rather *we*—now know that at one time the three women were friends. I've spent some time with Lady Leanan; this certainly looks like her—exactly like her. She admitted to me that they—she and Maude, were friends."

"Okay," declared Stacy, "this is getting pretty creepy!"

Ellen merely shrugged. "We also know that Diere and Leanan can travel between realms, just like Maude did as Steward. There are other photographs depicting the three of them together."

"So," observed Stacy, "there's evidence that they were friends, and that they were frequently *here,* in this realm. But the question remains; what really happened to break up this friendship?"

"What indeed?" echoed Ellen.

CH 2

SALIDAR COOLED HIS heels in a dimly lit, yet reasonably comfortable, windowless chamber to await his audience with Lady Diere. He was becoming increasingly worried.

From his perspective, he had fully complied with her instructions to deliver the scroll to Boltar, the innkeeper of the Crying Cup. Granted, he did not know where Padraic the Rogue was at the moment; but, he had discovered where Padraic would be in about a week.

An insidious worm of doubt began to twist in his gut; she had clearly ordered him to find the Rogue. He could only hope that learning of Padraic's *future* location would satisfy her.

Resigned, Salidar knew he had no choice but to play the hand he'd been dealt. He rocked back, balancing the simple chair teetering on its rear feet, and pondered his present circumstances. His only real concern, at least for the moment, was that he was unsure of what Lady Diere knew of his activities since they had last met. If, by any chance, she had learned exactly *where* he had been and with *whom*, this impending audience would not go well—not well, at all.

To his mind, it would be better if Lady Diere did not come to learn about the *wood nymph*, the Lady Stacy. He found himself uncharacteristically concerned for her welfare.

After they had narrowly escaped capture at the Crying Cup and transited to Storm Haven, they had been separated. He realized now that he should have expected no less.

Salidar had spent long sessions with the senior mage, Gallenius, giving him detailed reports of his recent activities in the service of the Lady Diere.

Lady Stacy and her *damned cat* had been closeted with the Guildmaster. Salidar was not then overly concerned for her safety—that should not be an issue within Storm Haven—but he nonetheless emphasized to Gallenius that she was to be shown every courtesy. After all, she *had* saved his life. He wasn't too sure about her cat, so he made no comment about the feline. He did not see Stacy again during the entire three days he spent in Storm Haven. Gallenius discouraged and deflected any questions about her.

Despite his disinclination—and subsequent procrastination—Salidar knew he had to return to Lady Diere. So, on the afternoon of the third day, he bid farewell to the Guildmaster and reluctantly left the safety of Storm Haven.

He transited to the Realm of the Dark Elves and made his way to Castle Diere without incident, arriving just before sunset.

Guards immediately took him to this small windowless room to await the Lady Diere's pleasure. The stout door closed with a *click* of the lock. He tried the door; as suspected, he was locked in.

Was that really necessary?

His accommodations were surprisingly sparse for the otherwise opulent castle. The only furnishings, a pair of simple wooden chairs tucked under the lip of a small table, an old yet ornate daybed, and a cold hearth, were barely illuminated by a set of wall sconces and a candelabrum.

He realized of course that she would make him wait; he had come to expect it. He sighed, thinking that in some ways she was almost predictable—*almost*. It would be most unwise to make any assumptions in her regard. She was not referred to, in secret of course, as the *Mad Elf* without reason.

Why had the silent elfin guards whisked him away so quickly to this secluded chamber? It was almost as if he was not to be seen in the castle. Or, was it to prevent him from observing? Was he not supposed to see something?

Rocking back and forth on the heels of the teetering chair, he smiled knavishly. His curiosity was now aroused; he considered doing a little unauthorized exploring—given the right opportunity, of course. He nudged his pack with the toe of his boot and chuckled; his lock-picking tools were well hidden within the thick seams of the leather.

He surmised that he could leave this room anytime it suited his fancy.

A LITTLE LATER, THE metallic *click* of the door unlocking snapped him from his reverie.

He fumbled in righting the chair, nearly losing his balance, and quickly stood as Lady Diere stepped into the room, shimmering in a sleek gown of pale amethyst trimmed in delicate black lace. Closing the door, she stood in regal silence as he bowed deeply and awaited permission to speak.

She acknowledged him with a cool reserve. “Salidar.”

“May it please you, m’lady, I have returned as you instructed to report upon my progress.” He held the low bow with apparent effort. He fully expected her to make this moment linger, presuming he felt discomfort in this awkward position.

“Rise, Salidar, and tell me!”

However unintentional, her impatience betrayed her; and, Salidar noticed.

“M’lady, I delivered the scroll to the hand of the innkeeper, Boltar, as you instructed. However, he offered no information as to the whereabouts of Padraic the Rogue. There was an incident thereafter, in the common room. A Dark Elf, a mage, commanded his retainers to seize both the scroll and Boltar, but a local patrol of men-at-arms and a vampire, the Lady Sabrina, interceded. A fight broke out; in the confusion I escaped—”

Diere interrupted. “Did anyone see you pass the scroll to Boltar?”

This was dangerous ground, a direct question. He paused as if recalling the circumstances, and carefully crafted his response.

"M'lady, we were well within the inn, in an alcove screened from view by a hanging cloth of homespun. For any to have seen, they would have had to have been in that very tight space with us. It was there that I transferred the scroll and questioned Boltar about Padraic. It would not have been possible to have been overheard or seen by those in the common room or the kitchen."

She stared at him without expression.

His face was a façade of earnest candor, but he sensed something was amiss. Perhaps his account was incomplete in some trivial way? His trepidation was clear. He had dared to lie by omission—if she knew or suspected such . . .

He strove not to twist under her gaze as he awaited her reaction. He was either doomed or not.

"Very well," she mused aloud. "You said the mage seized the scroll and the innkeeper. What happened next?"

"M'lady, the mage kept the scroll. He is called Atrellan, and claimed to be in the service of Queen Mab. He was not alone, two elfin warriors and four hard men did his bidding. The Lady Sabrina demanded that the innkeeper, Boltar, be released; and he was. Then Atrellan and Lady Sabrina argued; he cast some sort of sudden spell. There was a flash of light; all involved came to blows. I fled. I know not the outcome."

"I see." Her brow furrowed.

He waited, his expression bland, despite his festering anxiety.

She paused, seemingly deep in thought. Her hand rose to her chin and absently stroked her cheek. She suddenly pinned him with her penetrating gaze. Leaning slightly forward she asked, "And what have you learned about Padraic? Have you found him?"

"M'lady, I-I have not found his present whereabouts—but I have discovered where he *will be* a sennight hence, at the Fertility Festival in the Realm of Mer."

Her eyebrows rose in surprise, then dropped as a scowl marred her face.

Salidar hastened to add, "M'lady, you were correct in your speculation that he frequently travels in the wild realms, which makes tracking him most difficult."

She remained silent, obviously deep in thought.

"M'lady, if I may? It was your enhancement of my transit skills that enabled me to learn of his imminent plans. Such information was only available in the wild as you so shrewdly anticipated. I am most grateful for your foresight. I only hope that you find my services helpful."

She considered him as one might an interesting insect, just before dispatching it.

He had one hope—that she still needed him. He sensed that she was actually surprised that he had managed to escape the melee at the Crying Cup.

Had he been killed, it would have been *what—inconvenient?*

But then, had that been her plan all along? After all, was he not an incriminating element that could directly link her to the scroll—and therefore a threat to her that would have been eliminated? If it had not happened there and then, was this not something she would eventually have to contemplate, and see to? Would she seek to accomplish this by her own hand—or others?

He shuddered involuntarily; he could not afford to underestimate her. She was no fool, and no doubt saw through his smarmy praise. She knew what he wanted. He suspected she also knew he was somehow not being completely forthcoming. He was gambling that too much was happening, much too quickly, and she would have to adjust her plans once more. If he was right, she must take a chance as well and begrudgingly acknowledge that it would best serve her advantage to have him fully functional, at least for his next task.

"Salidar, it appears you have done well—so far. I want you to go back to Shadow; learn what happened to the innkeeper, Boltar. You will no doubt need all your faculties for the tasks I will set before you; so, I return your full sight to you. I shall also extend the transit ability enhancement by another moon; you may need that as well."

She murmured an arcane incantation as she made a series of small gestures.

At first he felt nothing; then a mild tingling began at the crown of his head, traveled downward through his body to his toes, and then back up again. He blinked involuntarily, missing the spot of illumination that flared briefly just above his head—and that Lady Diere had captured that mote of light during his moment of disorientation.

He was unaware that something had been taken from him.

With the return of his full sight, he was distracted by the glint of gold in the palm of her open hand.

Her next words grabbed his attention.

"I will also give you this ring, an enchanted bauble that you will use to contact me when you have learned the fate of the innkeeper. Merely rotate the stone's setting and I will arrange for your transit to a secure place for our meeting. Only do so when your task is complete."

She leaned forward, as if to drop the ring in his eagerly waiting hand, but suddenly closed her fist.

He tore his covetous gaze from her hand and looked into her cold eyes.

"Salidar, heed me well. You are not to return here, to this castle, unless I specifically tell you to do so. Am I clear?"

"Of course, m'lady, I understand."

Lady Diere held him in thrall a moment longer, and then dropped the ring in his outstretched hand.

He held it up to the candelabrum and stared at the square cut stone. The gem captured the dancing candlelight in its barely transparent tint of rich tea.

"This is a fine topaz, m'lady," he offered, with more than just a touch of awe in his voice.

"Well noticed, Salidar. Your restored sight suits you. That is indeed a fine topaz, one of the gems reputed to have been amongst a dragon's hoard. That is likely true, for it is capable of holding a spell."

A hint of envious greed that he could not contain flashed in his eyes. He cursed silently, in the knowledge this flare of avarice had not escaped her notice. *Or was that to be expected? Has she once again assessed a weakness and played me like a toy? She is so smug!*

"But beware!" she cautioned, raising a finger in warning, "The enchantment will work but once. You will need that ring once again when you find Padraic."

"Padraic, m'lady?" His confusion was evident.

"After you perform your first task, ascertaining the disposition of Boltar, I will place another spell in the ring that you will use to establish your *bona fides* when you contact Padraic."

"I am to *contact* him now, rather than merely find him? But why, m'lady?"

Her demeanor darkened; he realized his mistake. *Never presume to question her!*

"You need not concern yourself," she intoned icily. "Concentrate on the task at hand. I want you to understand just how important that ring is to me. Do not lose it! Fail me and I assure you my wrath will be *special!*"

He groveled. "M'lady, rest assured that I shall neither fail you, nor lose your ring."

"See that you do not. You should plan on departing for Shadow at first light. I will arrange for you to be fed. You may take your rest in this chamber. Now I have much to attend to, so I shall bid you good night. A servant will come and escort you to the kitchens."

He bowed deeply and murmured, "M'lady, you may rely upon me. I thank you for your hospitality."

When he looked up, she was gone and the door was swinging closed—almost shut.

He scrambled forward; but, the lock *clicked* just as his hand grasped the handle, an instant too late.

AS LADY DIERE MADE her way through the elegant halls, she gestured for a liveried household servant to walk with her. The young elfin maiden, attired in a belted black and silvered smock bearing the stylized image of crossed hawthorn leaves, kept her eyes downcast as she received her instructions.

"Malvana, a *guest* waits in the small locked chamber off the reception hall, a halfling called Salidar. You are to arrange an evening meal in the kitchens for him; but you are not to leave his side while he is out of that *guest room*. He is to go nowhere else. Return him to that chamber after his meal, and secure him within. At first light, you may release him and escort him to the outer portcullis. The gatehouse guards will be expecting him. He is to depart and carry out certain instructions. Come then and advise me of his departure. Do you understand?"

The maiden curtsied gracefully. "Of course, m'lady. It shall be done as you instruct."

As Malvana left her, Lady Diere considered looking in on George and his *tutor*, Daegon the Alchemist. She turned down the corridor that would lead to the chambers used for George's instruction, wondering if she needed to periodically monitor some of those sessions more closely.

Daegon, sent by Queen Mab, was to teach George the differences germane to the function of magic among the Council Realms and how these distinctions could affect the varying political positions each realm would likely take on a given issue.

From what little Diere had learned, this Daegon was considered to be quite astute in his field, alchemy, a so-called science of experimentation and observation in pursuit of the mysteries of both transmutation and an arcane device known as the Philosophers' Stone. However, he displayed an uncanny comprehension of the workings of magic, and more curiously, politics. Nonetheless, he claimed neither mage-like status nor political ambition, asserting that he was not a practitioner of either art.

There was clearly no denying that he was Mab's minion; he would bear watching.

Lady Diere found the training chambers unoccupied. This training session must have already ended. That was just as well, for she had much to do this evening. As she made her way to her own chambers, she firmly decided to make a concerted effort to personally observe George's training more frequently, especially those sessions conducted by Daegon. Time was growing short, and soon enough George would have to be sent back to the Realm of Man to receive the Council's anticipated summons.

THE SOFT KNOCK UPON the heavy door surprised Salidar. He assumed a servant had come for him; Lady Diere would not bother to knock.

With a small *click* and a flowing *whoosh*, the door swung open. A petite elfin maid in the livery of the House of Hawthorn gracefully stepped into the room. Her jet-black hair, pulled back past her delicate pointed ears, was woven into a single thick braid that hung nearly to her small waist. Haunting hazel eyes beneath thick dark lashes captivated him for several heartbeats.

She bowed her head and spoke with a musical lilt. "Good evening, good sir, I am to escort you to the kitchens where a meal has been prepared for you."

Almost smitten by her youthful beauty, Salidar steeled his cautionary resolve with the thought that she could easily be much older than she appeared. He straightened his tunic and nodded in return. "Thank you. I will gladly accompany you. May I know how you are called?"

She considered him a few seconds and smiled. "I am called Malvana, and I know you are Salidar. Shall we go?"

"Of course, Malvana, please lead on."

As he followed her, he tried to engage her in further conversation, but she politely declined to comment, suggesting that they wait until they were comfortably seated in the kitchens.

They entered one of the large adjacent rooms, evidently a crowded staff dining area. A fair number of liveried servants were finishing bowls of a rich brown stew, sopping up the dregs with hand-torn chunks of warm fresh bread. It smelled wonderful; Salidar realized that he was really quite hungry.

At Malvana's direction, they sat side by side on a long wooden bench near one end of an even longer table. A kitchen servant placed steaming bowls and ornately carved wooden spoons before both of them. Another deposited a thick round loaf of warm bread on the table.

The aroma of savory chunks of meat and root vegetables in a thick spicy broth set Salidar's stomach to growling. He ate with relish, while Malvana took delicate bites, and evidently found it amusing to watch him wolf down his food with such gusto.

Finally sopping up the last of his roux with gobs of fresh bread, Salidar asked, "So, Malvana, you are a servant in the household of the Lady Diere?"

She looked at him as if he had insulted her. Her eyebrows arched in indignation, she spoke deliberately, as one would to a dim-witted child bereft of manners and breeding.

"Sir, I am a *fosterling* in the household of the Lady Diere. I am of noble blood, daughter of the Earl of Tanist, the Queen's Avatar to the Council of Realms. As is our custom, I serve for a time within another noble house to learn the ways of management of a house. It is an honor to serve the Lady Diere—as you should well know!"

"Ah, please forgive me, m'lady," said Salidar contritely. "I was not informed of your status. I was only told by Lady Diere to expect a servant. I pray that you do not take offense at my regrettable ignorance."

Seemingly mollified she straightened her slight shoulders and sniffed, aloofly electing to concentrate on her stew with delicate jabs of her spoon.

Salidar expected as much; so, he ignored her.

Many diners had left the tables and drifted from the room. As their table cleared of staff, Salidar noticed a pair of men hunched together on either side of the table at the opposite end. Initially he could barely make out their muted voices; however, as more people left, the ambient noise in the room slowly diminished. He could distinguish their voices more clearly.

Something seemed familiar—something unusual about one of the voices. He leaned slightly forward, looking past Malvana, to get a better view.

As the men leaned back from their huddled conversation, he could see their profiles. One was a complete stranger. The other, he knew! The shock stunned him and the blood drained from his face.

George! By the gods, what is he doing here?

Salidar sat back immediately—had he been seen? Although he didn't understand why, he sensed that it would be better if George did not see *him*. Salidar was wracked with curiosity.

What was George doing here? Who was he sitting with? And why? Do I dare another peek? How can I not?

Salidar leaned incrementally forward once more. His *chaperon*, Malvana, seemed oblivious; so, he stole another glance at the two men.

Who is this stranger with George?

Just as that very thought formed in Salidar's mind, the stranger's head turned and his eyes locked on Salidar's own. His blood ran cold, and it took everything he had just to *blink*—break that contact—and look down into his own empty bowl. He shuddered as the breath he'd been holding escaped his cramping lungs.

Malvana touched his arm. "Salidar, are you all right? Be not concerned; I am not still upset with you. I took no offense—you had no way of knowing. I do not think it will be necessary to report your unintended insult. You are forgiven."

Confused for only an instant, Salidar looked past her shoulder to see that the other end of the table was now empty. George and the *stranger* were gone.

"Ah, m'lady, my apologies and my gratitude," he managed, trying to slow his racing pulse. That she thought his discomfort was for offending *her*—that was a gift he would not ignore. "I would be sorely distressed to find that I had offended such a stunning beauty. Thank you so much for your gracious understanding."

Malvana preened a bit under the not-so-subtle flattery.

Then he added smoothly, "I fear that I may have eaten a bit too much, far too quickly, as well. Perhaps we could walk about these lovely halls a bit after such a fine repast?"

"I am sorry, Salidar, but Lady Diere was quite clear that you are to return to your chambers after you have supped. Please come with me."

"Alas," he sighed dramatically, "at least I shall have the pleasure of your company a bit longer, m'lady. I willingly follow where you lead."

As they made their way back through the castle's halls and passages, Salidar did his best to memorize the layout.

Back at his room, as he bid Malvana a good night, he feigned a yawn and begged her forgiveness, pleading exhaustion.

She raised a single eyebrow in response, bid him a good night, and locked him in.

WITHIN HER OWN CHAMBERS, Lady Diere sat at a broad yet exquisite desk of burnished rosewood festooned with a delicate filigree inlay of golden wire. Deep in thought, she studied a series of astrological charts, hand-scribed scrolls, and an ancient grimoire that lay open before her. She had been analyzing the results of a spell; but, an unforeseen anomaly had manifested that she simply could not understand.

She contemplated the mote of pale light she had taken from Salidar as it hovered above the palm of her hand. Expanding to the size of a grapefruit, it pulsed slowly as wisps of ruddy elfin runes glowed and faded like faint tracings at the edge of the soft light. Soon a series of landscape scenes and faces flickered within. She carefully studied the images.

She assumed that Salidar was unaware that her offer to enhance his transit ability would have a price—a hidden *tracing spell*. His travels to other realms, and where he went within them, would be recorded by the spell, which she had retrieved from him a few hours ago. The problem was that there was a gap, not a blank spot exactly, but a period of about three days that was obscured.

This was the first time she had used such a spell, a very old and arcane bit of sorcery unknown by most contemporary practitioners of the *Art*. She could not find any indication that the enchantment had failed or faltered; therefore, she deduced that something must have interfered with the spell. She reexamined all aspects of the enchantment to the best of her abilities. There did not appear to be an error in the casting, nor in her analysis of the results. Therefore, it *had* to be focused interference, or perhaps a *counterspell*?

Was it accidental—or deliberate?

Had Salidar discovered this spell? Not likely, she reasoned; he did not seem that sensitive to discerning enchantments. No, she was certain he was unaware of the tracing spell. What if he had unknowingly gone somewhere that had an undue influence on the spell? He admitted to traveling in the *wild realms*; he had even bragged that he found the information he had sought there.

Clearly, something impacted the spell—something in the *wild?* Perhaps something tampered with the spell *deliberately?*

At that thought, her countenance grew dark and grim.

Who would so dare? I will not tolerate such interference! Nor can I use such a spell again until I know what has happened.

Lady Diere knew that she would find no more information in the reference material spread before her. There was only one more resource she could access, but that was not without its own potential peril—the Orb of the Old Ones.

She had learned that aside from its role as a scrying device, it was the repository of a vast amount of forgotten magical lore. Much was convoluted and utterly confusing; but, some of the less esoteric sorcery was comprehensible to her. She had made use of such thaumaturgy when it suited her. She had found the tracing spell there long ago, and thought it might prove potentially useful someday.

The orb did not differentiate between benign enchantments and those of dark malignancy; the intent of the user opened different paths and allowed access to pertinent resources. Lady Diere knew it was best to avoid certain perilous avenues—especially the dark regions of necromancy, not that dabbling in other aspects of the Black Arts inhibited her in the least.

She leaned back in her chair and considered that, to the best of her knowledge, she had exhausted all other means at her disposal, with no satisfactory results. She logically determined that her need was still great; otherwise, she would not consider consulting the orb so soon to find an appropriate counter to her compromised spell.

The last time she had used the orb, she had drawn unwelcome attention and an attack from some unknown and powerful entity. She did not relish another such encounter.

Closing the old grimoire, bound in the stiff leathered skin of some extinct carnivore, she stared at the remaining charts and notations without really seeing them. Her mind was focused upon what she truly feared—that Queen Mab was at the heart of the disruption of her spell. The simple truth was that she feared the queen more than she feared another attempted use of the orb. It was incredibly perilous to subtly manipulate the queen by arranging for carefully crafted bits of information to come to the attention of the queen's spies—dangerous indeed. In one sense, it galled Diere that she should be so wary of her cousin; but in another, it galvanized her will and prompted her to take decisive action.

She slipped from her chambers by a hidden way behind an ornate bookcase, emerging moments later in the secret chamber of the orb.

Steeling her resolve, she sought a calm inner state and cautioned herself to be most careful. She would only seek the specific information needed to penetrate the cloud that obscured her spell, treading the ethereal paths gently to attract no undue notice. Clearing her mind of all distractions, her goal clearly established and her mental shielding at the ready, she began her delicate and dangerous quest.

SALIDAR HAD LONG AGO trained himself to sleep for a few hours at a time and wake surprisingly alert. It was a technique that came in quite handy for a thief—or a spy.

Opening his eyes in the dim room, a lone guttering candle the sole light, he guessed that it was sometime after midnight. The routine bustle of the castle, at least that which he could barely hear from this locked chamber, had diminished to near silence in the depths of the night.

He was certain some sort of guard force was awake and on duty, but they would typically be more concerned with the castle's perimeter. Only the personal guards of the nobility were likely to be on post within the walls of the keep. He had no doubt that he could avoid them with the deft exercise of due caution.

His only other concern was that there might be a spell or enchantment that would alert anyone that he had left his guest quarters. Using the relaxed focus technique, he scanned the chamber, paying particular attention to the door and its lock.

He found what he had expected.

The room was warded. He recognized it immediately as an elfin *counter-transit spell,* the likes of which he had become all too familiar with of late. His search was quite thorough, but he found no other wards, no alarm or alert spells. He smiled at the irony. One could not use magic to depart the room; but, one need only defeat the simple lock by some mechanical means. His host would be none the wiser.

He smiled in amusement, acknowledging the little known fact that magic users' dependency and reliance upon the Arts frequently engendered a complacency that was often easily taken advantage of by a gifted opportunist, such as himself. He almost laughed aloud.

Retrieving his lock-picking tools from the hidden recess of his pack, he set about examining the lock. The relatively simple device was no match for his skills; it yielded readily. He slipped the small roll of tools into a hidden pocket within his waistband; he might need them again. He rummaged around a bit in the depths of his pack, and grinned when he found what he sought.

He took a small but thick brass nail and wedged it in the slot of the mortise faceplate. The door would now fully shut and appear secure, but the bar would not slide forward from the lock housing and engage the slot in the faceplate. Salidar could now come and go as he pleased, his absence undetected—provided no one tried to open the door.

That thought gave him pause.

He returned to his pack for a folded piece of parchment. From within, he drew forth a single length of hair plucked from a horse's tail. He gently tied one end of the thin strand to the door's inner handle. He held the other dangling end as he slipped from the room, and softly shut the door. The single hair was now wedged within the jamb, with only its very tip sticking out close to the smooth stone floor. Salidar ran his fingertip along the lower length of the doorjamb until he felt the tip of the virtually invisible hair. Should anyone open the door, the hair would fall free and hang loosely, almost undetectable, from the door's inner handle. He'd know someone had been there. It wasn't foolproof; but, it would suffice for what he had in mind.

Salidar stood silently in the dark hall, just listening. Very patient, he did not move for a long time. Satisfied that he was undetected, he carefully retraced his steps toward the kitchens.

He well knew that, as in most castles, one could almost always find access to anywhere in a keep from the kitchens.

Few candles remained lit so he found it easy to slip from shadow to shadow. He skulked silently with the practiced grace of a thief in the night.

The overt opulence and ostentatious wealth of Lady Diere's household would have normally been a significant distraction for him, but not tonight. What he craved was information, anything about George and the stranger.

The patter of soft footsteps came from a passage to his right.

Ducking into a deep shadow, he shimmied behind a musty tapestry. He held his breath so no movement of the hanging cloth would betray him.

The glimmer of diffused candlelight softened the nearby shadows as someone—no, two people—trying very hard to move quickly and quietly, entered the hall in which he hid. They passed unknowingly within inches of his hasty cloister, and continued in the same direction in which he had intended to proceed.

As the illumination waned, Salidar took a measured breath and elected to follow, his curiosity aroused.

Keeping to the darker nooks and crannies, as soundless as a shadow, he had no difficulty following his quarry as they led him through a warren of passages and up a series of steep stone stairs. As he huddled in the dark recess of a narrow landing near the base of a circular stone staircase, he heard the creak of infrequently used hinges.

A door had been opened somewhere above him.

Surely, he thought, they had ascended the inner wall of this tower—there was nowhere else to go.

He debated continuing to follow for only a moment; there would be few places to hide should they reverse their course and descend.

The slightest breath of cool night air brushed his cheeks; his excessive curiosity overwhelmed his caution.

In practiced stealth he ascended.

He found an iron-bound door of heavily weathered wood standing ajar at the top of the stairs. Hiding in the dark of the stairwell, he looked out upon the moonlit roofs of nearby buildings. Nudging the door further open, he saw a narrow flagstone walkway that led to a wider observation area. He recognized it as a parapet of sorts, obviously not in frequent use, judging by the windblown debris and copious dried bird droppings.

Seeing no one, he waited until a cloud passed over the face of the waning gibbous moon, and crept forward along a curving crenelated wall. Stealing a glance over the edge, he noted that this part of the parapet overlooked a stable yard and training ground to the rear of the main keep. He heard nothing more than the usual night sounds; the rustle of trees beyond the walls, the scratching of insects, and the occasional soft nickering of sleepy horses stabled below.

Taking advantage of the cloud cover, he stole along the wall until he came to two sets of narrow stone steps; one flight went up, the other down. Purely on instinct, he ascended a dozen stairs following the outer curvature of the tower.

The sound of hushed voices from somewhere below froze him in mid-step. The thick cloud slid from the face of the moon; the lower observation deck was washed in pale colorless light. He dropped to his belly on the stairs and peered over the edge.

Two figures stood below; one carefully unwrapped a small bundle as the other watched.

The night breeze carried their words to Salidar as plainly as if he stood beside them. He recognized the voices immediately.

George! And the other voice sounds like the stranger in the kitchen!

"All right, Daegon, just what are you going to do?"

"I? Why, *I* will do nothing. *You*, m'lord, will do as I instruct—yes, *you*. You are so eager to learn the ways of power; you shall have a taste of it. *You* will perform this rite."

Daegon produced a sleepy bird from within the folds of the bundle, a pigeon, and handed it to George.

"Now, m'lord, quickly dispatch the fowl," he urged, making twisting gestures with his hands.

"What?" George exclaimed.

"Come now, m'lord," derided Daegon. "Surely you are not squeamish about what must be done, or the sight of a little blood? Wring the thing's neck!"

George scowled and sneered contemptuously at Daegon. With a sudden wrenching snap, the deed was done. He held out his hand as the doomed bird twitched pathetically and then lay still upon his palm. His murderous gaze never left Daegon.

"Be careful, Daegon. You have no idea what I have done, or what I am capable of doing. There are many kinds of power. And in my world—let's just say that I'm not one to be trifled with."

"Of course, m'lord, I meant no disrespect. Perhaps, should the opportunity arise, you might instruct *me* in the ways of power of your realm. Such knowledge might prove *interesting* among the Council Realms."

"Oh, I already have a few ideas about that," responded George dryly, "but for the moment, I am here to sample this unique power you spoke of earlier. Isn't that why we're here, now?"

"Indeed, m'lord, indeed. We should proceed."

George hesitated. "Before we begin, tell me why we had to come up here, rather than do whatever it is in the training rooms. This trek was really necessary? Now I've got bird crap on the soles of my shoes!"

Daegon raised a finger in caution. "Please, m'lord, keep your voice down. It would be best that we are not discovered. We are compelled to perform this rite outside the walls of the castle keep because there are certain wards and protective spells within the walls that would interfere with the casting, and would alert certain persons to what we are about to attempt. That would not be good—for either of us."

Even Salidar heard the ominous tone and the inherent caution in Daegon's warning.

Nonetheless, George groused impatiently. "Whatever, let's get on with it. What do I do?"

"Cup the pigeon in both hands and hold it to your chest. Yes, like that, good. Now, I will whisper the incantation in your ear and you will repeat it *exactly* over the bird. The incantation will include the *true name* of the fowl. It is *very important* that you mimic precisely both my words and the inflections in my voice. Do you understand?"

"Of course! Damn it! Let's do this!"

Daegon leaned into George's shoulder and began whispering in deathly earnest.

Salidar could hear nothing but George's muted mumble as he repeated the incantation; no distinct words could be discerned or understood.

Salidar felt the night breeze change direction, falter, and stop dead still. The ambient temperature dropped; a sudden chill frosted the air. He could no longer hear any normal night sounds; no rustle of trees, no scratching of insects, no breath of life. It was as if all were held in a state of suspension. The hair on the back of his neck rose; he had a sudden impulse to flee. But he hunkered down into a tighter position, and dared another peek below.

George now held his hands forward, arms fully outstretched from his shoulders; the bird, cupped upon his palms, pulsed with a sickly greenish light.

The fowl flinched! A series of spasms, and the pigeon awkwardly righted itself—its head at an impossible angle. It took a couple of drunken steps before George closed his hands around it.

The alchemist stepped back and grinned.

"Well done! Now, command your servant." With a sweeping gesture of his arm, Daegon indicated the open sky. "Tell the bird to fly about!"

George tossed the bird aloft.

It flapped its wings erratically, and then settled into a familiar circling flight pattern, making ever-widening circles above their heads.

Salidar ducked from view. Soon the pigeon would be flying at his level; he feared discovery. He fought his rising panic and looked longingly at the descending steps, his only path of escape.

At Daegon's urging, George recalled the bird. It plopped gracelessly into his hands.

"Excellent, m'lord," oozed Daegon. "You will note that you have commanded your servant to act counter to its nature; pigeons do not fly at night by choice. You can command it to do anything—even to harm itself in your service."

His impatience forgotten, George was wide-eyed and obviously quite pleased with himself. It seemed to take a moment for what Daegon had just said to sink in.

"*Anything?* Even to the point of harming itself?"

"Indeed, m'lord," Daegon responded as he drew forth a small dagger and handed it to George hilt-first. "Hold this dirk in your other fist; command the bird to fly about and then impale itself upon the blade."

George tossed the pigeon aloft once more; the bird began circling.

Holding the dagger skyward in a stiff-armed stance, George audibly commanded the bird to impale itself.

It did so in the next instant, sending up a bloody puff of feathers, and a shudder down George's arm.

The surprised crime lord stood there aghast. Then, with a casual flick of his wrist, he sent the carcass tumbling away to crumple at the foot of the crenelated wall.

Facing Daegon, George said with a modicum of respect, "Now, I *am* impressed. That is power, indeed."

Salidar was shocked beyond words, but not beyond self-preservation. He *had* to be away from this scene.

As if in answer to his unspoken prayer, a dense cloud passed across the face of the moon and shadows merged with the night.

He quickly picked his way down the steep open stairs with cat-like grace and made haste for the weathered door to the inner tower stairs. A scant glance behind him showed no pursuit; therefore, he assumed—*hoped*—he had not been seen.

He had barely reached the foot of the long staircase when he heard the door above close. He knew George and Daegon had begun their descent.

Salidar wasted no time in unerringly making his way down through the warren of passages in the direction of his *guest accommodations*. He moved as quickly as his stealth would allow, his heart pounding. Every nominal creak of the old castle's timbers triggered a frightened flinching of his shoulders. His imagination ran rampant, attributing any sound to something unspeakably loathsome lurking in deeply shadowed ambush.

Finally, in a cold sweat, he found the door to his room. In the dimly lit passage, it appeared to have been undisturbed. The lone hair was as he'd left it. He slipped inside, untied the hair, and returned the lock to its normal function. In fact, he was grateful that the closed door was now locked.

Salidar had witnessed that which he had hoped never to see—an act of *necromancy*. His very soul shuddered at the thought, as if his earlier proximity to such horror had somehow infected him.

He had to get a grip; he needed his wits about him. The potential danger could not be greater. This *Daegon* had knowledge of the *darkest* of the Black Arts; and, he had started George down a most ominous path.

HIGH ABOVE SALIDAR'S locked chamber, a night breeze ruffled a distended clump of bloodstained feathers wedged against the rampart wall. The small mass twitched involuntarily, trying unsuccessfully to right its abused and broken body.

Its feeble efforts had not gone unnoticed.

A clawed hand gently scooped up the cursed bird, and a dog-like face sniffed at the tiny thing. The short muzzle drew back; a lip curled in distaste, a hint of fang briefly exposed.

With surprising dexterity, thickly gnarled hands gently wrapped the bird in a broad leather skin, stained with age and marked with ancient runes, then placed the bundle in a stiff bag with similar runic markings.

An ominously dark cloud wall, the massive vanguard of a cooling front, began to slowly slide across the face of the moon, pulling an obsidian blanket in its wake. Silvery highlights fled the land; and, bleeding shadows became a flood. Soon the blackest of nights would hold dominion.

Standing erect, the gargoyle tied the bag to a belt around its waist, and surveyed the darkening area of the parapet.

In the next moment, the last trace of argent light died; all was darkness.

Satisfied that it had memorized the pertinent details of what it had seen, to include the undetected spy, the gargoyle flexed a set of huge bat-like wings, stepped off the edge of the wall, and swooped into the stygian night.

CH 3

THE AFTERNOON'S BRIEFING was to be held in a conference room in the New Orleans Office of the U.S. Attorney for the Eastern District of Louisiana. Security was tight; all persons were screened upon entering the building. At the entrance to the conference room, a stern pair of Homeland Security Federal Protective Officers double-checked everyone's credentials against a list of invited personnel.

Trey and Hawk made their way around the long conference table toward some empty seats. The room was already crowded with representatives from a host of federal, state, and local law enforcement agencies. Trey nudged Hawk and indicated a knot of people standing near the far corner of the room.

Hawk recognized two of the four men, FBI Special Agent Jim Franklin and his boss, Assistant Special Agent in Charge, Manny Scherer. The other two men, fresh-faced and eager, stood rigidly attentive, obviously hanging on ASAC Scherer's every word.

Chuckling as he sat, Trey whispered, "Ah, the *Quantico Glow*—fresh from the academy, brand new baby agents. I'll bet New Orleans is their first office; and Manny can't resist molding these youngsters into the proper image."

"Don't you mean *his image*, Trey?" said Todd Simmons in a stage whisper as he and his partner, Deputy U.S. Marshal Willis Hebert, took the two chairs to Trey's left.

On Hawk's right, two more investigators, BATF Special Agent Bart Warner and Special Agent Kendra Sandler from Immigration and Customs Enforcement (ICE), sat down.

While Hawk and Trey laughed aloud, Bart Warner repeated the Deputy U.S. Marshal's comment to Kendra Sandler, who sputtered and chuckled.

As the laughter died, Jim Franklin looked toward the group and nodded in greeting, a placid smile on his face.

Manny Scherer pointedly ignored them.

They almost laughed anew, managing to hold their mirth to a few muffled snickers.

"Ladies and gentlemen, please take your seats, and we'll get started," said a tall bespectacled man of middle years. He brushed a shock of thick grey hair to one side and made only a minimal effort to straighten his rumpled brown suit as he stepped to the lectern at the front of the conference room.

"For those of you I've not yet met, I'm Paul Blakely, First Assistant U.S. Attorney. I'm about to turn this briefing over to Inspector Don Paglia from the U.S. Marshals Service Regional Fugitive Apprehension Strike Team, or the FAST squad as some of you know them. But first, I have a few remarks. Everything you are about to hear is to be considered *Law Enforcement Sensitive—Confidential* and is not to be shared outside your chain of command without informing this office first. Sharing within your chain of command should be on a need-to-know basis. Is that clear?"

Heads nodded around the quiet room.

Blakely stepped from behind the lectern assuming a more relaxed pose.

"As many of you are aware, there has been an ongoing OCDETF/RICO investigation that involves all three federal judicial districts in Louisiana. We have recently discovered related drug trafficking evidence in the Southern District of Texas—specifically, in Houston. We have also been examining a number of related state and local felony cases that may have inclusive value as *predicate acts* in our racketeering case. Now, what you may not know is that it appears that we may have just caught a major break. Now, with that as an appropriate segue," Blakely added smiling, "I'll ask Inspector Paglia to take over."

A wiry man of medium height, wearing a navy-blue polo shirt displaying an embroidered circled-star, the U.S. Marshal's badge, and khaki cargo pants, stepped to the lectern. His shaved head and prominent goatee were distinguishing characteristics. His voice was firm and clear, with the slightest hint of an old New England accent.

"Good afternoon. I'll cut right to the chase. A recent homicide in Chantilly Parish has led us to some very interesting intelligence. The victim has been positively identified as Suzi Origami. At the request of the Chantilly Parish Sheriff's Office, we located the victim's apartment here in New Orleans. Not too surprisingly, the entire building was leased in the name of a company that we already knew had strong ties to George Papadolis, AKA *Papa George*.

"In the course of a search pursuant to a warrant, which is still underway, a number of computers, external hard drives and storage media were discovered; all were encrypted. Our Forensic Information Technology personnel are in the initial stages of confirming the decryption and subsequent data analysis of what's been recovered so far; but for now, we have prepared a fairly comprehensive preliminary report of our findings.

"Here's the bottom line: as has long been suspected, Suzi Origami did commit murders for hire. And in some cases, she kept encrypted records, presumably for future blackmail or coercion purposes. We don't really know; at this point, we can only speculate as to her motivation. The important aspect is that some of these records directly implicate Papa George and some other organized-crime figures, many of whom are believed to be dead—but who knows? Further decryption might prove enlightening in that regard as well.

"We are faced with an inherent problem. The intelligence data gleaned, while reasonably comprehensive, is only circumstantial at this point. We must corroborate or refute each bit of information; and for that, we will need your help. All of you have open cases that are referenced in this data; that information will be provided to you. Please investigate it thoroughly and advise this office of your findings. Mr. Blakely has a team of Assistant U.S. Attorneys and analysts available to coordinate the results. Any *new and/or relevant* data will be immediately forwarded to any related investigation.

"You should expect that your cases, especially *older cold cases*, may lead in new directions.

"Remember that the pending federal case should in no way inhibit any state or local prosecution. There is not an inherent double jeopardy issue here, merely duplicate or concurrent jurisdiction. When warranted, the local District Attorneys and respective U.S. Attorneys will iron out issues of prosecutorial discretion and scheduling. Convictions in state and local courts can and will be added to the list of predicate acts in support of the RICO case. Now, are there any questions?"

A state police lieutenant raised his hand. "Can you give us some idea of exactly what is contained in these records?"

The inspector grinned. "I'm glad you asked that, Norman. How about the identity of the victim, time and place of the *hit*, the client who ordered it and sometimes even *why*. She frequently recorded the fee, and even body disposal. Will that work for you?"

The lieutenant smiled broadly. "Yeah, Don, I think that'll work just fine."

Another hand went up. "Inspector, I'm Fred Steuben, Calcasieu Parish S.O. Did you say *body disposal?*"

"That's correct, Fred. In fact, we've found repeated references to a small funeral home on the outskirts of Lafayette, Final Rest, Inc., that appears to have been very popular with Suzi Origami. We'll be visiting that establishment very soon—hopefully with a search warrant."

"Don?" queried a female voice from the back of the room.

"Eva? Sorry, I didn't see you back there. It's Eva Quantrell from DEA. Go ahead, Eva."

"I think we also have a meth case in which a funeral home near Lafayette has come up. If it's the same establishment, we'll need to talk before you apply for a search warrant."

"Not a problem, Eva. See me after we adjourn. Okay, people, are there any more questions at this point? No? All right, I have some handouts, copies of the preliminary report. They're marked CONFIDENTIAL and numbered. You'll have to sign for them.

"You are welcome to meet with one another in this conference room for the next hour if you'd like. I'll need to see the people from Chantilly Parish now, if you please."

As the briefing ended and the handouts were distributed, Willis tugged on Trey's sleeve. "Listen, we know what Don wants to talk to you about. So, if you don't mind, Todd and I will stick around."

Before Trey could respond, Inspector Paglia and Eva Quantrell walked up. At the inspector's gesture, they followed him into a small office.

Closing the door, he motioned for them to take seats.

"Trey, correct me if I'm mistaken, but don't you have an open case on a missing lawyer, uh, one Perry Wilkerson?"

"We sure do, Don. How is it related?"

"We found his name in Suzi's files, as a contracted *hit;* the client was Papa George. The body supposedly went to this funeral home I mentioned, Final Rest, Inc. Eva confirms that this is, in fact, the same place that's involved in DEA's meth case."

"Well, do we have enough probable cause," Hawk asked, "based on whatever is in Suzi's files, for a search warrant on the funeral home?"

"Yeah, that *is* a good question," added Trey. "The thing is, Don, I'm fairly certain that we've never heard of this place before in the Wilkerson case. It wasn't my case, but I did help out on it. In fact, we even interviewed Suzi Origami. She was supposedly an employee or executive of some sort in one of Papa George's casino-based private clubs, which has been closed for some time. But we never got anything *from* her or *on* her. So, I don't think there's anything in our file that would help with the PC."

Eva, who had been scanning the highlights of the preliminary report, shrugged.

"That's not going to be too much of a problem, Trey. We never did get to make a *buy* on the premises, despite a few attempts and periodic surveillance. However, we did get some fairly well-corroborated intelligence from other sources that bulk quantities of meth have gone through that funeral home on several occasions, and then on to known distribution points to the north and east. So, I think we have enough PC from our meth case, combined with some of this data from Suzi's files, that we should have no trouble getting a search warrant for documents and data."

That brought smiles all around. Among other requirements, search warrants must specify the evidence being sought. Personnel conducting the search can only look in places where such evidence can reasonably be found. For example, one cannot reasonably search for a motor vehicle in a desk drawer. However, a search for documents and/or data could be most comprehensive. The investigators knew that any other evidence of criminal activity found in the course of such an authorized and sanctioned search would be deemed admissible in a subsequent criminal proceeding.

Willis Hebert rummaged through a thick file folder and held up a mug shot for all to see. A swarthy, unkempt and unshaven man with a heavy bruise above his right temple stared listlessly at the camera; his slight shoulders slumped in an apparent pose of weary resignation.

Hebert's partner, Todd, pointed to the photo. "Now, we can add a little more to the mix. This is Theodore Rasmussen, AKA *Teddy Pots*. He's a federal parole violator wanted on a technical violation, missing reporting dates with his U.S. Parole Officer. It's an older case from back when the federal system still offered convicts parole. These days there is no federal parole; the time sentenced is pretty much the time served. The underlying case was possession and distribution—big surprise, right? Anyway, Teddy's been in the wind for almost three years. We haven't had squat on him in all that time."

Willis picked up the narrative. "A week ago, his P.O. passed us a tip that Teddy was seen near Breaux Bridge about a month ago driving a hearse. Teddy Pots is no *wheel man*—he's a *meth cook,* and an *old school* cook at that, with old ties to the late Fenton Brewster.

"I should mention that the P.O. warned us that Teddy used to be a real hard case who in his younger days liked to fight the police. Over time the meth has taken its toll; he's a shell of his former self. But like all *meth heads*, he's unpredictable and can still be dangerous. His P.O. thinks that Teddy's more inclined to just shoot first and run away."

Todd shrugged and summarized. "Anyway, with what Eva has in the DEA case, the info in Suzi's files, and the tip about Teddy driving a hearse, there are just too many coincidences not to have a closer look at that funeral home. It sounds to me like there's plenty of collective probable cause. So, if there's a search warrant to be served, we're on board."

"Okay, with Eva's help, I'll draft the affidavit for the search warrant," the inspector offered. "Eva, can you have your surveillance unit in place again by tonight? If we can get the U.S. Magistrate Judge to sign the warrant today, or even this evening, I'd like to hit it first thing in the morning, at sunrise."

"No problem," she agreed.

A knock on the door was followed by the entrance of Jim Franklin from the FBI.

"Sorry to interrupt. Trey, are you all going out to the Origami apartment to finish the search? My boss wants me to 'observe' in the hope something will help our end of the RICO case. I'll be glad to help any way I can. And I need a word with you."

"Oh, okay, no problem." Trey turned back to the inspector. "Don, we have to finish a detailed search of Suzi's apartment. Our CSI people and the NOPD CSI are already at the site. Will you need Hawk or me in the preparation of your search warrant affidavit?"

"No, I think Eva and I can handle that," Inspector Paglia responded, "but thanks anyway."

"Trey, need a lift?" Jim asked. "I understand you and Hawk rode down with your CSI people. I've got my *bu-car*, so why don't you both ride with me to the search warrant site? Then you can hook up with your CSI folks."

"Okay, Jim, thanks, that'll work. I've got to call our captain and bring him up to speed. Hawk and I have to read and digest what's in this preliminary report, but we can do that on the way."

Todd made a suggestion. "Listen, why don't we all just meet later at our Lafayette office, say five o'clock? We can work out our strategy and tactics. Do you need lodging for tonight?

Trey shook his head. "No thanks, our office already took care of our hotel rooms. I'm not sure we'll be through with the search by five; but, we'll get there as soon as we can."

"No problem," Todd assured. "We can also muster and stage there in the morning. I'll call my chief and get our Special Response Team on standby for tomorrow's operation."

"Good idea," the inspector acknowledged. "Okay, if that's it, we're done here for now."

ONCE IN HIS UNMARKED FBI cruiser, Jim paused before driving out of the secured parking area of the Federal Building and offered Trey and Hawk a cautious warning.

"Listen, if you're hitting that funeral home tomorrow, be careful. We've been aware of that place, trying for months to track the money trail in an unrelated matter. It was initially some irregularities with a post-hurricane FEMA contract, but now maybe even fraud and money laundering. We have yet to get a look at their books. Some very expensive, high-end lawyers have leapt to the corporation's defense—a disproportionate response, in my view. Unfortunately, we still have nothing solid at this point, but my gut tells me they have something to hide."

Trey nodded sympathetically at the notion of *trusting one's gut*, a well acknowledged yet unwritten norm among successful investigators.

"To be candid," Jim conceded, "the OCDETF steering committee would love it if you guys were to find anything incriminating. However, they're not willing to commit resources just yet. Personally, I think they're a little gun-shy of the threatened lawsuits. Be certain your search warrant and supporting affidavit are pristine."

"Don't worry, Jim," Trey assured him. "Don and Eva are preparing the affidavit, so you know it'll be *textbook*. Do you want in on the execution of that search warrant?"

Jim sighed. "I would if I could; but, my boss thinks we should sit back and see what you all can develop."

"Ah, I see—*plausible deniability* in the event something goes wrong, or we don't find anything?" Trey asked wryly.

Jim merely shrugged, and reiterated, "Just be careful."

"We will. Look, I appreciate your telling us about the FEMA thing. I'm sure Manny didn't suggest that you share that information."

Jim only smiled and shook his head.

AS JIM'S FBI CRUISER entered the downtown streets and filtered sluggishly through convoluted rush-hour traffic, Trey contacted Captain Miller and advised him of the latest information and pending plans.

Hawk studied the preliminary report as the blocks of the recovering city staggered past the cruiser's heavily tinted windows in the staccato rhythm of the stop and go traffic. The information gleaned from the encrypted files was surprisingly detailed. No less than a dozen murders were committed at the behest of Papa George; but they represented only those carried out by Suzi Origami. Had Papa George ever used anyone else for contract *wet work*?"

A sudden chill accompanied Hawk's realization that he already knew the answer.

Of course, Fenton Brewster was killed by Lady Leanan. Now that presents an interesting question—how does one bring a vampire to justice, and provide due process under the law?

SUZI ORIGAMI'S CONDO apartment was on the top floor of a converted warehouse, four levels above the Rue de Carondelet, and several blocks south of the Vieux Carre, the French Quarter. That the old stone and brick building had withstood the ravages of the recent twin hurricanes was a testament to its stout construction. A number of other old buildings in the same block had succumbed to the savagery of the storms. Some were now reduced to piles of broken rubble, mute monuments to nature's fury, shoved to one side like so many forgotten shards of the city's past.

The obvious police presence at the building had earlier attracted a small crowd of the curious; but, since nothing had appeared to have happened in the last hour, most of the gawkers had grown bored and dispersed.

However, local television stations' news crews had recently arrived in their garish vans, and were now busily unlimbering camera equipment. A female reporter noticed the arrival of the unmarked cruiser and made a hasty effort to reach the three men before they slipped into the building, but two uniformed NOPD officers unceremoniously stopped her at the front door.

The lone elevator was not running, so the three investigators had to take the stairs.

Trey winced as he negotiated the last few steps. "Four flights, *damn!* Oh well, I need the exercise; but, it's tough on my knees these days. I see the two of you are *huffin' and puffin'* as well. You guys are too young to be that outta shape."

Hawk and Jim scoffed and ignored the jibe; but, both were winded.

The stairwell opened onto the small elevator lobby. A uniformed NOPD officer met them there and checked their credentials. Each man signed the on-the-scene roster. Only authorized police personnel would be admitted to the floor during the execution of the search warrant.

There were two apartment doors in the brightly lit lobby area. Two loft apartments occupied the entire floor. Suzi's suite faced north; the other faced the south. Both doors were open; but, the southern suite was vacant and completely devoid of any furnishings.

Trey, Hawk, and Jim were handed crime scene gloves and booties by a CSI tech at the door. Once appropriately attired, they stepped inside and stared.

The interior was a study in austerity, a minimalist expression in black leather, chrome and glass. White walls contrasted severely with the black marble tiles of the floor. A chrome-framed black leather couch faced a vast expanse of tinted plate glass. A set of glass sliding doors trimmed in brushed aluminum took up half of the north wall, and accessed a small balcony.

Hawk stood transfixed, staring at the balcony. Its sole furnishing was a miniature bamboo table of knee height. Its delicate burden was a rectangular pot of dark green glaze that held an exquisite bonsai tree. He had no idea what sort of tree it was.

In truth, he barely saw it. His mind saw another balcony scene.

A wet, wind-whipped display of carnage and hopelessness, the silent horror of Suzi Origami's decapitation, her blank, lifeless—and yet, somehow knowing, stare . . .

A hand upon his shoulder broke the spell.

"Hawk, are you all right?"

"Yeah, Jim, I'm fine. Just thinking, that's all."

Hawk deliberately turned from the balcony and assessed the rest of the front room.

To the right of the balcony doors, the wall held a large flat-screen television and a set of small speakers to either side. Facing the same wall a few feet away and to one side, a glass-topped desk held two computer monitors, an elaborate curved keyboard, and an open laptop. Two component cases stood on the floor beneath the desk; one was slightly larger and more imposing. A 3"x5" evidence card, bearing "SERVER" and the date, had been taped to its faceplate. The other case bore a card reading "PC".

Two CSI technicians had removed the sides from both cases, and were busy digitally photographing the interior hardware and wiring.

Hawk stepped to the rear of the large room, where a galley kitchen sat ensconced in stainless steel trim, black marble countertops, and glass-fronted cabinets.

Next to the kitchen, in what appeared to be a dining area, Trey laid his gloved palm on a flat oval of thick glass that served as a stark table, surrounded by four chrome and black chairs.

Hawk was drawn to the wide length of scarlet ribbon draped across the glass. The partners shrugged at each other without comment.

"Pretty bleak, isn't it?" asked Sgt. Melancon, who appeared quietly at Trey's side.

"Yeah," grunted Trey, "not to my taste at all. It doesn't even look lived in. Are we sure she lived here?"

"Oh, we're pretty sure she did, or at least she *stayed* here," Mel responded. "I'm willing to bet she didn't spend a lot of time here though. We're pretty much through with the search; we're just double-checking at this point. So, go ahead and have a good look around; then we'll talk about what we've found. So far, it's not that significant—other than the computer data, of course. The IT techs tell me that they've gotten quite a lot from the drives while everything is on site, but there's more that's heavily encrypted. So, if it's all right with you, they'll box everything up and do a more thorough examination at their lab. Of course, they'll maintain the chain of custody."

"No problem," acknowledged Trey. "We may as well see the rest of the place."

The upper loft held the sleeping area, another study in minimalism. Against one obsidian glass wall a low bed jutted forth, covered in white silk sheets. Pillows of sable and crimson lay at its head in staggered precision. Just above, a finely detailed grey kimono, deeply filigreed with golden thread, seemed to float upon the face of the dark wall as it hung displayed on a horizontal bamboo rod.

A hinged-frame lithograph, depicting an early seventeenth-century shogunate castle, hung ajar, revealing a wall safe standing open and empty.

A large walk-in closet and its built-in chests held some clothing, but not the volume they expected to find.

There was a well-appointed and spotless bathroom. A mirrored medicine cabinet was empty; no cosmetics, no pills, nothing. A solitary toothbrush and unopened tube of toothpaste sat in a delicate crystal glass to the side of a waterfall faucet near the edge of a pebbled glass sink bowl recessed into the black marble countertop.

A small linen closet held folded sheets and towels, and unopened hair care products.

Returning to the main floor, the detectives were drawn back to the galley kitchen. The narrow space was somewhat dwarfed by the refrigerator-freezer. The stainless behemoth held stacks of frozen dinners, six-packs of bottled fruit drinks, and a large carafe of cold water. There was no fresh food, no perishables. A modest pantry held rice, sugar, and an assortment of herbal teas; green and jasmine teas were predominant.

"That's one huge fridge for one person," Hawk remarked.

"Maybe," Trey allowed. "Notice how all the food is the kind that keeps?"

"Yeah, you're right. It's like a cache."

"That's kinda what I was thinking. Notice anything else?"

"Like what? This place is pretty spare; there's not a lot here."

Trey made a sweeping gesture with his hands, as if to encompass the entire condo. "The clocks, check them out."

Hawk focused. The sole nod toward interior ornamentation appeared to be a varied collection of digital clocks. There was at least one in every room or area; and, all were synchronized to the second.

"Whoa . . . Okay, that's a little creepy."

Trey smiled and canted his head. "Yeah, I know. Maybe it's a little insight into the mind of an assassin—you know, timing, precision—some food for thought, eh?"

They concluded their examination and sought out Sgt. Melancon.

"Okay, Mel," Trey announced, "we're done. What did y'all find?"

"Well, you already know about the computers and data storage. Additionally, we found sufficient traces of occupancy to postulate that this was likely her primary residence—that is, when she's in New Orleans. But, as I said, we don't think she spent all that much time here."

"Find any weapons?" Hawk asked.

"No, we found no weapons. However, we did find a little over five thousand in cash and three bogus foreign passports—Canadian, French, and Japanese—in that wall safe upstairs. They are excellent forgeries, fresh with no visa stamps, and all bear alias names."

"Well, the passports are Homeland Security and State Department violations," Trey observed. "We'll have to notify DHS and State's Bureau of Diplomatic Security. Did you find any other paperwork?"

"We found a business card for a property management company and a couple of receipts for pieces of furniture, but no personal mail—not even bills—no personal photographs or any suggestion of family members, and no address book or any banking information. Of course, she could have accomplished most, if not all, of that online; although, that's probably encrypted as well. There's no documentation related to her computer gear or any electronics. Based on what we've found—or more specifically, *not* found—I don't think it'll be easy if you're planning to make any sort of next-of-kin notification."

"What about those receipts? Was there any personal contact information?" Trey asked.

"Very little, they're from a local outlet store that's been out of business for a little over two years. They invoice the couch and the desk, and show her name and this address for delivery. She paid in cash, by the way—no other paper trail. We found these receipts in the back of a kitchen drawer, like they were shoved in there and forgotten. They bear her signature, as Suzi Origami, dated four years ago.

"We haven't found a copy of the condo lease. But if she kept a copy, we think she might have scanned it to a file in the encrypted data. She certainly seemed to rely a great deal on her computers."

"What about the business card your guys found, the property management company?" Trey probed.

Mel handed Trey a piece of notebook paper. "The card is tagged and bagged; but here's the information. The number is good; my guys checked with the phone company. It's listed to a local realty firm, only about two blocks away."

"Thanks, Mel. We'll follow up when we're through here. What else have you got?"

"You may have noticed the small alarm pad by the door. It's nothing special; all the apartments in this building have the same basic system, just perimeter windows and doors. It's not even monitored; that's an option she apparently declined. It wasn't activated when the FAST unit made the initial entry.

However, there are small wireless cameras in the interior spaces, tucked up in ceiling corners—see those little domes? Their placement pretty well covers the entire apartment; we suspect they connect to her computer system."

"So, that's her version of a security system?" Trey speculated.

"More than likely, we think. They're not hard-wired, and not powered at the moment. So, there's either a remote switch to activate them; or, any batteries may be dead. We'll know more once we get her system analyzed."

"Okay, anything else?"

Mel nodded. "Yeah, a coupla things. We know that each apartment comes with an assigned parking space in the adjacent parking garage, but there's no vehicle parked there. It doesn't look like the space was used much, no accumulation of oil stains or tire marks. There are no security cameras in the garage either, almost like someone, maybe the tenants, valued privacy over security."

"Damn," Trey groused. "So, she had no wheels here, huh?"

The CSI sergeant shrugged. "Doesn't look like it. Hold on a sec'. Hey Cassie, any luck finding any car keys?"

Across the room, the CSI tech looked up and shook her head. "No joy, Sarge. We found no keys or any info on a personal vehicle. We ran her name, and the alias names from the bogus passports, through DMV, but nothing popped—no registrations and no DLs."

"That figures; her name is probably an alias anyway," mulled Trey thoughtfully. "But there's more, Mel, isn't there?"

Mel just grinned. "I'll let Cassie tell you the rest. Cassie, you done? Tell the detectives what you've found, *not found*, and what you think it might mean."

She peeled off her latex gloves, dropped them into a discard bag, and joined her sergeant.

"Well, a few things struck me as odd," Cassie began, flipping open a small notebook. "A woman who could afford to live here would probably have multiples of stuff. I looked in her bathroom, her medicine cabinet, all the usual places, right? So, where's her stuff? Her fragrances, potions and lotions? Where's her make-up? Is this a woman who doesn't use *any* cosmetics? Where's the usual assortment of non-prescription medications? Where's the aspirin? Is this someone who never gets sick, never gets a headache?"

Hawk took a breath, a question on the tip of his tongue; but Cassie held up a hand to forestall any interruptions.

"Okay, maybe she'd take some of that stuff with her—at least what would fit into her purse. And that's another thing—we found no purses, no bags! Women usually have more than one, and lots of accessories and jewelry. But we found *nothing!*"

Trey and Mel exchanged an amused glance as Cassie flipped up a page in her notebook and took a deep breath.

"And then there's her clothes—there's this great closet space, but not enough clothes, or even the right kind! I mean, if she really *lived* here, she'd have a more summer-oriented wardrobe—cotton and light fabric stuff. You know how hot it can get! And that brings me to her *shoes*—there are more boots than shoes! That's just not right for this climate. I only counted *six* pairs of shoes and boots *combined!* Can you *believe* it?" She huffed skeptically as she flipped to the next page.

Hawk wondered about the importance of the shoes. He didn't think that he ever owned more than six pairs of footwear—including boots. He almost raised the obvious question. Fortunately, Trey urged Hawk, with a subtle shake of his head, to remain silent.

Cassie gestured to the kitchen. "Y'all saw what food's in the kitchen, right? Some of those frozen dinners are old—really old, well past their *use-by dates*. So does that mean she ate *every* meal out? Okay, I know that you can always find great food in this town; and, you could conceivably eat out every night.

So, where are the *take-out boxes* and *doggie bags?* There's nothing like that in the fridge—not even anything in the trash bins!"

Cassie pointed across the room. "That red runner on the dining table is actually a vintage—and exquisite—silk *obi*, a belt-like sash for a kimono. It may, or may not, go with the kimono we found displayed in the bedroom.

"We also found an interesting collection of sunglasses, at least ten pairs, in an ornately carved chest. None appear to have prescription lenses, just plain glass or plastic optics. There are half a dozen umbrellas and parasols in a vinyl case in her closet. Some of the parasols are antiques and quite valuable.

"And finally, we found a bonsai tree on the balcony, the only plant. She could leave that for weeks; it'd get plenty of rain on the balcony. However, it does require periodic attention."

Closing her notebook, Cassie summarized. "Anyway, my point is that we can infer almost as much about our victim by what we haven't found as that which we have found. She may have stayed here; but she didn't really live here, not in the classic sense."

Jim, who had been quietly listening as he stood to one side, gently nudged Hawk and whispered, "Damn! She's good!"

Hawk smiled and nodded affirmatively. "Yeah, she is. Based on her assessment and what we can see, this feels to me like a high-style extended-stay hotel or something."

"Yes, it does," Trey agreed, "but there's no luggage."

"Exactly!" Cassie confirmed. "Women like nice luggage, and usually have more than they can use at any one time."

"I'm in general agreement with Cassie," said Sgt. Melancon, with just a trace of pride evident in his voice. "I think we're missing something here. But for the passports and the computer data, we're not finding what we'd expect. It's almost as if she expected this place to be found—maybe even searched. Who knows? Our victim doesn't even have a landline phone; the IT guys said that it appears she used some sort of *Voice Over Internet Protocol*. We don't know if she had a cell phone; we haven't found one, or any related bills either."

"That doesn't make sense," Hawk remarked. "She should've had a cell phone at least, probably a *pre-paid burner*. I know we didn't find one with her body or in the casino suite. We never did find a purse; and we looked."

"Keep what we do know in mind," Trey cautioned. "And Cassie, correct me if I'm wrong. First, let's speculate a little. My gut says if Suzi had a cell phone, she either kept it on her person or may have carried it in her purse. If she had a car, her purse might be in it.

"Now the known facts: there's no evidence that she owned a car, no registration, no current driver's license in her name, or any of the known aliases. The Tribal Police never found an unaccounted-for car at our scene. There may not be a car.

"We're speculating that Suzi carried a purse; the truth is that we don't know for sure. I just can't rationalize a purse as a foregone conclusion. Keep in mind that neither a purse nor any luggage was found at the original scene. Of course, we speculated that whoever killed her may have taken a purse and any luggage, kind of a weak robbery motive; but there's no evidence to support that. In fact, our sole witness, Howard Simms, the hotel's day manager who checked in the group she was with at the front desk, did not recall her having a purse or any luggage. So, focusing on the purse and luggage might be a dead end.

"However, I think the cell phone idea holds water; and her killer may have taken it. I can't imagine her not using a cell phone; although in this case it might be something more sophisticated or technical than I can comprehend. So, I think we can agree that she at least had access to one, or something equivalent, right?"

"Right," agreed Mel. "You may be on to something. This computer installation is a very sophisticated system. We know that her network includes, at a minimum, the hardware we found here; a server with multiple drives, a desktop PC, a laptop, and assorted storage media. We have no way of knowing what she may have in the way of *cloud* operations and storage—not yet, anyway. We don't know if she had a tablet; we found no evidence of one.

"Her internet connection is via a privately owned satellite that's the property of a Japanese conglomerate; the dish is on the roof. The IT guys are trying to figure it out, but they tell me the software is proprietary, and encrypted as well. They do know this system is *VOIP* capable; and, they're pretty sure she's using a very sophisticated *VPN*, uh, *Virtual Private Network.*

"There's no question that she's making ample use of wireless tech, like all those little dome cameras. Even that television on the wall is *WiFi* connected to her computers.

"Unfortunately, we have no idea what this system was really capable of, at least not yet. The tech wizards suspect that she may have done some serious hacking. They're sure they'll know more given the time to fully analyze this system."

Trey shrugged and sighed. "Okay, I guess we'll just have to wait for their report. I see you left a copy of the search warrant and the evidence receipt on the dining table. Is there any more we can accomplish here and now?"

Mel scanned the room one last time and glanced at Cassie. She shook her head. The CSI techs had finished boxing the computer equipment and indicated that they were ready to go, as well.

"No, Trey, we're done here. We can all clear this scene."

"Okay, give Hawk and me about fifteen minutes or so to run down this lead on this property management realty company, then we'll ride to Lafayette with y'all."

The CSI sergeant nodded. "That'll work."

Trey turned to the FBI agent. "Jim, I'm sorry we didn't find anything more helpful for your case. You can always join us tomorrow on the other search warrant at the funeral home. Care to meet us all in Lafayette this evening?"

"Thanks, I appreciate the offer; but, I'm sure my boss expects me back in the office with a full report of today's events."

"Well now, you tell Manny hello for us—we're his biggest fans, don't y' know, okay?"

Jim just grinned and shook his head. Shaking Trey's outstretched hand, he remarked, "You be careful tomorrow—all of you. Have a good night."

"Be safe, Jim," Trey called out as the agent disappeared down the steps.

Turning to the CSI sergeant, he said, "All right, Mel, we'll help you take your gear down, and then go do our interview. I want to try to get a copy of the condo lease. Then we can head to Lafayette. There's a new restaurant off Pinhook Street that Willis told me about that we ought to try, *Enola's*, I think."

"Sounds good to me," agreed Hawk. "I've never had a bad meal in Lafayette, or New Orleans, come to think of it."

Mel and Cassie echoed his sentiment as they trundled their gear down the stairs to their vehicle.

ONCE MOST OF THE CSI team and their NOPD colleagues had cleared the scene, Trey paused on the sidewalk and scanned the area. He noticed with no small degree of satisfaction that the local news crews were gone, no doubt since there had been nothing to see and no official willing to be interviewed. He figured they were chasing another story for their evening deadline, something more along the lines of *if it bleeds, it leads.*

He grimaced; *if they only knew, jeez.*

He reached for his cell phone. "Give me a second, Hawk, and I'll try the realty office."

"Okay, I'm gonna help Mel and Cassie load up."

Calling the realty office, Trey was surprised at the immediate commitment of cooperation.

He and Hawk found Mrs. Anne Cormier waiting for them in the reception area of the office. A tall distinguished woman of middle years, Mrs. Cormier was the proud mother of a newly minted New Orleans police officer, a daughter who had recently graduated at the top of her academy class. In her mother's perspective, helping law enforcement authorities was not only a civic duty, but an honor and privilege.

In anticipation of their need, she had already prepared and produced a copy of the lease in question. She was only too happy to cooperate—and gush about her daughter.

Trey managed to ask a number of case-related questions; however, Mrs. Cormier had little more pertinent information to add. They thanked her profusely, and congratulated her daughter's accomplishments.

The fiercely proud mother positively beamed with satisfaction as she bid them farewell.

"Nice lady," observed Trey, as they headed back up the street to the waiting SUV.

"Yeah, and she saved us having to get a subpoena," countered Hawk.

"Maybe," cautioned Trey. "We'll still have to get one if this leads to something. You know we'll need the original document; this is only a photocopy."

"At least it has Suzi Origami's signature and the name of this real estate holding company Don told us about. So, that confirms another link to Papa George. But we're really no closer to solving her murder, are we?"

"Not yet," Trey confirmed. "And we're no closer on our other victim's case, *Jane Doe*, remember?"

"Oh, yeah, I haven't forgotten. We don't even have an ID on her yet—or a clue that might link or sever the two cases."

"True, but we're better off than we were. I can't shake the feeling that some important door has been opened. And it looks like a lot of other open cases are going to be closed."

"Yeah, I guess we'll just have to wait and see." Hawk stuffed his hands in his pockets, and kept his thoughts to himself.

THE CONCRETE RIBBON of I-10 slipped endlessly beneath the tires of the heavy westbound traffic. Seated in the rear of the unmarked SUV, Hawk stared blankly at the rush of lush growth that bordered the interstate. His mind was elsewhere.

This case was clearly strange enough on its own, but how could he ignore that George Papadolis was somehow at the heart of this, this—*what?*

Just what the hell am I involved in? Why do I feel like everything is off-kilter? And everyone involved is in some sort of jeopardy? I'm worried for Ellen.

Traffic thickened again as the SUV passed through Baton Rouge and crossed the wide Mississippi, but thinned out considerably beyond Port Allen. The landscape began to change, sinking incrementally below the paved level of the elevated interstate highway as the vehicle continued its unabated pace in a futile chase of the lowering sun.

They had entered the causeway portion of I-10 that traversed the Atchafalaya Basin, a massive collection of floodways, swamps, and wet forests that resembled a forgotten slice of the Cretaceous. The lengthening shadows and saffron-tinted light heightened the sense of transformation.

An old memory rose unbidden, yet vivid, of traveling this road once before, over a decade ago.

Hawk had been eastbound then, and the traffic had slowed perceptibly as people gawked at some unfortunate *road-kill* carcass lying on the spare shoulder, against the low concrete railing. At first he thought it was a large dog, but as he neared and passed he was shocked to see it was not a dog, but a panther, dark and dusky. It was huge, over eight feet in length from its muzzle to the tip of its thick tail. Awesome, even in death, there was no doubt it had been magnificent—and deadly—when alive. Such large feline predators had long been thought to be extinct in the swamps; but, there lay rather blatant evidence to the contrary.

That simple experience was both a surprise and a sort of rude philosophical epiphany. Some comfortable assumptions and expectations with which he had grown complacent were suddenly called into question. Perhaps his reality was not what it had seemed, not what he had been told and thus expected.

And now, his perception of reality was once more—*what? Evolving? What does it all mean?*

With a firm mental grip, he shook off such ruminations; he could immerse himself in the philosophical analysis later. What he needed to do, here and now, was to concentrate and focus on the issues at hand; that meant Papa George.

Suzi had killed for him, and so had Leanan. Just how far did his influence reach?

Hawk was coming to appreciate just how darkly twisted and evil, yes *evil,* this individual, George Papadolis, actually was.

I can't afford to underestimate this man. Just how utterly dangerous might he really be? What is he capable of—in this world, or any other?

CH 4

A GENTLE BREEZE TEASED Ellen's hair and cooled her coffee as she leaned against a pillar on the front porch. Tuesday morning had arrived under the herald of a bright azure sky with nary a trace of cloud. She let her eyes drift over the splashes of colors vying for attention in the diverse gardens, and willed herself to put all other thoughts aside.

Just savor the moment.

She had decided to take this day to relax, recoup her energy, and organize her thoughts. In truth, she had plenty to think about. Today she would begin to record the things she thought worthy of mention in the journal, as Maude had asked. She sensed that this was important. It was certainly no imposition for one who so enjoyed writing.

The screen door banged open as Smokey shot onto the porch, screeched to a halt, and promptly sat down as if nothing unusual had happened.

Ellen laughed and bent to pet him. She glanced up as Stacy and Mark came out to join her, each clasping a mug of hot coffee.

Mark held the door open for a moment longer as the dogs followed him out, promptly finding favorite spots on the smooth boards to lie down. Stacy and Mark opted for the rocking chairs.

Rubbing his stomach and grinning widely, Mark broke the silence.

"That was an excellent breakfast! I'm stuffed. I couldn't eat like this all the time; I'd put on way too much weight. So, what's on the agenda for today?"

"Nothing, really," Ellen offered with a sigh. "I want to take it easy; do some thinking, some writing, maybe take a walk."

At the word *walk* the dogs perked up and looked right at her, in obvious anticipation, their ears alert.

Stacy laughed aloud. "Oh-ho, now you've done it! It looks like we'll be going for a walk! I guess it wouldn't hurt to work off some of your mom's pancakes, now would it?"

"That sounds pretty good," agreed Mark, "but I don't want to be gone too long. I want to finish up with the truck this afternoon. You wanna go now?"

"At least give me time to change shoes," Stacy countered, pointing to her feet. "These flip-flops won't do for the woods."

"We have plenty of time," Ellen observed. "I want to finish my coffee. And we've got to let my mom know."

"She might want to go with us. Let's ask her," Stacy suggested.

"We can ask, but I think she and Madeline have something planned for today," Mark cautioned. "She was on the phone with her when I came downstairs this morning."

Ellen and Stacy just looked at one another.

"Mark," Ellen said soberly, "I think we need to talk—the three of us—but let's do it on our walk, okay?"

Stacy looked over her coffee mug, raised her eyebrows, and nodded affirmatively at Mark.

He simply shrugged his shoulders in mute acquiescence.

THIRTY MINUTES LATER, on the wide sun-dappled path in the forest, Mark came to a sudden halt.

"Aunt Millie did what? She told Madeline? Why? Th-that's, uh, that's . . ."

"We know, Mark, we know," soothed Stacy. "But it's done now; so, deal with it."

Ellen held out her hands in supplication. "Mark, I can kind of understand that Millie *had* to tell somebody—someone of her own generation in a sense. I know that Madeline is older—but you know what I mean.

"Think about it. Truth is that we are going to need a great deal more information; that means research in a fairly esoteric area. So, who better than Madeline? She's already provided a good deal of information about Maude, Diere, and Leanan—some of it from firsthand experience."

"But don't you see?" he argued. "She'll almost assuredly tell her husband, Armand. This sort of research falls well within his bailiwick—it's his expertise. Don't you remember what he talked about the night of Maude's wake, when we were all up in the loft of the bookstore?"

Ellen did remember, and found herself nodding; Mark did have a point.

"Besides," he rationalized, "a couple who've been together and happily married as long as they have probably *always* share, telling each other *everything!*"

"What?" Ellen balked. Honestly, she'd never thought about that. "Really?"

"Oh, Ellen, I think he's right." Stacy nodded. "I'd probably tell *my* husband—if I *had* one. And if the shoe were on the other foot, I'd want to be told. I'm not sure I'd be too forgiving if my spouse were to try to hide the existence of other realms in the Multiverse from me. Do you know what I'm saying?"

"Yeah, I think I do." Ellen sighed. "But what can we do about it? I mean *the cat's out of the bag*, so to speak—uh, no offense, Smokey."

"Well," Mark offered, "I suppose all we can do is keep the number of people who do know to a minimum; and, get everyone to agree to some sort of mutually agreeable *containment strategy*. We can't let this information get out of our control. It could potentially be dangerous—perhaps for everyone, not just us."

They walked on in silence.

This path would have taken them toward the cabin, but Smokey dashed off to the left on a less obvious track. Out of curiosity, Ellen followed. Within minutes, the faint path seemed to come to an abrupt halt at the face of a bluff, then meandered off to the right.

Ellen stood very still, several paces from the base of the bluff, as a strong sense of déjà vu washed over her. She had been here before, in a dream. Nonetheless, she remembered it.

She stepped forward and felt another sensation, an overwhelming urge to be away from here. The closer she approached a thick screen of overgrowth and honeysuckle vines, the stronger it grew.

That's very unpleasant! But there's something here—a cave? I can sense it!

In her dream, Max had prevented her from exploring further; but now, both dogs merely sat to one side and watched her. Smokey simply wound through the fragrant honeysuckle maze and disappeared beyond the vines.

"What is it, Ellen?" Stacy came to stand beside her friend. "This place feels, uh, I don't know—*strange,* kind of *weird.* Come on, let's go."

"Hold on. I think—no, I *know* there's a cave here, behind all this honeysuckle and *stuff.* Smokey just went in there."

"*Stuff?*" Stacy chuckled. "Ellen, that's *privet.* This looks like it was planted. See how all these trunks are in a straight line? The honeysuckle is wild and just overgrew the privet. You're right; something's behind this. Let's see if we can get through here. Mark, hold these branches back, would you?"

"I've got them," Mark grunted. "Are you sure you want to do this? This feels *funny*, kinda *off-putting*. I don't like this at all; we should stick to the plan and keep moving. I've got things to do. Hey! There *is* an opening back there. Oh crap! It *is* a cave, dammit!"

"Huh? What's wrong, Mark?" Stacy pressed.

"Uh, well it's just that, um," he hedged, "I'm not all that fond of caves, uh, lately, you know?"

"Oh, I get it—it's okay, Mark," Ellen assured her cousin. "This isn't the Shadow Realm; we're home now. Everything should be okay, shouldn't it? Besides, Smokey went through here; it didn't phase him at all. So, I'm sure it's safe; you know, you gotta trust Smokey. Just hold these branches back; Stacy and I will go through first."

"Yeah, gotta trust Smokey," Stacy echoed. With an impish smirk, she reached out and stroked Mark's cheek. "Don't worry, lover, we'll protect you."

The women slipped past Mark and stood at the entrance to the cave. Ellen took a step forward, and immediately experienced a sudden sense of stomach-lurching disorientation. She paused for a moment.

That was awful! I certainly wouldn't want Stacy or Mark, or even the pets to experience that sensation. Maybe I was just dizzy.

The dogs simply walked past her, then began sniffing the dirt floor just inside. Stacy followed, and stood with Ellen. Mark resignedly pushed his way past the stubborn privet to join them.

"Well, ladies, I take it back; that wasn't so bad." He held up a small flashlight. "Shall we explore?"

Stacy smiled and produced a penlight of her own.

Ellen grinned and dug in her pocket for a key fob that incorporated a small LED light; its spot of white light darted about on the dirt floor. "I should have guessed that we'd all come equipped."

Mark sighed. "I don't think I'll go anywhere without some sort of light source ever again."

The women smiled in moot agreement.

He held up a small plastic lighter in his other hand. "And you never know when you might need a little *fire*."

“My, aren’t you the well-prepared *Boy Scout*,” teased Stacy. “I guess that beats rubbing two sticks together in the dark!”

The three flashlights provided modestly adequate illumination for them to proceed deeper into the cave. The flat dirt floor was undisturbed, save for Smokey’s recent tracks, and free of debris. Walls of rough stone tapered to a rugged ceiling high above their heads.

They soon confronted a blockage, a rippled wall of boulders. They panned their lights over the face of the wall, but there seemed to be no way past.

“Hmm, dead end. Looks like an old cave-in,” Mark mused aloud. “Wait, I think it might be deliberate. Look, there are traces of old mortar between these stones. This was built here, and crafted to appear as if the cave came to an abrupt end.”

Smokey materialized from the shadows; the dogs gave him a cursory sniff.

“Smokey,” asked Stacy, “where have you been?”

In answer, the cat simply turned and walked into a deep pool of shadow, disappearing once again.

Mark followed him. “Well now, isn’t this clever. Over here, there’s a passage.”

Behind a large outcropping, which hid the entrance from view, another short passage descended for several yards and opened into a much larger space. As Mark disappeared from view, the women grew quiet.

“Hey, there’s a lantern here,” he announced from the darkness.

There was a muted clicking. Soft yellow light flared, brightened, and settled into a golden glow. Soon there was another, and another.

Stacy nudged Ellen. “A Boy Scout and his lighter to the rescue, eh? Come on, let’s go.”

“I found three old hurricane lanterns full of oil, so we have more light.” Mark handed Ellen and Stacy each a glass-globed lantern as they joined him. “I have no idea how long these have been here, but they work." He nudged Stacy with his elbow and grinned smugly. "Now, weren't you lucky that *someone* had a disposable lighter and was, what was that word—*prepared?*"

As Stacy rolled her eyes, Ellen laughed, only to be answered with a pale echo of her chortle, suggesting a sizable expanse of subterranean space.

Stepping further into the chamber, they raised their lamps high to maximize the light, and were stunned into silence.

This cave was far bigger than they expected; it appeared to be a perfect hemisphere. The floor was a dirt-free patchwork of flat stones, cunningly fitted together without the benefit of mortar. The walls were smoothly hewn rock, girdled a few feet from the floor in a continuous series of bas-relief carvings depicting stout individuals in mail armor brandishing axes and battling fantastic beasts.

"Whoa," murmured Mark. "Will you look at that. That's really something."

They approached the wall and held their lamps close.

"This is amazing," Stacy breathed as she ran her hand over the stone surfaces of the figures.

"The workmanship is awesome," Ellen agreed, hefting her lamp. "The details are exquisite."

Mark stepped back and scanned more of the walls. "Look, they go on and on."

The women saw that he was right. These carvings appeared to comprise a ring about the chamber, at waist height.

Just below the ring of carvings, half a dozen short-legged tables were pressed against the curving wall. Most of the dust-coated tables were bare, but some held assorted small barrels, glass jars, and unfamiliar tools and devices. A number of short chairs and stools were pushed under some of the tables.

"You know," Ellen surmised, "this space isn't merely a *cave;* it's a *chamber* because it's obviously been crafted by someone."

Stacy wandered toward the center of the space and held her lamp aloft. "Hey guys, what is this?"

A series of shapes hidden by dust-covered tarps stood near the center of the vast chamber. Without hesitation, Stacy jerked the tarps free and revealed towering copper metal vessels, festooned with coiled piping, patinated ornamentation and brass valve handles.

A guffaw startled Ellen, until she realized it was only Mark. He began to laugh, a hearty belly laugh that left him wheezing.

Finally catching his breath, Mark sputtered, "I *don't* believe it! But, of course! It makes so much sense now!"

Stacy tried to glare at him, but found it impossible not to smile. "And just what are you talking about, *Mr. Hilarity?*"

"Forgive me, ladies, but *this,*" he said as he held his lantern high and indicated the metallic monstrosity with a sweep of his other hand, "is a *still!* A rather old and elaborate version, but I think it's a still nonetheless."

Ellen gawked at her cousin. "You mean for making *moonshine?*"

"Possibly." He bobbed his head. "It's for the distillation of some type of alcoholic spirits, assuredly. I don't know all that much about it, but I do know that whatever liquor you make depends on the ingredients you have to work with. For example, moonshine is typically made from corn."

Mark stared in open admiration as he walked around the device. "This is really something. It's *huge!* There would have to be a heat source big enough to . . . Hmm, now that's a little strange."

"What is?" Ellen asked.

Mark used his flashlight to scan a depression in the floor just below the largest copper vessel. "As far as I know, heat is required to cook the mash in the distillation process. But I don't see any evidence of a fire, no charcoal or even ashes."

"So maybe they swept out the ashes?" Stacy proffered with a shrug.

"Maybe, but I doubt it," pondered Mark. "There's not a trace of ash; nor do I see any fuel source, no pile of wood or coal. Yet, I can see that the base of this vessel is discolored as if from great heat. Look, the stones in the wall of the depression directly below are glazed—that would take a lot of heat."

"Well, if there was a fire," Stacy reasoned, "wouldn't there be smoke? Where would that go? I don't see any vents in the ceiling, do you?"

Raising their lights they craned their necks, but could discern only a smooth expanse of stone far overhead.

"I don't see anything," Ellen admitted, "not even any soot stains up there."

Obviously intrigued, Mark stepped back and slowly washed the flashlight beam over the entire assembly of the distillation device, mumbling pensively. "There's just something too strange about all of this."

"*Duh*, no kidding," Stacy retorted.

He walked a few paces to either side, scrutinizing details as he moved. "Anyway, this is really some amazing workmanship—somebody really knew what they were doing. I think the vessels and coils are copper, but these fittings are brass. And I think this plate, some sort of ornamentation with printing or characters on it which I don't recognize, is made of *gold!*"

"Really? Does that mean this is somehow sanctioned, or legal?" Ellen pondered aloud.

"I seriously doubt it." Mark shook his head, and swept his hands about the chamber. "It's very unlikely this was any sort of legitimate distillery. It would have to have been licensed, routinely inspected, and subject to a host of taxes. No, someone made a lot of *illicit* booze here."

"Does this mean that Maude was a *bootlegger?*" asked a wide-eyed Stacy.

"Maybe." Ellen grinned. "We always knew she was a bit of a *pistol*."

"Oh, I think we can speculate that she was definitely involved," observed Mark. "Remember the *hot-rod* Chevy in the garage? That car was set up to transport illegal booze, of that I have no doubt. And this location is so well hidden; well, you can't say it doesn't make some sense. Although, I doubt she could have done it on her own. This type of operation would have required some help, some kind of infrastructure. However, everything about it would've been kept secret to protect it."

"Uh-oh," mumbled Ellen.

"What is it?" asked Stacy.

"Maybe nothing, but I just had a thought. Let me try something."

"Oh yeah, I get it," Stacy blurted, "the easy eyes trick!"

"Huh? What?" Mark wondered aloud.

"Really, Mark? We already explained relaxing your focus." Stacy scoffed in mild exasperation.

"You could have just said that, instead of 'easy eyes trick', you know," he mumbled in a sulk.

"Now hush! Let Ellen do this—it takes some concentration, you know?"

Standing to one side of the room's center, Ellen smiled. *Concentration? Uh, not so much anymore.*

She let her eyes relax their focus. Within a few heartbeats, a soft blue glow became apparent to her where the curved wall met the smooth floor, and the frieze along the wall began to glow in bright blue neon intensity. She stared in astonishment as the articulated figures slowly moved in patterns of mortal combat. Above the silent tableau, on what had been the blank stone wall and ceiling, unfamiliar runes pulsated and morphed into ever-changing new shapes.

This was not the same as the light she had seen at the cabin. This light was *blue*, not *red*. The runes were different—*a different language?*

Slowly turning to see the entire chamber, she beheld the still—or rather how it may have looked in operation. At the base of the largest vessel, within the dip in the floor, a ghostly blue light blazed in a roiling, yet contained, intensity. Concentrating, she could discern a crystalline shape at the heart of this trapped energy.

What is that? A gem? It's at least the size of an orange! I sense the capability of energy containment, and a kind of managed or controlled release, much like the emerald Stacy had been given by the Guildmaster, a spell contained within. But what about this vision? Was this truly a glimpse into the past, or merely an imprint of lingering residual energy? Until I more fully understand, perhaps I'd best keep this to myself.

Closing her eyes briefly, she allowed the azure light to dissipate. Upon opening her eyes, she beheld the chamber as it had been, only dimly illuminated by the oil lamps and flashlights.

As she turned to Mark and Stacy, she spied a cerulean trace, a residual glow of faint blue, now fading, around one of the closely set flagstones in the floor. Kneeling over the now darkened flagstone, Ellen placed the palm of her hand flat upon its cool surface and closed her eyes.

"Ellen!" Stacy cried in alarm, "Are you all right?"

"I'm fine. I think I saw something. Give me a minute." She calmed herself, slowed her breathing, and sought her metaphysical center.

Mark, obviously puzzled, started to speak, but Stacy silenced him with a finger to her lips.

In the depths of Ellen's mind, a picture formed. The image was this very place, but in another time altogether. She saw Maude kneeling over this very stone, softly speaking an unheard incantation. Then the image of Maude looked directly at her, smiled and nodded affirmatively. In the next instant, Ellen was back in the present moment, her hand still pressed upon the wide stone.

She looked up at Stacy and Mark, their concern obvious, and smiled.

"Everything is all right," she assured them. "There is something below this flagstone, something important that Maude placed here—at least I *think* she did. But whatever it is, I'm certain she wanted me to have it. Do you think we can get this stone up?"

"We can try," said Mark. "The fit looks pretty tight. Let me see what I can find to use as a tool."

There were a number of unfamiliar hand tools on some of the tables. Mark settled on what appeared to be a chisel, a sort of round wooden mallet, and an iron bar almost the length of his arm. He knelt and placed the chisel in a narrow space between two flagstones, hefted the mallet, and prepared to strike—but Ellen suddenly stopped him.

"Stop! Wait! I think there's some sort of protection, or at least I think we should expect it."

"What?" Stacy blurted, quickly looking about. "You mean like a spell?"

"Huh? How can you tell?" Mark asked, holding the mallet poised to fall. "Can you *see* something?"

"No, not exactly—call it a *hunch,* or a *deduction,*" Ellen explained. "Maude wouldn't go to the trouble of hiding something without somehow *protecting it* from being found by the wrong sort of people, now would she?"

Mark and Stacy looked at each other in sudden concern and then apprehensively at Ellen as she raised a finger in caution.

"Listen, neither of you felt anything, like a sudden disorientation when you entered the cave opening, did you?"

They glanced at one another and shook their heads.

"Well," Stacy offered, "I thought the place felt *strange* or *weird* and kind of *uncomfortable;* but, I didn't feel *disoriented.*"

"Yeah, kind of uncomfortable," Mark agreed, "like I wanted to leave—but not disoriented."

Ellen nodded. "Well, *I* did. I remembered thinking that I hoped you all wouldn't feel the same discomfort; and you didn't. I suspect there was some sort of *avoidance spell* on the cave entrance; and I managed to, uh, *turn it off*, I guess. Look, just bear with me; I think I'm supposed to be figuring this stuff out on my own. So, let me try something with this stone—*before* you apply any force."

Mark stood, and Ellen took his place kneeling over the flagstone.

Closing her eyes and holding her hands out flat, just above the surface of the stone, she let her awareness encompass the stone, its adjacent brethren, and finally the entire floor. To her surprise, she sensed that the entire floor—no, the *entire chamber*—hummed with a formidable level of trapped energy. It bore a familiar format, that of a potent transit spell. She realized that any attempt to force the chamber to yield its protected secrets would trigger the spell. The interlopers would be instantly transported, no doubt to someplace very unpleasant.

"Oh man, it *is* protected—big time! Don't do anything!"

"Another spell?" Stacy asked. "Can you turn this one off, too?"

"Huh?" Ellen balked. Could she turn this spell off, too—as she had with the avoidance spell?

"Well, can you?" Mark echoed.

"Good question. I dunno; but I may as well try."

Ellen closed her eyes, concentrated on the trapped energy, and visualized holding it in check, a sort of suspended animation. She imagined the swirl of energy slowing and stopping, held in abeyance. The essence of the crafting manifested a certain familiarity; she sensed that she was beginning to recognize Maude's hand in the casting of the overall protection spells.

She then tested the chamber through her ever-questing awareness and found it quiescent, at least for the moment. Opening her eyes, she sighed.

So far, so good. Now, how would Maude have dealt with this stone? It would have been simple.

She closed her eyes once more and focused her will upon the flagstone. She visualized it rising from its placement within the floor and coming to rest to one side of a gaping hole.

Stacy's gasp and the clang of the dropped chisel as it fell from Mark's hand were sufficient stimuli to startle Ellen. She opened her eyes to see that the flagstone now lay next to a dark recess in the floor.

"If I hadn't seen you do that, I'd never believe it!" exclaimed Mark.

Stacy hefted her lantern near the edge. "Hey! There's a box down there! It looks to be only a couple of feet deep. Mark, can you reach it?"

Prone on his stomach, he could just grasp a metal handle on the box top. He grunted and strained; it barely budged, only twisting a bit in his grip. "I can reach it, but I can't lift it. Damn! I can only get one hand on the handle. Hey, look! It's not just one box; there's another beneath it. This hole is deeper than a few feet, and it's lined with very smooth stones. We're going to need something like a block and tackle to lift the top box out, or maybe even both, if they're equally heavy, I would think."

"Maybe not," mused Stacy. "Ellen, can you try, like you did with the stone?"

Ellen broke into a wide grin. "Sure, I don't see why not. Stand back—just in case."

She focused her awareness on the pit and its contents and was surprised to find a familiar energy signature. *More of Maude's crafting? Yes, of course it is.*

Ellen couldn't help but smile; somehow she now knew exactly what to do. Gathering some of the residual energies from the spell she held in stasis, she focused on levitating each box out of the pit and setting it down on the floor of the chamber.

It worked.

"Oh man, that was way cool!" squealed Stacy, grabbing Mark's arm—who was, for the moment, speechless.

There were actually *three* grey metal boxes, unmarked cubes of about eighteen inches, each the size of a small chest. They appeared to be similar to large bank safe-deposit boxes, but with metallic push-button releases and handles on their tops.

Ellen opened the first; its top flopped back on a long piano hinge. As she held her lantern high, the three friends were once again stunned into silence.

Mark quickly opened the other two boxes and stood wide-eyed as spots of reflected lantern light dimly danced upon the domed ceiling of the chamber.

The chests brimmed with coins, thousands of coins.

"No wonder they were so heavy," breathed Mark.

"What is this?" gasped Stacy. "Like a treasure, or something?"

"I don't know," whispered Ellen, as she picked up a handful of coins to examine them more closely.

Mark did the same, flicking on his flashlight to better scrutinize the cache. "Well, well, well. In a sense, this *is* a treasure. I only see late issue coins, not any real antique stuff like *doubloons* or *pieces-of-eight*. But I do see American gold and silver coins from the nineteenth and twentieth centuries."

"But this box over here is different," observed Ellen. "These aren't American coins."

"Let's see," said Mark eagerly. "Wow! These are German marks, Austrian kronen, South African Krugerrands, and Swiss francs. All the coins in this chest are gold."

"Well, this one is full of coins, too," Stacy added. "I think they're all gold, silver, and copper. But I don't recognize any of them. Of course, it's hard to see in this light."

Mark joined her and shone his flashlight on the strange coins. In the enhanced light, they could see that these coins were unique, indeed. Many depicted heraldry—shields bearing coats of arms—and runes on the other side. Some depicted only runes on both sides.

Stacy picked up a handful and sorted out a number of copper coins. "I think I've seen some like this before, in Shadow. Salidar paid the innkeeper, Boltar, with *coppers* like these for our meals. I'll bet these coins are the common currency of the different realms!"

"Yeah, that would explain why they're in this chest, separate from the coins used in our realm," Mark mused.

"Then it would also make sense that the other coins are separated," Stacy observed as she dropped the coppers back into the chest, "because one chest contains only gold coins that we don't often see, the collectible kind like the Krugerrands. And the other chest contains coins that we *do* see in everyday commerce, you know, like dimes, quarters, dollars, and fifty-cent pieces."

"Hmm, I'm not so sure," responded Mark as he scooped up a handful of coins from the chest Ellen had opened.

"What do you mean?" Ellen asked.

"Here, take a good look at these coins," he said, sprinkling a few into their open hands. "See the gold ones? Well, the United States went off the Gold Standard in 1933, and no more gold coins were minted for general circulation. Look at the dates, nothing after 1933. Now look at the silver coins; the US stopped minting true silver coins in the mid-sixties. I doubt we'll find any dates later than 1964.

"Now, here's my point; these coins are worth a great deal, far more than their *face value*. I think we have discovered what amounts to a small fortune; and, that doesn't take into account all the gold coins minted here in our realm in the other chest."

Hands on her hips, Stacy smiled at Mark. "And just how is it that you know so much about coins?"

Mark grinned back and admitted, "Actually, I don't. But a guy I work with, another associate attorney in my firm, is an avid *numismatist,* a coin collector/trader. He knows all about valuable coin trading and makes a tidy sum on an occasional sale of a rare coin. There's a lot of money in the collectible coin trade, uh, no pun intended."

Ellen let the coins in her palm slip through her fingers, tinkling as they dropped back into the open chest. She assumed Maude never fully trusted banks, having lived through the Great Depression, so she must have stashed these coins here, well protected, yet readily available. "Okay, so what do you think all this means?"

"Well," answered Mark, "among other things, it could mean that our problems with the *back taxes* owed on the farm are effectively solved. But we should be discreet and very careful. No one can know about these coins."

"I'm not sure I understand," said Ellen, her confusion evident.

Mark weighed a handful of coins as he answered. "I can convert this small amount into a considerable amount of cash, quite legitimately, by having my friend offer certain of these coins for acquisition on the collectors' market. The trick is not to offer too many coins, or too often. A coin's rarity has a significant effect on its market value; so, it wouldn't do to suddenly flood the market with examples of an otherwise very rare coin."

"Okay," she acknowledged. "I can see how that makes sense."

"Of course, it would be best to move slowly and deliberately; only liquidate those assets that we deem as absolutely necessary. You could even use some of the cash to get the farm and all back on to a self-sufficient level."

"The farm and all? What are you talking about?"

Mark pointed to her. "Look, you haven't come right out and said so; but, I suspect you intend to live here, don't you?"

She paused for only a moment. "I admit it has been on my mind. After all we've seen and learned, it would be kind of hard to be the Steward and not live here. So, yeah, I guess I do intend to live here."

Mark nodded. "Well then, Ellen, you'll have to have some sort of income; and, these coins are *not* the way to do it."

"What do you mean?" she pressed.

He dropped the handful of coins back into the chest. "Think about it. You'll need some sort of cash flow to maintain the farm, pay the bills, to include the taxes, and just survive. Have you given any thought to stuff like this? You know the rest of us have jobs and lives to return to, and—"

"Ouch! Mark," Stacy cried, coming to her friend's defense. "That's a little harsh, don't you think? Ellen's got a *life!*"

Ellen reached out and placed a hand on Stacy's arm. "Hey, it's okay. Let him finish. I think I know where this is going."

Mark sighed and apologized. "I'm sorry if I seem to be too blunt. But seriously, have you thought about any of these issues?"

"Not really," she admitted. "I think I got preoccupied with being the Steward of this place—I admit I'm in awe of it. Now that you've brought it up, I realize I haven't considered all the practical aspects and logistics of actually living here."

"Well, it is a farm," remarked Stacy, "with the most astounding herbal and flower gardens I've ever seen. It could really be a nursery or some sort of, oh, I don't know, maybe an herb and flower wholesale business. Oh my goodness—you could do the whole thing *online!* It'd be great!

"Oh, wait! You could collect and sell seeds—that's a big thing these days! I've read lots of articles about heirloom seeds. Ooh, we could design these cute little seed envelopes. Your mom and Madeline could help figure out what we've got. Cute little envelopes would be a lot easier to ship than flowers, you know?"

"Actually, that's an excellent idea," agreed Mark. "Considering that we have the farm already, it'd require less of a start-up investment. I think you'd still need the appropriate business licenses, a website, and a shipping contract. Of course, you would most likely need some help."

"Well," admitted Ellen, wiping her hands on her jeans, "it certainly is a lot to think about. But for now, shouldn't we secure these chests and return them to their hiding place? I'm pretty sure I can reactivate the protection spell."

Mark and Stacy nodded sagely. For the time being, that sounded like the best plan.

However, Ellen, still deep in thought, paused. "You know, it all does make some sense. Mark, maybe you should select a handful of the coins you think will work best for us, and do as you proposed with your friend. It *would* be wonderful to alleviate this tax burden. You *are* certain that this is all legal?"

"Quite certain, El'. Pursuant to Maude's last will and testament, these coins are now *your property* to do with as you see fit. You'd have to declare the profit from any sales, of course, but that's an income tax issue. There's no question as to your ownership of anything found on the property."

Reassured, Ellen smiled. "Fine. Select the coins, close up these boxes, and let's see if I can do my levitation trick once more to hide them again."

"That works for me." Mark started picking through the coins. "I certainly don't need to chance a hernia hefting these boxes."

Ellen's skill with levitation had not diminished, and the three chests were soon secured beneath the replaced flagstone. It was no great matter for her to reactivate Maude's protection spell, either. In fact, it seemed easy, almost *natural.*

Standing outside the cave's entrance, just beyond the privet and honeysuckle, Stacy asked, "Can you make the avoidance spell work again, too?"

"I think so," Ellen said softly. "Try taking a few steps closer to the privet."

"Ugh," spat Stacy, quickly retreating after two short steps. "That's even worse than before! What did you do?"

"Oh, sorry. I thought to enhance the intensity a bit. But maybe that's too much?"

"No, leave it," urged Mark. "We don't need anyone snooping around. Leave it strong."

Ellen shrugged in acquiescence and turned toward the path.

Smokey and the dogs were already trotting toward home; the three friends followed.

Musing aloud, Ellen asked, "So, who do you think built that chamber?"

"Good question," observed Mark. "The workmanship was really something. I got the impression it was really quite old."

"Do you mean the stonework or the *still?*" teased Stacy.

"Actually, both," Mark retorted and chuckled. "Although I'll bet the stonework was done before the booze was brewed."

Softly, Ellen said, "I could sense old magic there. When I did the relaxed eyes trick, I could see the energy; it was *blue*. I probably should have mentioned that; I guess I got distracted with finding the coins and all. Anyway, the carved figures seemed to move in the blue light. It was different from the light we saw at the cabin, that was *red*. The runes were different, too. I had the sense that they might be a different language, different from the runes I saw in the red light. I'm not really sure."

"Did you all notice how low the tables were, the chairs, too?" Mark asked.

"Dwarves!" announced Stacy. "It has to be! Dwarves crafted that chamber, and probably built the still! And I'll bet their magic must be blue!"

Ellen and Mark stared at her in awe.

"What makes you say that?" asked Ellen.

"Well, the figures in the carvings that went all around the wall were short and stocky, the chairs and tables were obviously made for someone of short stature; and of course, Dwarves are famous in folklore for high levels of stone craftsmanship. And I wouldn't be at all surprised to learn that they were excellent brewers or brewmasters—or whatever you'd call someone who runs a still."

"Uh, that'd be *distillers*," offered Mark, obviously surprised.

"Somehow, Stacy," Ellen reasoned, "I get the sense that you're right—*Dwarves.*"

"Interesting company our Aunt Maude kept," observed Mark dryly.

"Interesting, indeed," agreed Ellen.

CH 5

THEODORE RASMUSSEN, AKA *Teddy Pots*, was bone tired. He'd been up for the past three days and he realized he'd need to *crash* soon. He knew not to do any more crystal. Besides, they were almost finished here. He was getting too old for these marathon cooking sessions, but this was to be his last—at least in this lab. They were supposed to shut down once this batch was done.

He looked up from the small desk and his laminated checklist. To his right, two tired men moved carefully and deliberately around vats, buckets, propane cylinders, and a web of rubber tubing within the confines of the crowded room as they went about their monitoring tasks. All three of them wore stained grey coveralls and rubber boots. Professional-grade respirators covered their lower faces; the masks were critical because the fumes could be intense during the cooking process. This was no *stove-top cooker;* this was a full-blown meth lab.

The work was very dangerous, but very, very profitable.

Right now, Teddy craved a cigarette; but, that was out of the question in here—unless he had a death wish. However, his craving would not be denied. He stood to draw the attention of his coworkers, mimed puffing on a cigarette, and pointed to the door.

One of the masked men nodded and waved him on.

Teddy wound through a maze of stacked rolls of paper towels, bolts of cheesecloth, and around a leaning tower of ice chests. He pushed through a series of clear plastic sheets suspended from the ceiling to get into the next room. Once within, he made for the lone door that was the sole exit from that end of the building.

He stepped outside and carefully closed the door. He liked the darkness, and felt that the night welcomed him. Tugging his mask free from his face, he let it flop against his chest. He walked a few steps away from the building, stood arms akimbo in the night breeze, and savored the fresh air. Lighting a cigarette would have to wait a few minutes until the fumes permeating his clothing dissipated somewhat.

The waning night was cool and clear. The setting moon seemed to barely kiss the western horizon. Teddy could see that the bright orb would sink into the dark embrace of the shrouded tree line in the time it would take him to smoke a cigarette, maybe two. But for now, it shone almost three-quarters full, so he had ample light to see by.

The employee parking area in the rear of the building was empty; and the wooded area beyond was quiet and dark. He was alone but for the occasional sounds of crickets and tree frogs. Sunrise would come soon enough, but this was a placid moment, a quiet time that put him in a reflective mood.

This had been a sweet deal for him. He'd had the run of the funeral home since the owner's death a little over two years ago, when the crackhead son had inherited the business. Rudy, the dilettante heir, had been suckered into some bad loans by Fenton Brewster—money no doubt wasted on more crack cocaine. Of course, when the addict couldn't make the weekly *vig*, the legitimate business was history. Now Rudy was a token front man, and as much an empty shell as his father's once solvent mortuary business.

Under Brewster's barely hidden control, the legitimate enterprise had quickly degenerated into a money laundering, drug distribution, and rather ironically, an illicit body disposal operation.

But all that was changing.

The rumor was that Fenton Brewster was dead; and, he'd died owing Papa George quite a lot on an outstanding loan. To owe Papa George was not good; failure to pay him was fatal. He could and would take anything and everything the poor soul once had. Teddy knew full well that Papa George knew all about Brewster's funeral home operation. And if Brewster *was* dead, it was only a matter of time before Papa George stepped in.

Teddy didn't plan to be part of the *management transition and consolidation*. He'd finish this last batch of meth to effectively conclude this current contract, and then disappear. He was good at that, very good. Besides, he didn't want any part of the grief he knew was coming.

He fumbled in his coveralls, trying to reach his cigarettes. Finally successful, he fished one out and carefully lit it. Cupping the butt to conceal the glow, an old survival habit from years on the run, he savored a deep drag and thought he might try someplace else on the Gulf Coast—maybe Florida? No one knew him there. He wondered idly if he'd miss this place or the people, not that he cared about any of them.

On the other hand, he hadn't heard from Suzi in the last few weeks; that nagged at him. She might well be the closest thing he had to a friend. Even if she didn't have a job for him, she did keep in touch. They had a mutually beneficial, and for him, quite profitable arrangement. She did contract *wet-work;* he did the clean-up and disposal. He never knew or really cared what she was paid for each job; he earned five grand whenever she used his services. Having access to a hearse was a real help in this business.

A little over six months ago, Fenton Brewster accepted a deal with a South American cartel that was diversifying and was very interested in establishing full-scale methamphetamine production. Teddy was one of the best old-school meth cooks still around. So, Brewster had Teddy set up a full-scale lab in the funeral home's crematorium, and made him take on two client-apprentices, Ramon and Pablo, of no last names of course, to learn the trade. When this lab was done cooking, they were supposed to go back home, somewhere south of the border, and set up their own lab operations.

Teddy would not be sorry to see them go; they gave him the *creeps*.

Brewster didn't tell Teddy much about the two men—in fact, hardly anything at all—only that he was to teach them how to set up and cook in a full-scale lab. Teddy assumed that Brewster didn't really know too much more either. But over time, Teddy had learned some things, none of which made him feel any easier around Ramon and Pablo.

They were too quiet for one thing, not just that they hardly ever talked; it was that they never made any unnecessary sound or noise. They could move like ghosts. And their eyes, so cold—they looked *through you*, and seemed to convey *you are nothing; I could kill you on the spot.*

Teddy pegged them as mercenaries, or at least ex-military types. But that was really a no-brainer since each wore a holstered pistol and kept a short-barreled AK-74 within reach almost all the time. There was no mistaking the way they handled those assault carbines; they were professionals, or at least had been at one time.

Early on he'd made the mistake of insisting that they not bring their "AK-47s" into the lab. He received an immediate lecture, in surprisingly almost accent-free English, on the differences between the earlier AK-47 in 7.62x39mm, and the later Soviet design enhancements of the AK-74 in 5.54x39mm. He had no real clue what they were talking about, but he was smart enough not to interrupt.

Nonetheless, he repeatedly warned them about the danger of firearms, even cell phones, around the chemicals used in the cooking process. Any flame, a single errant spark, could be disastrous. They would just stare at him with the dead-eyed gaze of serpents, then ignore him. But to their credit, they never caused an incident within the lab, and otherwise followed his instructions precisely, even eschewing cell phones while working.

Their presence also put a crimp in his usual special body-disposal jobs, like those for Suzi. Normally, he'd use the crematorium; but, with the lab set up in there that was no longer an option. So, he'd been forced to take advantage of the on-site cold storage; it was getting crowded. Twelve body bags could not be explained when the paperwork on only eight existed. As soon as they broke down the lab, he was going to take care of that problem, and then fade off into the sunset.

The only good news was that Brewster had paid him half his fee up front; the rest was to be forthcoming after the job. That was their usual arrangement. But Teddy hadn't liked the way the deal had been proposed, so he doubled his fee at the outset. The fact that Brewster hadn't even blinked or argued should have been another red flag. That could only mean the front money investment from the cartel must have been huge. Maybe Teddy should've asked for more?

As he finished the cigarette and ground the butt beneath his heel, the faint *crunch* of tires on gravel snagged his attention. At first he saw nothing, so he drifted silently away from the building toward the tree line, the better to view the area to the front of the connected buildings. He was all the way to the trees when he saw the two darkened vans roll quietly into the front parking area and take up positions near either corner of the main building. Another vehicle without lights entered the lot; this blacked-out van turned in his direction, obviously headed for the employee parking in the rear.

Teddy melted into the trees and crouched in the underbrush. He didn't think he'd been seen, but he wasn't willing to take the chance. He wanted nothing to do with whoever was in those vehicles; they were acting too much like *pros*. It could be the *cops*—or worse, it might be the cartel's *competition*.

Now *that* would be very, very bad.

He began to pick his way through the thick growth, going deeper into the trees. He wanted distance from whatever was about to happen.

The thought of warning Ramon and Pablo never even occurred to him.

A QUARTER MILE AWAY, parked in the weed-strewn lot of a defunct gas station, an idling SUV served as the operation's Command Post. A dozen silent people in and around the dimly lit CP listened intently as an encrypted radio softly crackled with ambient static. No one was immune to the rising tension and focused anticipation.

The Special Response Teams, designated Alpha One, Two, and Three, had just been deployed in their special tactical vans, and should be in position at any moment.

The unmarked federal units waiting on the outer perimeter, designated Bravo One through Bravo Four, could monitor the radio traffic as well.

Most of the marked units on the outer perimeter—from the state police, sheriffs' departments, and local municipal police agencies, designated Charley One through Charley Eight—could not normally monitor the encrypted radios. So, six hand-held encrypted federal radios had been assigned to the Charley Team units manning the four checkpoints on the only roads that accessed the funeral home. However, those extra radios still weren't enough for everyone, so many uniformed personnel crowded around the nearest federal cruisers to listen.

"CP, CP, Alpha One . . . Alpha Team vehicles in position, inner perimeter established. No other vehicles in the parking lots; no movement detected. Standing by."

Sitting in the front seats of the USMS SUV, Hawk and Trey twisted to watch as Eva Quantrell, seated behind them, made a few hurried data entries on her tablet and announced, "All set; we're good to go. The surveillance has been updated, too."

She turned her tablet so the others could see a schematic floorplan of the target buildings displayed, to include the immediate grounds and parking areas. And now, with her latest data input, the positions of the Alpha Teams glowed from the screen.

Sitting next to her and nodding appreciatively, Inspector Paglia reached for the radio, keyed the mike, and broadcast the latest information. "Alpha units, Alpha units, CP . . . Surveillance advises that a rear door on building three was opened and closed approx ten minutes ago. Floorplan indicates that's the embalming lab. We may have an *unsub* in the rear, unconfirmed."

"CP, CP, Alpha Three . . . Copied surveillance update and have current visual on that door. It's closed and the area appears clear. No movement and nothing in the rear lot. No change since our arrival."

"Alpha units, Alpha units, CP . . . Maintain positions and stand by. CP will make designated landlines now."

At a nod from Inspector Paglia, a tech, crammed into the vehicle's third-row seat amid a host of communications gear, activated a preprogrammed dialing sequence on his laptop. The home phone of the owner of record, Rudolph Broussard, began ringing; not surprisingly, it went to an answering machine. A prerecorded message was left. A second dialing sequence was automatically activated; the main line to the funeral home began ringing. It did not go to an answering machine or service; it just kept ringing.

"No answer yet," the tech reported, "letting it ring."

"Are we good to go?" Trey asked.

"Not yet," Paglia warned. "This search warrant must be executed during the hours of daylight—at sunrise at the earliest. We've still got some time before we can *knock and announce*."

"We can't just make a forced entry?" Hawk asked.

"No, this is not a *no-knock* warrant," Eva explained. "The judge wouldn't authorize it. Absent extenuating circumstances, meaning officer safety, we have to *knock and announce* our presence and intentions. We try to inform the owners of the property about the search warrant immediately before its execution, and of course ask for their cooperation. If anyone else is there, like whoever might have immediate control of the property, we inform them, too. That's why we're using recorded telephone notifications, and recording any responses which will serve to document compliance via a digital record."

"Of course, the Special Response Teams, the designated Alpha units on the scene," Paglia reminded, "will physically make the appropriate announcement—if it's safe to do so—and proceed to secure the target buildings. Once secured, the search teams, the designated Bravo units, will enter and conduct the actual search."

"At least, that's the plan," Trey grumbled. "Let's not forget Murphy's Law. We should—"

"Hold on," the tech interrupted. "Someone picked up the phone inside the funeral home. Wait one—they hung up, halfway into the recorded announcement."

That was not considered cooperation; tactics would be appropriately modified.

"Alpha units, Alpha units, CP . . . Phone notifications attempted; message left at owner's home. Be aware; phone answered and deliberately disconnected within target. Occupant is non-cooperative. Sunrise imminent. Execute!"

On the inner perimeter, van doors silently slid open and black-clad tactical personnel poured forth to take up positions covering all windows and doors of the three connected buildings. Most of the doors were locked, but two members of one team checking the garage found an unsecured overhead door.

"CP, CP, Alpha Two . . . We have an unsecured, now open, garage; hearse and flower car inside, no keys. We have an unsecured door from within the garage into the interior."

"CP copies. That door opens into a short hall that T-intersects with a wider hallway. The wide hallway accesses first-floor rooms of the main building, building one. At the end there's a connecting hall to building two that holds a stairwell to the second floor. Standby."

"Alpha Two copies."

"Alpha One, Alpha One, CP . . . Knock and announce at the front door; then hold position and maintain cover. Alpha Two, form your stack and attempt a soft entry. Clear first floor of building one and advise. Alpha Three, cover Alpha Two's entry/exit point and follow. Alpha units acknowledge."

"Alpha One, copy."

"Alpha Two, copy."

"Alpha Three, copy."

For three long minutes the radio was silent. Even though everyone listening knew that Alpha Two was now silently clearing and securing the first-floor interior rooms of the main building with practiced precision, the prolonged absence of any communications chatter was unsettling. Even the tension in the Command Post, the cramped SUV, was growing as darkness faded over the marshlands and swamps of the Atchafalaya Basin to the southeast.

IN ONE OF THE U.S. Marshals Service cruisers, designated Bravo Two, Todd made a quiet remark to his partner, Willis, as they sipped tepid coffee from cardboard cups and stared into the graying dawn.

"I can't put my finger on it, but I've got a bad feeling about this."

"Yeah," agreed Willis, "me, too. Something just feels *off*."

In the back seat of Bravo Two, CSI Tech Cassie Spenser nudged Sgt. Melancon. "Sarge, what's with the open radio protocol? I'm not familiar with it."

"It's pretty simple really," the sergeant responded. "Since the frequency is encrypted, the feds can speak pretty openly, without a lot of confusing codes. When you transmit, you call twice and then identify yourself, see? Say the call sign of the designated unit you want to contact twice, identify your call sign once, and follow with the message."

She nodded; and he continued.

"It's fast and efficient; and being encrypted you generally don't have to worry about your comm traffic being compromised. The other thing is that the tactical team members, the Alpha units, use earwigs and voice-activated mikes for their individual portables. So, once they commence the operation they tend to remain silent, otherwise they'll transmit. They'll use a lot of hand signals. That's why it's so quiet on the air right now."

"Oh, yeah, that makes sense."

The sergeant pointed to the cruiser's mounted radio control head. "And of course a unit's mobile radio, like this one and the one in the CP, is a lot stronger and can override a portable transmission."

"Okay, now I understand, thanks."

The radio suddenly squelched to life, and everyone involuntarily tensed.

"CP, CP, Alpha Two . . . Building one, first floor; viewing rooms, chapel, restrooms, and garage are secure. Some interior lights are on. We're ready to open the front doors for Alpha One."

"CP copies . . . Alpha One, Alpha One, CP . . . Stand by as Alpha Two opens front doors."

"Alpha One copies."

"All units, all units, Alpha Three . . . We have movement at the rear door of building three. One adult male stuck his head out, did a *sneak peek* at the rear lot, and ducked back inside, slamming the door!"

"CP copies, Alpha Three . . . Maintain visual but have personnel change positions to make any intel gained from the *sneak peek* obsolete."

"Alpha Three copies."

"Alpha One and Two, One and Two, CP . . . Acknowledge movement intel at rear of building three."

"Alpha One, acknowledged."

"Alpha Two, acknowledged."

IN THE USMS SUV SERVING as the operation's CP, Inspector Paglia looked over to Eva Quantrell and asked, "The door Alpha Three referred to, is that the same one surveillance noted opening before?"

"Affirmative, the embalming lab. They reported that no one was actually seen; but, they didn't have an unobstructed view—hence, the caution of a possible unsub in the rear. Whoever poked his head out just now might be the same guy."

"Maybe, but make no assumptions," Paglia cautioned. "What more has to be cleared; the offices, casket showroom, embalming lab, and cold storage?"

"Yes, two offices and a small storeroom are on the south side of building two, opposite cold storage. The casket showroom and the lounge area are on the second floor of building one. The embalming lab is in building three. And there's also the crematorium; that's the small appendage to building three, the one with the tall chimney, no outside door, and no windows."

"CP, CP, Alpha One . . . We're in; we'll clear the second floor of building one. Alpha Two is holding at building two, hallway intersection by the stairwell."

"CP copies."

THE ALPHA TWO TEAM leader crouched in the well-lit hallway and studied the matte surface of a closed metal door and its seal-equipped jamb. "CP, CP, Alpha Two . . . We've encountered a secured interior door on the west side of the shorter garage-access hall, building two. It's stainless, and padlocked. We think it accesses the cold storage."

"CP copies . . . We confirm that the floorplan identifies that door as another access to cold storage. Opposite cold storage are a storeroom and two offices. The embalming lab should be at the west end of the long hallway at a right angle to your position—"

The overhead lights in the long hall went out.

A fusillade of full-auto gunfire erupted from the embalming lab's main doors and ripped down the long empty hall, punching dusty holes in plastered walls and exploding a wall-mounted display case. Clouds of shattered glass fragments and shredded prayer cards rained on the men crouched nearby in the adjacent hall.

The team's point man braced his ballistic shield at the wall's corner and activated the shield-mounted floodlight. The long hall flared with light. He felt pistol rounds smacking into the ballistic shield and hissed over his shoulder, "Shooter's not close! Fire's coming from the doorway at the end of the hall!"

"CP, CP, Alpha Two—Taking fire from the embalming lab, long hallway past cold storage! Returning fire!"

IN THE CP, INSPECTOR Paglia looked at Hawk, and simply said, "Go!"

Hawk slammed the big USMS SUV into gear and roared toward the firefight.

Despite the frantic ride, Inspector Paglia managed to issue tactical commands. "Bravo units, Bravo units, CP . . . Converge and find cover. Charley units, lock down the outer perimeter! Emergency vehicle access only!"

ALPHA ONE HAD JUST finished clearing the second floor of the main building when the firefight began. Reacting to the sound of gunfire, members of Alpha One poured from the stairwell into the short hall across from Alpha Two, and maintained cover out of the line of fire.

With a few quick hand signals, men from each team began firing controlled submachine gun bursts down the hall in an alternating sequence with 12 gauge shotgun blasts. The suppression fire from the two H&K UMP .40 caliber sub-guns and the two tactical shotguns effectively stopped any further incoming fire from the embalming lab.

At the same time, Alpha Two personnel broke the lock on the stainless door into cold storage. Once inside they found another door from within cold storage that accessed the embalming lab. It was closed but not locked.

The team leaders hatched a simple strategy and immediately executed their plan.

From cover, Alpha One commenced a boisterous assault upon the main doors of the embalming lab. Amid loud shouts and salvos of small-arms fire, the detonations of flash-bang grenades rocked the long hallway, while Alpha Two made a dynamic entry into the embalming lab through cold storage, hopefully flanking the shooter.

The diversion worked; the flanking maneuver caught the shooter by surprise in the smoky confusion. Turning to aim in the direction of the entry team, he was trying to insert a fresh magazine in his assault rifle.

Multiple short bursts from the nearest Alpha Two personnel immediately cut him down.

A second man lunged in through the crematorium door in the rear wall, firing indiscriminately with a pistol. He fumbled with something in his other hand, lobbed it toward Alpha Two, and disappeared back through the same door.

"Grenade!" shouted the team leader.

All of Alpha Two immediately dove for cover.

The antipersonnel device bounced several times, rolled to a stop beneath an embalming table, and lay there inertly.

Alpha Two quickly realized the grenade was a dud. The ring had pulled free of a defective pin, which remained wedged in the spoon housing.

Weapons-mounted flashlights splashed harsh light upon the door marked "Crematorium" through which the second shooter had fled. It stood ajar; but the bright beams could not penetrate the plastic-shrouded darkness within.

Barely rising to a crouch, the Alpha Two team leader panned his flashlight around and quickly assessed the situation. His personnel were uninjured. The first shooter was down, most likely dead from multiple gunshot wounds. At a silent command, team members disarmed him and handcuffed him anyway.

"Alpha One, Alpha One, Alpha Two . . . Two shooters; one down, and one ran into the next room. The lab's secure; you can advance and clear the storeroom and offices."

"Alpha One, copy."

"CP, CP, Alpha Two . . . One subject down in the embalming lab; no team injuries. Second armed subject possibly barricaded in a room marked 'Crematorium' on the west end of building three. Can you advise of any other access or exits?"

"CP copies, Alpha Two . . . Be advised, the floorplan shows no other access or exits from the crematorium."

The Alpha Two team leader realized there was a strong chemical odor drifting through the dim room, mingling with the traces of formaldehyde and the haze of cordite—something vaguely alarming.

He was not the only one to notice. Another team member whispered, "What's that smell?"

The muzzle of an AK-74 emerged unseen from the shadows behind the slightly open crematorium door.

RAMON SQUINTED INTO the murk, holding his breath. He tried to pinpoint the locations of his adversaries and decide the order of their elimination. Their weapons-mounted flashlights and lasers easily compromised their positions. Years of training and experience dictated his tactics.

Smiling coldly, he performed his last conscious act.

He pulled the trigger.

AS THE SUV CAREENED into the parking lot, and slewed to a stop, there was a sudden blinding flash, a tremendous *WHUMPH!* A simultaneous pressure wave rocked the vehicle on its suspension. A massive roiling ball of angry orange flame rose into the shocked morning sky.

The vehicle's occupants stared in disbelief. Acrid smoke shrouded everything but the lancing tongues of sickly colored flames. Debris rained down indiscriminately.

Their shoulders hunched, Trey and Hawk jumped out and took covered positions behind the opened SUV doors. As the smoke began to clear, they could see that the aft section of building three, the crematorium, was simply *gone.*

The embalming lab was ripped open to the sky; sickly colored fires flared skyward from within its cracked and roofless walls.

The adjacent cold storage unit had suffered severe damage as well; its huge roof-mounted refrigeration unit now lay in the parking lot, an unrecognizable lump of twisted metal. The outer walls of cold storage were shattered rubble; what was left of the roof was slowly collapsing.

A dozen black body-bags lay scattered about like discarded dominoes. And worse, many of them were torn open, disbursing their grisly contents haphazardly about the scene.

Inspector Paglia, the radio microphone clasped in a white knuckled grip, hunkered beside the idling SUV and urgently issued orders. "Alpha units, Alpha units, CP—everyone check in!"

There was nothing but static and erratic interference.

The shaken tech in the third seat cried out, "Sir, I can clear that up! Give me a second!"

"Damn it!" Paglia cursed. "I need a sitrep!"

Without hesitation, Eva, Hawk, and Trey ran into the acrid haze, toward the vague shapes of those Alpha team members coughing and stumbling forward through the drifting smoke. The selfless rescuers, their own eyes stinging and throats burning, supported and pulled the staggering victims away from the destruction and into the clear air and relative safety of the parking lot.

It took several long minutes to account for all personnel. Unfortunately, there were casualties.

Alpha Two suffered two dead and three wounded, all from the blast. Alpha One had two wounded with flash burns. Alpha Three had three lightly wounded from blast shrapnel. All the surviving Alpha Team members were having residual hearing problems. Those who could still function effectively concentrated on first aid and rescue efforts.

Eva stood beside a scorched van and tried to catch her breath. She tried to wipe the soot and ash from her face and hands, but her damp wipe did little more than smear the residue. "Damn! Damn! Damn! It *had* to be a *lab*! I should have known there'd be a lab! I should have called for our lab team! This is *all my fault!*" She fumed and fumbled with the straps on her ballistic vest.

"Stop it, Eva!" warned Inspector Paglia, as he handed her a half-liter of bottled water. "Drink this. We don't know it was a lab; there was no intel to that effect. At best, we only suspected distribution. We still don't know for sure. Funeral homes use a lot of chemicals too, you know. This may be anything from an accident to an IED; we just don't know at this point. And we don't have the time for recriminations. Get focused, now! The fire department is en route, and if we want to get a good look before they drown everything, we need to do it now!"

"Okay—okay! I'm all right," she assured him. "I'm just *pissed!*"

"Fine! Then channel it into doing something constructive. Come on. Secure your vest. Let's take a look around—and be careful! We don't need more casualties."

So, the inspector, Eva, Hawk and Trey carefully prowled through the destruction, avoiding any of the lingering fires. Unfortunately, they could make little sense of the devastation. Hawk discovered the charred and twisted remnants of a barreled AK-type receiver. He pointed it out, but left it in place for the evidence recovery teams.

The two shooters were tentatively presumed dead. The handcuffed body of the first shooter was discovered; the other may have been vaporized in the blast. The authorities would have to rely on the evidence recovery teams to confirm his demise.

There was little more they could really do. The distant sounds of sirens and bellowing air horns grew louder by the second.

With the arrival of the fire department, Inspector Paglia sought out the ranking official to explain the circumstances and request minimum disruption of what was now a crime scene. The seasoned fire chief, a former arson investigator, knew his business. His crew had the fires out in a matter of minutes, leaving most of the scene intact.

Once the rescue units and ambulances had transported the casualties to the hospital, the fire chief approached the Command Post to see if there was anything else they could do.

"You know, this isn't anything official, but I think you definitely had a meth lab here—a big one. We found partially burnt remnants of what I suspect will turn out to be empty blister packs of ephedrine-based cold tablets, empty cans of brake cleaner, and empty lithium-battery blister packs. You wouldn't recognize most of that stuff in its current condition, but I think your CSI people will confirm it, too."

Hawk was puzzled. "I can understand the cold tablets and the lithium; but, why brake cleaner?"

Eva spoke up, her voice tired and wan. "For the *toluene,* brake cleaner is an easy source."

"Well, if you folks don't need me," the fire chief said, "I'll clear the scene, and leave my truck captain in charge. I'll send my arson investigators to assist. I'm sure BATF will be involved; we've worked with them before." He gestured to a knot of firemen milling around a rescue unit and a pumper truck. "These two trucks will stand by in the event of any flare-ups or any injuries. I'm sorry for your casualties."

"Thank you, Chief," said the inspector, shaking the chief's hand. "We deeply appreciate everything that you and your people have done for us."

With a sad smile and a brief nod, the fire chief walked away.

Inspector Paglia turned to face the entire scene of destruction and chaos. He gestured toward the bulk of the main building that was still standing, surprisingly intact. "All right people, we've still got a search warrant to execute, a crime scene to preserve, and reports to file." His voice softened perceptibly as he added, "And some of us will have some difficult notifications to make."

TWO MILES TO THE SOUTH, Teddy Pots hunched low in the thick brush along the two-lane country road. Soaking wet from a dunking in an unseen bayou, he shivered in the cool morning as he scanned for traffic in either direction. Nothing was on the road.

Since he'd stopped walking and had settled in to wait a while, his exhaustion was catching up with him, and his mind drifted a bit. He thought about how fortunate he'd been so far this morning.

Hell yeah! My momma didn't raise no damn dummy!

He knew nothing good was coming as soon as he saw those blacked-out vans pull in the parking lot. Good thing he'd never gotten around to quitting smoking and he'd craved a butt right then. Oh yeah, one look was all he needed. He'd split that scene without a second thought.

He'd been creeping quietly through the woods as quickly as he dared when he heard the explosion. He spun around in time to see an enormous fireball rise in the graying mists of the dawn, almost a mile away. Teddy knew immediately what must have happened—but that didn't slow his imagination.

I done warned them fools! Who was in them damn vans anyway? Did they see me? Are they on my trail now? They gonna use dogs?

He really didn't like dogs, nor they him. At the thought of dogs, he'd abandoned any attempt at stealth and ran pell-mell through the woods. In his rising panic, he didn't even try to avoid the sticky sago palm fronds and poison ivy vines.

He felt himself lose contact with the ground, legs pumping, and was suddenly underwater. The unseen bayou was not that deep, so he readily gained his feet, sputtering and coated with spring algae and duckweed. Climbing the steep bank on the other side, his chest heaved as he tried to catch his breath. At the top, he collapsed to his hands and knees, sucking in great gasps of air.

As he calmed down, he thought he heard something—something on the very threshold of his hearing that grew incrementally more distinct. *Sirens! Cops for sure!*

Galvanized to action he stood and quickly looked around; he was alone. He had to *get a grip!* Panicking wouldn't help!

His nose wrinkled. He stunk from his bayou bath; but he realized it was probably an improvement over what he smelled like from working with the chemicals in the lab. His breathing mask was gone, probably at the bottom of the bayou. His boots sluiced with water, so he sat and pulled them off to drain them. He stood and peeled off his soaked coveralls. He wore jeans and an old ratty Harley-Davidson T-shirt beneath; both were wet but not so foul.

After shaking his boots out, he put them back on, going bootless was not an option. He went through the pockets of the coveralls and found nothing but wet lint, duckweed, and a soggy wad that used to be a pack of cigarettes. He found that beyond sad. He really wanted a smoke right now; it would help to calm him down.

Balling the coveralls up, he tossed them into the bayou and watched for a moment as the sluggish current took them slowly downstream.

Let them dogs chase that for a while!

He struck out again through the thick woods, but changed his course and began to head north and west. He was no fan of walking anywhere; but, it sure beat sitting in a jail cell. So, he trudged on.

He knew he would eventually strike a road; then he'd hitchhike. He needed a ride out of the area, and soon.

Sniffing his shoulder, he couldn't really tell what he now smelled like, the lab or the bayou, not that either one would be good. His jeans were still quite damp but the Harley T-shirt was drying out. He didn't own a Harley. He'd never even ridden a motorcycle; he didn't know how. The truth was that he'd stolen the shirt from an old roommate long ago.

With a start, he realized he was becoming distracted; he needed to snap out of it. The lack of sleep was taking its toll. He was on the run, and could be in real trouble if he wasn't careful. He stopped dead still, suddenly worried that he may have become disoriented and walked in the wrong direction, maybe even back the way he'd come. He had to keep it together! He heard no pursuit, but he wasn't sure.

No dogs! Please, no dogs!

So, certain he had the morning sun at his back, he walked on. Within an hour or so, he broke through the swamp brush and came upon this lonely road, a paved two-lane running north and south. He settled in for what might be a long wait, and counted himself lucky just to be free of the thick bracken.

THE MORNING CREPT BY.

There, in the distance, he saw something moving on the long flat road, a faint shimmer with a hint of mirage. It grew steadily larger as it approached in the northbound lane.

What? A pickup truck, with two people inside?

He had to make a decision.

If he exposed himself now, and they were cops, it was over; he was caught. Even if they didn't connect him to the meth lab, he knew there was a federal warrant out for him on some penny-ante parole violation. He had five years on an old dope conviction hanging over him—and that's one nickel he never wanted to spend.

What to do—what to do? Aw, t' hell with it—at least they're going in the right direction.

He stepped to the roadside and stuck out his thumb.

To his mild surprise, the truck slowed and rolled to a stop. The passenger, a stocky middle-aged man with a grey ponytail and a *salt and pepper* beard, leaned out over his tattooed elbow and spoke in a thick Cajun accent. "*Ça va; où vas-tu?* Where y' goin', bro?"

"Uh, north . . . up t' Alec'."

The man nodded at Teddy's T-shirt. "Y' ride break on ya?"

"Huh? Uh, well yeah, b'n broke down a while."

The passenger scrutinized him closely and almost imperceptibly wrinkled his nose. He then glanced at the driver and they had a mumbled conversation.

Looking at Teddy, the passenger said, "Well, we can getcha far as Carencro, an' den y' can thumb it up I-49. Gots t' ride inna back; an' we ain't makin' no stops. Been offshore a mont' an' be deadheadin' to d' house."

"Dat's cool," slurred Teddy smoothly as he climbed into the bed of the truck, and settled in with the haphazard collection of duffel bags, toolboxes, fishing gear, and two large ice chests.

He had gambled and come up lucky once more—not cops, but offshore oil workers on their way home after a month on an oil rig platform out in the Gulf. They'd get him just north of Lafayette, which was good. But they'd drop him on U.S. Interstate Highway 49, which was *not* so good.

The Louisiana State Police and various sheriffs' patrols were thick on I-49. He'd never make it trying to hitchhike, at least not on the interstate. He'd be better off trying his luck on a state highway, Route 71, an older, rural two-lane that ran north all the way to Arkansas.

Teddy chewed his lip. True, the older highway ran roughly parallel to the newer interstate, but it didn't begin until it intersected with an east/west state highway, Route 190, about twenty miles north of Carencro and ten miles or so east of Opelousas.

Sighing, he resigned himself; he'd just have to deal with that.

As the truck picked up speed, the wind whipped around the cab and set his hair and shirt fluttering. The clean fresh air felt good, and smelled good. With that thought, he sniffed his Harley T-shirt and recoiled; he hadn't realized how rank it was. No wonder they had him ride in the back. For that matter, it was a wonder they'd picked him up at all.

Then he saw it, the decal, a Harley-Davidson trademarked *bar and shield* symbol on the rear window glass. He realized they mistakenly thought he was a fellow biker, down on his luck. He smirked; but for this tattered and stinking T-shirt, he might still be on the side of the road.

He knew not to question good fortune whenever it came his way. So, he settled in for the ride and kept his profile low. Although he might not comprehend the term, he was a consummate opportunist, and firmly believed he would make the best of whatever fate had in store for him, or at least stay one step ahead.

CH 6

SALIDAR'S ARRIVAL IN the large empty building that served as the general entry point into the Realm of Shadow was far more cordial than that of his last visit. Instead of being beaten into unconsciousness by a troop of men-at-arms, he was rather graciously greeted, albeit somewhat ironically, by the same squad on guard duty.

"Ah, a good morning t' ye, good sir. Salidar, tis it not?" asked the gruff sergeant.

"Uh, indeed so, Sergeant," Salidar responded warily.

"Come to see the baron, have ye—or just to witness the execution? A fair number of travelers have come for the event."

"Of course, I will pay my respects to the baron. But tell me, Sergeant, what is this about an execution?"

"Ach, have ye not heard, good sir? A few days ago, one of our patrols captured the bloody murderer of the Baron Frederick Von Kestel's late father—*may he feast with the gods*. The execution tis today, at midday, in the courtyard of the baron's castle."

"An' how do y' kill that what's already dead?" spat a soldier under his breath.

"Enough of that talk!" bellowed the sergeant. "Tis not your place to question the doin's of the baron! If'n his lordship decrees it an *execution, then so be it!* Now back to y' posts—all of ye!"

Turning back to Salidar, he cleared his throat and spoke considerably more courteously. "Pay that lout no mind, good sir. Tends to speak w'out thinkin', he does—and of things he *ought not*."

"Think nothing of it, Sergeant," Salidar said smoothly, his interest aroused. "If you could spare a few minutes, I would hear more about how your brave lads captured this *murderer*."

The sergeant seemed to think about it for a moment. "Aye, good sir, that I can do. Walk with me for a bit."

They walked the length of the hall in silence as the rest of the squad members manned their posts and resumed their assigned duties. Once outside in the bright morning light, the sergeant scanned the immediate area and kept his voice low.

"I ken y've been a guest of the baron, and of the Lady Leanan; so, I'll confide in ye what little I know, though tis not much."

Salidar held his thoughts to himself; and, as he hoped, the sergeant continued.

"Morning before last, one of the lads on patrol was approached by a farmer, a stout sort who tills a patch to the south about a two hours walk from here. The landsman complained a beast took his mule in the night. Now, there's not many beasties that will go for a mule, knowin' how contrary they can be, and *kick*—ah, like nothing else!"

Salidar smiled knowingly and nodded. "Aye, there's truth in that."

"Well now, the patrol, to the farm they go and find a blood trail. Ain't much, but leads it does to the low mountains in the west where it peters out on the rocky plains near the old barrow hills. Most like y' know that no one goes there, near them hills—*haunted, some say.* Others hold them hills to be the burial mounds of the *Old Ones—cursed, no doubt,* but who knows? Anyway, the lads find a faint trace of trail that leads *into* the barrow hills. But stout of heart they be, so they follow."

The sergeant stopped walking and faced Salidar. He stared over Salidar's shoulder, as if considering whether or not to continue. He looked Salidar in the eyes, seemingly having made his decision.

"Understand, good sir, that I have served as a baron's man-at-arms for many years. I have seen much, and fear little. I care not what any may think of those cursed hills, be they natural or no. I have a cousin who serves on that patrol squad; and, I trust what he had to tell me."

"I understand, Sergeant, please go on."

"Aye. He said that they found a cave in one of the largest hills; but, twas neither natural cave nor hill. Twas an entrance—dug out by sheer strength—into a tomb! Aye, the barrow hills *are* tombs, of something long dead, as many have guessed. There was a stench—the remains of the mule carcass, y' see—so they knew they were on the trail of the right beastie . . . "

The man's voice trailed off. He stood there momentarily lost in his own thoughts.

Salidar sensed that whatever the patrol had found had unnerved those men sufficiently to render the sergeant conflicted and unsettled, even at the very memory of this second-hand account.

I must know; but, I must tread carefully.

Salidar prodded gently. "Found their *beastie*, did they?"

"Aye, that they did, an *ogress,* well hidden within the many-chambered tomb. Only, dead she be—or so they thought."

What—a female ogre?

Salidar knew that ogres were exceptionally rare; very few had been sighted in the last century. They were long-lived and rather solitary; considered dull of wit, they were consistently ill-tempered. It was thought the last of them had either been slain or had migrated into the *wild,* generations ago.

The ruling vampire clans had made a concerted effort to rid Shadow of ogres; they were considered unacceptably dangerous to vampires. In fact, ogres and vampires shared a strong mutual animosity, much like that between vampires and the Were. This enmity was also ancient and well entrenched; however, the root cause was long lost in dim antiquity. Of course, there was ample speculation, but no one knew for certain.

There was, however, one undeniable fact; unlike their distant cousins, the more common versions of trolls, ogres were immune to the effects of sunlight and could hunt in darkness *and* daylight. Since vampires were particularly vulnerable during the hours of daylight, ogres were reasonably perceived as significant threats.

Salidar was obviously surprised, and he let it show in his voice.

"An *ogress?* I must say, Sergeant. They were certain? And it was *dead?*"

"Doubt me not, good sir," the man-at-arms replied firmly, "for I do not doubt my cousin. He swore that she appeared dead, rather, to have been dead for some time. But rose up and fought them, she did! Had she not been so thin and weak, they might not have captured her in a beast net. Once ensnared, collapsed once again, she did, as if dead. They detected no heartbeat. Regardless, bound her firmly, they did, not trusting their own senses."

"I see," said Salidar, "but how did they know she killed the Baron's father?"

"Ah, the ring, y' see? Within the desecrated tomb, the patrol found a number of *trophies* from her kills; grisly indeed, were some. Among them, the baron's signet ring, aye, twas not found with his mangled body in the wood not far from where we now stand."

Musing to himself, Salidar mumbled, "Hmm, she could've *found* the ring."

Not realizing he'd been heard, he was surprised when the sergeant softly responded.

"Aye, but twas still on the *finger*—the bone freshly gnawed."

Salidar's stomach involuntarily lurched. He could only stare at the sergeant, who slowly nodded his head in affirmation, and resumed his tale.

"They brought her, all trussed up, to the baron. He identified the ring. Still appeared dead, she did; but they took no chances. Bound her to a stake in the castle courtyard, they did. Suspecting some sorcery, the call for a mage, the baron did send, to examine her, y' see?

"Lady Leanan and Magus Jalash-el came that night at the baron's invitation and examined the ogress by torchlight."

"Did they reach any conclusions?" Salidar inquired.

The sergeant shrugged his shoulders.

"Perhaps, I know not, firsthand like; but, soldiers talk . . . We heard from the household guards that the baron met with the mage and Lady Leanan long into the night. In the morning, the baron announced that the ogress had been declared guilty of murdering his father and other crimes, and twas to be burned at the stake. That *execution* tis to take place today."

"Ah, I see," Salidar observed. "So, the baron made no mention of any sorcery at work here, or anyone else being involved?"

The sergeant shrugged once more. "I was not told so. Perhaps ye can ask him y' self when ye pays y' respects?"

"Thank you, Sergeant, I shall follow your advice," he said, executing the slightest bow. "If there's nothing else, I shall be on my way."

"Safe journey, good sir," the sergeant said, and then added a warning. "Best keep to the road. There be some sign of a bear in the forest of late, a big one."

"I shan't tarry, Sergeant." Salidar waved. "I hope to be with the baron before mid-afternoon. Good day to ye."

SALIDAR MADE GOOD TIME, and came within view of the baron's estate shortly before noon. He was not the only traveler on the roads enjoying this bright sun-washed day; many people were making for the baron's castle, most with some degree of haste.

Eager to see an execution, he guessed.

In truth, the circumstances surrounding this event were significantly unusual, and thus bound to cause some heightened interest. He'd heard others on the road talking amongst themselves. The rumors were running rampant; *a monstrous ogre . . . no, a bloodthirsty troll . . . nay, some unknown demonic beast . . . to be executed by sorcery . . .*

He knew, of course, it would have been flatly impossible for the soldiers involved in the capture not to talk about it. Even if they tried to be circumspect while discussing it among themselves, it was inevitable that they'd eventually be overheard. And soon enough, the countryside was aflame with the news, however muddled or exaggerated it had become.

So, it came as no surprise that a fairly large crowd had gathered at the foot of the drawbridge. Individuals were carefully scrutinized and questioned by a brace of guards before being allowed to traverse the stout span and enter the courtyard of the castle.

Castle, indeed . . . Salidar mused as he moved slowly with the press of farmers, merchants, and serfs towards the drawbridge. He still considered it little more than a well fortified and walled manor house; but to these poor people, it was no doubt a *castle.*

He looked up to find a guard blocking his path; he'd reached the security checkpoint while moving along with the steady flow of people without realizing it. The guard had been conversing with each person. Salidar hadn't noticed that the merchant shuffling before him was briefly questioned and allowed to pass. Now, it was his turn.

"Good day, good sir, state your name and business."

"I am Salidar. I'm here to pay my respects to his lordship, the Baron Von Kestel."

"Are you here for the execution as well, good sir?"

"I hadn't planned on it; but, I might observe while I am here. Is that permitted?"

"Of course, good sir. But I must ask, do you carry any magical charm, or device?"

"No, I do not," replied Salidar, obviously puzzled, "and why would you ask?"

"Orders, good sir, orders," the guard said firmly. "None are to be admitted if they carry any token of magic; even good-luck charms are to be left outside the castle walls. It's just a precaution, good sir. Is the baron expecting you?"

"Uh, no, this was an unanticipated visit. But we are acquainted. I am sure he will see me when he learns I am here," Salidar said with confidence.

"Very well, sir. You may pass. See the sergeant inside the courtyard, beyond the portcullis. He will see that his lordship is told of your arrival."

Salidar nodded and started out across the stout drawbridge. He remembered the last time he was here, in custody and ignominiously bound. This drawbridge had then been *invisible* to him, until the horse he rode trod upon it. Not so today, it appeared normal in all respects. Nor did he sense any spell at work here. He thought that strange, given that he knew the baron routinely employed magical defensive measures.

As he passed within the courtyard he noticed a large number of people milling about and talking, albeit guardedly. Some more enterprising individuals had set up a number of small stalls and were selling toasted oat cakes, strips of tough dried meat, honeyed fruits, and watered ale. It was almost a fair-like atmosphere, yet subdued. The large number of uniformed men-at-arms contributed to the sense of anticipatory tension.

He pushed through the crowd surrounding the stalls and found himself facing the nearly vacant central area of the courtyard.

No person would venture any closer to the center, not that a ring of dour-faced guards would have permitted it. For there, in the very center, slumped a large body bound in twin chains of cold iron and tarnished silver to an upright stake, the girth of a stout bridge post. A short shroud was snugly tied about the form, covering the upper body above the waist; yet the outline of broad shoulders and a squat head could easily be discerned.

The breeze shifted and a slight odor of decay wafted toward Salidar. It was enough to thin the nearer crowd. Even the closest guards grimaced in distaste.

Salidar tried to stay upwind as he sought out the guard sergeant. He introduced himself and asked that Baron Von Kestel be informed of his presence. As expected, he was politely told to wait.

As he patiently complied, he studied the crowd. There was a pervasive undercurrent of unease among the people, even the guards were conspicuously wary. It was as if storms were gathering, subtle tensions building just beyond the horizon of an otherwise cloudless sky.

He had the unsettling feeling that he was being watched; he could feel the focused gaze of another upon his back. Never one to ignore such an instinct, which had served him well innumerable times, he casually turned and scanned a sea of faces while appearing to examine a wind-chime merchant's wares.

Across the courtyard, a large bearded man dressed in disheveled homespun was staring at him. As the man took a step forward, another man, his back to Salidar yet a farmer by his clothes, stepped into the big man's path. A small cloaked woman appeared and tugged at the huge man's wrist, pulling him aside and saying something in haste. The big man's full attention stayed upon the small woman as the farmer casually turned and looked directly at Salidar.

Wilhem!

Salidar recognized him immediately, and assumed the woman, whom he could no longer see, was Frieda. The huge bearded man was now nowhere to be seen. Both he and Frieda had disappeared into the crowd.

However, Wilhem still stood there. When he had Salidar's full attention, he swiped the side of his nose with his index finger and gave a slight shake of his head—a *Guild* sign!

Ignore us—make no contact.

Salidar returned an answering sign—he tugged on his ear—to indicate that he understood, and resumed waiting among the nearest stalls. His mind raced.

What were they doing here? It must be Guild business. And who was that giant of a man? And more importantly, why was he staring so intently at me?

There was nothing more he could do but concentrate on the task at hand. He needed to stay alert and focused. He composed himself and casually scrutinized the subtly enhanced defenses incorporated in the renovated designs of the manor keep, all the while being careful not to draw undue attention from the ever-present guard force.

Unfortunately, his wait was a bit longer than he expected. He was considering sampling a copper's worth of watered ale, when a deep voice behind him rumbled forth, startling him.

"You are Salidar, good sir?"

He turned to see a very large man-at-arms in light armor awaiting his answer. Clearly surprised and caught off guard, Salidar could only nod affirmatively.

"Very good, his lordship will see you now. Please follow me, good sir."

Salidar fell in behind the soldier, and entered the keep. He mentally scolded himself for letting *anyone* come up behind him that easily—especially a hulking man-at-arms. *I can't ever afford to be that distracted—not in Shadow! That could be fatal!*

Following the man-at-arms up a short staircase and through a number of halls, Salidar was impressed. The soldier moved with the grace of a large cat, and was just as quiet, even while wearing mail and light armor.

The man-at-arms finally stopped before a tall set of ornately carved wooden doors that Salidar immediately recognized from his last visit. The massive soldier knocked briefly. At the sound of a muffled *"Come"* from within, he pushed one of the great doors open.

Salidar entered alone and found that the room held true to his memory; as before, it seemed more of a library than an office. However, on this bright afternoon, no fire crackled in the great fireplace, nor was an abundance of lit candles needed to illuminate the room. Sunlight poured in from the mullioned windows set in the far wall, warming the polished oak surface of the broad table that served this minor lord of the region as a desk.

The Baron Von Kestel was standing in front of the table with his back to Salidar. Hunched forward and focused on an open tome, he was not alone. A graying yet distinguished older man in the scarlet robes of a high mage stood on his right, equally intent upon the pages of the ancient book.

At the click of the door closing behind Salidar, the baron straightened and turned to face his visitor. Attired in formal robes, he wore the implements of his office; an intricate golden chain supporting the pendulous seal of the Von Kestel family, and the twisted gold and silver torc about his neck that signified his noble status and allegiance to the House of Lamia, the ruling house of Shadow.

Striding toward Salidar, open hands extended, he smiled. "Ah, welcome Salidar. I presume you are here once again in service to the Unseelie Court, as before?"

"Ah, yes, it would appear so, your lordship," Salidar answered and bowed, thinking, *indeed, in a manner of speaking.*

"Oh, where are my manners? Do forgive me," the baron said, shaking his head and turning to the wizened mage. "Salidar, allow me to introduce Magus Jalash-el, Magus Primus of the Shadow Mages, Senior Mage of the House of Lamia."

"M'lord Magus, this is an honor," Salidar said, bowing once more. He bit his tongue to say no more. He needed his wits about him now. This was no trifling magician; this was the most powerful human adept in the realm.

"Ah, yes . . . Salidar," intoned the mage, pursing his lips as he silently assessed the new arrival for a few moments. A wave of recognition seemed to pass over his careworn face.

Salidar thought his heart would stop. He felt a trace of cold sweat break out upon his brow before the mage deigned to resume speaking.

"Harrumph, I believe I recall the Lady Leanan mentioning that she had worked with you," Jalash-el said slowly, "on *court business*, of course, on another occasion."

Salidar had little choice but to brazen it out. "Quite true, m'lord, but it would be inappropriate for me to discuss any such matters further. You understand, of course."

"Quite so, quite so," the mage readily agreed, seemingly satisfied.

However, Salidar thought the aged adept appeared somewhat preoccupied or distracted. His next comment clearly indicated that the mage had obviously made an erroneous assumption regarding Salidar's presence.

"Well, as you will soon see, you may assure the Unseelie Court that the Baron Von Kestel and the esteemed House of Lamia are more than capable of dealing with the task at hand. This *abomination* will be but ashes in the cleansing light of the sun this very day, any trace of such foul sorcery banished to oblivion!"

The baron put a calming hand on the arm of the older man, and offered to pour wine for his guests.

As he did so, he spoke casually, but there was more than a hint of tension in his voice. "You see, Salidar, Lady Leanan has kindly offered the Magus Primus to conduct the rite of execution since there appears to have been some sort of dark sorcery involved."

As Salidar took the proffered goblet, he saw a trace of fear in the baron's eyes, and a spark of uncertainty mirrored in the distracted gaze of the mage. Something frightened these men to their very cores; however, he could see that they were evidently determined to face, and overcome, whatever haunted their thoughts and concerns.

Salidar glanced at the open book upon the time-burnished table, an ancient grimoire of dark magic, its stiff pages heavy with ominous lore. His mind leapt to the conclusion that *necromancy* was the unspoken nature of this alluded *dark sorcery* that so worried these men. Of course, he'd had his suspicions since he'd first heard the tale of the ogress. But now, it could surely be nothing else.

"I am certain the Court has every confidence in you both, m'lords," Salidar said smoothly, and raised his goblet in a toast. "To your health, m'lords, and to the complete success of your duty this day!"

"Hear, hear," echoed the baron as the three clinked goblets and sipped their wine.

After a moment, Salidar ventured a question. "M'lord Magus, I understand that no charm or implement of magic is to be allowed within the walls today. May I assume that you advised this precaution?"

"Indeed so, sir," Jalash-el responded. "The rite of execution that I must perform is rather involved and comprehensive, the complete immolation of the ensorcelled creature and the black spell itself."

Salidar's eyebrows rose in impressed surprise. This was no small undertaking.

The mage sighed, took a sip of wine, and stared into the cold hearth. "The dark spell will fight me. It will resist most strongly; any source of power in use within the immediate vicinity might be involuntarily drained and absorbed in the spell's defense. It will be challenge enough, as it is. I cannot allow anything to aid its resistance."

"Ah, I understand completely, m'lord," Salidar assured him. "I am certain you shall prevail."

So, that would explain the suspension of the baron's special defensive measures. He's taking no chances, but this may be far more dangerous than he realizes. I would be well away from here.

The baron took the opportunity to change the subject, and inquired further of Salidar. "May I ask, Salidar, if you would care to be my guest for the night, or have you other pressing business?"

"That is most kind of you, m'lord, but I do have another task to complete, which may take some time, I fear." He paused, in deference to a curious thought—*why not? Who knows what else I might learn?*

With a casual toss of his wrist and a lowered voice, he made it appear that he shared a confidence. "You see, I am to determine the status of Boltar, the slain innkeeper of the Crying Cup."

"Ah, of course. I have only just learned of the Council's formal request," remarked the baron. "Magus, you've known for some time?"

"Only since the night before last, my dear Baron." The mage sighed with a slight bow in Salidar's direction. "I suppose I should not be surprised that the Unseelie Court would initiate a separate inquiry."

Salidar shrugged and remained silent.

Jalash-el paced about the room, seemingly deep in thought, and then as if he suddenly remembered Salidar's presence, he turned to face him. "Please forgive an old man, Salidar, I would not have you think me rude. I mean no disrespect to the Unseelie Court. In fact, I believe I may be of some assistance in your task."

The mage gestured to the chairs at the front of the hearth, and looked inquisitively to his host.

The baron nodded. "Of course, Magus, let us be seated. I shall refresh our cups."

Once they settled in the comfortable chairs, Jalash-el took a long sip of his wine and cleared his throat.

"Attend me, Salidar. As I am certain you have already been told, the body of Boltar presently lies in the castle of the Lady Leanan. Our investigation of the circumstances surrounding his death is still incomplete. Lady Leanan has requested more time to resolve the issue. I should mention that she is most eager to speak with *you* about this matter, as well."

Salidar's eyebrows rose in surprise, but he said nothing as the mage continued.

"It is indeed unfortunate that Queen Mab of the Dark Elves has seen fit to formally request through the Council that his body be surrendered to her. She insists that he is suspected of treason against her realm, conspiratorial involvement in a coup plot, and so on. But I am sure you know of all this.

"We are aware that you had a role in ferreting him out. Please, take no offense—we do not question the motives or activities of the Unseelie Court. I merely state the obvious. Surely you can see that we have a vested interest in learning precisely *how* and *why* our realm came to be involved in this sordid affair, can you not?"

Salidar had to be very careful.

What—'ferreting him out'? Ah, clearly they think I acted as an agent of the Unseelie Court then, and still do. It is more likely to be to my advantage to allow that misconception to persist, without confirmation or denial. Nor can I lie; an adept of this level would no doubt sense it immediately. I must opt for the truth—carefully parsed though it may be.

"M'lord, I understand your position. In fact, I sympathize; but you must understand that I have no role in the formulation of *policy*. I am but a tool, given certain tasks to perform to the best of my abilities. Surely you can understand?"

"Of course, of course . . . It is just that my mistress, the Lady Leanan, has been recently frustrated in her efforts to resolve the matter." The elder mage sighed heavily. "I only hope that at some point, at least, we will be fully informed, and all our questions answered."

"I understand, m'lord," Salidar said cautiously.

"Forgive an old man's impertinence," pleaded Jalash-el, "but I must ask a question. Do you know if the Council intends to grant m'lady's request for more time, and delay the transfer of the body?"

"No, m'lord, unfortunately I do not know," responded Salidar honestly, and then dared to offer a bit of speculative advice. "Nor would I be too hopeful; her majesty, Queen Mab, is not known for her patience."

Jalash-el again sighed heavily. "Indeed, alas that is unfortunate. I have no doubt that there is more afoot here than meets the eye. Nonetheless, assuming the Council does not grant m'lady's request, I will likely be instructed to make the necessary arrangements for the transfer of the body of Boltar to the realm of the Dark Elves upon my return to the castle of the Lady Leanan. Salidar, you may assure the Unseelie Court that we will comply with the Council's formal request."

Salidar bowed slightly, but kept silent.

"Magus, the enchantments you found on the body will remain *intact?*" asked the baron.

"Of that, I have no doubt," answered the mage. "To be so is a designed intention, I am certain. To what ultimate end, I have no idea."

"What can you tell me of these *enchantments*, m'lord?" Salidar dared to ask.

"Only that there are two," Jalash-el shook his head sadly, "a common stasis spell—Boltar is a Were, of course—and a very dark and complete *mind-wipe spell* that has robbed the corpse of its *true name*."

Salidar suppressed an involuntary shudder. This was very dark sorcery indeed, perhaps not as deep an abyss as *necromancy*, but well within the nethermost depths of the black arts. To suffer the loss of one's true name was surpassed in significance only by the loss of one's immortal soul.

Salidar looked to the two men and solemnly observed, "This is an ominous business, to be sure."

They sipped their wine slowly, commiserating in silence.

The baron finally spoke, "Gentlemen, the noon hour has slipped by unnoticed. I confess I have no appetite. I have been overly concerned with what must soon take place. However, I can call for a meal if either of you hunger; but, forgive me if I do not join you."

"I have been fasting in preparation for the rite, my lord baron," the mage reminded him, "so, be not concerned for me."

"You are most gracious, m'lord," added Salidar, "but I hunger not. If I might inquire, when shall the rite commence, m'lords?"

The baron looked to the magus, who rose and walked to the windows. He studied the position of the sun in the afternoon sky for a moment and sighed resignedly.

"It appears I can commence the rite in a few minutes; there will be minimal shadows in the courtyard. Baron, you can alert your guards to move the people back a few paces."

"Very well," agreed the baron, standing. "Salidar, I am expected to oversee the rite from my balcony. You are welcome to join me and observe from there."

Salidar stood as well and executed a slight bow.

"Thank you, m'lord, it would be an honor." *Although I would much rather be miles away, it seems that I am now compelled to stay. They assume that I am supposed to observe on behalf of the Unseelie Court—I can now do little else.*

The baron signaled to a guard captain and gave him his orders. The mage left to make his way down to the open courtyard. The baron and Salidar stepped out onto the balcony and beheld the milling crowd below. Salidar surreptitiously scanned for Wilhem and Frieda in the throng. He sensed they were present, but he did not see them.

Magus Jalash-el appeared on the lower steps of the keep and stood still in the sunlight. Whispering a soft incantation inaudible to all but himself, the mage descended the last few steps and entered the courtyard.

A number of anxious people noticed the mage and nudged others; conversations soon dwindled to mere mumbles. The crowd stepped back and grew completely quiet as he walked further out onto the sun-baked stones.

Jalash-el approached to within two paces of the slumped and shrouded figure chained to the stake. Raising his open hands to his face, he began to chant in a low register as he slowly extended his arms and swung them out to his sides. Pale amber light began to pulse in the palm of each hand in cadence to the rhythm of his chanting.

Coming no closer, the mage began to move to his right, counterclockwise, in a measured side-step shuffle that was almost a dance. He gently waved his outstretched hands in a distinctive and continuous pattern until he had slowly and rhythmically circumnavigated the captive three times. Pale traces of amber light hovered in the air wherever his hands had passed, mimicking a Celtic basket-weave pattern.

The mage came to a stop before the unmoving figure. From within his robes, he took three vials, each slightly smaller than the size of his fist, and placed them on the ground at arm's length behind him. He mumbled another incantation over them, then picked one up and held it briefly to his forehead.

Facing the bound figure, the mage stepped off to his left, clockwise. He retraced his circular path, and sparingly sprinkled the entire contents of the first vial, salt, in a large circle. He then repeated the pattern, in a slightly larger concentric circle in the opposite direction, with the contents of the second vial, oil. He reversed direction once more and repeated the pattern to craft the outermost circle, dispensing the contents of the third and last vial, water.

Jalash-el stood back from his original position, well beyond the concentric circles he had just completed. He opened his arms widely, and clapped his hands sharply. The vague pattern of amber light suddenly flared into a woven cylinder of fierce incandescence twice the height of a man.

The crowd stumbled back and shielded their eyes.

Jalash-el clapped his hands again. A silver shimmer arose from the ring of spilled salt and melded with the bright amber weave.

He clapped his hands a third time. Tongues of blue-white flames erupted from the ring of oil. As they flared upward in frenzy, colors along their questing length morphed from azure to yellow-orange and rampant reds in complementary enhancement of the pulsing glow of silver and amber.

Jalash-el clapped his hands one more time, and the ring of puddled water began to boil. Steam rose to form a circular cloud that hovered near the top of the outer circumference of this magnificent display of magic. The cloud roiled within itself and darkened. Then it began to rain, but only upon that circular boiling puddle from whence it came.

Jalash-el stepped back a pace, closed his eyes, and pointed with both hands at the bound figure within the pulsating screen of thaumaturgy.

"By the powers of Air, Earth, Fire, and Water . . . I, Magus Jalash-el, Magus Primus of Shadow and House of Lamia, call forth that which is unnamed and bound within this desecrated shell. By the powers of all the elements, I command that this unknown shall be *contained and known!*"

The bound figure began to twitch and jerk, spasmodically twisting against its bindings. Its struggles grew more frantic, as if it were becoming more conscious of its surroundings and did *not* like it, a predator trapped by its prey.

It was nearly impossible to see more than a straining outline beneath the tightly tied shroud through the sorcerous screen of containment spells.

Suddenly, the figure went completely still, and shuddered once. A stygian mist began to form like an aura clinging to the form of the bound figure.

There was a faint sound, a keening that swelled, rose to a harrowing shriek of despair, and culminated in a mind-numbing screech of frustrated rage.

A convulsive spasm snapped the figure upright and aware. Instantly, its mighty struggles began anew as its demonic howls furiously ripped at the sky.

People in the crowd held their ears and pressed back against one another.

With growing alarm, Salidar could see trickles of blood from Jalash-el's nose and ears. But the mage stood resolute, chanting a binding incantation, focused on containing the roiling dark spell.

With a sudden surge of strength, the chained form seemed to bulge; the tarnished silver links stretched and snapped, scattering upon the courtyard stones. The taut shroud ripped apart revealing a monstrous decomposing form, its festering squat head covered in long disgustingly matted hair. The cavernous mouth opened in a roar of psychotic glee.

Sudden winds sprang up and whipped about, toppling baskets of food and raising stinging dust. The crowd broke, scrambling over upturned carts and collapsed stalls, trampling one another in their panic. Only the men-at-arms kept their wits about them and prevented more injuries as they funneled the frightened masses out of the courtyard.

Jalash-el dropped to one knee and winced. Despite his obvious pain, he never interrupted his chant or lost his focus.

The dark mist thickened about the grotesque ogress, obscuring the desiccated form and sightless dead eyes as she strained against her remaining bonds. Tendrils of the foul vapor jabbed forth, probing and testing the strength of the conjured elemental walls of containment.

Jalash-el flinched and faltered with each attack.

Salidar, near panic himself, reached for the baron's arm and rasped, "M'lord, I know you are a magic user! Can you not do something? Help him!"

The pain the baron felt was evident in his face as well as his voice.

"Would that I could, Salidar. But *that* is precisely what he warned me against. Anything I might try would only strengthen the evil he now combats! And I caution you—if you have any such skills, use them not! You would only assure his defeat!"

The elder mage was now on his hands and knees, blood dripping freely from his nose and ears; but he never gave up chanting and maintaining the elemental spells.

The cold iron held; neither the black spell nor the raging she-beast could overcome the ferrous chain.

The dark mist slowly rose from the body of the ogress. As it steamed off in a vapor, the exposed portions of her body grew still; her feet, legs, hands, and arms went slack. The last wisps of vapor trailed from her distended nostrils and her head lolled upon a slack shoulder. At last, she was still.

The foul mist could not escape the walls of containment. It gathered in a noxious cloud above the chained corpse and roiled in frustration.

Jalash-el struggled to stand; although none dared come to his aid, he managed.

His heart pounding, Salidar gripped the balustrade until his knuckles whitened. A quick glance at the baron confirmed that he was equally transfixed by the drama unfolding below. All either of them could do was watch.

Jalash-el swayed slightly as he stood erect, and brought his outstretched arms just above shoulder height. While carefully maintaining his focus on the many spells in play, he spoke in a clear voice, using a language not heard in a millennium.

The strange thing was that, *in his mind,* Salidar clearly understood what was said. The mage again called upon the elementals—Air, Earth, Fire, and Water—to witness the evil befouling their appointed realms. He asked that they implore the sun to eradicate all trace of this dark energy, and its foul vessel.

Between his next two heartbeats, Salidar experienced what he could only later describe as shockingly unbelievable.

I saw—I know, I saw! The sun reached out with a fiery finger to vaporize the dark mist and the body of the ogress, leaving only a slack chain of cold iron, and an unharmed—not even singed, wooden stake!

Jalash-el stood alone in the silent courtyard. The swirling weave of elemental spells was gone. Only a pile of iron chain about the stake remained; no trace of the mist or the ogress was to be found.

At a signal from the baron, men-at-arms rushed to the mage and supported him as they led him into the keep.

Forcing his grip on the balcony railing to ease, Salidar realized he'd been holding his breath. His heart pounded in his ears. He had just witnessed an extraordinary event, a staggering example of bravery. He had seen necromancy defeated by a human mage—a lesson he would not soon forget.

Perhaps there's yet hope. I have learned much, but not yet enough.

His thoughts awhirl, he stared vacantly into the distance, absently fingering the topaz ring.

He blanched!

Ye gods! The ring! It holds a spell! I had forgotten about it. Did it contribute to the dark spell's defense? Have I unwittingly contributed to this brave adept's near defeat? I did not use the ring, so I can only hope it played no role.

But has its purpose been compromised? If so, what will Diere do to me? I pray its integrity and intention are intact; I have no choice but to proceed as if so. Damn the fates!

JALASH-EL WAS TAKEN to a room off the great hall on the lower floor, and closeted with the baron's healer. No one other than the baron was admitted.

Several hours passed before the worn and weary baron emerged and gave instructions to his staff.

Salidar waited patiently until the baron acknowledged him and bade him to approach.

"Forgive me, m'lord, I intend no intrusion," Salidar proffered. "May I ask how the magus fares?"

The baron gave him a wan smile tinged with relief. "The healer says he will recover. He will be weak and will require assistance in the process. Performing the rite of execution was a great strain upon him; and, he is not a young man."

"He is certainly a courageous man, m'lord," observed Salidar. "I have never seen the like. I have never heard of anyone doing what I saw him do."

"Aye," agreed the baron, "there has been little call for such workings, not for a very long time. I count us as quite fortunate that he was successful. I shudder to think of the alternative."

"Indeed, m'lord, indeed." Salidar could not imagine what they would have done had the mage failed.

"Well, Salidar, you must take advantage of my hospitality this night. For as you can see," observed the baron, gesturing to the windows above, "the sun sets within the hour. And I expect a visit by another guest, the Lady Leanan."

Salidar's blood went cold, but he remained expressionless.

"You are most gracious, m'lord. I am, of course, honored to accept your hospitality."

"Excellent," the baron declared, and gestured for a servant to attend him. "Darla, please escort my guest, Salidar, to the visitor's suite in the east wing, and see to his comforts."

The demure young woman approached and curtsied.

"We shall dine in two hours, Salidar," said the baron, with a tired smile. "By then, I am certain we shall both have recovered our appetites."

The servant led Salidar to the guest suite, arranged for wine at his request, and took her leave.

SALIDAR MADE SHORT work of the wine; he really needed a drink. Resigned to his circumstances, he reclined upon the bed and stared at the ceiling, watching as daylight faded and shadows crawled forth in the dimming light.

He lit a solitary candle and pondered what he should do next.

There was no point in returning to Lady Diere—not yet. He sensed that there was more to learn.

And besides, there was no way to avoid Lady Leanan. He had mixed feelings about her. She trusted Lady Diere as little as he did; but, that didn't mean he trusted the Sidhe. She was dangerous and deadly on her own. However, could she prove useful?

To entertain such a thought was bold indeed; one misstep with her could be fatal. But in truth, what choice had he? She was coming to check on her mage, of course—and she wanted to see *him.* He had better adjust to it, and soon; it was almost full dark.

THE SERVANT'S KNOCKING woke Salidar from a light sleep. The lone candle guttered low.

"One moment," he mumbled as he made his way to the door. Upon opening he found the servant girl, Darla, curtsying at the threshold.

"Please excuse the intrusion, good sir, but dinner is to be served and you are expected at his lordship's table."

"Ah, thank you, my dear. You need not wait for me; I know the way. I shall be there presently," he assured her with a smile.

"As you wish, good sir," she replied, dipping slightly. She turned and disappeared down the well-lit hall.

A quick glance upward at the suffused illumination from no apparent source confirmed his suspicions.

Aha! Wizard's Light is once again in common use. The baron must have authorized it once the rite of execution was completed. To forgo even that minor magic during the rite was no doubt a wise decision.

Let's see what the rest of the evening has in store. There may yet be more to learn.

SALIDAR FOUND THE BARON seated alone in the grand dining room. Two liveried servants stood to one side. "Ah, good evening Salidar. I trust you are a bit rested, and perhaps hungry?"

"Quite so, your lordship. Thank you for your gracious hospitality."

"Come, come; be seated. The wine is chilled and I am told we have a fine goose for supper."

The baron nodded to the servants.

At that gesture from his lord, a servant poured wine into crystal goblets; another rolled a tureen cart forward. With a distinct flourish, he uncovered the tureen and allowed the baron to savor the aroma and visually inspect the contents.

Sniffing deeply, the baron smiled. "Ah, excellent! You may serve the soup."

The long table was set for only two; so, Salidar felt compelled to ask, "The Lady Leanan will not be joining us, m'lord? I thought she was expected?"

"Oh, she arrived a short time ago. She will join us later." The baron sipped from his goblet. "She is presently with Magus Jalash-el. She was quite concerned for his well-being, of course."

"Of course, m'lord, I quite understand."

Over the course of the meal, Salidar made the expected periodic complements in regard to the fine repast, but any substantive conversation between them was conspicuously absent. He could only speculate that the events of the day weighed heavily upon his host. It was, after all, the final overt act of a man mired in grief and loss, yet doggedly in pursuit of closure in the matter of his father's death.

As they finished the plum pudding dessert, the Lady Leanan entered the room. Attired in a black and silver gown cut in a style convenient for traveling, she carried a supple leather jacket across one arm. Her free hand absently fingered the soft silver fox fur of the collar. She appeared to be deep in thought.

The baron leapt to his feet, and Salidar followed suit.

"Ah, m'lady, please join us." The baron bowed deferentially.

"M'lady," echoed Salidar, bowing deeply as well.

"Good evening, gentlemen. Baron, let us retire to your study, where we might converse more intimately."

"As you wish, m'lady."

As he turned to lead the way, the baron signaled briefly to the servants who prepared a tray of crystal goblets and wine bottles. Salidar immediately recognized a large black bottle of great age, one that held the Lady Leanan's favored beverage.

A small welcoming fire blazed happily in the great hearth of the baron's study, and the three seated themselves comfortably before it. The servants poured and served each their preferred refreshment, then left them alone.

"If I may, m'lady," began the baron. "How did you find the magus?"

She stared into her goblet and sighed heavily. "He is still very weak, but he will recover, in time. The rite of execution taxed him greatly. In truth, it was a near thing."

"I, for one, m'lady, was impressed with his skill, and his courage," offered Salidar.

"Be not a fool, Salidar!" she snapped. "The dark spell he narrowly defeated was already weakened, as was its host. That ogress was half decayed. Had that been a fresh corpse at full strength—or had its foul author still been in direct control, all of you would likely now be dead."

"M-m'lady," Salidar stammered, "D-direct control? I-I do not understand. Do you mean—"

"Let us not mince words here!" She pinned him with her stare. "This was *necromancy*—that *forbidden black art!* We all know it! In fact, all who witnessed the rite of execution, in their hearts, know it; although, few would ever admit it. Most will delude themselves that it was some other dark magic, some skewed sorcery gone awry. They cannot deal with the ominous reality; perhaps, that is just as well. We need no panic, do we, Baron?"

"No, m'lady, we do not," he responded, his voice edged in sadness.

She sighed once more, sipped crimson from her goblet, and stared into the fire. The men remained silent.

"We do not yet even know the scope of the problem," she admitted. "When Jalash-el and I first examined the ogress the night of her capture, we could see that the black spell had been cast at least a year ago, but *abandoned* for six months, or more."

"Forgive me, m'lady," begged the baron, "*abandoned?* What does that mean?"

"That means, my dear baron, that this ogress, dead at least a year, was under no control for at least the last six months. From that point on, she no longer drew sustaining dark energy from the sorcerer, so she started to decompose and reverted to her natural instincts—to hunt and kill—not for food, per se, but for the *life energy* of her victims. Sadly, that was your late father's unfortunate fate."

The baron remained stoic, but his expression was grim as he accepted the truth of her words.

"Be grateful that she was not more successful at killing," the Sidhe cautioned. "That she was captured at all is evidence of her weakened condition. Had she slain more frequently, her corruption would not have been so advanced. She would have been much, much stronger."

They sat in the thickening silence and sipped from their goblets. The firelight fluttered in its flickering dance and held the gazes of all three. Each saw something different in the flames, something very personal, the echoed essence of some private dread.

"I fear this will not be the last example of such foul sorcery," Leanan said softly, her initial anger spent.

Salidar bit his tongue; he dared not speak. He knew so little about what was going on around him that he felt overwhelmed. He harbored a strong suspicion about the identity of this sorcerer, this *necromancer*, but he did not yet know how to turn this to his advantage. Nor did he know whom to trust; and, that was his *biggest* problem.

"What then can be done, m'lady?" ventured the baron.

"We must be vigilant," she warned. "And act swiftly when so directed. Notify me of anything unusual—*anything!* We may have little or no warning before another incident."

She savored another sip and continued. "Now, in regard to the magus, I have brought a carriage. He will return with me this night. Baron, if you would be kind enough to see to the preparations, I would spend some time with your guest, Salidar. We have some . . . *court business* to discuss."

"Of course, m'lady, I shall attend to the magus personally," agreed the baron, rising. "If you will excuse me?"

Salidar stood as the baron departed. Gesturing to Lady Leanan's drained cup, he raised his eyebrows in an unspoken question. She nodded affirmatively.

He also refilled his own goblet, knowing he might need the *liquid courage.*

She nodded once in thanks as he returned her brimming crystal cup.

They sat for a moment in silence, just gazing into the fire.

"We both know something very dangerous is underway, do we not?" she asked quietly, her eyes locking upon his.

"I suspect so, m'lady," he agreed.

"You gave the scroll to Boltar. He now lies dead in my castle; yet you survive."

The irony was not lost upon him; he maintained his silence.

Her gaze drifted back to the fire and she sighed. "Let us consider what else we know, shall we?"

"M'lady?" His unease did not abate as she stared into the flames.

"We know that Atrellan, a mage in service to Queen Mab, seized the scroll and returned with it to the Realm of the Dark Elves. It appears that the enchantment upon the scroll has yet to do anyone any harm. I find that curious. Equally curious is that Atrellan and his mercenaries were there, waiting for Boltar to come into possession of the scroll. And now, Queen Mab has issued a formal request through the Council for Boltar's body. You know we have little choice but to comply. The spells will be discovered and suspicion will be cast upon the Realms of Shadow and Were. I find all of this to be too well choreographed to be coincidence."

Salidar did not respond, notwithstanding that he found himself in complete agreement with her assessment. Bartering information was second nature to him; he would withhold even his concurrence unless he saw an advantage.

But was there not advantage, however subtle, in drawing more information from the Sidhe? He would have to be very careful. She would be a formidable enemy—and yet, perhaps an interesting ally. Had she not once proposed *trust*?

His thoughts spun to a stop as she broke the silence.

"Salidar, a woman was with you, called the Lady Stacy. What can you tell me about her?"

He paused for a moment and tried to perceive if any truth spells were at work here; but he sensed nothing untoward. And yet, this could perhaps be the opening gambit in furtherance of establishing the uneasy alliance he envisioned. Thus, he decided that this was not the time to dissemble, but rather an opportunity to be seized.

"M'lady, I can only tell you what I saw—and what I suspect. I was foolish enough to be caught by a *tangletree* in the Forest of the Damned; she happened along and freed me. I saw her touch the tree without being harmed; I have no doubt she *communicated* with it. The tree released me—not a moment too soon! The ants were nearly upon me! We then traveled together to the Inn of the Crying Cup, where I delivered the scroll to Boltar. We fled when the fight started, and shortly thereafter became separated. I have not seen her since."

"Very well." Leanan sipped from her goblet. "I suspect you knew you were followed and observed. Your account comports with what was reported. Now, tell me what you suspect."

Salidar hesitated; he had told Lady Diere *nothing* about Stacy.

"I'm waiting, Salidar."

"M'lady, I think the Lady Stacy is some sort of *wood nymph*. She surely has some sort of relationship with *trees*. And she had this strange grey cat; but somehow I sensed that it was more than a mere pet. I asked if it was her *familiar*, but she said it was her *friend and associate*. I sensed power there."

His last comment hung between them with a heavy degree of certainty. Leanan's countenance betrayed nothing save the slight rise of a single elegant eyebrow that almost escaped his notice.

"But even stranger yet, m'lady, I think she has traveled or at least visited the Realm of Man. I base this speculation on her clothing, her manner of speech, and . . . I caught a glimpse of a piece of man's *technology, a cell phone.* It is a device that—"

"I *know* what a cell phone is, Salidar," she frostily interrupted.

"Of course, m'lady." He groveled. "I intended no disrespect."

"Enough! Do you think she has anything to do with Lady Diere? Was it mere happenstance that she came along just when you needed rescue?"

Salidar was plainly surprised by the question. He had never even considered that Lady Stacy might have been a pawn, willing or otherwise, of the Lady Diere. No, it just did not fit, notwithstanding her timely appearance and his subsequent rescue. He had no proof, but he felt certain that there was no relationship between the two.

"No, m'lady, I believe the Lady Stacy has nothing to do with Lady Diere. I have not mentioned her to Diere. And, I think it was purely by chance that she found me in the grip of that tree. I have no proof, of course, but I *feel* the truth of it."

"Actually, I agree with you," she said smugly, "but then, I am better informed. And you would do well to heed my words."

Despite his inherent fear of her, Salidar sensed that his strategy, however dangerous, was working. She was about to share information with him, as he had just done with her. The first overt steps toward a mutually beneficial agenda, or even better, a potential alliance, *however tentative*, were now being laid. His confidence growing, albeit incrementally, he felt he need only continue to play the role he knew so well, that of *conspirator*.

"Of course, m'lady, you have my full attention."

"Lady Stacy *is* from the Realm of Man, and is a close friend of Lady Ellen Doyle, the new Steward of the Grand Portal of the Realm of Man. Lady Stacy came here through some accidental means, and Lady Ellen, with two companions, came looking for her. Lady Stacy was found near the forest the following morning and was restored to her friends."

"Indeed, m'lady, I find that good news. I would not have wished any harm to befall the Lady Stacy."

"Indeed? Perhaps it would be best if you were to give the Lady Ellen and her companions a wide berth. It is my understanding that they have returned to the Realm of Man. Did not Lady Diere decree that there would be no more attempts upon the life of the Steward?"

"She did, m'lady," Salidar responded, confused, "but *'a wide berth'*? I do not understand."

"The Steward and her companions are well aware of your role in the attempt upon her life, and the role you played in the death of Fenton Brewster—"

"But *you* killed Fenton Brewster!" he blurted. "Uh, forgive me, m'lady. But how could they know any of this? And what difference would it make?"

Her brow knitted and her eyes flared. "You would be wise not to interrupt me again."

"Your pardon, m'lady." He dropped to his knees in supplication. *Had he overplayed his hand?*

She let him kneel there for a long moment, and then relented.

"Get up, you fool! Refill my glass, then resume your seat. I will explain further."

He did as she asked, in contrite silence.

She made him wait nonetheless, while she savored several languid sips of her crimson beverage.

"Now, as to the *difference* it would make, these acts of which we speak are *crimes* in the Realm of Man, as you well know. One of the Steward's companions, known here as Lord Hawk, is some sort of law enforcer in that realm, and he is not without some degree of power in *this* realm. The other companion, known as the *Counselor*, has already slain Damien the Cursed and assimilated his power. I do not know how he did this, but there can be no doubt that he is dangerous."

This was indeed news to him. *Could it be these men were hunting me as well?*

Lady Leanan sipped thoughtfully from her warm goblet.

"Remember that *cat* you mentioned? That sounds very much like a companion of the late Maude Delafaire. That was no mere pet, but a being of *power*."

Hearing his suspicions confirmed was no comfort. A knot of unease began to churn in his gut. A cold breath of uncertainty teased the hairs of his neck.

His head snapped up when the Sidhe continued.

"I should mention that they also suspect that you were involved in the death of the last Steward. These people are not to be underestimated. Make no mistake, Salidar, they would fiercely protect the current Steward, and I suspect the Lady Stacy as well. And given the opportunity, they would hunt you down for your *crimes*."

Salidar paled, took a long drink of wine, and then found his voice.

"M'lady, you may rest assured that I have neither plans to visit the Realm of Man in the near future, nor any intention of harming the Steward. My sole remaining task is to deliver a message in Mer. Then I am *done* with Lady Diere as far as I am concerned."

She smiled coyly. "Ah, Padraic the Rogue, I presume, at the Fertility Festival?"

"Quite so, m'lady, but how did you know?"

She smiled, sipped from her cup, and considered him as one might a rather dense child.

"An easy deduction, actually. You see, I know Lady Diere quite well. Consequently, I could anticipate that sending you to the Fertility Festival to seek out the Rogue would be her next move, as it is an event he always attends. It is what I would do, were I she."

"M'lady, I fear that I still do not understand—"

"Salidar, it is not necessary that you understand."

His confusion evident, he drained his cup. He needed a moment to assimilate this information, so he stood and pointed to Lady Leanan's goblet.

"No, thank you, Salidar," she said as she rose, and draped her leather jacket over one shoulder, the silver fur of the collar soft along her cheek. "I must be going. It will be a slow carriage ride with the magus in his frail condition this night. I would appreciate it if you were to keep me informed of what Lady Diere may ask of you—especially as it may impact my realm. But listen carefully; do *not* come to my castle. Things are presently *unsettled* within the administration for the moment. Just send word of where and when we can meet. Do you understand?"

"As you wish, m'lady, but . . . " He hesitated and fidgeted.

"Yes, Salidar?" She paused at the door, her patience waning. "Now what is it?"

"M'lady, uh, these people from the Realm of Man, they do not know me, except for the Lady Stacy, of course. But, I know humans. They may *suspect* or *guess* at someone's involvement in these *so-called crimes;* but, you said they '*know*'. . . How is that possible, m'lady?"

She faced him and stepped closer. Staring coldly into his wide eyes, her smile was feral.

"It is really quite simple, Salidar—I told them."

CH 7

STACY KNEW SHE'D OVERSLEPT, and thought it an absolute luxury. When she finally got herself motivated, she dressed in grey sweatpants and a UCLA T-shirt, and wandered into the kitchen. She had to step over Max who was sleeping just inside the doorway; Sophie was curled into a cinnamon ball nearby, softly snoring. Smokey was, of course, nowhere to be seen.

Millie was on the phone. She waggled her fingers at Stacy and pointed to the coffee pot as she continued her conversation. "Yes, that'll be fine. I'll be here all day . . . That'd be fine, and today would be *so* great. Bye-bye."

Millie hung up, scribbled a note on a slip of paper, and turned toward Stacy, who was already sipping her coffee, her eyes closed in savory satisfaction.

"Good morning, sleepyhead. Did you enjoy sleeping in?" Millie grinned as she sat upon a nearby stool.

"Uh-huh." Stacy put her cup down and stretched her arms over her head. "I hardly ever get to do it at home. It felt great. Where is everybody, and who was that on the phone?"

"Oh, that was just the power company."

"I thought I heard a truck earlier, or maybe I was just dreaming."

"Well, there *was* a truck when the TV was delivered this morning. And then the satellite TV people came out to install the satellite dish. I told them to keep the noise down because you were sleeping."

"Huh? What TV?" Stacy asked over the brim of her coffee mug.

"Oh dear, I think I spoiled the surprise. It's Mark's idea; he wanted it to be a surprise for everyone. Well, Ellen doesn't know yet, so please don't say anything."

"Oh don't worry, Millie. I won't. A satellite dish, huh? How big is it?"

"You know, I was worried that it might be one of those great big ones; but, it's a little thing—not much bigger than my large pizza pan. It's on the roof; but, you don't notice it unless you're looking for it. You see, there's no cable service available out here, and over-the-air TV reception is spotty; so, it has to be a satellite dish. Now we'll have internet access, too."

"That's cool." Stacy drained her cup.

"And let's see, what else?" Millie pondered. "Oh yes, the phone company man was here first thing this morning, too. Remember, we called about getting a phone in the cabin?"

"Uh-huh. The cell phone coverage can be spotty out there." Stacy poured another cup of coffee, and perched on the stool next to Millie. "So, he did it already?"

"No, he came out to see what would have to be done. Ellen walked him out to the cabin and back earlier this morning. He found that there was an old conduit already laid but there were no wires in it. It looks like we can get telephone service to the cabin without too much trouble. He called it a *POTS* line—plain old telephone service."

Stacy snickered. "Really?"

"Yes, really. I also called the power company just now and they said they'd have to schedule someone to come out to inspect that conduit—they might be able to use it, too. I'm waiting for them to call me back; I'm trying to get them to come out today. Anyway, if it'll all work out, we can have electricity and a landline telephone at the cabin."

"Well, that'd be outstanding," Stacy agreed. "Where's Ellen now?"

"She and Mark took the truck into town to run some errands. They decided to let you sleep."

Stacy was suddenly overcome by a jaw-stretching yawn. Rolling her shoulders, she straightened her back; perhaps she wasn't as awake as she thought. *Hmm, coffee's still too hot.* She added a bit more milk, and echoed Millie. "Errands?"

"Yes, well, let's see." Millie started counting off on her fingers. "Mark insisted that the truck had to be inspected; and Ellen really wanted to drive it. They had to meet the lawyer, Mr. Fornier, and go to the bank to straighten out the accounts. And then they had to go to the funeral home to pick up Maude's ashes. The funeral director, Mr. Sheldon, is supposed to meet them."

"Mmmph, I'm glad they let me sleep," mumbled Stacy, as she let her head droop.

"Oh, I also called to confirm our airline reservations. I assume we're still going home to Los Angeles tomorrow, right?"

Sipping her coffee, Stacy sighed heavily. "Yeah, I *have* to be at work on Monday, although I'd much rather stay here. This has been really wonderful—wait, that didn't come out right. I mean, it's sad that it was Maude's death and Ellen's accident that brought us here. But once we got past that, and Ellen's recovered and all, I've met some very interesting people, and had a pretty good time."

"Interesting people? Oh, you mean like Mark?" Millie teased.

"Who?" Stacy blinked and shook her head. "Oh, him? Well, maybe I do find him a *little* interesting."

"Ha! A little?"

Her hands open in surrender, Stacy grinned. "Okay, I like his company; he is fun to be with."

Millie leaned forward, her tone soft yet sincere. "I don't mean to pry; but, do you think it could get serious?"

Stacy stared into her coffee mug for a long moment.

"I don't know, maybe . . . I really do like him—a lot. On the one hand, it seems like it's happening so fast. On the other, this whole visit has been kind of unreal, almost overstimulating, like an exciting vacation that you probably shouldn't tell anyone about. Do you know what I mean?"

"Yes, I do, I certainly do," agreed Millie wistfully. "Although I'd just as soon pass on all that *excitement*, if you don't mind. But aside from that, I must admit I'd forgotten how much I liked it here. The pace is so relaxed. I have great memories of my childhood; so much reminds me of simpler and happier times. I just feel so, I don't know, *at home*, I guess. I don't really know how else to express it."

Stacy tilted her head. "I guess we can always come back, you know, to visit."

"I suppose that's one way of looking at it," mused Millie. "But it seems more like I've always lived *here* and I'm really just visiting Los Angeles. You see, I followed a man out there thinking he was *the one*. Of course, he wasn't; but, that was a long time ago."

"So, that's been one long visit, hasn't it?" Stacy offered a wry smile.

The phone rang; Millie jumped up and answered it by the end of the second trill. "Hello? Oh hi, Detective. No, she isn't here. She and Mark went into town . . . Not really, sometime this afternoon, I expect. Oh, of course she has her cell phone; so, I'm sure she wouldn't mind. You're welcome. Bye-bye."

Millie hung up and stood beaming at Stacy, who couldn't help but return her conspiratorial smile.

"Isn't that sweet?" effused Millie. "Hawk just called to *check* on Ellen. I think those two *like* each other, too."

"You *think?*" Stacy guffawed, trying not to spill her coffee.

Sputtering with laughter, Millie refilled her cup. "Okay, let's get a grip. Now, what would you like for breakfast? I have bacon, eggs, pancakes, and I can whip up some grits."

"What are *grits?* I'll try some—I think," Stacy said gamely.

"Sit back," Millie directed, "and I'll demonstrate all you ever wanted to know about that staple of the southern breakfast. *Grits it is!*"

A FEW HOURS LATER, Mark and Ellen returned. Mark held the doors open for Ellen as she solemnly made her way into the library and placed the rose-colored marble urn upon the mantel above the hearth.

Millie and Stacy stood quietly in the doorway.

"Welcome home, Maude," Ellen whispered.

"Yeah, welcome," echoed Mark. "It is indeed a homecoming."

"That mantel is the *perfect* place for her," Millie added, "although some might think it morbid. I think it's just fine."

Stacy approached the mantel and gently ran her hand along the fine grain of the polished cypress wood. Her eyes lost their focus for a moment and she smiled. "The house welcomes her as well. Now it feels *complete;* it's once again a home."

Everyone smiled at the sentiment.

Stacy stepped back and asked, "Can anyone else feel anything? Anything about the house?"

They were quiet for a moment. Ellen realized each person was looking within, opening respective perceptions and experiencing the sensations, however subtle. *Even I feel comfortable with all of this.*

"I just feel that this is somehow *right,*" Mark offered. "That's the best I can explain it."

Millie stepped to Ellen's side and hugged her. "This would have made Maude very happy. You did good, sweetie. Now, who wants lunch?"

Ellen could only chuckle and shake her head; but she realized she *was* hungry. So, she let her mother lead her toward the kitchen.

"Oh, by the way," Millie remarked, "that nice young detective of yours, Hawk, called for you earlier. I told him to try your cell phone. Did you talk with him? Is he coming by here today?"

Ellen stiffened and her voice grew somber. "Yes, I *did* talk to him, but he's not coming by. In fact he'll be busy down south for the next few days."

"Ellen, what's wrong?" asked Millie firmly.

"He was part of a team conducting some kind of drug raid that didn't go well. He's fine, but four people were killed. Two of them were police officers; eight or nine other officers were hurt."

Millie gasped. "Oh no! What happened?"

Ellen shook her head, her expression grim. "He couldn't tell me much; just that there was gunfire and an explosion. He said he'd call when he knew 'the arrangements'; I think he was referring to *funerals.*"

"Oh honey, I am so sorry." Millie hugged her daughter. "We had no idea. We had the new TV on for a while but we didn't hear anything about it."

"What new TV?" Ellen asked.

Millie blanched, her hands covering her mouth. "Oh no—now I've gone and done it! Mark, I'm so sorry to spoil the surprise."

Mark just chuckled and shrugged. "No harm done, Aunt Millie, I didn't think I could pull off this big a surprise for very long. So, they delivered the TV and did the installation while we were gone?"

"Yes, and I think you *have* surprised Ellen," observed Millie. "But I'm afraid I also blurted out the secret to Stacy this morning."

"It's okay; I'm still surprised!" exclaimed Stacy.

"Come with me to the parlor," Millie urged her daughter. "They installed the television in there."

In the parlor, Ellen confronted her cousin. "Mark, you know I can't afford such an extravagance; and I thought we weren't going to be conspicuous with our spending."

"Think of it as a housewarming present. Don't worry; I can afford it on my own. Look, if you're going to be living here, you're going to need to be connected to the rest of *this* world; you need to know what's going on and all. Besides, I got a great deal. The satellite service even comes with wireless broadband internet access. Don't fret about the cost; technology advances by leaps and bounds, and hardware prices drop pretty consistently. I didn't buy the fanciest or the latest, but it is nice. And, I just want you to be happy, and informed."

"Is it okay to mount it above the mantel?" she pressed. "You know that's a working fireplace, right?"

"They said it'd be fine," Mark assured his cousin. "Besides, it comes with a stand; so, we can always have it moved if you want."

"All right, enough with the TV already," interrupted Millie firmly. "Now, you all come into the kitchen and we'll have lunch. This TV is not going anywhere. Besides, we have more to talk about, like what you two accomplished this morning in town."

Ellen rolled her eyes and sagged with an exaggerated sigh. "Okay, Mom, alright already. Well, first we got the truck inspected. I drove, of course, because I'm an excellent driver."

Mark coughed, and Ellen playfully punched his arm as they passed through the dining room.

"Well, I am! I wanted to get a *feel* for the vehicle that's gonna be my primary transportation. Actually, the truck runs pretty good. Only thing is the air conditioner doesn't work; but the truck still passed the state inspection."

As he pushed the kitchen door open, Mark felt compelled to explain.

"You don't need a working air conditioner to pass inspection. But I would've fixed it if I could've found the required refrigerant. Old systems like that take R-12; but it's obsolete now and tightly controlled under EPA regulations. It's very costly to convert the system over to the newer refrigerants. So, you may have to make do with *strato-freeze*."

Millie burst into laughter.

Stacy and Ellen glanced at one another in obvious confusion.

"*Strato—what?*" Ellen echoed.

"What's so funny?" Stacy asked.

Millie caught her breath and dabbed at her happy tears. "Oh my, I haven't heard that in years! Oh girls, that term, *strato-freeze,* just means you roll your windows down! Mark, you're a rascal!"

His smug smile earned him an exaggerated eye-roll and none-too-subtle elbow nudge from Stacy. "Tsk! Mark, you are so incorrigible! So, what else did y'all do?"

"Quite a bit, actually." Mark sat and continued to describe their morning. "After the inspection, we went by the lawyer's office. I spent a little time discussing my application to the Louisiana Bar with Claude Fornier. He also gave us the appropriate copies of the court documents we needed for our meeting with Mr. Foster, the bank manager."

"It went real well at the bank," Ellen added. "We set up new accounts for the farm. Mr. Foster transferred the balance of Maude's funds and closed her accounts. We also arranged for a pair of safe-deposit boxes."

She and Mark exchanged knowing glances; a selection of assorted coins would be kept in those readily accessible safe-deposit boxes.

"After that," Mark hastily added, "we met with Mr. Sheldon at the funeral home to pick up Maude's urn. Then we came home. And Ellen did drive very well, pretty much the entire time."

Ellen shot him a raised-eyebrow look. "I'll take that as a belated compliment, thank you.

"So, Mom, what else happened around here while we were gone? I know Stacy was sawing logs when we left."

"Indeed she was," Millie confirmed, "so she missed all the excitement. Let's see . . . You know about the TV and satellite dish. Oh, I've been talking to the power utility cooperative; and you already know about the telephone company. Hopefully, it'll work out, and you'll soon have electricity and landline phone service at the cabin."

"The phone line is probably a good idea," Ellen allowed. "I've begun to wonder if the portal isn't sometimes messing with our cell phone reception out there."

After lunch, they assembled in the front parlor where the new flat screen television had been installed above the fireplace. It resembled a large mirror with a slightly dark tint, an illusion shed the instant Millie activated the power button on the remote control. The high definition digital picture was crystal clear, and visually stunning.

The satellite reception offered well over three hundred channels; so, it was no challenge to find a New Orleans news channel covering the drug raid and explosion near Lafayette.

A dispassionate reporter's laconic commentary accompanied distant panning shots of the destruction's aftermath. Flashing lights of firefighting apparatus drew the eye as emergency responders moved about carefully. It was obvious that this was the *post mop-up* phase of the operation.

They watched in silence, recognizing no one among the emergency and law enforcement personnel in the newscast. A band of text crawled across the bottom of the screen, repeating a headline like a weary mantra; "Illegal Drug Lab Explodes! Four Dead! More Injured! Funeral Home Burns!"

Ellen couldn't watch any more. "Excuse me, I need some air."

She left the room and made her way to the front porch. Leaning against a shaded post, she gazed out across the colorful gardens and sighed. The gentle warmth of the afternoon was soothing. Small breezes teased one another across the swaying swath of bright blooms, further calming her.

The screen door opened and closed behind her; she heard the footfalls of her friend.

"Ellen, are you all right?" Stacy asked solicitously, her hands cupping her cooling coffee mug.

"I'm fine . . . I'm just glad that Hawk's all right, and sorry that some of the other officers were killed or hurt." Ellen stepped down upon the stone steps and sat down.

Stacy sat beside her. "I understand. Look, he's all right—he *called* you to tell you he was fine, see? He didn't want you to worry; that tells you he *cares* about you. You have to step back from the situation to see what he's really showing you. He's worried about you *because* he cares about you. As I see it, this is not exactly a bad thing, is it?"

"No, I suppose not, and I *do* like him. I'm, um, fond of his company."

"Oh, for crying out loud!" exclaimed Stacy. "He's not some random *hookup!* He's perfect for you! He's single, good-looking, smart and kind! Ellen, he *dotes on you!*"

"Dotes?" Ellen echoed, fighting not to smile through her incredulity.

"Well, okay, maybe not *'dotes'*—not yet—but he certainly cares for you," asserted Stacy. "You can't tell me that you don't feel the same way about him."

"Oh, you mean the way you and Mark feel about each other?" teased Ellen playfully.

"Moi?" Stacy sputtered in mock horror, as they both collapsed in laughter.

"Now, now—glass houses and all that!" Ellen teased.

"Okay, okay, I plead *nolo contendere*, your honor." Stacy mimicked Mark all too well, bringing about a new round of laughter.

"Oh yeah," Ellen spouted, "don't you look guilty!"

Stacy caught her breath. "All right, all right. Not to change the subject, but let's *do* change the subject. You know, there is something I need to ask you."

"What?" Ellen regained her composure.

Stacy glanced over her shoulder as she heard the screen door creak open; but it was only the dogs and Smokey who joined them on the porch. She put her empty mug to the side, which the dogs just *had* to sniff before laying down.

"Remember in the cave with the still, when you did that *telekinesis thing*, lifting the boxes and all?"

"Telekinesis?" echoed Ellen. "Yeah, I guess it was. What about it?"

"Can you still do it—here, I mean? Like, can you make my empty mug rise off the porch?"

"I don't think so—hold on." Her brow furrowed, Ellen concentrated, and then sighed in resignation. "Nope, but that doesn't surprise me. See, I think I could do it at the cave, because Maude left me, um, the tools, sort of, to do it there. I sensed that I could access the spells involved, and manipulate them."

"That makes sense," Stacy allowed. "I'd bet Maude set it up so you, her successor, could do so."

"Yeah, I think that's it," Ellen confirmed as the cat nuzzled under her elbow and crawled into her lap. She absently scratched behind his ears, and he began a hypnotic purring.

"You know your mom and I are leaving tomorrow," Stacy reminded her. "We're on the same flight back to L.A. in the early afternoon."

"Yeah, I hadn't forgotten . . . I just didn't want to think about it, that's all."

Stacy reached out and hugged Ellen's neck. "Aw, you're gonna miss us . . . Before we go, there's something you and I are supposed to do today, Thursday—remember?"

"What? Oh yeah, Storm Haven, right? Sorry, it sort of slipped my mind."

"You still have the gem, the emerald, don't you?"

"Sure, it's upstairs in my room. Why?"

"We should do this *now,* this afternoon," urged Stacy. "I get the feeling that we're running out of time, or something. Somehow I know this is important, so let's get the jewel and go. You can probably summon a transit globe there in your room, right?"

"Actually, I can't, or at least I shouldn't, not in the house. I've been doing some more reading in the journal; it seems the more I read, the more there is yet to be read. I know that doesn't make much sense, but just listen. The house is warded; some *very strong* and *very old* enchantments protect it. Almost no major magic will work within its walls, and I think that could include transit spells. We'd be better off going to the cabin and working the spell in the circle of standing stones. Some equally strong old enchantments there are designed to protect the user of the circle. Do you understand?"

"I get it," Stacy assured her. "So, we get the gem, go to the cabin, and transit from there, right? Oh, wait a minute! Remember what the Guildmaster said about being discreet? I don't think we should tell anyone where we're going, if we don't have to."

"Yeah, that would probably be best, I think. We can tell Mark and my mom that we're just going for a walk."

Of course, the dogs alerted at the mere mention of a *walk* and elected to go along.

Smokey was not to be left out. So, when they went, he followed.

ON THE TRAIL, STACY explained the protocols for entry into Storm Haven and demonstrated the secret signs expected upon arrival. She went on to describe what she had seen on her earlier visit, so Ellen would know what to expect.

The dogs ranged ahead, but Smokey stayed close, as if he was listening to Stacy's explanation.

At the cabin, Ellen told the dogs to *stay.* She and Stacy entered the circle of standing stones. Smokey, of course, was underfoot.

Ellen's merest thought brought the large familiar globe into shimmering existence. At her whim, it enveloped them, expanding to the edge of the standing stones. Once again they were in a vast space with a sea of floating globes before them.

"Wow!" exclaimed Stacy. "You're really getting good at this!"

Ellen chuckled. "Yeah, it did seem a little easy. Now, let's see what this bright emerald will do for us."

She held the vibrant gem in her fist and concentrated on summoning a transit sphere, with no thought as to a specific destination. As the image formed in her mind, her hand began to tingle. An orb began to form before them, with various shades of green light washing across its surface. The globe reached a state of solidity and the flowing green tints cleared from its surface. Ellen opened her hand to find the jewel bereft of its inner light, its energy spent. She slipped it into her pocket and smiled at Stacy, who now stood with Smokey in her arms.

"Okay, Stacy, shall we? It seems that Smokey will be joining us."

Stacy hugged the cat and grinned, eager for the adventure. "Oh yes, by all means—I don't think he'd stay behind anyway."

THEY PRESSED INTO THE globe and found themselves in the austere arrival chamber of Storm Haven. Thanks to Stacy's coaching, they executed the entry protocols flawlessly, and were admitted into the adjacent reception room.

Ellen had been forewarned; but, she was nonetheless a bit surprised at the black-clad guards armed with shotguns posted around the perimeter of the large chamber. They kept to their posts as two tall men in grey robes approached. One was hooded and gloved, but not the other.

The two men bowed. The hoodless one extended a formal welcome.

"Greetings, m'ladies, and welcome to Storm Haven. I am Gallenius, Senior Mage of the College, and this is the Guildmaster."

Inclining his head toward his companion, he continued. "Guildmaster, may I present the Lady Stacy, who has returned to us, and the Lady Ellen Doyle, Steward of the Grand Portal of the Realm of Man and heiress to the Lady Maude Delafaire. Oh, I see that Smokey has decided to grace us with his presence once more, as well."

Ellen could not see within the Guildmaster's hooded robe, his face was obscured by a veil of shimmering dim lights and shadow, but his voice was warm and confident, if a bit metallic.

"I bid you welcome, m'ladies, and Smokey. Lady Ellen, thank you for honoring our invitation. We have much to discuss; and I am sure you have many questions."

Ellen had been finding herself increasingly assertive, and she responded pointedly. "Thank you, Guildmaster. I would like the answer to a question now, if you don't mind. Why can't I see your face?"

The chamber grew very quiet, the air dead still.

Gallenius drew a breath as if to speak, but a gesture from the Guildmaster forestalled him.

"I shall indulge the Lady Ellen, Gallenius. M'lady, the identity of the serving Guildmaster is a closely held secret, for many reasons. In fact, the very existence of Storm Haven is a secret, a very large and difficult one to keep, to be sure. But the very survival of a multitude of beings hinges on maintaining that secret. I must ask that you display the utmost discretion in regard to what you already know, and what you will learn here today, as many lives may depend upon it."

Ellen stared at the man and assessed his words. She was inclined to reserve judgment, and was about to declare her reservation when Smokey wound around her ankles, trotted to the Guildmaster and leapt into his arms.

Clearly, *he* trusted the man; and that was her tipping point.

"Very well, Guildmaster, you shall have my discretion."

"Excellent, m'lady, you have my deep appreciation. Now if you will forgive me, I must ask for the return of the gem you were given to use in your summoning. Please, give it to Gallenius."

"Of course." Ellen retrieved the emerald from her pocket and dropped it in Gallenius' outstretched hand.

"Thank you, m'lady," muttered Gallenius. "These stones are all too rare; we have far too few to spare."

"They are capable—or at least that one is—of holding a spell, aren't they?" she observed.

"Indeed so, m'lady," he answered, smiling. "Such gems are believed to have been among a dragon's hoard, a long time ago."

Her eyebrows rose, but she kept her thoughts to herself.

"Now, m'ladies, if you would be kind enough to accompany the Guildmaster and me, we shall meet in more comfortable surroundings and see to your refreshment. This way, please."

They followed the men to the Guildmaster's office, which to Ellen's mind could have served as a library or grand study. Heavily laden bookshelves covered the walls; she found that this put her at ease. Perhaps it was the warmth of many books, or the sense that knowledge was esteemed here, if for no other reason than its own sake, that contributed to her comfort.

They took seats at one end of a long table covered with books and charts. A younger man in a tan robe offered to serve goblets of honeyed wine and tall glasses of a fruity, yet tart, lemon-scented drink.

Ellen declined the wine and opted for the tart drink. She sipped tentatively, and found that she rather liked it.

"I think it might be best if we were to simply give you an overview of the history of this realm," suggested the Guildmaster. "Will that be acceptable?"

Ellen glanced at a nodding Stacy and smiled. "Yes, please go on."

The Guildmaster spoke at length, with the occasional supporting comment from Gallenius. It reminded Ellen of a civics lecture. However, the importance of secrecy became apparent; should any of the eight council realms become aware of Storm Haven, its continued existence would be in jeopardy. Well, perhaps with one exception, the Realm of Dragons had been a silent enigma for the last five hundred years.

When the Guildmaster began to speak of the *professional* relationship between Storm Haven and Maude Delafaire in her capacity as Steward, Ellen became thoroughly intrigued. She sensed a subtle subtext in his recitation. It was almost as if there was something he was reluctant to tell her.

A flash of sudden insight focused her thoughts.

I am being tested! He is probing. He is unsure of something. Something about Maude? Or rather about me in the role of Steward? No, it's something more personal . . . Aha—of course! The clothing in her closet!

As the Guildmaster paused for a sip of wine, Ellen asked, "Guildmaster, would you care to visit my home at some time of your convenience?"

The unexpected invitation momentarily surprised the Guildmaster, but he responded smoothly. "Thank you, m'lady, but I never leave Storm Haven."

"Ah, but you have in the past," countered Ellen. "You have even been in my home; of course, it was my Great Aunt Maude's home at the time. And, I suspect you were the *serving* Guildmaster at the time. You even left some clothing there, didn't you?"

No one moved in the deafening silence. Stacy stared wide-eyed at her friend. Only Smokey, lying splayed upon a nearby chart atop the table, remained nonplussed. Ellen smiled sweetly, but never took her eyes off the Guildmaster.

Gallenius leaned forward and placed his cup upon the table. Ellen noticed a slight tremor as he extended his arm; it soon affected his shoulder—it was *twitching*. His breathing altered, coming in small gasps and spurts. She suddenly realized that he was *laughing!*

Soon both he and the Guildmaster were laughing aloud.

"Oh my," gasped Gallenius. "She is very good!"

"Indeed," agreed the Guildmaster.

Now Ellen was on confident ground, and she knew it. "Gentlemen, let us dispense with the subtleties and have a free exchange of information. I don't think any of us have the time to waste."

The Guildmaster put his drink down and stood. Bowing slightly toward Ellen, he said, "Well met, my Lady Steward. I can see why Maude chose you to succeed her."

Ellen remained expressionless as he continued.

"Let us be frank. Maude was a dear friend, both to me and this realm. And yes, I visited her quite often. She had a hand in molding a motley group of thieves, smugglers, other ne'er-do-wells, and no shortage of honest refugees into a confederation of mutual yet clandestine support, based in a safe and hidden refuge, the likes of which had never been seen among the *wild* or the Council Realms.

"We are the information brokers, the storehouse of all available knowledge, and the collectors of secrets. We are the hope of all those beings who would be free."

Resuming his seat, the Guildmaster spoke with similar passion for some time as he explained in considerable depth much of the inner workings of each of the known realms.

Ellen had many questions, and he answered each with complete candor—even those about Salidar, however unpleasant that topic was for him.

Finally, Ellen synopsized her understanding of the key issues, and he generally confirmed her comprehension.

However, she felt compelled to inquire further in several areas.

"So, as it pertains to Delafaire Farm, a contingent of Light Elves, the rough equivalent of junior botanists in training, essentially served as Maude's gardeners in exchange for free access privileges to her forest?"

"Quite so, m'lady," Gallenius interjected, "until she died. They—the Light Elves—have been, ah, somewhat reluctant to approach you, as the new Steward, about continuing the traditional arrangement. You are largely an unknown factor to them, you see."

Pursing her lips and knitting her brow at that revelation, she nonetheless continued to probe. "And this also holds true for a group of Dwarves who would distill alcoholic spirits, using the still I found on my land?"

"Actually, m'lady, they are a *Guild,* the Dwarven Guild of Brew Masters and Distillers. They did construct that still. But they deferred distillation operations when Maude was incapacitated three years ago."

"I see," Ellen acknowledged. "Are there any other groups, guilds, or beings that I should know about—I mean those with whom Maude may have formed agreements or extended any other similar privileges?"

Gallenius looked to the Guildmaster and shrugged.

The Guildmaster held up a finger. "Perhaps the *Mer—the water people?* As I recall, they were quite fond of visiting the lake near the cabin."

"Mer-people, dwarves, and elves!" Stacy exclaimed, nudging Ellen. "You've got to continue the arrangements—let them all come back!"

"Don't worry, I will," responded Ellen, smiling at the notion.

"It may not be quite that easy, m'lady," warned the Guildmaster. "You have not yet presented yourself to the Council during a formal meeting to introduce yourself as Steward. It is a mere formality—you are effectively the Steward since Maude selected you and you accepted. However, it is critically important that you observe the formal protocols of the Council, otherwise the other races will be very reluctant to deal with you. Many among them tend to be staunch traditionalists."

Ellen leaned forward. "May I assume this is the same Council that now has a vacant Chair of Man? Is that not the same position that George Papadolis wants?"

"You are correct on both points, m'lady," acknowledged the Guildmaster.

"Where and when," she asked, leaning back in her chair, her voice strangely flat and devoid of warmth, "does the Council meet?"

The Guildmaster nodded to Gallenius, who then answered her question.

"Upon the next full moon, about three weeks hence. They meet in a solitary place—one must transit there—but it is well known. You could find it easily, I am sure."

"If I may, Lady Ellen," the Guildmaster inquired. "Could you please tell us how it is that you are so well-informed about this man, George Papadolis?"

Ellen considered and crafted her answer carefully. Stacy listened wide-eyed.

"He is a native human of my realm, a known criminal referred to as 'Papa George'. I have reason to believe he is wanted by the authorities even now for questioning in regard to a murder. Furthermore, if your intelligence network is as good as you say, you should already know that I have met and dealt with the Lady Leanan in the Realm of Shadow. She too has confirmed his hand in murder. She strongly suspects that he acts at the direction of a Dark Elf, the Lady Diere. I am not overly trusting of Lady Leanan, and certainly not Lady Diere." She leaned forward for emphasis. "But understand this; there's absolutely no way Papa George can be allowed to ascend to the Chair of Man."

"All the more reason for you to appear before the Council at the earliest opportunity," intoned the Guildmaster.

"Gentlemen, rest assured I have every intention of doing so." Her voice rang with conviction. "Do I just appear, unannounced? Or is an invitation required?"

"An invitation would be the proper protocol," advised Gallenius, who cast a glance at the Guildmaster. "It would be our pleasure to *arrange* that very formality, through our own channels. It would appear to have come from the Council itself—in fact it actually will."

Ellen smiled. "I'd appreciate that."

"M'lady, please consider Storm Haven your ally," the Guildmaster urged. "It would please me greatly to establish the same type of mutually beneficial relationship that we enjoyed with the last Steward, your Great Aunt Maude. Please, do not hesitate to call upon us—as we would not be reluctant to call upon you."

Ellen stood, smiled, and extended her open hand. "Your candor pleases me, Guildmaster. I accept your offer. Shall we shake hands? It is the custom among my people, as I'm sure you know."

The Guildmaster stood, hesitated but a moment, and then took her hand in his gloved one. He grasped and shook it firmly, but then surprised her by raising her hand toward his hidden face, briefly simulating a chivalrous kiss.

"And this, as you may not know, is the custom among our people, m'lady."

"Duly noted, my friend," said Ellen, in mild chagrin. "May I ask a favor? Once I have appeared before the Council and formally confirmed my status, could you discreetly arrange for me to meet with the appropriate representatives of the Light Elves, Dwarves, and Mer so that we may re-establish those arrangements that Maude had formerly put in place?"

"That would be a singular honor, m'lady," the Guildmaster said as he bowed.

Ellen smiled. "Of course, that will include getting my Aunt Maude's version of an *Underground Railroad* up and running as well."

Ellen may not have been able to see him smile, but she felt it.

"Thank you, m'lady. I thank you on behalf of our entire realm."

"One final question," posed Ellen, "and then we really must return. I have heard and read repeated references to the *Old Ones.* What can you tell me about them?"

"Ah," exclaimed the Guildmaster, "that is Gallenius' area of expertise. I shall let him enlighten you."

Gallenius urged them to be seated once again, mumbling, "Oh, where to begin? It is almost all legend, you see." He took a moment to collect his thoughts. "Much of what I shall tell you is speculation based upon a collection of legends, oral traditions, and commonly accepted myths. But within this hazy cloud of supposition we believe the flame of truth endures. So, please bear with me.

"It is told, and believed by many, that in ancient times the Old Ones were essentially very powerful entities, or perhaps simply more evolved beings who strode from realm to realm unhindered, doing as they chose.

"We do not know their form; descriptions of their appearances varied wildly from different accounts. Perhaps, like the Were, they could change shapes—no one truly knows. But we suspect they were not like humans, or any other known race. We do not even know if they had corporeal bodies; although, it is thought to have been very likely.

"We *do* know that they were sentient and, as I said, very powerful. They had a great command of what is referred to as *magic* or *sorcery*.

"We know they were unique as *individuals*. They were known by many individual names, ascribed by the different cultures that knew of them. However, it became universally forbidden to speak any of their names, for reasons that will soon become clear.

"Some Old Ones disdained contact with those they considered lesser beings, any life-form other than themselves. Some Old Ones didn't really care but found amusement in the lives of such lesser beings, and were content to merely observe. However, there were a few among the Old Ones who frequently meddled in the mundane lives of those they considered lesser beings.

"At that time, there were many diverse races or tribes of these *lesser beings*, as perceived by the Old Ones, far more than we are commonly familiar with today. A multitude of sentient life-forms were represented; giants, goblins, and so on, to include hybrids like the centaurs and fauns, in addition to the broad diversity of beings still around today. Of course, a fair number of them still exist, but are now considered rather rare. Oh yes, there were the Dragons, as well.

"Sadly, many of these races have disappeared from the known realms, with some exceptions, of course. For example, goblins still inhabit almost all the known realms, but are very shy and secretive. It is thought that they are likely few in number these days. They were known to assiduously avoid contact with anyone not of their immediate clan or tribe. Ah, forgive me, I digress.

"Now it came to pass that there were those among the Old Ones who fancied themselves *gods* over the lesser beings. They would occasionally demand *worship* and *sacrifice*. These Old Ones were typically those who frequently interfered and meddled in the lives of the unfortunate. Some took an inordinate interest in the infliction of hardship and pain, most often only for their own amusement. Worse, they often disagreed and argued amongst themselves—so much so, that they would use lesser beings as proxies to stage fights, conflicts, and sometimes lingering wars.

"Others among the Old Ones found these activities distasteful and distanced themselves from their evil brethren. Over time, the more aloof of the Old Ones faded from memory; many speculated that they had moved on to a higher plane of existence. The simple truth is that no one knows what actually became of them.

"Life in all the known realms became very harsh and untenable for all those still under the thumbs of the remaining Old Ones. As you would expect, strong resentment festered—always carefully hidden, of course—and bred a determined commitment to resistance.

"A very wise and learned group of beings representing a handful of realms met clandestinely and plotted to rid themselves of the Old Ones. They developed a careful and methodical strategy of rebellion; but it would take time, and happen right under the arrogant noses of these *self-appointed gods.*

"Before I continue, I must tell you of the Dragons."

"Oh, yes!" Stacy exclaimed. "This is really getting good!"

Gallenius smiled, and warmed to his tale.

"We believe that the sentient Dragons are as ancient as the Old Ones; but, the Old Ones never held any dominion over the Dragons. Of course, legend holds that the Old Ones tried to subjugate the Dragons, but they failed. Scholars of Dragon lore believe that the Dragons as a race generally opposed the Old Ones whenever their paths crossed. It is believed that the Dragons were as competent in magic and sorcery as were their adversaries.

"Early on, the Dragons became aware of the plot by the bolder realms to throw off the yoke of the Old Ones, and they quietly observed developments. Typically aloof, the Dragons were little concerned with anything beyond their home realm. However, they did not trust the Old Ones, and so kept a wary eye upon them.

"It was soon evident to the Dragon Lords that all was not going smoothly among those representing the rebellious realms. There were frequent arguments among the plotters in regard to tactics in support of their overall strategy. Some thought they were moving too slowly and were impatient; others had trust issues with their co-conspirators and threatened to withhold cooperation. At some point the Dragon Lords intervened and imposed some order on the participants, encouraging mutual cooperation and enhanced secrecy. Fortunately, the representatives of these realms listened and complied."

"Well *duh!* I imagine it would be pretty stupid to ignore a dragon's advice, right?" interjected Stacy.

"Ah, quite so," Gallenius agreed with a bemused smirk. "The Dragon Lords also advised a slight modification to the conspirators' strategy; acquire as much of the Old Ones' sorcerous lore as possible. In other words, learn to use the Old Ones' own magic against them. So, this was the path the rebellious realms pursued, ultimately with great success.

"The Elves proved to be quite adept at gleaning the spells and incantations of the Old Ones merely by careful observation. But as many have since suspected, the Elves kept some of the magical secrets for themselves. To this day, they are the preeminent magic users.

"Over time—actually generations—the rebellious realms were successful. A secret cabal of mages was formed to conduct the final great work. It was performed under the dark of the new moon, while the Old Ones were preoccupied with an annual festival of self-aggrandizement.

"It is said that at the break of the new dawn, a cataclysm ensued. In the chaos, the remaining Old Ones were suddenly swept up by a mighty wind bearing a cloying grey mist, an aberrant mutation of a nefarious mixture of their own dark sorceries. They were seen no more.

"And thus, with the Dragon Lords' considerable assistance, the Old Ones were banished to another plane of existence, a sterile grey place, spare and empty but for themselves. There, it is said, they remain trapped, constantly bickering with each other, always plotting and planning ways to return and take their vengeance.

"For this reason, the speaking of any of the individual names of any of the Old Ones has long been forbidden. Names can hold great power; it would be potentially disastrous for an Old One to be inadvertently summoned forth from banishment. The Dragon Lords are said to have insisted upon this taboo.

"Now as I said, much of the strongest magic—especially that practiced by the Elves—had its origins in the lore of the Old Ones. But of course, it too has evolved over time and been refined to a large extent. The occupants of other realms have learned much of these esoteric arts as well. In fact, most beings have some capacity for magic, depending, of course, on which realm they are in at that moment and their personal skill level. Things can be quite different in realms other than one's home, as I am sure you know."

A question occurred to Ellen. "Gallenius, may I assume that these original rebellious realms were those who are now represented on the Council?"

"Well, actually yes, m'lady, but the Council was not formed until much later—albeit millennia ago—by those seven realms. The Dragon Lords were also invited. So, there are actually eight chairs on the Council; although, the Dragon Lords have not sent an avatar in over five hundred years.

"In conclusion, that is essentially what we know and suspect about the Old Ones."

"I see," said Ellen. "This has been an enlightening visit, indeed. If there is nothing further we can accomplish here and now, then gentlemen, we should return home. Thank you, for your hospitality and your patience. We still have much to learn."

As they all stood, the Guildmaster spread his gloved hands. "M'ladies, it is I who should thank you. I feel we have renewed a vital bridge between us. And I wish to express my deepest condolences on the death of your Great Aunt, my dear friend Maude. I think she would approve of our agreement this day. We shall not delay you any longer. I am sure you are eager to get home. Gallenius will accompany you to the departure chamber. Again, m'ladies, you have my deepest thanks."

The Guildmaster bowed deeply and left the room by a narrow door in the rear wall.

Ellen scooped up Smokey and nodded to Stacy. "We've gotta get back."

Gallenius swept his arm toward the wider entrance door; they followed him from the room.

Once in the spare departure chamber, the senior mage eloquently expressed his gratitude. "My deep thanks as well, m'ladies, especially for your pledge of secrecy. I wish you health and safe journey. I bid you farewell."

Ellen raised a lone eyebrow. "I pledged *discretion*, Gallenius. But you may rest assured your secret is safe with us."

"Ah, semantics—well played, Lady Ellen. Your Great Aunt Maude could display such wit as well. I think we shall get along just fine."

Ellen simply smiled in acknowledgment and summoned a transit globe with no difficulty.

IT WAS BUT THE PASSAGE of a moment before they found themselves back in their home realm, on the sun-dappled grass amidst the standing stones.

The dogs bounded off the cabin porch and came trotting up to greet them.

"Wow, that was an experience!" exclaimed Stacy. "I wish we could have stayed longer!"

"I would've liked to stay a little longer, too. Maybe next time. Oh wait, that's right; you're leaving tomorrow. I hope you have a nice flight," Ellen teased.

"Ha!" Stacy squealed, and then squared her shoulders and jutted her jaw. In her deepest mock *terminator* voice, she uttered, "I'll be back!"

CH 8

WHEN SALIDAR TWISTED the topaz in its setting as he'd been instructed, he didn't have long to wait. In the span of a few heartbeats, he found himself standing weak-kneed in a solitary cone of light surrounded by darkness. Momentarily disoriented, he nonetheless knew immediately where he was, and who had brought him here.

Sighing, he also knew she would make him wait.

Such petty mind games . . . Would she ever tire of such trifling banality?

As he expected, it was several moments before Lady Diere elected to appear at the edge of the light. She stepped forward and stood aloof in a severe gown of pale purple, trimmed in burgundy lace. Its décolletage plunged nearly to her waist revealing a narrow slash of pale skin.

He acknowledged her with a deep bow, but held his tongue, waiting for her to speak.

"Rise, Salidar," she said imperiously. "Report what you have learned."

"May it please you, m'lady, I have learned that the body of Boltar, the innkeeper, is now in the possession of the Administration of Shadow, more specifically, in the custody of the ruling House of Lamia.

"Furthermore, Queen Mab of the Dark Elves has formally requested, through the Council, that the body of Boltar be turned over to her. She insists that this action is critical to the unmasking of a treasonous plot against her throne. The authorities in Shadow are conducting an inquiry into the circumstances of Boltar's death. I understand they are not yet satisfied."

Lady Diere pursed her lips. "I see. Will the House of Lamia comply with the Council's request?"

"They will, m'lady, for they know they have little choice, notwithstanding the incomplete status of their inquiry. However, I suspect there will be some delay."

"They would not dare to ignore the Council!" She fumed in sudden frustration and spun to one side. The cone of light widened perceptibly to compensate for her sudden movement.

"M'lady, if I may?" he ventured cautiously.

"Go on," she spat, unaccountably angry.

"I do not believe the delay to be intentional, or even avoidable. While at the castle of the Baron Von Kestel, I had the opportunity to speak with Jalashel, the Senior Mage of the Shadow Realm. It was he who advised me of the Council's formal request, and of his intention, as authorized by powers within the realm's administration, to make arrangements for the transfer of the body as soon as he returned to the House of Lamia. He further assured me that the Administration of the Shadow Realm has every intention of compliance.

"However, shortly after our discussion, he was injured—to a fairly severe degree—during a rather strenuous rite of execution. He was seriously debilitated; but, he is now recovering."

"Rite of execution?" Lady Diere echoed, her interest now clearly aroused. "Explain!"

"M'lady, the baron's men captured an ogress who had been wreaking havoc in certain rural areas, and is believed to have killed the baron's father. The magus and the baron believe that the ogress was ensorcelled in some way—in truth, I would not disagree. I saw her, an unwholesome thing. In fact, she indeed appeared *dead*—no, rather *long dead!* It was hardly a surprise that the ruling house determined that a mage should conduct the rite."

"You witnessed this rite?" Lady Diere asked, her voice now subdued and her focus intent.

"I did, m'lady," he whispered as an involuntary shudder wracked his frame, "although I rather wish I had not. It was quite difficult for Jalash-el; he succeeded, but at a cost."

She walked about in a small circle for a few moments, obviously deep in thought. Finally she faced him and pointed an elegantly manicured finger in his direction. "Salidar, tell me truly, do you think this ogress had been ensorcelled by *necromancy?*"

"M'lady, I am no mage. I know not for certain; but, I strongly suspect so—*most strongly.*"

He watched carefully to gauge her reaction.

Can she not know what Daegon and George have been up to, upon the battlements of her own castle?

"This is disturbing indeed." She pinched the bridge of her delicate nose. "It has been rumored that Queen Mab has a mage among her minions who is familiar with such *forbidden black arts*. Have you heard anything more in this regard?"

His heart skipped a beat and his mind raced! "Uh, no, m'lady, I have not."

He sensed no truth spell; nonetheless, he was withholding certain information. He well knew he was not supposed to have known George had been at her castle, much less to have seen him. But then again, she had asked not what he had *seen* or *observed*, nor what he might *suspect*. Here, he walked a fine line; he prayed she would not question him any closer.

"You are to keep your ears open. I would be told of any such news immediately." She leaned into his face. "Do I make myself clear?"

"Perfectly, m'lady," he answered, in wide-eyed innocence.

She strode in a small circle once more, pursing her lips in thought.

He tried not to fidget or show his innate fear of her; but, being this close to her, it was nearly impossible. He would be glad when this interview was at an end.

At length, she faced him once more. "You are certain the body of Boltar will be sent to Queen Mab, notwithstanding any unforeseen delay?"

"I was so assured, m'lady. I believe they will comply, despite any delay."

He was growing curious at her overt concern for the disposition of this body.

Did she want Mab to get Boltar's body? Just what was her game here?

Lady Diere appeared lost in thought again. She stood very still, staring at a spot in space just above his head.

Salidar found that more unnerving than when she paced.

Mumbling to herself, she breathed, "There is still time, yes, still time."

Looking him in the eyes, she held out her hand. "Give me the ring!"

He slid the topaz off his finger. As he dropped it into her waiting hand, he noted how its inner light seemed to have paled drastically since he had used it to transit to this place.

She cupped both hands around the ring and brought them to her lips. Turning her back to him, she chanted softly into her hands. Although Salidar could just barely hear her voice, he could not discern her words. After a moment, she turned and held out her hand to him. Upon her palm, the dark coffee-hued gem glowed brightly with a rich internal radiance once again.

"I have refreshed the stone with another spell. You are to travel to the Realm of Mer and find Padraic the Rogue. You will have several days before the festival begins. Try to seek him out before the crowds grow too thick, if at all possible. Give him the ring; it will confirm your *bona fides* and verify that I have sent you. You are to *invite* him to visit me, here, in this place. The ring will work as before and transport him to this specific location. Should he decline," a flare of pique bloomed within her eyes and quickly vanished, "you are to use the ring to return here and so advise me. Do you understand?"

"Yes, m'lady . . . But, if I may ask, what am *I* to do if he *does* use the ring?"

She thought for a moment. "He *must* use the ring; he cannot access this place without it. See that he does so, and you may stay in Mer and enjoy the festival. I will summon you when I need you."

"As you wish, m'lady." He bowed deeply from the waist.

This was unexpected, *a bonus!* To spend time in Mer, especially during the most celebrated festival held on the idyllic islands of that Aquarian realm, was hardly an imposition. He would certainly look forward to having some free time, perhaps even a week or more—provided, of course, that Padraic would accept Lady Diere's invitation. He held his low bow, and his breath, fervently hoping she would ask no more of him.

In seeming answer to his prayers, she mumbled a soft incantation, and waved a hand dismissively. "Now, be on your way. I have other business to attend to."

In the next instant, he was gone.

THE WERE LORD SAW HER, alone in the cold cone of light, and stepped in her direction. As he drew near, the rasp of his footsteps over the smooth stone and the swish of his robe betrayed his approach.

She turned and smiled. "Welcome, Lord Addecus, I appreciate your prompt response."

"Ah, Lady Diere, I have been expecting your sssummonsss," he responded as he broached the edge of the light.

The illumination widened just enough to include him. Typically attired in his usual shapeless robe, he blinked as his pupils narrowed to mere slits in reaction to the enhanced scope of light.

He bowed his head only a bit in deference to her—*not quite* a slight, but a duly noted sign of diminished respect. To his surprise, she either didn't notice, or chose to ignore it.

No reaction whatsssoever? What game isss thisss? Or rather, doesss sssomething elssse preoccupy her attention?

"Addecus, time grows short and there is much yet to accomplish," she began without preamble.

He remained silent as she began her habitual pacing.

"The Council will issue a summons within the next few days commanding George to appear before them at its next meeting for consideration as a candidate for the Chair of Man. *Gods be cursed!* I am not certain he is ready."

"Indeed, m'lady? What givesss you sssuch paussse? Hasss he not been tutored under your sssupervisssion thessse passst weeksss?"

"That is true. In addition, Queen Mab saw fit to send her alchemist, Daegon, to assist in the tutoring—ostensibly to speed the process. I have observed several of these sessions with Daegon; and, I am unsettled. This *alchemist* has a singularly intuitive grasp of the politics of the realms. I wonder where Mab found him? Bah! At this point it matters not."

"M'lady? I am confusssed. I know nothing of thisss alchemissst, Daegon. But, am I to undersssstand the queen troublesss you in thisss regard?"

The Dark Elf smacked a fist into the palm of her hand, and stared into the pervasive darkness. "The queen—ha! I *know* she grows impatient, too eager to grasp control of the Council. She intends to use George—and anyone else—as her pawn. She is pushing to accelerate his election to the Chair of Man. I suspect even at the very next meeting, if possible."

"Ah, I sssee. But, what of the pawn, George? Hasss he not asssimilated and retained sssufficient knowledge upon which he might be tesssted?"

She tugged on her sleeves in mild irritation and absently smoothed the ruffled lace. "It is not his retention of the appropriate knowledge that concerns me, Addecus. It is his *loyalty* that gives me pause. I am not at all certain that he is ready to be so loosely supervised. I do not fully trust him."

"Nor do I," agreed the Were Lord, "although I cannot sssay precisssely *why*."

"Nor I." She shrugged resignedly, flicking her wrist. "Alas, it is far too late in the game. I must now send him back into the Realm of Man, to receive the summons."

"Ah, yesss, the sssummonsss. Well, the Council can be rather sssticky about the resssidency requirementsss. May I asssume you will need sssomeone to ssstay clossse to him, much like before?"

Her smile turned feral. "Yes, I think so. I was thinking of Ling. He knows her—but not too well—and would likely be reasonably comfortable with her."

Addecus nodded; he had been thinking along similar lines—although somewhat deeper.

"I trussst there will be no *vampiric interference*, thisss time, m'lady?"

He knew his question bordered upon insolence. He was smugly satisfied to see the effort with which she stifled the irate reflex of an angry retort.

Nonetheless, the chill in her voice frosted her words. "Hear me, Addecus. The Realm of Shadow has no further role to play in the matter before us."

"Ah, I sssee. In that cassse, I am sssure it can be arranged with Ling, m'lady. Where and when?"

"At dawn tomorrow, I will send George through one of the New Orleans portals."

"I beg your pardon, m'lady," he interrupted, "I have only recently learned there isss only one portal now functioning in New Orleansss, the one in the old graveyard. The othersss no longer exissst; no one knowsss why. Perhapsss a resssidual effect of the hurricanesss, or sssome unfavorable celessstial alignment? Who can sssay?"

He was pleased to see that this clearly came as a shock to her.

Ssso, you are not asss well-informed asss you would have me think.

It was known that fixed portals, or entry points, between realms did occasionally stop working, fail to appear, or even wink out of existence. However, it was rare and *not* understood. Equally surprising, a new portal could suddenly appear, perhaps even remain stable for millennia and then, without warning, simply disappear.

When a new one was discovered, it was typically kept as a closely held secret, at least for a while. Soon enough, other beings would discover and try to use the portal. This would most often be a source of argument and strife among those would-be travelers until things could be worked out. And sometimes, like now, only a sole portal remained in place in a highly traveled area; this mandated mutual cooperation amongst the realms. The potential alternative was acceptable to no one.

"That is unfortunate. Very well, the cemetery portal must suffice," she decided.

"Ling will meet him there, m'lady," Addecus assured her guilelessly, but his thoughts were running on a more convoluted path. After all, the welfare of his own realm was foremost in his mind.

Diere raised a finger in caution. "There may be some problems with the authorities, in light of his involvement in past incidents. George has assured me that he has a place in mind that is unknown to the police of his home realm. He will await the Council's summons there. Do you have any questions?"

"Not at the moment, m'lady. Ssshall I make the arrangementsss?"

"Yes, by all means," she said firmly. "I shall inform George."

Addecus bowed, somewhat more deferentially than upon his arrival, and backed out of the light.

There was but a whisper of sound, like the subtle *pop* of a soap bubble, and he was gone.

GEORGE PAPADOLIS FELT the familiar tug of a summoning on his consciousness. Moments later, he stood unsteadily in a shroud of darkness; he hated the transition.

"Oh, George," Diere cooed. "Join me, won't you?"

He saw her in the cone of light and hastened to her. As he breached the edge of light, he missed her brief flare of ire when she saw that he wore the dark robe of a magician. He didn't suspect she would find such attire an unwitting gesture of arrogance, if not hubris. Oblivious and somewhat cavalier, he nonchalantly executed a modest bow.

"Greetings, Lady Diere. You called?"

Her voice was strangely flat and devoid of emotion.

"George, your tutoring has come to an end. Your instructors inform me that you have done well; even Daegon has reported favorably on your progress. He has returned to Queen Mab, and I am sure he will so advise her, as well. Tomorrow, you will return to the Realm of Man. You must be there when the Council issues its summons; which I expect in the next few days. You will stay there until you appear before the Council. Do you understand?"

"I can't go back right now. There are some *complications.* I want to—"

His throat slammed shut! He couldn't breathe, much less continue to speak! He was suddenly thrown up into the air by an unseen force, and held in some sort of spread-eagled stasis, unable to move. Below him, he could see only Lady Diere.

The delicate features of her elfin face drew down into a mask of venomous rage; her eyes smoldered with an unholy blaze. Power rolled off her like boiling ocean waves and crashed against him, the relentless pounding of merciless surf. He shuddered under the impact.

Worse, her harsh words stung like the splash of acid on his wincing form.

"FOOL! How *dare* you defy me! I care not one whit what you want! You will do exactly as you are told—no more and no less! Test me again, and you shall rue your very existence!"

He was on the verge of passing out. Small bursts of multicolored lights were appearing on the periphery of his failing vision. His lungs began to spasm; and he spiraled into blackness.

HE DID NOT KNOW HOW much time had passed. He lay in a crumpled heap, his face dampened in a shallow puddle of his own drool. He was alone in the uncaring pool of light, or at least he *thought* he was alone. He straightened his limbs and took stock. Nothing was broken, but every muscle in his body complained; he was *beyond* sore. He managed to sit up. Ashes slipped from his shoulders to fall in small puffs upon the stone floor; the magician's robe he'd worn was gone. His throat throbbed and his breathing was ragged.

He realized that he had seriously screwed up. He hadn't exactly *defied* Lady Diere—at least not to his way of thinking. But it didn't really matter; *she thought so*. Consequently, he suffered for it.

He stood slowly, rocking slightly as he found his balance. He'd gotten careless; he should have known better. He would neither forget this lesson, nor *forgive*.

"Now, where were we?" echoed from the darkness.

He cringed at the icy tone of her voice; but otherwise, he dared not move.

"Ah yes, you will return to your home realm tomorrow. You will be met—your *bodyguard* expects you. When a messenger from the Council delivers the summons, you will follow its directions precisely."

She finally emerged from the shadows into the light. "Now I will ask you once again—do you understand?"

He bowed as deeply as possible, holding the subservient position with difficulty, as he answered in gasps. "I . . . I understand . . . p-perfectly, m'lady."

She smiled as if nothing untoward had transpired between them.

"Much better, George. Now, heed my final word . . . Never presume to style yourself a mage without my leave—*ever!* This is the last time you will see me before the Council meeting. Malvana will see to your departure at dawn. Go now."

He backed away from her carefully, disappearing in the shadows. At a slight gesture from her, he was gone.

DEEP WITHIN ADDER CASTLE, Lord Addecus sat with Ling as they savored a pale wine before a small fire in an enormous hearth. They were alone in the Great Hall.

"M'lord, I understand my role in what is about to happen. But, might I ask?" she inquired thoughtfully.

"Of coursssse, pleassse do," responded the Were Lord affably.

"Why, m'lord, am I to take those two *idiots*, Iggy and Bubba, with me? They are more trouble than they are worth!" Ling exclaimed, and then hastily added, "Please, forgive my outspokenness, m'lord."

Not surprised by her candor, he was rather pleased with her confidence in speaking her mind. He prefaced his response with a patient smile.

"Well, Ling, for one thing, *becaussse* they are sssuch trouble. Their petty thievery and missschief have been the caussse of much conssternation and grief for my guardsssmen sssince you brought them here. No, no—tisss not your fault; nor do I imply sssuch.

"I thought they would prove more usssefull than they have. Ssso, I arranged for a more comprehensssive *mind-wipe ssspell* to be adminissstered; they are now conssiderably more compliant. They are not quite reduced to the level of *dronesss*, but they are clossse. They ssshould now follow insssstructionsss to the letter, no more and no lesss. My magesss asssure me that they *will* in fact do ssso.

"Perhapsss you ssshould conssider them asss George would, merely additional *mindlesss mussscle*. But remember, any commandsss given them mussst be carefully consssidered beforehand. Do you undersssstand?"

"Yes, m'lord," responded Ling dutifully, yet clearly unhappy about the prospect.

Addecus was not yet finished. He smiled, for he rather enjoyed surprising his favorite protégé.

"Alssso, I arranged for their appearancesss to be altered, ssso they will not be recognized in the Realm of Man. It isss merely an illusssion sssupported by a *ssstasssisss ssspell* that only affectsss their facial featuresss. It will not hold beyond the next full moon—or beyond their deathsss."

"*Beyond their deaths*, m'lord?" Ling repeated, a gleam growing in her eyes.

"Indeed, my dear Ling," he agreed, smiling. "When you have determined that they have completely ssserved their usssefulnesss in the Realm of Man, you may disssposse of them asss you sssee fit. However, do ssso only in the Realm of Man—in no other place. Do you undersssstand?"

Ling's countenance was positively awash in feral glee. She rose and bowed deeply to the Were Lord.

"Absolutely! It shall be my pleasure, m'lord. Thank you."

Addecus could almost swear that he could hear Ling softly purring.

CH 9

AS MARK DROVE TO THE airport, he noted that his three passengers were uncharacteristically quiet, lost in their own thoughts. Millie and Stacy were leaving today; and soon enough, he'd be returning to New York. Ellen would stay at Delafaire Farm; but once he left, she'd be alone. He found that a bit unsettling; but, he didn't understand just why.

He parked in the short-term lot.

As Millie alighted, she gazed one last time at the bucolic countryside beyond the airport and sighed.

"You know, I am going to miss this place."

"Aw, come on, Mom," Ellen remarked. "You can always come back to visit, or even to stay. You know the house is huge; there's plenty of room."

Millie just stared at her daughter, and smiled.

Mark removed the luggage and shut the car's trunk. "Listen, why don't you all go ahead and get in line at the ticket counter. I'll be along in a minute with the rest of the luggage."

"I'll give you a hand," offered Stacy, smiling at Mark. "There are only a couple more bags."

"You're sure?" Millie asked. "We can help, you know. There's plenty of time. I don't think there'll be much of a line. We only have to pick up the electronic tickets and check our bags."

"Yeah, you two go on," Stacy urged. "We'll be there shortly."

Ellen caught Stacy's wink, and nudged her mother along. "Okay—let's go, Mom."

STACY WATCHED AS MOTHER and daughter walked toward the terminal. Nodding in their direction, she whispered to Mark, "Give them a few minutes—they need to talk."

Mark just grinned at the obvious irony. "And we don't?"

"Oh, is there something on your mind?" she teased.

He set the bags down and took her hand. "Stacy, I would very much like to *see* you. Um, no, it's more than that, uh, I mean *be with* you. This isn't . . . Oh damn! I'm not good at expressing *feelings*. But, I mean at one point I thought I'd *lost* you—not that you were *mine*, in that sense—I mean, I had no right—"

She reached up and placed a finger across his lips. Balling his collar in her other hand, she tugged him closer. "Mark, just shut up and kiss me."

And so he did, and found that no words were needed. Nor could such an inadequate medium ever describe how they both felt at that moment. They were their own universe, blissful and safe.

WATCHING FROM THE TERMINAL, Ellen and her mother smiled.

"Well," Millie observed, "I can't say I didn't see that coming."

Ellen nodded. "Yeah, at times it was like watching a pair of high school kids. But I think they really do make each other happy, at least from what I've seen."

"Well, having someone who makes you happy," Millie said wistfully, "*is* important."

"But Mom, isn't it better if you make each other happy—as a couple, I mean? Shouldn't it be *mutual?*"

"Oh, of course, sweetie, but life isn't always perfect. Sometimes we can only hope, and make do as best we can."

Ellen winced. "Oh man, that's almost *depressing.*"

She nodded toward Mark and Stacy crossing the parking lot. "Oops, time to change the subject, Mom; here they come."

"Oh, I wasn't necessarily talking about *them*. You have to think about your own life, too."

"Me? We're not going there. Listen, Mom, I was serious about you coming back. You know you really could live here—after all, it *was* home, once."

Millie took Ellen's hands and smiled. "I know, sweetie, and I appreciate the invitation. I want to tell you that I have really enjoyed our time together. You've turned into a fine young woman, and I'm proud of you. No, I'm not trying to embarrass you—I mean it. And I *do* plan on visiting you; but I'm not sure I'm ready to move back here. After all, I have my own life in Los Angeles, a career, such as it is, and a boyfriend."

Ellen could not help but cringe at the mention of a boyfriend. Perhaps it was nothing more than a residual reaction to what had once been a source of divisiveness for them in the past, Millie's succession of boyfriends she thought she could fix. But now, to be honest, the impact was minimal and passed quickly. Ellen was no longer the judgmental teenager who perceived her mother as a source of embarrassment. They were both adults, entitled to their own lives and decisions. Ellen recognized the maturity of this assessment, and accepted it unconditionally.

"Mom, I understand." She gently squeezed Millie's hands. "I just want you to know that I love you, and you've always got a home with me. So, just give living here some thought, okay?"

"All right, Ellen, I will—I promise. Look, the *lovebirds* are almost here."

"Mother!" exclaimed Ellen in exasperation, but grinned when she saw the twinkle in Millie's eyes.

Mark dropped the bags at their feet and remarked, "Say, this line is moving pretty fast. Do you all have everything you'll need, picture IDs and such?"

Millie and Stacy rummaged in their purses as the line moved steadily forward.

"Yeah," commented Stacy, "we're all set."

Suddenly it was their turn at the ticket counter. Their bags checked and tickets in hand, they hugged and said their more decorous good-byes in the lobby.

Just before Stacy and Millie joined the shuffling security line, Millie turned to her daughter. "Ellen! Don't forget Madeline!"

"I won't. Have a good flight! Call us when you get in!"

Within the next few minutes, her mother and Stacy were through the security checkpoint and swallowed by the busy crowd streaming down the inner concourse.

WALKING BACK THROUGH the terminal, Mark asked, "What about Madeline?"

"Oh, she called this morning. She's collected some research material for us. So, if it's not too much trouble, can we stop by the bookstore on the way home?"

"Sure, that's not a problem."

On the drive, Ellen's cell phone rang; it was Hawk calling.

Mark tried to be discreet and not eavesdrop, but there is little privacy for a personal call in the confines of a car. From her subdued tone and monosyllabic responses, he could sense that all was not well.

When she ended the call, he asked, "Is everything all right?"

"Yeah, I guess."

"I'm sorry. I didn't mean to pry."

"I know . . . It's just that he's really sad, you know? They have to attend the funerals today. I've come to realize that a law enforcement funeral is a pretty big deal. It has really affected him."

Mark drove on in silence for a few minutes.

"You really like him, don't you, El'?" At first he thought she hadn't heard him, sitting there lost in thought, staring at her hands folded in her lap.

She looked up, staring through the windshield. "Yeah, I guess I do. I think . . . I think he might be special to me."

Glancing at her, their eyes briefly locked.

She asked, "Do you know what I mean?"

"Yeah, I think I do."

She smiled, a little self–consciously, and sighed.

Mark returned her smile. "He's a good guy. I trust him. So, I guess it's all right if he wants to date my cousin."

"Ha! Like *you* get any say!" She responded, clearly grateful that he'd lightened the mood.

THEY FOUND MADELINE tending the front desk at the bookstore, her nose buried deep in a paperback. Delighted to see them, she ushered them to the rear of the store where her husband, deeply engrossed in some sort of puzzle, was seated at a long library table.

"Armand!" she called to him. "Ellen and Mark are here! Say hello!"

He glanced up, looking over his glasses, and smiled. "Hello, you kids! Come, have a seat. Now I have an excuse to put this damn thing down." He tossed a folded newspaper to one side.

Ellen's curiosity overcame her, so she pointed. "What is that?"

Madeline gestured at the newspaper. "It's the local paper's *sudoku* puzzle. He *hates* them; but, he won't stop trying to solve them."

Scrunching his face, Mark asked, "Then why?"

"Because Zack can do them like *that!*" Armand responded with a sudden snap of his fingers. "There's a *trick* to these infernal things—there *has* to be!"

Madeline rolled her eyes and reminded her husband, no doubt for the thousandth time, that his dear friend Zack was, among other things, a brilliant mathematician.

It was obvious that Armand had heard all this before. He just smiled and blew her a kiss. Turning back to Ellen, he nodded to the discarded newspaper and mumbled. "Sudoku—my foot! They ought to call those things *stick it to you!*"

Madeline's patient smile betrayed her tolerant amusement as she turned to her guests. "Don't mind him. Now, would you like some sweet tea? I have some fresh."

"Thank you," Ellen answered, "that'd be nice."

"Armand, would you get that stack of books we put together on the other table? I'll fetch the tea."

The books were primarily an assortment of folklore, mythology, and history. There were half a dozen hard-backed texts, a few handwritten notebooks, and a set of bound pamphlets that were dog-eared and worn. The specific topics were diverse; scholarly dissertations on cultural myths, comparisons of similar legends within oral traditions, and several anthropological field studies.

Armand seemed slightly chagrined as he laid the collection before them. "As you may have surmised," he began tentatively, "I helped Madeline seek out some of this research material. I hope you find it useful."

Ellen stared into Armand's eyes. "She told you, didn't she?"

It was more of a statement than a question.

To Armand's credit, he did not flinch.

Ellen could sense that there was steel in the character of this wizened old man. In some unknown and unexplainable way, that realization comforted her. She was further impressed with Armand's response.

"No, Ellen, she did not; she didn't have to. We've been together for so long we can almost read one another's minds—*almost*. We each respect the other's word when given to protect a confidence. Maude often shared things in confidence with me and with Madeline, sometimes together, sometimes not. We have never betrayed a trust."

Mark placed his hand on Ellen's arm. She acknowledged that this was just as he'd predicted. They now shared an unspoken understanding, and a decision.

"Armand, we have every intention of fully including you in our research efforts," she assured him. "We are smart enough to know that we hardly know anything. We would welcome your expertise."

"Thank goodness," chimed Madeline, returning with a tray laden with tall glasses, a sweating crystal pitcher of iced tea, and a plate of lemon crisp cookies. "That will certainly make my life around here more bearable." She winked at her husband. "Don't worry dear, we'll talk later."

"Of course. Ellen, you should also know," cautioned Armand, "that Maude sometimes confided in Zack and Marie, as well. I think we told you that she used to refer to us, collectively, as her *think tank*."

"What my husband is trying to say," Madeline offered, deftly pouring the sweet tea, "is that we are here for you, as we were for Maude. We will help you in any way you ask; but, you *do* have to ask. We never pry; we are always discreet. Think of us as a research resource with access to a considerable knowledge base. Do you understand?"

"Yes, I believe I do," Ellen responded thoughtfully, and glanced at Mark.

He nodded affirmatively, as he accepted the tall glass from his hostess. "Thank you. I must admit it makes perfect sense to me. The term *think tank* describes it quite well. But I do want to ask, what will we find in this material, these various selections, that you've collected here?"

"Quite a bit, actually," Armand answered and paused for a sip from his own glass. "You are delving into an area rich in folklore and legend; it's quite fascinating, actually. You really should make yourselves familiar with many of the more common traits and threads woven throughout the traditional lore. The more commonality you find, the more likely a factual basis may exist, however distilled. There are even local tales and legends held by indigenous peoples that you may find interesting, especially since some are believed to have taken place within Maude's—forgive me, I mean to say *your* forest."

"Our forest?" exclaimed Ellen, a rather specific suspicion growing. "Like what, for instance?"

"Oh no, my dear," Armand cautioned with a chuckle, "I wouldn't want to spoil your reading. Don't worry, you will enjoy it. We will have ample time to discuss the details, once you've finished the assignment, of course."

Madeline gently tapped her husband's shoulder and playfully scolded him. "Now, Armand, you are *not* teaching a course, so drop the *sagacious professor* routine. We are here to help, understand?"

Her husband merely smiled sheepishly and shrugged his shoulders.

To Ellen and Mark, she added, "Don't fret, I've stuck lots of little sticky notes in places of pertinent interest. The reading is not as cumbersome as it appears. And there is quite a bit that, well, let's just say, it would be very much to your advantage to know."

Ellen smiled. "Have no worries, Madeline—I love to read. Although I do have some material I'm presently engrossed in, I'll be happy to sink my teeth into this as well."

"I have to return to New York early next week. I should be back in a few weeks or so." Mark pointed to the assembled books and pamphlets. "Would it be possible to take some of this stuff with me? I could read it on the plane and at home."

Armand and Madeline looked at one another. Something—a flash of concern, perhaps—flickered across their faces for an instant.

Armand held out his open palms. "Mark, I'm sorry, but that would *not* be a good idea. Some of this material is *special* and *irreplaceable*. Think of it as precious. Some of these books, all of the pamphlets and notebooks, are the originals. And in most cases, there are no copies. We do not lend these lightly. It is imperative that they stay in this bookstore, or within the walls of your house at Delafaire Farm. Trust me, it *is* that important."

In the somber silence, Ellen experienced a small epiphany. *Of course!* She could almost hear Maude's chuckle deep within her mind.

Reaching out with her awareness, she let her eyes relax and slip out of focus. Just as she suspected, faint tracings of ruddy light pulsed around the structural lines of the building. Tiny delicate runes rode the subtle flow, barely discernible in the soft glow.

Ellen reached out to Armand and Madeline and clasped their hands. Both of them seemed mildly surprised by the simple gesture, but it was Ellen's question that stunned them.

"Armand, Madeline, is *Tomes and Scrolls* protected? *Warded?*"

They looked to one another for a long moment, and finally turned back to Ellen. Neither one spoke, but they began to nod their heads affirmatively, in unison.

Ellen smiled, released their hands, and reassured the couple. "It's fine. I suspected as much. Maude told you, didn't she?"

Madeline found her voice. "More than that, Ellen—she *did* it. She performed some little ceremony with soft chanting, kind of like that new age stuff, or so I thought at the time. We didn't mind; it seemed to make her happy. But the truth is that we've never had a problem here, not a shoplifter, or even a broken window. Everything has always been just fine in and around this building, just as she said it would be."

"And you also know that our house—Maude's house—is warded as well," deduced Ellen.

Mark followed her logic, adding, "And that's why you feel these books would be safe there, at least as safe as they are here."

"Yes, precisely," acknowledged Armand.

"I understand," Mark conceded. "Rest assured that they will go nowhere else."

"Thank you, thank you both for your understanding." Armand sighed, obviously relieved.

"Ah, it is we who should thank you," said Ellen, "for we have a lot of work to do. As ignorant as we are about so much of this stuff, I suspect we'll be keeping you really quite busy."

"Excellent!" Armand exclaimed, grinning. "Then I'll be more constructively occupied and have no time for those mind-numbing numeric conundrums foisted upon the unsuspecting public!"

"Huh?" Mark's befuddlement was obvious.

Ellen smirked and nudged her cousin. "He means the sudoku puzzles."

ON THE RIDE HOME, MARK asked, "So, El', do you intend to start reading the research material right away?"

She thought for several moments before responding.

"Not immediately, I've got some writing to do in the journal. How about you? Are you going to start reading?"

"Well, it depends. I still have a few things I want to do on the Chevy before I have to leave next week, Monday afternoon actually. I might get started on some of the reading material this evening."

"That reminds me, Mark. Thanks again for getting the truck running. I'd be at a real disadvantage here without transportation."

"No problem, I've always enjoyed working on vehicles."

She smiled. "I bet you got that from your dad."

"Yeah, probably . . . You know, El', it will take me a while to make arrangements with my firm, and to convert a few of the coins we found into liquid assets. I'll call you, of course, and keep you informed. But, it'll be at least ten days, maybe two weeks, before I can arrange to come back. I'm concerned that you're going to be alone for a while. Will you be all right?"

"I'll be fine. The dogs and Smokey will keep me company. And, I've got lots of reading to do, remember?"

"Yeah, but I'd feel better if Hawk was here. Did he say when he'd be back?"

"No, but he said he'd call. I'm pretty sure he'll be back by next week."

"Well, I hope so. I know I'd feel better knowing he's around."

"Me, too."

She smiled at her own admission. She *would* feel better, *much better*, indeed.

MILES TO THE SOUTH, Gulf breezes began piling a blanket of heavy clouds that swaddled the city of New Orleans in stifling humidity. It was practically a daily event in late spring; an afternoon thunderstorm would almost be a welcome relief.

Vito scanned the sky from the driver's window of the long limousine and tried to estimate how soon the rain would fall. His only real concern in this air-conditioned behemoth was how badly a hard rain would snarl traffic in the Crescent City. For the moment, the black limo glided unhindered along Canal Street like a silent barracuda slipping through shadowed shoals.

He had been roused from sleep this morning by an urgent call from his exotic, yet enigmatic, passenger, Ling. The boss, Papa George, needed him and the car. Ling would be at the hidden garage.

She had not been alone. She'd been barely noticeable in a shapeless grey raincoat that dreary morning, accompanied by two bald men attired in black suits. Even now, seated in the limo's jump seats, they were as still as twin statues, their eyes hidden behind dark sunglasses. They remained stoic and silent, unless she told them what to do. There was something unnerving about them.

Vito shrugged; they were not his concern.

Vito was a wheelman, one of the best. His skills were good enough that he could have raced professionally; but having a criminal record, a bad one, was sufficient to render that notion a pipe dream. Papa George had recruited him years ago, and helped with the lawyers' fees on a murder rap that Vito had barely beaten—only after certain witnesses went missing.

Vito was loyal; he knew his place, and didn't ask questions. Papa George liked it that way; and Vito knew it.

A few lone drops of rain plinked upon the windshield, questing scouts of an imminent barrage. Vito knew it would not be long in coming.

Ling spoke up from the back of the limo. "Vito, make the next right. Then do a U-turn in the block and park by the cemetery entrance."

He nodded and executed the maneuvers with calm precision. The long limo hissed to a stop right where Ling had indicated. The rear doors opened and the two men exited, each with a furled umbrella at his side. Ling stepped out and mumbled something to them that Vito could not hear.

Leaning down so that she could see him through the open door, she said, "Vito, keep the motor running. I'll be right back."

He nodded, and she closed the door. He watched as she and one of the men disappeared into the cemetery.

The other man stood vigilant at the curbside of the vehicle, watching the empty street. No other traffic or pedestrians entered the block.

Vito became aware of a gentle mist, punctuated by a few big ploppy drops, wetting the windshield and slightly distorting the view. He had barely flicked the windshield wipers to an intermittent setting when he sensed movement to his right.

Ling and her escort were returning; they were not alone. Another form huddled with her under the black umbrella held forth by her stoic minion. They walked briskly toward the limousine.

The rear door opened, and Ling stooped and entered, followed by George Papadolis and the two silent men in black, their damp umbrellas furled once again.

As he made himself comfortable, George acknowledged his driver. "Hey Vito! Long time—it's good to see you."

"Boss, it's good to see you, too. Where to?"

"Uh, hold on a minute."

Vito watched in the mirror as George jabbed a thumb at the two bald men seated in the limo's jump seats. "Okay, Ling, who are these guys?"

"Just more muscle, sir, who will follow orders precisely," Ling responded succinctly.

"Well, I guess we can't be too careful," George grunted.

Ling bowed slightly, as if she had received a complement. Vito saw her smug smile.

"Vito," George rumbled, "We'll need somewhere quiet and safe. Remember Brewster's fish camp?"

"Uh, yeah, I think so, up on Toledo Bend?" Vito glanced again in the mirror at George, as the misting rain increased to a steady drizzle.

"Right, let's go."

"*Fish camp?*" echoed Ling, unable to keep the incredulity from her voice. "Please excuse me, but we are to go *camping?* I don't—what are you talking about, sir?"

"Relax, Ling," George assured her. "It's just a term that refers to a rather nice waterfront home on a very large reservoir. It's isolated and very secure; and best of all, no one knows about it. It used to be in the hands of a *former associate,* but he no longer has a use for it. It'll serve us quite well. You'll see."

"Very well, sir." A hint of reservation tinged her voice.

As the sleek vehicle pulled away from the curb, George commented, "We should make a stop and get some provisions before we leave the city. The limo would attract too much attention if we had to stop at some *mom 'n' pop* store in the sticks. Vito, find a big grocery store, and we'll let Ling's men do a little shopping. Do we have cash?"

Vito grunted. "As always, Boss, in the console."

"Sir," Ling offered, "it might be best if I and one of the men went into the store. The two of them might draw attention, and be remembered."

George smiled and leaned toward her. "My dear Ling, has it ever occurred to you that *you* draw attention and might be remembered?"

Ling smiled. "In the rain, I will be nearly invisible in my hooded raincoat."

She flipped up her hood drawing it tight, slipped a pair of large sunglasses on, and allowed her shoulders to slump forward. Her entire form seemed diminished. Her exotic aspect had completely disappeared. She now resembled any frazzled housewife trying to avoid the rain.

George laughed. "Ha! Damn, woman! You are good! By all means, go shopping."

A FEW HOURS LATER, Vito carefully maneuvered the long limousine up the serpentine gravel drive that took them to the camp.

Camp was indeed a misnomer; a stone and cypress mansion sat atop a bluff overlooking the Toledo Bend Reservoir. Little of the view could be seen through the incessant rain; but, the steady torrent also assured an unseen arrival.

They dashed from the vehicle to the covered porch, where they shook the rain from their umbrellas and coattails.

George paused at a small digital push-button panel in the wall, a security and entry system. He punched in a code and a small red light blinked several times and turned green. He entered another code and the door unlocked with a *click*.

Vito saw the small light began to blink red again. George didn't notice it as he pushed the door open; but Ling had. She stopped him before he could enter, and pointed to the flashing red light. "Sir, what does *that* mean?"

George stared at the blinking light, as if trying to recall its meaning.

Vito knew. "Boss, someone's here!"

Ling pulled George away from the door, and pointed to the men in black. "Someone is here. Find them. Hold them. Go."

The two men slipped silently into the darkened house.

Ling stepped across the threshold, and turned to George and Vito. "Wait here, just inside the door; do not let it close completely. I will return, sir."

Without waiting for any reply, she vanished into the dim interior.

George and Vito stood just inside the vestibule and held the door slightly open as she had instructed. Straining to catch the slightest sound, they heard nothing.

In just over a minute, Ling appeared out of the silent darkness and grinned evilly. She had shed her shapeless raincoat and was nearly invisible in a black turtleneck and black slacks. "We have him, a lone man, in a lower-level room. Come this way."

She spun on her heel and disappeared into the gloom; and George immediately followed.

Vito, however, began turning lights on as he followed, making his way through the house. He suppressed a barely perceptible shudder. He was not fond of the dark, especially when *she* was slinking around in it.

THE INTRUDER'S FACE ground against the rough concrete floor as the hand on the back of his skull pressed down mercilessly. Pinned by two silent bald men, he whimpered and tried to thrash about to no avail. He squinted as the room was suddenly awash in fluorescent light. He sensed someone leaning over him. His face was wrenched toward the harsh light. His ear felt the passage of a husky breath.

"Who are you?"

He froze at the guttural yet feminine voice. Its predatory, almost eager, quality raised the hairs on the back of his neck. His eyes went wide with fear; he couldn't speak. He could not see past the silhouettes of this deadly woman and the two hulking men holding him down with such little effort.

His mind raced; a sudden realization flared like a solitary match in an abyss.

They don't know who I am! Maybe they're not cops? I don't think they're from the cartel—at least I hope not!

That fledgling spark of hope died when the deep, yet vaguely familiar, voice of an unseen speaker echoed in the vast room. "Boss, I think that's *Teddy Pots!*"

"Brewster's *meth cook*?"

"Yeah! He looks like *shit;* but that's him."

The woman spoke, her disappointment evident. "You know this . . . *person?*"

"Yeah, Ling," admitted George, "we know who he is. Let him up, and let's play *twenty questions.* If I don't like the answers, you can dispose of him."

Teddy was raised to his feet and released; although the two goons stayed within easy reach. He instantly recognized Papa George and his driver, Vito. He didn't know the creepy woman all in black; but, she somehow instinctively scared the hell out of him.

George nodded to Vito, who stepped in front of Teddy, literally towering over him.

Visibly shaking, Teddy took hitching breaths and blinked up at the big man.

Despite the frightening depth of his voice, Vito spoke evenly and with great patience. "Teddy, tell us why you're here; and don't leave nothin' out."

Faced with a dubious reprieve, Teddy gulped and hesitantly began his tale. He made a reasonable effort to comply with the warning, except for certain tidbits he thought best kept to himself. His disjointed and rambling style of response unfortunately led to several inadvertent tangents, but Vito kept him more or less on track. Eventually, his account wound to a close.

Vito nodded and stepped to George's side. He spoke softly, but Teddy could hear.

"That jibes, Boss. It's been all over the news. Some cops were killed and more were hurt. Of course, he could've heard about it on the news, too."

"Yeah, maybe, but I knew about Brewster and the funeral home; and the meth angle fits," George reasoned. "Besides, Teddy's not smart enough—know what I mean?"

The hulking driver smiled and nodded.

George cleared his throat and addressed the frightened meth cook.

"So, Teddy, let me see if I've got this straight. You got away just before the raid, and the explosion. Then you made your way here, because this is where Brewster told you to hide out if things went south. That's why you had the security codes. Does that about sum it up?"

"Uh, y-yes, sir," Teddy managed.

"And you weren't followed? No one knows you're here?"

"N-no, sir, not followed; an' I don't t-think anyone even knows about this p-place."

"You *idiot!*" fumed George. "*We* know about it! And you know why? Because it's now *my* place! Even if Brewster swore to you that he told no one else—somebody else obviously knows!"

Teddy shrank within himself; this situation was going from bad to worse. The last person he wanted to have anything to do with, *Papa George,* was in this very room, and was now *royally pissed off.*

Vito spoke up. "What do you wanna do, Boss?"

"Shut up—let me think!" George began to pace.

Teddy's knees began to knock as the woman loomed over him from behind and deliberately let her husky breath float across the back of his neck. Just knowing she was that close unaccountably terrorized him. His eyes squeezed shut; and a thin stream of urine trickled down his leg, darkly staining his already filthy jeans.

Vito grimaced and stepped back as the acrid stench assailed his nostrils.

The woman also leaned back, wrinkling her nose; but the smugly satisfied smile never left her face.

George stopped pacing.

Teddy held his breath.

"For the time being," George began, "Teddy can stay. But I want to know exactly *who* is liable to come looking for him. Now, just *who* might that be, Teddy?"

"Uh, c-cops, maybe? I think I g-got an old warrant out on me for some t-technical jam-up on an old p-parole deal."

George started to step into Teddy's face, but one whiff of the frightened man's pungent aroma stopped him abruptly. Standing an arm's length away he asked a more probing question.

"Is anybody *else* looking for you, Teddy? Like whoever was in on that meth deal? You know, like Brewster's partners? Somebody had to front Brewster the cash to set up a lab like that, *because I didn't!* See, he already owed me; he couldn't come to me for more money. So, he went to somebody else—somebody who had to know about you, the cook. So, who's going to be looking for you to make good on the deal? Oh yeah, they'll be looking for you to make good, because Brewster's dead! But then, you knew that, didn't you?"

Teddy had one hope, one card left to play; but, it was a good one, and almost entirely true.

"Uh, I d-don't know exactly who they were. I know they spoke Spanish—the t-two guys I taught to cook, I mean. B-but they died in the lab explosion. The others, I saw them first—the raiders, I mean, before they saw me. No one saw me slip away." *That I know of, that is.*

George narrowed his eyes and stroked his chin. "These *guys* you taught, you're sure they're dead?"

Teddy's head bobbed enthusiastically. "They g-gotta be! No one coulda lived through that—it was *huge!* Everyone'll think *I* went up in the explosion, *too, if* they even knew I was there. Nobody will be looking for me."

George considered that for a moment, and then glanced at Vito.

The big driver simply tilted his head and shrugged his shoulders.

The woman watched the exchange with apparent growing disappointment.

"All right, Teddy, you can stay, but go upstairs and get cleaned up." George's expression soured. "And find some fresh clothes—you stink!"

Teddy scrambled; he couldn't get away fast enough, especially from *her!* Papa George was bad enough, but *that woman*—she was very, very bad news.

GEORGE NODDED WITH approval once the food was stored in the refrigerator and pantry. "That should hold us for a few days. Damn, it's chilly in here. Vito, put some coffee on and break out the bourbon."

"Irish coffee? You got it, Boss."

Ling stepped up to George and inquired. "Sir, I must ask, this *Teddy,* why do you let him live? He is clearly a danger to you."

George considered his bodyguard.

"Ling, understand that I am not in the habit of explaining my decisions; but I will indulge you this once. He is more of an asset than a liability, even though he *is* a wanted man. You see, Teddy Pots is a very talented man. Admittedly, his single talent is the very efficient large-scale preparation of methamphetamine. And that makes him a valuable asset—*a good earner*. I can see how he would potentially fit nicely in my plans."

Vito cleared his throat to get George's attention; George raised his eyebrows and nodded.

"One thing, Boss, that parole violation beef, an *old one,* he said. That means a warrant, right? So, *state* or *fed?* Know what I mean?"

"I am afraid I do not understand," interjected Ling. "What difference would it make?"

George pursed his lips, wagged a finger at Vito. "Good point—that could be a problem. Tell her."

Vito turned to Ling. "Look, if it's just a *state* warrant, especially if it's an old one, then it's likely that just his state parole officer is lookin' for him—if at all. And that's only if the parole officer's caseload isn't too big. But if it's a *federal* warrant, his federal parole officer *and* the marshals will be lookin' for him. They'll *never* quit hunting him."

"Right now," George cautioned, "I'd be more concerned with the *other parties* involved in this meth deal—the ones who lost their *investment*."

Vito nodded once.

However, George could see that Ling didn't get it—and she should have. A competent bodyguard should understand the implications. He'd have to think about that.

Clearly Vito got it; he shrugged as he made a laconic observation for her benefit.

"Yeah, you know those *other parties*—they don't always play by the rules."

CH 10

SALIDAR HAD ALWAYS liked the Realm of Mer, a world dominated by water and aquatic life. There was land, of course, but no massive continents, just a host of islands of many sizes. Some were quite large, covering hundreds of square miles; but, most were smaller. It was not unusual to find both active and slumbering volcanoes among them. All offered a wide diversity of terrain, flora, and fauna. And all, but for a very few of the most inhospitable islands, supported some sentient population.

However, on this occasion, only one island held Salidar's interest, Essa, one of the largest in the tropical regions, also known in this realm as *The Mother's Island.*

He leisurely made his way along its southern shore toward the port city of Derinseum. It was there that the largest, most elaborate Festival of Fertility would be held in five days time. The annual festival was observed throughout the realm, of course; but here, on the Mother's Island, he knew it just had to be experienced to be fully appreciated.

It's like Mardi Gras in New Orleans and Carnival in Rio de Janeiro, but better!

Celebrated continuously for a week, the festival was a boisterous exaltation of thanksgiving for the generous bounty provided by nature from both sea and land. For that week, only the simplest of social rules were observed; essentially one could do whatever one would, or could afford. However, unwelcome coercion was forbidden; neither harm nor force was permitted.

Of course, it went without saying that such a libertine approach and epicurean philosophy had no little effect on the robust birthrate enjoyed by all the realm's inhabitants. Yet the diverse population never grew beyond the ecology's capacity to support such life and still readily renew its resources. It seemed to be a world in perfect harmonious balance.

The closer Salidar drew to the city, the more people he noticed traveling in the same direction. It came as no surprise; he knew others had been making their way here for some time.

Indigenous habitants arrived daily, many having covered great distances over unpredictable seas, in all manner of seagoing vessels. They came from other islands, keys, atolls, and archipelagos, both nearby and from the far reaches of the realm. They often sailed together in traditional tribal fleets, a colorful pageantry of diverse sailing vessels.

This was a world of oars and sails. Most land-dwelling residents were competent sailors by the time they reached adolescence.

The vast majority of the population lived in the equatorial and tropical regions, although some hardy souls preferred the colder regions to the far north and south. Nonetheless, every tribe, clan, and family observed some form of the annual celebration. Many looked forward to participating in the most eagerly anticipated festival held on Essa.

It had become an unofficial rite of transition to adulthood for the young of the realm who had attained their sixteenth summer; they enthusiastically sought passage on the swiftest of their families' ships. Others, like the Mer, for whom the realm was named, and the aquatic Were, simply swam in large family pods, and endeavored to keep their young and rambunctious offspring under close, yet benevolent, supervision.

Salidar felt confident that he would perform his task here without undue hazard, and then be free to enjoy himself. He anticipated no threat. The Mer administered the realm. These amphibious humanoids oversaw the oceanic world with pragmatic efficiency and little to no interference in the affairs of its citizens. The individual islands were generally self-supporting and independent, each enjoying some version of home rule. There was no inter-island strife to speak of; simple trade and inter-island commerce were relatively brisk.

The aquatic Were, lycanthropic humanoids capable of metamorphosis into seagoing mammals such as porpoises, dolphins, and smaller whales, sometimes offered their services as guides and escorts to merchant vessels. Considered good luck, such offers were keenly sought; and, such services were well compensated. However, the Were of this realm were not great in number; only four clans were represented.

Salidar was privy to another little known fact; both the aquatic Were and the Mer had a sort of rapport, much like a mental link, with some other denizens of the sea within their immediate vicinity. In some cases they could even call upon these creatures to assist a crewman fallen overboard or aid a floundering vessel. Unfortunately, this rapport did not extend to all sea creatures; the more aggressive predators, like sharks, were not overly susceptible or even amenable to such rapport. In fact, intentional mental probing tended to exacerbate their ill-tempered nature. They were best left alone.

Salidar knew that despite the carefully managed image of carefree holiday ambiance supported by the Mer Administration, the realm was not without its problems. Aside from the unpredictability of the ocean world's weather, the predominant difficulties facing the inhabitants of the realm were twofold, and very likely often related: rampant smuggling to avoid inter-island commerce taxes, and worse, the occasional instance of piracy, a blight not even the resourceful Mer could eradicate.

The independent islands were well aware that not only was their shipping at risk from pirates, but many a village had been raided by marauding bands of buccaneers. Some of the unfortunate victims were often severely injured and left for dead; but, many simply disappeared, or were enslaved.

Consequently, most of the islands had some sort of loosely organized naval militia. Residents would periodically drill and occasionally press a vessel into service to patrol the shores of their home island. Nearby islands formed mutual assistance pacts, to support one another in times of pirate raids. Salidar knew that while such raids were infrequent, they were often swift and brutal, and usually over by the time any help arrived.

Needless to say, the Mer Administration was always reluctant to publicize any such events.

Salidar had learned that lately the pirate threat seemed to have diminished. Few recent raids had been reported; the militia drills had grown lax. Most islanders were now focused on the approaching Fertility Festival, and were content to leave current security concerns in the hands of the Derinseum Watch, a nominal police force employed by the Merchants Association, the defacto governing body of Essa.

At one time, long in the past, Derinseum had been a walled city, its deep harbor defended by a garrison of professional marines. But now, many of the old walls had tumbled, fallen blocks scavenged for use in newer construction of shops and dwellings. The marine garrison had long since been disbanded, its barracks deteriorated to the point of potential collapse.

These days, Salidar noted, all the old gates stood open and rusted in place. Only a few of the city's watchmen were in evidence along the quays and docks.

The deep harbor was already crowded with sailing ships resting at anchor. Small launches and dories were rowed about, shuttling passengers and goods.

Salidar marveled at the host of sailing vessels: tall-masted windjammers towering over wallowing galleons and merchant frigates; sleek schooners and cutters; nimble sloops and ketches; flat barges and scows; stout brigantines and delicate junks. The cries of seagulls floated through a cacophony of creaking rigging, punctuated by the flap of an errant sail, blending in a rhythmic counterpoint with the happy shouts of working crews, all contributing to an almost tangible sense of expectation.

As the freshening ocean breeze died, Salidar became aware of a subtle stench of rotting seaweed trapped in shallow pools of stagnant water. *Ah, as expected at low tide, much like most harbors*. Wrinkling his nose, he turned inland and started walking uphill into the heart of the city, his boot heels softly crunching upon the crushed oyster shell and gravel roadway.

The wider streets were lined with colorful stalls and booths, much like a huge market or municipal fair. Merchants of all types proudly displayed their wares: bolts of dyed cloth and elegant embroidery; shell necklaces and trinkets; exotic fragrances and oils; and good-luck charms of all sorts. Doors to taverns stood open as patrons wandered in and out, pewter mugs awash. Wine, mead, and ale flowed quite freely. Vocal vendors pushed rickety carts laden with coconuts and tropical fruits. The sweetly tantalizing aroma of toasted honey-cakes wafted through the milling throng.

Salidar found the wide diversity and colorful dress of the crowd mildly disorienting. There was already a burgeoning festive atmosphere, despite the fact that the celebration was still officially days away.

He noticed that quite a few visitors from other realms were already present in the city. He passed a group of Light Elves haughtily examining a silversmith's wares. Within the same block, he saw groups of dwarves attired in full guild regalia from the Dwarven Realm boisterously toasting one another with sloshing mugs on the broad steps of an alehouse.

Smiling in amusement, Salidar moved on, stepping to one side as a centaur trotted down the street.

He was reminded that the Realm of Mer boasted dozens of well-known fixed transit points, *portals,* to and from other Council Realms, and easily used by almost anyone with a smattering of talent. Most of these portals were land-based; but not all, more than a few were to be found at sea. The realm's administration typically monitored the use of these known portals. However, during the Fertility Festival such scrutiny was more or less abandoned; always challenging, it would have been an impossible task under the circumstances.

Even more daunting was the little known fact that there were also dozens of *unfixed* portals that could drift about, especially at sea, altering their locations for reasons not understood. These could be quite dangerous. Some were not stable in the least, and periodically winked in and out of existence. Some were quite large. It was speculated that whole ships had been swallowed, sometimes to reappear in other realms—or more ominously, never to be seen again. It was even rumored that the first pirates appeared in the Realm of Mer centuries ago, most likely through such a rogue portal.

Pausing in the shade of a flowering mimosa tree, abuzz with flitting hummingbirds, Salidar sat with his back against the trunk and considered the situation. He now had to admit that finding Padraic the Rogue in this already crowded city would not be easy; and worse, the number of festival participants would only increase.

Trying to search during the celebration would be nearly impossible; benign chaos would reign. He *had* to find Padraic before the festivities started; but, he was momentarily at a loss as to *how.*

He knew he needed a reference point from which to begin. There were a few taverns worth checking; and he did need lodging. He pondered the wisdom of contacting the *Thieves Guild* for assistance—no, not wise. He was reluctant to involve Storm Haven in what was, after all, one of Lady Diere's schemes.

So, he sat in the pleasant afternoon, trying to formulate a strategy, while watching all sorts of beings wander by, completely unaware that he was being watched as well.

A FEW BLOCKS AWAY, a centaur stood in a livery stable and held a quiet conversation with a tall thin man dressed in a loose fitting robe of light cotton dyed a pale green. To his side stood a young woman half his height, delicate yet stunning in the manner of a certain ethereal beauty, wearing a gossamer flaring shift that heightened the sense of promise of her barely hidden charms. Her allure, pointed ears, and webbed fingers readily identified her as an *Undine, a water nymph.*

The tall man had to look up slightly as he addressed the centaur. "You are certain it is he, Tullos? There is no mistake?"

"Rest assured, old friend," the bass voice uttered. "I was as close to him as we are now. I am certain it is he—although he has arrived sooner than we were told to expect. Selene, you agree?"

In a light voice reminiscent of the faint liquid music of a babbling brook, the undine answered, "Aye, there is no doubt. He is here, and alone."

The tall man nodded and made a flat sweeping gesture with his open hands crossing before him, palms down. This definitive act, commonly used among his people to indicate a firm resolve, disclosed that his fingers were webbed as well. "So be it. We will not tolerate any trouble, or any disruption of the festival. We have been quite clear on that point."

Selene smiled at the Mer Lord and soothed his concerns. "M'lord Antonius, we anticipate neither trouble nor disruption of any kind on the part of Salidar. We intend only to observe his activities—without his knowledge, of course."

Tullos chuckled and grasped his old friend by the shoulder. "Antonius, you worry too much. The sole purpose in apprising you of this situation was to preclude you from such fruitless concerns and to set your mind at ease. We have heard of no specific threats to the festival, or we would have so informed you. Even the Guildmaster, who sends his regards, hopes that you will *lighten up*. So, do not worry."

Antonius smiled and shrugged in return. "Forgive me, my friends. It is my curse as a senior member of the Administration to always anticipate the worst, especially when things have been going so well. Please thank the Guildmaster for me. As always, we are indebted to you for your services."

The centaur waved a hand dismissively. "Ah, think nothing of it. Tis but what we do, and are thusly well compensated. Nonetheless, I will happily convey your gratitude. Be at ease; all is well. If need be, we will contact you."

"Of course, now I must return before I am missed," responded Antonius. "I wish you good fortune, my friends, fair winds and following seas."

"Fair winds and following seas, m'lord," Tullos echoed.

Antonius departed the stable, leaving the centaur and nymph alone.

Tullos snorted and asked, "The sprites are still watching Salidar?"

"Yes, but they are easily bored," cautioned Selene. "I'll relieve them at dusk and have the spriggans keep watch."

"The *spriggans?* Let us hope they resist the temptation to tease and torment him in his sleep—you know their nature."

"Aye, that I do!" She laughed. "Be assured, they've been warned. You know that *Twit* keeps tight reins on his lads. They very much want to stay for the festival. So, I've told them that we expect their best behavior on this mission. Nothing less will do."

"Very well, let us see how this plays out. We will meet here, later tonight, an hour after moonrise. Be on your guard, Selene. We know of nothing conclusive, but something is afoot here—I can sense it, notwithstanding our assurances to Antonius. Remember, be careful."

She smiled at her friend and tossed, "As always!" over her slight shoulder as she disappeared from the shadowed stable.

Tullos shook his head as if to dispel a sense of unease. He had not exaggerated his concern that he felt that something unwelcome was just over the horizon. He wondered if it had anything to do with Salidar's unexpected early arrival. He had little to do but watch and wait—and of course, think. Given time, he could reason almost anything out. He had the patience, but would he have the time?

DEEP WITHIN THE HEART of the Realm of the Dark Elves, Magus Atrellan, the Senior Elfin Mage in the service of Queen Mab, paced apprehensively in the outer reception area of the queen's private study. He knew not the reason for her terse summons; but, he sensed that she was angry, or at least displeased. That alone was sufficient to churn a Gordian knot of anxiety in his gut.

He had fallen into her disfavor upon his return from the Realm of Shadow with the mysterious scroll purported to hold the secrets of a treasonous conspiracy. However, he had *not* returned with the suspected traitor, Boltar. The queen was not pleased, for she had demanded both. He had produced only one.

That was the crux of the matter. Without the presence of the intended recipient, Boltar, the scroll could not be read. Protected by a strong privacy enchantment, as were most messages sent by courier, the scroll had resisted opening.

At the queen's urging, Atrellan, truly a formidable mage in his own right, had finally managed to force it to unroll, only to find that it appeared blank. He knew better. There was no doubt that the scroll still jealously withheld its secrets, despite his untiring efforts to coax them forth.

Frustrated in all his endeavors to break the enchantment, Atrellan was finally forced to admit defeat. Boltar was the key; he—*or his body*—must be in close proximity to the scroll, and only then would its hidden secrets be revealed. He pondered upon the problem, but to no avail.

Wrestling with the issue only led to more questions.

How did Queen Mab know that there would be a spell upon the scroll? How did she know that the presence of Boltar would be required to render it inert? How can she be so certain that the scroll contains the details of a treasonous conspiracy? For that matter, how did she know that Boltar—and the scroll—would be there, at the Crying Cup, and at that time? How did she come by that information? Has she spies skulking in the shadows? Surely, she has some means of gathering such information. Ye gods! This train of thought can be dangerous—I should desist from any further speculation.

Footsteps in an adjacent hall drew his attention. He stopped pacing and drew himself up to his full imposing height—after all, he had an image to maintain, regardless of the queen's presently cool disposition toward him. He would not tolerate any disrespect from mere servants or underlings.

The alchemist, Daegon, rounded the corner.

Atrellan's mood soured darkly. He had little use for those who pursued *alchemy*. He considered it a pale imitation of true magic, a feeble attempt by lesser minds to comprehend the mysteries of sorcery, and at best, a dubious crutch for the untalented.

He held Daegon personally in equally low regard—and not just because Atrellan suspected the alchemist was some sort of *halfling*. Atrellan considered him an incompetent bumbler, always fussing with his so-called *experiments*, accomplishing little or nothing worthwhile. He could not understand what the queen saw in this blundering buffoon, or why she had taken him into her service. It rankled him no end. He considered it a borderline insult to such a highborn elf as himself.

Daegon bowed and greeted the senior mage formally. "M'lord Magus, I bid you good day."

Atrellan, a stickler for the homage he felt due his station, barely acknowledged the bowing man.

"Hmmph, Daegon. What business can you have here?"

"M'lord, I respond to Her Majesty's command to attend her."

"Here? Now?" Atrellan was unaccountably offended that this charlatan would intrude upon his pending—and presumably private—audience with his queen. This was simply not acceptable, not at all! His mouth twisted in distaste.

"Quite so, m'lord," Daegon responded without a trace of smugness.

Before Atrellan could respond, his sense of umbrage building, the door to the queen's study swung open. A large warrior-elf in mailed armor, the queen's ever-present bodyguard, stood in the threshold and scrutinized them.

"Her Majesty will see you now—both of you."

Daegon nodded courteously to the warrior-elf. In deference to the senior mage's ranking status, Daegon gestured for Atrellan to precede him, a matter of courtly protocol which Atrellan would have insisted upon in any event.

Attired in a high-necked gown of shimmering amethyst trimmed in tatted black lace, Queen Mab sat at a small writing desk, busily making notations with her quill on a piece of parchment. She ignored the two as they held deep bows and awaited her pleasure. Finishing her notes, she finally turned in her seat and deigned to notice her summoned vassals.

"Gentlemen, you may rise. Daegon, you may report."

Atrellan's nostrils flared involuntarily and his jaw muscles twitched as he heard his queen acknowledge this *halfling* first. He fought to hide his warming indignation.

Daegon nodded. "Majesty, I have completed the tutoring of the individual as you have commanded. I think he is ready to appear before the Council."

"Well done," the queen acknowledged. "I understand the Council's summons will soon be issued. Tell me, how did you find his potential competence in politics, his skill in the *craft,* and most importantly, what of his loyalty?"

"My Queen, I think he was well chosen. He *is* quick of mind. He readily assimilated and retained the knowledge that was provided. He has an intuitive understanding of politics, and its manipulation. However, in matters of *magic,* he has little innate skill and less craft, yet he is eager to acquire more. So, to the extent that he senses an advantage in that regard, he will remain loyal."

Atrellan was quite shocked to hear Daegon render an opinion regarding magic—notwithstanding that the queen had asked. This was *his* field of expertise! He almost visibly bristled; but, he wisely maintained his composure. It would not be unusual for the queen to deliberately toy with him by playing to his prejudices. He knew that she was well aware of his disdain for alchemy, and perhaps more so for Daegon personally.

Queen Mab smiled. "I understand. I am pleased, Daegon." She gestured to a divan. "Be seated."

She then turned to the elfin mage, and briefly paused as if gathering her thoughts. However, when she spoke, the pleased tone was conspicuously absent from her voice.

"Atrellan, I am informed that the body of the traitor, Boltar—the one you failed to recover—is to be released from the Realm of Shadow. The House of Lamia is complying with the formal request that I was compelled to make through the Council. You do understand that such a request was required only because of your failure to follow my commands, do you not?"

Atrellan dropped to one knee, eyes downcast, and mumbled, "My deepest apologies, Your Majesty. I shall not fail you again. Please, tell me how I may serve you."

Eyes flaring, her tone harshened. "You will serve me by following my simplest instruction as if it were my strongest command! I will not tolerate any further ineptitude *or* faltering performance on your part! You will do precisely as you are told—where, when, and how you are told! Heed me well, elf. Your next misstep may be your last!"

From the corner of an eye, Atrellan could see Daegon seated to one side, witnessing this humiliation. Daegon's face betrayed no emotion; nonetheless, the alchemist's very presence was an affront to Atrellan's besmirched dignity. That Daegon saw this utter debasement gave Atrellan's bitter resentment and mounting anger a focal point. Something deep within his shamed and fevered mind roiled in fear and self-loathing—a synapse twisted and snapped. What had been low regard and disdain for Daegon now festered, mutating into an infected and irrational hatred for the halfling.

But the queen must not know! I must hide my hatred—aye, nourished in secret—until the moment is right! Then—yes, only then—will redemption and revenge be mine!

The queen's voice slowly penetrated Atrellan's seething rage, drawing his focus back to her words. She had apparently been speaking for some moments; but, he'd been lost in the churning fury of his own bile. Only now did he come to understand what she was saying.

". . . and thus, since I understand that Magus Jalash-el is still very much weakened from his recent encounter with the ensorcelled ogress and the subsequent rite of execution he was compelled to perform, I have decided that you *both* shall make arrangements to meet with him at the portal he has named, and there assume custody of the body of the traitor, Boltar. Take it to an appropriate place and examine it carefully—both of you. I understand it holds more secrets that I would know. I am not yet aware of what time frame Jalash-el has in mind, but I feel the sooner, the better. Go now, and make your preparations."

Atrellan rose from his kneeling position, and Daegon joined him. Together, they bowed to Queen Mab and backed away. Atrellan ground his teeth as they returned to the reception area.

"M'lord, my schedule is open. I can depart whenever you prefer," Daegon offered solicitously. "I have very few preparations to make. Can I be of any service to you? Would you like me to contact Magus Jalash-el?"

Atrellan fought to maintain his composure, and responded blandly, "No, I think not. I will make the appropriate contact with Magus Jalash-el. I will also prepare the place of examination. These things take time, and require considerable skill. I shall inform you when all is in readiness."

"As you wish, m'lord," acceded Daegon, bowing slightly. He then turned and walked down the hall.

Atrellan watched him go. A scowl pinched the senior adept's face; his pointed ears reddened in constrained fury. As the scowl faded, a placid self-satisfied smile rose in its place; but, there was no disguising the evil glint in Atrellan's squinting eyes.

Oh yes, I have the most appropriate preparations to make—especially for you—you presumptuous halfling fool! How dare you relish in my chastisement! I'll not have you recount that which you should never have seen! You overreach yourself at your own peril—you supercilious Scaramouch!

WORLDS AWAY, IN THE Realm of Shadow, three people sat hunched over the rough planks of a simple tavern table, their voices low and guarded.

"Miska, you must *not* attempt something so foolish. You will surely be caught! Wilhem, *tell* him!" urged the smallest of the group, a woman whose intensity belied her size.

"Aye, friend Miska," the man seated next to her agreed. "Frieda speaks truly; you would only deliver yourself to the vampires. Was not what Hilde told you enough? How can you still doubt?"

The big man splayed his elbows atop the table, leaned forward and rumbled softly, "Ah, my friends, you have been patient with me, and I am grateful. But you do not understand—I must *see* for myself! Only then will I know for certain if this *Boltar* is truly my brother, Ivan."

"Miska, if you try to sneak into the castle of the Sidhe," declared Frieda with finality, "then you are doomed. The sun sets in only a few hours; it would take you longer than that to journey there, well past full dark. You would surely be faced with the resident vampires, in addition to the guard force."

Miska grinned and winked at the diminutive woman. "Worry not for Miska, dear lady, for I, too, have my secrets."

She leaned across the table until she was almost nose to nose with the big man, and whispered breathlessly, "Do you mean, perhaps, that you are of the *Were, Miska of the Ursus Clan?*"

His eyes widened in shock. He would have pulled back, but her small hands shot out and grasped his beard, holding his head in place.

"But . . . uh . . . how do y—"

"It matters not!" she hissed into his face. "When we found you at the Crying Cup, Hilde had almost come to grips with her grief—but you tore that wound open with your insistent questions. Aside from having little consideration for a grieving woman, did you think that making such impassioned inquiries about Boltar—an accused traitor and conspirator, would go unnoticed? Why did you think we were so adamant that you leave immediately and travel with us? The Eastern Patrol frequents that inn—they *bunk* there! When we were at the Baron Von Kestel's castle, the day the mage performed the rite of execution on that cursed ogress, you wanted to talk to a man you saw, thinking he might be this *Salidar* that Hilde had described. Then you tried to approach the mage to ask about Boltar—but we stopped you both times, remember? Don't you realize that the mage could have discovered your true nature with very little effort? You are not in any way shielded!"

She released her grip and leaned back, sighing in exasperation. She looked into his stunned face and felt a trace of sympathy for the confused man. *You poor lumbering oaf—no, we could not permit you to interfere with Salidar, nor would we see you commit unwitting suicide.*

As if her husband had read her mind, and her emotions, he spoke quietly. "Miska, do you not know that the castles of vampires are *warded?* You would be discovered as soon as you crossed the gate's threshold. The Were are not well regarded in this realm. You would be made a prisoner—at best."

However, Miska was obviously determined. "Friend Wilhem, I do not expect that you will understand. I must know—the honor of my clan demands it! Tis common knowledge that the body of this Boltar lies in that castle. I *will* see for myself—even if it costs me my life."

Wilhem and Frieda exchanged a meaningful glance; they would not dissuade Miska from this path, and they knew it. They both leaned forward once more, the resignation evident in their expressions.

"Very well." Wilhem sighed. "Miska, we wish you luck—you will need it."

"We must be away, Miska," Frieda added. "We are to be elsewhere before sunset. Be assured that your secret is safe with us."

"I understand. I am sorry, but I must do what I must do," Miska said with finality. "You have been fine traveling companions, despite your strong opposition to my quest."

"Before we go," Frieda whispered, "there is one thing . . . "

Miska's eyebrows rose. "Yes?"

She lowered her voice even further. "You must be willing to forget us—for now. I can help you with that. Are you willing?"

He was puzzled, but he nodded affirmatively.

"Just look into my eyes and relax . . . "

She began a nearly inaudible chant in an old and secret language. Its rhythm and tonality seemed to sweep him into a pleasant euphoric state. She knew Miska would soon feel almost weightless as he drowned in the depths of her dark eyes. Nor would he notice as Wilhem sprinkled a pinch of white powder into his flagon and topped it off with ale.

SOMETIME LATER, MISKA finished the dregs of his drink, and looked about the small tavern. He was growing tired of brooding by himself. Wasn't there something he had planned to do? Slowly it came back to him: Ivan—*Boltar?* Now he remembered. He must see for himself, soon. *In fact, why not now?*

Leaving a few coppers on the rough table, he left the tavern, and stepped into the late afternoon sun. Looking around, he got his bearings and set off in the direction of the Sidhe's castle, leagues away. Minutes later, seeing no one about, he slipped into the woods and searched for a secluded spot suitable for his transformation.

He had spent little time lately in bear form; and, he had kept that to a minimum. He'd found that it was conducive to keeping his wits about him—even when transformed. One happy result was that he'd contrived a way to keep clothing with him in a pack he kept suspended from his shaggy neck. He'd once caught a glimpse of his reflection in a pool of still water; he looked like an overgrown pet who'd escaped its leash. He had *huffed* at the image; and, it dawned upon him that he had just *laughed* as a bear. Until that moment, he hadn't realized that his sense of humor could now survive the transformation, a rather pleasant surprise.

He made good time through the forest and arrived at the castle about a quarter hour before sunset. In a thick copse of young pines off a well-traveled road he returned to man form, and donned his clothing. Then he sat just inside the shadowed tree line and watched as people returned from working the fields, making their way up the dusty track toward the castle. It was clear to him that everyone wanted to be within its walls by nightfall.

As the minutes slipped away, the number of people on their way to the castle dwindled to a sparse few.

A worn man of advanced years, pulling a small cart, came struggling up the rutted road and passed quite close to Miska's position. A number of sacks teetered upon the unstable cart as the fragile wheels haphazardly negotiated the dried and crusting wagon wheel ruts. A sudden lurch to one side sent two sacks tumbling to the dusty surface.

The old man turned to see Miska pick up the fallen sacks and deposit them back upon the cart.

"My thanks, good man," wheezed the tired farmer. "This road grows, ah, steeper with every trip."

"Aye, it does that, landsman," Miska replied with a grin.

The man bobbed his head in weary agreement.

"But, tis not so far now," Miska noted and held up both hands in offering. "Allow me to help push?"

The man nodded gratefully and plodded on with Miska pushing the rear of the cart.

Thus, Miska passed into the gatehouse passage. He stumbled a bit and could walk no further as the cart trundled on. It was as if he had stepped into quicksand; he couldn't move his legs. His arms briefly flailed about, but then slowly dropped listlessly to his sides, useless. He sensed movement above and he tried to glance up. The last thing he saw was a silvery net descending. Everything went dark.

MISKA DID NOT KNOW how much time had elapsed. He was very groggy. His head was spinning and he could not seem to get his balance. Disoriented yet aware, he realized he was seated; but, he could not move. As his eyes tried to focus in the dim light, a headache of such throbbing intensity was born in the back of his skull that his stomach was on the brink of nausea. He closed his eyes, concentrated on his breathing, and tried to calm his churning gut.

Even in his suffering, he was dimly aware that he was not alone. He could hear the clink of mailed armor and a set of muffled voices.

"He's coming around. Notify her ladyship."

Moments later, his discomfort easing considerably, Miska squinted his eyes open.

A pale woman with luminous green eyes and a cascade of red hair seemed to float into his field of view. Still groggy, he now saw that he could not move because he was restrained by silver manacles and leg irons. A silver chain bound him to a stout wooden chair bolted to the stone floor of a dungeon cell. The only illumination was from wall-mounted torches, whose flickering light danced off the mail of the men-at-arms standing warily nearby.

The guards stepped back a pace as the woman approached more closely and stood before him. She spoke in calm clear tones, as if this were a simple conversation rather than an interrogation.

"So, Miska of the Ursus Clan, tell me why you have come to visit."

He would normally remain silent, and divulge nothing—but, he could not. He found himself wanting to tell this beautiful woman why he was here, all about his brother, Ivan. And so, he babbled on, not understanding in the least why he did so.

If she asked a question, he answered unreservedly. Part of his mind rebelled that his own tongue would betray him so easily. He was utterly confused and crestfallen. The only redeeming factor, he realized, was the irony that he needed to remember no fanciful fabrications, for he had only spoken the truth and divulged all he knew about Ivan.

Then she surprised him.

"Miska, I believe you . . . and I will help you. If you were to see the body of this *Boltar*, would you know for certain if it is your brother?"

"Yes, I would." He heard the hope in his own voice.

"Is it possible that you might not control your emotions, and possibly react poorly, perhaps even resorting to violence?"

He was compelled to respond truthfully. "Yes, it is possible."

"Then here is what we shall do," she said casually. "I will arrange for different restraints that will allow you to move about. But since they are of silver, you do understand that you will not be able to *change*—even if you were to lose control. I will ask that you maintain control over yourself to the best of your ability. Do you understand?"

"I do . . . I must *see*—I must *know.*" His voice had taken on a pleading tone.

"As must I," she responded, turning toward the door.

At her departing gesture the guards carefully switched the restraints. He was allowed to stand. A silver chain now encircled his waist, his hands manacled, wrists together in front, and locked to the chain. A long length of chain dropped from the waist chain to the short length of links between the silver leg irons on his ankles. He could walk, taking short mincing steps; but, he could not raise his hands above his waist, nor move them more than a few inches from in front of his stomach.

He was slowly led to another torch-lit chamber, where the mysterious red-tressed woman waited. She was not alone. Aside from another brace of guards, a tall thin man in the robe of a mage sat upon a small bench. The woman leaned over him protectively. He did not look well; a pair of attendants hovered anxiously nearby.

"Jalash-el," she asked solicitously, "I am concerned that you have not sufficiently recovered from your ordeal. Are you certain this will not overly tax you?"

The mage appeared to respond more firmly than he felt. "I am fine, m'lady. It is important that this matter be suitably witnessed. Which begs the question; should not the Lady Sabrina be here as well?"

The woman sighed. "She attends to Gunther; he is quite unwell. She has taken him to her manor house. His injuries are severe; and, he is wracked with fever. He slips in and out of consciousness, and is still unable to describe what happened to him."

"Ah, I understand," said the mage. "Shall we proceed?"

At the woman's gesture, the guards guided Miska to a long table, upon which a shroud covered a reclining figure, no doubt the body he had longed to see.

She glanced at the seated mage and nodded. He returned her nod, indicating he was ready.

She came to stand beside Miska and laid a cool hand upon his arm. "Miska, this may not be easy for you. As I said, you *must* maintain your composure. Are you ready?"

Although the circumstances were not what he could have imagined, he found her concern somewhat comforting. He was somehow determined to cooperate; after all, she was providing him with that which he so dearly sought.

"Yes, I am ready."

The shroud was drawn away and torches were brought to bear. The flickering firelight gave the illusion of movement to the dead man's face. For a moment, it looked as though he might open his eyes and speak; but of course, he did not.

Time seemed suspended; the room felt compressed in a leaden silence until Miska let out a mighty sigh that ended in a hitching sob.

"Oh, Ivan . . . He is . . . my brother."

The torches withdrawn, the shroud was drawn back over the corpse.

Tears streamed down Miska's cheeks as he was shuffled away from the table and led before the seated mage. His worst fears had been realized, yet it was somehow a hollow confirmation. Perhaps because, in his heart, he had always expected to discover that Ivan was dead. And his grieving, however subtle, had truly begun a long time ago. Now, he felt strangely detached . . . empty.

Then he realized the mage was speaking to him.

". . . have no idea at this point who or what was responsible, and unfortunately, the Council's request, on behalf of Queen Mab, has interrupted our inquiry . . ."

The mage rambled on, but Miska heard only a slowly diminished droning, his mind slipping into a thickening fog. Moments later, he was dimly aware that he was being led to a cell; but this was a different cell, much larger and illuminated by many torches.

There he was alone for several hours.

SOON ENOUGH, THE WOMAN stood before him once again; but, she did not speak until she was certain she had his attention. "Miska, I am not sure what to do with you. There is someone I must consult; and, I may require your presence. Wait for my summons."

In the next moment, she had disappeared.

Morose and befuddled, he had no idea what she had been talking about; but, he certainly wasn't going anywhere.

STANDING ALONE IN A solitary cone of light surrounded by a stygian darkness, Lady Leanan concentrated on another summons, one she never envisioned she would have to make. Then she waited . . . and waited.

She had almost given up when she sensed his presence, somewhere off in the impenetrable shadows, lurking, watching, and apparently making no effort to come forward.

If he was inclined to make her *wait,* her ire beginning to smolder, well, she was not going to put up with . . . She caught herself—this was no time to let one's temper inhibit communication; too much may be at stake. If necessary, she would make the first overture.

"Lord Addecus . . . Come forward. Please, it is urgent! We *must* talk!"

Suddenly he was there, at the edge of the light, casting about—no doubt to confirm that she was alone, and that this was no trap.

"I have come, alone, asss requesssted. But, why here? Where isss Lady Diere? Your urgent messsage wasss quite cryptic. What isss it?"

"Addecus, I know we have had our differences, but something of portent is happening—something that I suspect far overshadows our incessant bickering. Let us put our differences aside for the moment. I think this may be too important. Can we not come to terms, at least for the purposes of this meeting?"

Addecus regarded her from the edge of the darkness and kept his silence.

She knew her urgency had alarmed him—and that he would be loath to let her perceive it. She didn't have time for this.

"Addecus, something is happening—something very wrong! You must at least agree to listen!"

"I am prepared to lisssten."

"That is all I ask," Leanan assured him. "First of all, Lady Diere knows nothing of our meeting. This is the last place she would expect either of us to meet—without her. Now, I do not pretend to know what she is up to; nor do I know or understand your involvement with her. But I feel I have to trust you—and you will just have to trust *me*."

"Go on," Addecus said flatly.

"Bear with me; I shall explain, for I now have little doubt that Diere is at the heart of the matter. As you likely know, she has called upon me to undertake certain actions at her direction, ostensibly on behalf of the Unseelie Court, and perhaps the Council itself. But I now strongly suspect that neither the Court nor the Council is involved, and that she pursues her own agenda. I am concerned that her plans, whatever they may be, will prove to be detrimental to my realm—if not to the overall *balance* of *all* the Council realms. Furthermore, I am now convinced that the Realm of Were is involved."

Addecus stepped fully into the light and let his hood fall back. He leaned toward her menacingly, his pupils narrowed to vertical slits in the harsh light.

"What do you mean that the Realm of Were isss involved?" he demanded.

Leanan leaned into his face and spat, "I mean that you are either completely in league with her; or, you are about to become another victim, sacrificed upon her altar of expediency!"

"What are you talking about? You have proof of sssuch treachery?"

"Yes, Addecus, I believe I do. You are familiar with Salidar, her halfling minion, are you not?"

"Yesss, I am familiar with that bungling fool. What of it?"

"You may, or may not, be aware that he was tasked by Diere to deliver an ensorcelled scroll to the innkeeper, Boltar, at the Crying Cup in Shadow. There was an altercation involving Dark Elves, including the mage Atrellan, and men from the Eastern Patrol. The Lady Sabrina confronted the elfin mage, who insisted that Boltar was a traitorous conspirator, and that the scroll held the damning evidence. The confrontation escalated and a melee ensued. Two Dark Elves were killed, and Atrellan escaped with the scroll. Boltar was killed. And it seems Salidar escaped without a trace—"

Addecus interrupted, "I fail to sssee how my realm isss involved."

"Patience, Addecus," Leanan warned, holding up a hand. "There is more. The Dark Elves were supported by some mercenaries; two were captured alive and questioned. Their mission was twofold; to seize the scroll *and* Boltar—or his *body*—and bring both to Queen Mab. There is clearly a link between the scroll and the body of this Boltar."

"The name Boltar remindsss me of sssomething," Addecus said pensively. "Two and a half centuriesss ago, there wasss a Dark Elf by that name who led a futile insssurrection againssst Queen Mab ssshortly after ssshe asssumed the throne—a coincidence?"

"Perhaps," allowed Leanan, "but I think not. 'Boltar' is an alias, I suspect, intended to arouse suspicion and draw Queen Mab's attention. As for the man, he is not human, but *Were,* Ivan of the Ursus Clan. For the moment, I have his body. We have found two spells upon it; a common stasis spell, and a very dark and deeply hidden mind-wipe spell. However, I must soon release the body to Queen Mab, by order of the Council. I can only delay compliance for so long."

"I sssee. Thisss isss ample caussse for concern, indeed. It isss not wissse to draw the attention of the Queen of the Dark Elvesss, essspecially if ssshe ssseeksss to ferret out traitorsss—real or imagined. There can be no doubt that Queen Mab will dissscover the ssstasssisss ssspell and that the body isss Were. Ssso, the Realm of Were will be implicated in the sssussspected plot—asss will the Realm of Ssshadow, for you have already drawn elfin blood."

"Now, you can see my concern. It would not go well for either realm." Leanan let the implications sink in.

Addecus stood silent for several moments. "Thisss isss all very interesssting; but, it may be fraught with ssspeculation. You claim to have *proof?*"

"Indeed, but I thought it best that we have our conversation before I brought him forth. He did not need to hear all that I have conveyed."

The Were Lord nodded sagely at her discretion, and listened to Leanan's account of Miska's arrival at her castle.

"Finally," she cautioned, and seemed to shudder involuntarily. "There is something else I must tell you."

"Yesss?"

"Queen Mab is rumored to have a *necromancer* in her service. Of that I have no *proof*, of course, but the captured mercenaries were convinced of it."

The Were Lord's jaw dropped; words failed him.

"I know," she conceded. "This would be a most unsavory turn of events. Necromancy had once very nearly doomed all the known realms—as you well know."

He winced at the mention of those dark memories.

Leanan nodded in commiseration. "Now, if you are ready, I'll summon my proof."

Within moments a dazed and hulking figure, draped in silver chains and restraints, stepped forth from the darkness and now stood before them in the widened cone of light.

"Lord Addecus, I present Miska of the Ursus Clan, late of the Realm of Were, brother to Ivan of the Ursus Clan, who is now confirmed deceased, and was formerly—and falsely—represented as Boltar."

Taken aback, Addecus straightened. Leanan knew the Were Lord now mentally probed the disheveled man.

"Ah, I sssee he isss indeed of the Were."

Addecus considered the silver chains with distaste, and noted the man's apparent disorientation. "What isss wrong with him? Why isss he in thossse foul ressstraintsss?

Leanan laid a hand upon Miska's arm, a gesture of sympathy.

"He has been under the influence of an immensely powerful *truth spell* for several hours. As an adept, you know that there are certain lingering residual effects from so long an exposure. Nonetheless, he will be quite well in a few hours. As for the restraints, bear in mind that he *did* attempt to breach the defenses of my home. And, he has admitted that under the circumstances, specifically the great emotional burden of identifying his dead brother, he might have difficulty controlling his emotions and potential subsequent events. And we just could not have that, now, could we?"

Addecus sighed heavily. "I underssstand taking pragmatic precautionsss; but I ssstill find the sssilver ressstraintsss offensssive. Isss he *marked?*"

"No, I have not tasted him, nor do I intend to. I have found him to be quite cooperative and forthcoming. Under the circumstances, I am even inclined to overlook his *indiscretion* at my castle gate."

Addecus looked at her with a newfound modicum of respect, and nodded his head. "I would appreciate sssuch a gesssture of good will, on hisss behalf, of courssse."

"Of course," she acknowledged with a wry smile. "There is more of interest in some of the details. For example, I have listened carefully to Miska's tale of how his brother, Ivan, took a mercenary job as a courier's guard, and disappeared shortly thereafter, possibly in Shadow—"

Addecus interrupted her with a raised hand. "When wasss thisss? And I want *him* to anssswer, if you pleassse."

Leanan smiled and gestured to Miska.

The big man narrowed his brows in thought and mumbled, "Um, three? Yes, I think three years past, maybe a little longer."

"Tell me, Missska of the Urssusss Clan, are you now certain that you have found your brother, Ivan?"

Addecus watched for any reaction carefully, but only a resigned sadness clouded the big man's brow.

"Yes, I am certain."

Addecus stroked his scaly chin and paced in a small circle. He came to a stop before the Sidhe.

"Leanan, I am sssatisssfied for the moment; sssend him back. We have more to dissscussss."

She nodded in understanding. "Miska, I will now send you back to wait for me. I shan't be long." Closing her eyes by half, she whispered a small incantation; the big man receded into the shadows and faded from sight.

Alone with her once more, Addecus resumed his pacing, mumbling under his breath, "The implicationsss . . . the implicationsss . . . Damn the godsss! The implicationsss . . . "

Leanan arched a lone eyebrow. "It seems you have picked up Lady Diere's habit of pacing."

That stopped Addecus in his tracks. "I am *nothing* like Lady Diere! Damnation! Do you realize what thisss may imply?"

"I think so," she answered cautiously, "but I would like to hear your thoughts."

"You mussst underssstand sssomething—the Urssusss Clan isss not large; but, they are among the mossst powerful of the Were. They are *werebearsss* and enjoy sssignificant immunity to mossst common magic. They hail from the mossst remote highlandsss and when traveling are notoriousssly sssolitary individualsss; yet they are extremely clossse-knit asss a clan. Fierce fightersss and competent mercenariesss, they tend to resssissst authority jussst for the sssake of belligerence. It isss unheard of for a clan member to go missssing for any sssignificant length of time—certainly not three yearsss! There isss sssome very ssstrong sssorcery at work here—there mussst be! To my mind, there can be no doubt."

"What is the significance of the *three years* elapsed time?" she asked.

"I am not sssure; it may only be coincidence—but perhapsss not. I am told that I have a sssomewhat overly sssussspiciousss nature. Be that asss it may . . . A little over three yearsss ago, Lady Diere sssought my opinion on a matter of sssome arcane ssspellsss and potionsss that ssshe had acquired—I know not how. I learned sssoon enough that her intent concerned Maude Delafaire, Ssssteward of the Grand Portal of the Realm of Man. At the time, Diere wasss interesssted in finding an undetectable and protracted processs of debilitation that would culminate in Maude'sss death—which did, in fact, recently happen.

"Diere intimated it wasss sssimply a clandessstine bid for Maude'sss posssitionsss of power, the Ssstewardssship and the Chair of Man. However, I alwaysss sssussspected that there wasss a persssonal element asss well. But I now wonder if Maude'sss ssslow demissse wasss Diere'sss sssole intention. Sssome of thossse ssspellsss could have had other usssesss, and sssomewhat different effectsss upon other beingsss. Whether or not the two circumssstancesss, Maude'sss death and thisss *Ivan asss Boltar* matter, are related, I do not know. However, I would not be sssurprisssed."

"And as I recall," Leanan added, "Salidar was also involved in the matter of Maude Delafaire, was he not?"

"Oh yesss, he wasss quite involved, much to the detriment of Lady Diere'sss plansss at the time. He demonssstrated unauthorized initiative, thusss botching her carefully woven ssstrategy involving both Maude and her heir. And now, he isss involved once more in sssomething he ssseemsss to know more about than anyone elssse. Asss you sssaid, *he* carried the ssscroll, *he* gave it to Boltar, and *he* essscaped unharmed. Isss there not a pattern here?"

They were both silent for a moment, lost in their own thoughts.

Leanan began speaking softly and pensively, almost as if musing to herself. "You make a good point. Salidar appears to be inept, and often bungles; but he always manages to survive. He does *her* bidding; but, does *he* have an agenda?"

The Were Lord merely shrugged. "I do not know."

"Addecus, before we allow our speculation of Lady Diere to go too far, I should tell you that I have also been cautioned that Queen Mab is entirely capable of orchestrating such an elaborate scenario herself, culminating in a hunt for traitors and conspirators to effectively be rid of problems or rivals."

Addecus nodded in agreement. "That isss posssible. It may be that Her Majesssty hasss ample reassson to be concerned. I have often sssussspected Lady Diere of coveting the throne of the Dark Elvesss. Ssshe hasss even hinted asss much. Although, in retrossspect I doubt that isss any sssecret."

"Aye, tis no secret," agreed Leanan. "Diere and Mab, the former Celeste, are cousins in the House of Hawthorn. They have been rivals for generations. Although, as I recall, Diere did not oppose Celeste's bid for power those many years ago."

"The moment may not have been opportune," observed Addecus. "I know that Lady Diere isss mossst eager to have her pawn, the human, George, assscend to the Chair of Man. Ssshe intendsss to control him, or ssso ssshe asssertsss. On the other hand, perhapsss Queen Mab ssso intendsss. I know the Queen isss aware and sssanctioned the plan—or to be more precissse, ssshe sssanctioned the plan asss proposssed by Lady Diere."

"So, it appears that the current crisis may be laid at the feet of either Lady Diere or Queen Mab. Or, of course, we could be completely wrong." Leanan shrugged. "Our realms face jeopardy from an as yet unknown source."

"Posssibly, but," Addecus slowly shook his head, "I think it unlikely. Lady Diere hasss alssso hinted at reversssing the Council'sss decisssion to forbid *hunting and harvesssting* in the Realm of Man were ssshe to come into sssuch a posssition of power. Sssuch a proposssal pleasssesss sssome—but I have ssstrong ressservationsss about sssuch an idea."

"She cannot be serious!" Leanan exclaimed in shock. "Has she any idea how the Realm of Man would react? These are not the superstitious peasants of centuries ago! They can now be dangerous beyond measure—I *know!* I know all too well."

Addecus could only nod in sad agreement.

"I fear that isss true. On the other hand, Lady Diere may only be trying to entice sssupport and cooperation."

"We can hope," she said wistfully. "Although I cannot imagine any but the weakest of minds even considering such folly. But then, it has been many years since most beings of Faerie have dared to wander in the Realm of Man."

"Mossst beingsss, perhapsss," he warned, "but not all. You know sssome ress-side there ssstill, hiding in plain sssight."

She shrugged, conceding the point.

"True, but aside from those best not spoken of, we must focus on the issue at hand. Certainly Lady Diere should be aware of the capabilities of mankind; she spent much time in that realm, although perhaps not so recently."

"Leanan, do not overlook the obviousss; whether or not Diere isss at the heart of thisss matter, sssomeone isss manipulating beingsss of ssseveral realmsss, for reasssonsss we do not yet underssstand. Sssomeone believesss that they have sssomething to gain. We mussst try to learn who cavortsss be-hind the ssscenesss—and why—lessst we be played for foolsss."

Leanan sighed. "I fear we have already been played for fools."

Addecus straightened. "Perhapsss—but we are now aware of the game. Now we have our own ssstrategiesss to devissse. Missska can offer a degree of proof, at leassst that thisss careful and manipulative undertaking required prodi-giousss ssskill in magic and wasss long in planning—" He stopped, seemingly in mid-thought. "How many know of Missska and Ivan—or that Boltar truly isss Ivan?"

"Too many, I fear—far too many."

"Forgive me for ssstating the obviousss, but you do realize that Missska now represssentsss a threat to sssomeone'sss carefully laid plansss. Whoever it isss will eventually learn of him—and no doubt try to eliminate him. Ssso, what isss to become of him now?"

Of course, she had not overlooked this possibility. She was more interested in seeing if Addecus arrived at the same conclusion, and by what reasoning process.

Now she was pleased, and to a small degree somewhat relieved. It appeared that his involvement was not as sinister as she had feared. His obvious concern for the welfare of Miska, his fellow Were—and indeed, for his home realm—was considerably reassuring. He could be trusted—at least to a point.

Leanan raised a solitary finger. "Oh, I have a place for him in mind, where he will be quite safe."

"And free of thossse foul ressstraintsss?"

"Absolutely! He will be treated no less than an honored guest—after all, his well-being is important to both of us."

"I sssee; am I to know where?"

"Certainly, once I have made the arrangements," she assured the Were lord. "You need not worry."

"Very well then, we are to trussst each other, are we not?"

"We are," she confirmed and smiled, "and none should so suspect."

"Indeed." Addecus smiled as well, a less attractive gesture to be sure, and raised a point. "Of courssse, you mussst realize that meansss the next time we meet—particularly in the company of othersss—we mussst resssume our normally acrimoniousss bickering."

"Naturally. It does seem to upset certain people so. I shall look forward to it, m'lord."

"Asss ssshall I, m'lady, asss ssshall I."

"Fare thee well, m'lord."

They turned away from each other in mutual amusement, and stepped into the surrounding darkness, each carrying a bit more respect for the other as they disappeared.

CH 11

SHERIFF FRANK TATUM pursed his lips and blew softly across the top of his brimming coffee mug. He should have known better; the CID squad room coffeemaker always kept the drip brew too hot for his liking. The powdered creamer did nothing, of course, to cool his steaming cup. Whoever had the task of making the Monday morning coffee tended to make it a bit strong for his taste; but, he liked it anyway. Deciding that a little patience was the wisest course, he leaned forward from the creaking side chair and set his hot mug on the edge of Captain Lou Miller's desk to let the drink cool for a bit.

He could see into the squad room, where CSI Technician Cassie Spenser nudged her boss, Sgt. Melancon, and pointed to the coffee pot in an unasked question. The CSI supervisor just shook his head; clearly, he knew better. She took the hint and resumed shuffling some paperwork while trying to ignore Tribal Police Officer Sammy Caldwell, who kept stealing shy glances at her as he stood awkwardly near the captain's office door.

The sheriff bit back a smile; it was entirely too obvious that the young policeman desperately wanted to strike up a conversation with the attractive CSI investigator. Frank suspected the rookie officer dreaded embarrassing himself among all these other policemen, especially since this was probably the first major-case meeting to which he'd been invited, and the first time he'd been assigned to serve as his agency's designated representative. He kept alternating glances at Cassie and the open spiral-bound notebook in his eager hand, its page still blank.

Frank almost chuckled aloud. *Oh, to be so young again. Ah, here come my detectives—time to get to work.*

Trey and Hawk, each holding a coffee cup, meandered through the squad room, greeting the assembled investigators.

At the captain's beckoning gesture, everyone rose and slowly funneled into his office.

The captain did a quick head count and motioned for Hawk to retrieve two more chairs from the squad room.

"Everyone take a seat. We all have a busy morning; and, the sheriff and I have another scheduled meeting within the hour."

Sheriff Tatum nodded and gestured for Hawk to close the door. "All right, Lou, let's get started."

The captain cleared his throat before he spoke.

"Ahem . . . People, we have a lot of material to cover. We'll start with the two homicides at the casino parking garage. You all know Officer Sammy Caldwell from the Tribal Police; he's been assigned as liaison for these cases. We've received a number of reports back from the lab. I'll let Sgt. Melancon bring you up to speed. Mel?"

"Thank you, Captain. First of all, the initial reports essentially indicate that there is no trace evidence that links the two scenes; however, by no means does that rule out the possibility. It just means that we found no physical evidence of a link. The medical examiner, Dr. Pritchard, performed autopsies on both victims. The victim found on the lower level is still unidentified. The other victim, found on the roof level, has been positively identified via DNA. That decapitated body, and the severed head found on a seventh-floor balcony of the hotel, belong to Suzi Origami.

"Cassie, please pass out the photo ID sheets."

The CSI tech handed everyone a printout bearing a photograph, actually a rather unflattering mug shot, and what little-known ID data that had been confirmed relating to the late Suzi Origami, as the CSI sergeant continued.

"I'll come back to Suzi in a minute. Dr. Pritchard recovered tissue samples from both bodies that we now know didn't come from the victims—different DNA signatures. It *is* possible, even *likely,* that these DNA samples represent our perpetrators—"

"Hold on, Mel," Trey interrupted. "Did you say 'perpetrators' as in *plural?* More than one? We're going with two perps, as of now?"

"That's right, Trey. Aside from that of the victims, the other two DNA signatures are distinctly different; and, each is found at only one scene. In fact, we had to go back to the scene on the lower-level garage floor, Jane Doe #1, and search again at the M.E.'s request. Dr. Pritchard wanted to rerun the DNA testing. Apparently, the trace samples he got from the wounds on that body were somehow contaminated, and may have skewed the test results."

Sammy Caldwell hesitantly raised a hand. "I'm sorry, Sarge, but could you explain what made Dr. Pritchard think the sample was contaminated? I *know* we kept that scene—well, *both scenes*—secure, at least from the time the bodies were discovered."

"I'm sure you did. I'm not in any way casting aspersions on your department's performance," Sgt. Melancon said. "I'm just telling you what the lab found. And in this case, it was a DNA sample with too many chromosomes."

"Now I'm confused," remarked Frank. "Can you explain, Mel?"

"Certainly, Sheriff," Mel responded and leaned back in his chair. "You may already know that human beings have forty-six chromosomes in their DNA. Comparatively speaking, that's a fairly high number according to biologists. This particular sample in question displayed eighty-four chromosomes—thus, the assumption of contamination. I'm told that nothing, at least nothing that we know of, has eighty-four chromosomes. So, the M.E. suspects that something, most likely an animal, is responsible for contaminating the scene."

"So, you're telling us that something else—something with uh, *thirty-eight* chromosomes—was also at the scene of that murder?" clarified the sheriff.

"So it appears, but we don't know for sure," cautioned the CSI sergeant.

"Well, what has thirty-eight chromosomes?" asked Trey. "What are we looking for?"

"Well, we have an idea; but, before I get into that, there is one more lab report I want to discuss," Sgt. Melancon said. "We took some air samples at the lower-level Jane Doe #1 scene before a thunderstorm rolled through. There was an unusual scent or odor that a number of our personnel noticed."

"Yeah," interrupted Hawk, "I thought I smelled something, too. But, as I recall, it was just on the lower-level scene, Jane Doe #1—not both."

"Well, you were right," acknowledged the CSI sergeant. "We had noticed that, too. So out of an abundance of caution, we took air samples at the other scene, the garage roof level where Suzi Origami's body was found, with negative results. There were no similar odors or scents noticed at that location. Now as for the sample we *did* get, the lab could not nail it down precisely, but they *can* identify it as a pheromone, and a fairly pungent one at that. I'll let Cassie explain further. Cassie?"

"Thank you, Sarge. The lab believes it to be *feline* in origin, most likely related to the *Great Cats*; but, they admit that there doesn't seem to be a specific match. Give me a second."

She consulted a computer printout.

"Okay, the closest pheromone characteristics they could find were among the *panthera pardus* and *panthera japanesis.* Those are leopards, very rare, considered endangered, and typically found in upper Asia Minor and Northern China respectively. Both species of big cat have thirty-eight chromosomes in their DNA.

"The only large cat of comparable size indigenous to North America is *felis concolor,* the mountain lion, puma, panther, or cougar. It's the same cat, just with different names common to different cultural regions of the U.S., Canada, and Mexico. However, the pheromone of the mountain lion, while similar, is significantly different from the sample taken from the crime scene."

Trey scratched his head and asked, "So, we're looking for someone who might have a big cat? As what—a pet that attacks people? What about escapes from zoos, animal sanctuaries, traveling circuses? Anything like that?"

"There have been no such reports," admitted Sgt. Melancon. "The evidence points to an animal, whether wild or not. According to the M.E., something savaged the body of the decedent both *before and after* actual death occurred. I would not rule anything out at this stage."

Hawk interrupted. "Are you saying that the cause of death is an animal attack?"

Sgt. Melancon shrugged. "Dr. Pritchard is tentatively identifying the cause of death as 'traumatic dismemberment and subsequent blood loss'. As you can imagine, he's reluctant to be more specific."

"Is that it, Mel?" asked the sheriff.

"Yes sir. "

"Ah, Mel, you had more about Suzi Origami, right?" prompted Lou Miller.

"Oh, right! Thanks, Captain. Aside from being a homicide victim herself, we know for certain that Suzi was involved in plenty of criminal activity, to include contract murders. We executed a search warrant on Suzi's last known residence, in New Orleans, and recovered a lot of information. Of course, much of it was encrypted data on computer hard drives and storage media, which by now, a good portion thereof has been deciphered. I'll ask Sgt. Basset to pick it up from this point. Trey?"

"Thanks, Mel. Uh, if y'all will give me a second." Trey flipped open a spiral-bound notebook and squinted. Rolling his eyes in exasperation, he fished around in his jacket pocket for his reading glasses.

Hawk stifled a chuckle and grinned at his partner, who scowled back and then ignored him.

His reading glasses settled upon the bridge of his nose, Trey continued with the briefing.

"This decrypted information led us to the Final Rest Funeral Home near Lafayette, the illicit body disposals, the meth lab, and the subsequent raid and explosion that, as you know, the media covered.

"The media does not yet know the details of what we found; since no official statement in that regard has been issued—and won't be, pending the ongoing investigation. I shouldn't have to remind everyone that all aspects of this case are confidential. Refer any media inquiries to the sheriff.

"Now, the good news is that we've corroborated a great deal of what Suzi kept in her records. All related intelligence data, to include corroboration reports, have been passed on to the concerned law enforcement agencies. We are now starting to get considerable confirmation feedback, and I should add, the gratitude of those agencies."

Flipping to a new page, he continued.

"We only recovered the body of one of the two shooters at the funeral home. Sufficient trace evidence strongly suggests the other shooter's body was destroyed in the explosion. DEA intelligence has developed tentative IDs on both men; however, this information has yet to be corroborated, pending further investigation into suspected cartel connections. So, for now the IDs aren't being released.

"A number of unidentified bodies were found at the scene of the funeral home, deceased persons who, most likely, had nothing to do with the meth lab. Most were initially in body bags, but many bags were damaged, ripped open in the explosion.

"I know that finding bodies at a funeral home should come as no great surprise, right? However, we did not find sufficient paperwork to explain all of them. It was clear that some were victims of unreported violence, and had been deceased for some time. These bodies were not yet embalmed, and were likely held for an indeterminate time in cold storage, according to the M.E.

"From among those bodies, we believe that we've made a preliminary identification, via dental records and partial fingerprints, of the body of Perry Wilkerson. You might remember that name from one of our *missing persons* cases. He was a lawyer, and used to be a senior partner with the firm of Savoie, Wilkerson and Fornier. Well, according to the M.E.'s postmortem report, it's now a confirmed homicide.

"And of significant interest, Suzi recorded in her files that she 'eliminated' Wilkerson on the orders of Papa George. So, we now have a pretty solid *contract murder* case on George Papadolis."

"Let me interrupt you for a moment, Trey," said the sheriff. "You know all this is confidential. It will eventually become part of a federal RICO case. Sammy, you can inform your chain of command. However, please tell your chief to call me. We need to keep this on a need-to-know basis.

"Captain Miller and I are meeting with the district attorney later this morning about the Wilkerson case. I've already called him, and he initially indicated that, in his opinion, we should probably wait for a positive ID, by DNA, and then take it to the Grand Jury for an indictment. He doesn't want to move too precipitously by seeking an arrest warrant based solely on a bill of information citing a preliminary identification of the victim. He thinks the ID may be too tentative. He'd rather get the warrant based on a firm victim ID via DNA that can be articulated in an indictment. We're gonna talk to him about that."

Trey spoke up. "I don't think anybody has tabs on Papa George at the moment, anyway."

"Maybe," said the sheriff, his smile growing, "but that doesn't mean we can't look for him. You see, while you all were in New Orleans and Lafayette, Sammy here, got a *material witness warrant* for George Papadolis, as the registered guest of the suite in which evidence of a homicide was found."

"Well done, man!" Trey acclaimed as he bumped fists with the tribal policeman, and winked at Hawk.

The sheriff held up a hand to get everyone's attention. "And on top of that, he gave it to the U.S. Marshals; it was accepted as a task force case. It's now in NCIC. By the way, the OCDETF crew is delighted; Papa George is still *number one* on their hit parade."

Frank smiled and nodded to Sammy. "Solid thinking and good initiative."

The young man appeared grateful for the attention, but a bit embarrassed as well. He mumbled something about "just doing my job" and looked down when he caught Cassie smiling at him.

That did not go unnoticed by the amused others in the room.

Hawk's cell phone rang. He caught the captain's attention and pointed to his cell phone. Lou nodded; Hawk stepped out of the captain's office to take the call.

Frank let them settle down before he continued. "Okay Trey, did you have more?"

"Just one more thing, sir. Your mention of the U.S. Marshals reminded me that the fugitive they thought might be at the funeral home—the parole violator, Teddy Pots, was not found. The marshals have good identifiers on him; so, they've confirmed he's not among the remaining unidentified bodies. However, it does appear from recovered trace evidence CSI found, to include fingerprints in and on the hearse, that he had been there fairly recently. So, that corroborates the tip they received that Teddy had been seen driving a hearse."

Sgt. Melancon raised a point. "If I might add, Sheriff, we now suspect that Teddy was part of Suzi's body-disposal solution, especially considering his access to a hearse and crematorium. We haven't decrypted all of Suzi's data files. Cassie tells me we may have a series of e-mail links between Teddy and Suzi that may provide some pretty conclusive proof. We'll know more in a few days."

Trey nodded. "We think Suzi used pre-paid cell phones, *throwaway burners;* and, we're pretty sure Teddy did, too. We tried to subpoena her toll records;

she used a very sophisticated internet phone service based in Japan. Unfortunately, they've declined to honor the subpoena, and we can't compel them. Our federal friends have offered to make some efforts on our behalf, but caution us to not get our hopes up. These sorts of requests take time and some deft diplomacy; so, for now, we wait. In the meantime, finding an e-mail link could be a real break."

"All right, if that wraps up your report, Trey, I have a couple of things on other cases," mentioned the captain.

Sammy Caldwell stood, saying, "I can step out, Captain, if you'd prefer."

"No need, please stay. I hope you and your department's resources may be helpful in some of these matters. We'll use good intel whenever and wherever we can get it," the captain admitted.

"Thank you, sir." The young man resumed his seat. "We'll do whatever we can to help."

"We appreciate it," answered the sheriff.

His phone call finished, Hawk stepped back into the captain's office. Once in his chair, he locked eyes with Trey, smiled, and silently mouthed, *Ellen.*

Trey nodded as the captain continued.

"Detectives Jones and Burroughs have so far hit nothing but dead ends in the Fenton Brewster case. Some guy posing as a lawyer, and using the name 'Salidar', was his last visitor at the jail. They can find no record with the bar of any attorney by that name. They have photos taken from the video surveillance at the visitors' entrance and the front desk; but no one they've interviewed recognizes the guy. We'll have copies made available for other agencies. At the moment, we only want to question him as a *person of interest,* but we have to find him first."

The sheriff was not happy with the stalled status of the Brewster case. It was time to turn up the heat.

"Listen up," he began, "I want this guy Salidar found; he's not a ghost. Get with your CIs and other street sources—somebody's gotta know something. That includes reaching out to other agencies and task forces. Okay, Lou, sorry to interrupt—please go on."

"Speaking of task forces and the U.S. Marshals," the captain continued. "Todd Simmons called earlier this morning; they've received the DNA results from the truck in the Doyle traffic case. That truck was originally reported stolen in Alexandria, and is definitely linked to the Carlos Cantu homicide case in New Orleans. Todd hopes to drop off the report here later today if he and Willis can get out of court early enough. Basically, the report confirms our suspicions that Wilson 'Bubba' Cutler and Ignatius 'Iggy' Simpson were likely in the stolen truck at the time of the collision."

Lou consulted his notes briefly and continued. "Todd also told me that New Orleans PD has secured a warrant for *Bubba* for the Carlos Cantu homicide, the registered owner of the stolen cab. Of course, *Iggy* and *Ratso* are still wanted for escape from the federal halfway-house in New Orleans during the hurricanes."

"Once we have the DNA report," the sheriff interjected, "Trey and Hawk can get with the D.A. and proceed to get warrants charging both fugitives with the attempted murder of the taxi's passenger, Ellen Doyle, and the arson of the stolen cab."

"Of course," added the captain, "if we could find the body of the taxi driver, missing from the hospital's morgue—who we are reasonably certain is Orlando 'Ratso' Ratalondo, *Iggy's* old cellmate, we could charge them with his death, too."

"Captain, if I may?" asked Sgt. Melancon. "We still have tissue samples taken from the decedent—the burned corpse—at the scene of the collision. A sample was sent for DNA testing; so, even though we don't have the complete body now, the test results confirmed the identification of 'Ratso'. That will probably be sufficient for the Marshals Service to close their escape case on him. But more to the point, we all know that this wouldn't be the first time a homicide case was prosecuted without a body."

The captain shrugged. "I know. But this isn't our call; it's up to the D.A. to decide. I'm sure the sheriff and I will be discussing it with him later today."

The sheriff stood and stretched, his lower back throbbing with a minor dull ache.

"Forgive me, I'm getting stiff . . . If that's it, Lou, I have one final thing to mention. I got a heads-up call from Sheriff Picard in Lafayette Parish, just before I got an e-mail from his office. Actually, all the Louisiana Sheriffs will get the same message via e-mail. He's got a fresh double homicide near Carencro that's probably gonna hit the afternoon news cycle. Two white male victims were found tortured and killed in a mobile home, in a rural trailer park. Both bodies were bound with duct tape and coat hanger wire, and both victims had *Colombian neckties.* Nothing was apparently stolen; no robbery, no drugs or paraphernalia were found, and no other leads. Sheriff Picard's e-mail asks for any information, or similar case circumstances, street rumors, scuttlebutt—really, anything at all. He's got nothing at the moment."

The captain just shook his head. "We've got nothing like that. We've *never* had a case like that, at least not that I know of."

"Excuse me," interjected Sammy, "but what's a 'Colombian necktie'? I don't think I've ever heard the term."

Sgt. Melancon looked to the captain, who shrugged and nodded.

"It's a nasty way to die, usually the last act in a torture session." Mel began. "The victim's throat is slashed. Depending on the skill of the killer, the victim dies fairly quickly from shock and loss of blood to the brain, or he slowly drowns in his own blood. The victim's tongue is excised postmortem, staged through the throat laceration, and left distended. It's intended to send a message and set an example."

The office grew very quiet; the horrible imagery was powerfully macabre.

Finally Frank spoke, breaking the spell. "I haven't seen or even heard of anything like this in years, not since the days of gang wars and feuds among South American drug cartels—at least not stateside."

"Yeah, I remember too," added Trey in a low voice. "The cartels didn't invent the *necktie;* they just adopted it during the internecine drug wars. As I recall, it was first seen in the late forties during the civil unrest in Colombia known as *La Violencia*. It was occasionally found in Cuba as well. It was pretty effective in discouraging informants and keeping gang members in line. It was sometimes threatened in order to extract information. But like Mel said, it was most often used to send a message; *don't talk, betray, or cross us*. It became something of a cartel signature."

The sheriff nodded. "Yeah, and in this case, it may have been a home invasion; but, it wasn't a robbery, since nothing seems to have been taken, and no drug indicators. Since there was evidence of torture, it could be that somebody wanted information, or silence, or maybe even payback."

"What do they know about the victims?" asked Hawk.

"So far, just the basics." Frank shrugged. "Two men, one was in his mid-thirties, and the other about fifty. The names and all the ID details are in the e-mail; I'll forward it to y'all. Both victims worked on an oil rig in the Gulf, had been offshore for about a month, and had only been home a few days. The younger guy, divorced, owned the trailer; the other man was single and lived in a camp on a bayou about a mile away. Neither one had a criminal record; although, both had some minor traffic infractions. And as I said, there was no sign of apparent drug use. Autopsies are pending. I'm sure we'll be getting more information as the Lafayette Sheriff's Department investigates more thoroughly. For now, that's all I have; watch for the e-mail."

"Well," said Capt. Miller, standing, "I think we've covered everything. If there are no questions, we'll adjourn and get back to work."

A LITTLE LATER IN THE squad room, Trey nudged Hawk and asked, "The phone call from Ellen—everything all right?"

"Oh, yeah." Hawk grinned. "I'm going to meet her at the airport and take her to lunch. Mark's flying back to New York early this afternoon."

"I see," Trey acknowledged. "So, she rides with him and needs a ride home? Right, Romeo?"

"Nah, she's got her truck. She followed Mark; he had to return his rental car. We're just gonna meet to see him off, and then go somewhere for lunch, no big deal. And don't call me Romeo."

SEATED ON A WIDE BENCH in the broad airport lobby, Ellen gazed through the tall tinted windows as Mark waited in line at the ticket counter. She watched the few approaching vehicles slow to a stop at the terminal entrance, and drop off departing travelers with their baggage.

She was looking for Hawk; he'd promised to meet her here. Hopefully, he would arrive before Mark had to leave. She was glad that Hawk and Mark had become fast friends. She took that as a token of approval on Mark's part of her undeniable attraction and deepening feelings for the detective.

Mark plopped down next to her, breaking her train of thought. She'd been so lost in her musing that she hadn't even realized that he'd finished up at the ticket counter.

"Well, it looks like I'm good to go." Mark sighed, checking his tickets and baggage claim checks. "I'll call you when I get home."

"Do you have to go through the security checkpoint right away? Can you wait a few minutes for Hawk?" she asked, with just a touch of pleading in her voice.

"No need." He grinned and pointed just over her shoulder. "Here he comes now."

She turned in her seat to see Hawk almost upon them. She stood and was enveloped in his warm hug, one that she returned and was a bit reluctant to release.

"Hey now," teased Mark, "I'm the one leaving!"

Without releasing Ellen, Hawk stuck out his hand.

"You get a handshake. Your cousin is prettier; so, she gets a hug, you see. Sorry I'm running a bit late; I had to park my car down near the Airport PD office in an assigned space. The walk back to the terminal plumb wore me out; Ellen's just gonna have to hold me up."

She laughed and pushed Hawk away playfully.

They passed a few minutes seated on the bench discussing Mark's plans for his return in a few weeks time. More travelers crowded the lobby and the lines grew at the ticket counters.

Mark glanced at his watch and nodded to the line growing at the security concourse. "I think it's time for me to go." He stood and hugged Ellen, and then pulled Hawk into a backslapping bear hug. "Well, it's been real, man—well, sort of. Thanks for everything, Hawk—and please, look out for her."

"Don't worry, I will. Hurry back, Mark."

Mark picked up his briefcase and joined the queue at the security concourse. The line moved surprisingly quickly, and with a last wave, he disappeared into the crowd.

Hawk took Ellen's hand. "Are you all right?"

"I'm fine—it's just that I'm going to miss him. I hadn't seen my cousin for years; then I spend a couple of weeks with him and it's like all those years just fade away. I'm fine, really."

"I understand. He'll be back, don't worry. Now, what are we doing for lunch?"

Ellen gave him a small pained smile. "Would you mind if we just picked something up and went back to the house?"

"We can do that. Do you like boudin? You know that spicy Cajun sausage with rice and meat?"

Her face broke into a bright smile. "Oh, I haven't had that in *years*—but yes, I like it!"

His smile mirrored hers. "Then I know just the place to pick some up, Tippet's; it's pretty much on the way. I'll walk you to your truck. Sit tight until you see me in my cruiser near the parking lot exit. Then you can follow me, okay?"

"Sounds good!" Ellen thought it was a great idea; of course, it was probably the company.

As they walked through the airport, Hawk described their destination.

Ellen was content to just listen to the soothing easy cadence of his voice. She already knew he was a gifted storyteller. She relaxed and let his words animate the images forming in her mind.

Tippet's General Merchandise was typical of the rural emporium commonly thought of as a *mom-and-pop* general store. An old family business, the store had been in the same location for generations, just off an old parish thoroughfare that had long been eclipsed by the newer nearby interstate.

Huddled under a canopy of cottonwood trees, it offered a diverse range of essential items from hardware to honey, buttons to bait, the sort of things found useful by local farming families and weekend sportsmen. Right in front, in the midst of the dirt parking lot, a lone island held an old and dented pair of derelict gas pumps, still displaying the nostalgic price of forty-nine cents per gallon.

Tippet's didn't sell gasoline, hadn't for decades. Horace Tippet decided in the mid-seventies that it was just too much trouble, and wasn't worth the headache—what with the new confusing environmental regulations, and all.

Horace's father and grandfather built the original store and the small cottage out back in the late 1930s from reclaimed barn wood, stout white oak, old but solid. The two rustic buildings served as a home and a family business for three generations of Tippets. Sadly, Horace and his wife, Carrie, were childless; and, as they were now in their seventies, they knew the old store would come to its end with them.

On the store's exterior, a collection of sun-bleached metallic signs, ads from a bygone age touting forgotten brands of colas and marshmallow pies, hung rimmed in rust along the silvered coarse wooden walls. It appeared that the faded signs had been there for so long that they actually contributed to the very structural integrity of the weatherworn building. A porch roof of roughhewn cypress shakes protected the local whittlers from the spring and summer rains; and within the store, a potbellied stove warmed their old bones in the damp chill of Louisiana winters.

The store had long been something of a communal gathering place, especially on lazy afternoons. Miss Carrie would always have some sweet tea handy for the ladies; prolonged visiting and gossiping could just leave a body parched on a warm day. Mister Horace would gladly share a smoke and pass the time with the gentlemen on the front porch. The truth was that Miss Carrie could *not* abide her husband's cigars. She just would not permit smoking around her bolts of fabric and dried-flower displays; and, this was long before it had become illegal to smoke in a commercial establishment.

HAWK PULLED HIS CRUISER alongside the defunct gas pumps and parked. He motioned for Ellen to park there, too.

As she did so, she noticed that he took a moment to look around, a worthwhile habit that most street cops develop, he had once explained. Situational awareness, he called it. She smiled. It pleased her that she was becoming comfortable with these little habits of his, some of which she thought might be wise to adopt.

Satisfied, he glanced at Ellen as she climbed out of her truck. "Do you remember this place?"

She looked around, and cocked her head. "It does feel familiar; but it might seem so from your description, I'm not really sure. It *has* been a while, you know."

"Come on," he urged. "It's Monday, so Miss Carrie should have a batch of fresh boudin ready."

Two elderly men in bib overalls, who sat chewing tobacco and whittling on the front porch, nodded genially as Hawk and Ellen stepped upon the worn boards. Hawk nodded back and smiled, pulling the screen door open for Ellen. A small bell tinkled as they entered.

As soon as she stepped inside, Ellen felt like she'd stepped back in time. Scents of old polished wood, candle wax, cinnamon, and soap vied for her immediate attention; it was wonderful. Thick wooden shelves held assortments of handcrafts, carved wooden kitchen utensils, and all sorts of small items she couldn't even identify. Bolts of fabric stuck out of a warren of diamond shaped racks along one wall, and an old-fashioned soda fountain fronted the opposite wall. Mason jars of jams, preserves, and local honey were arrayed on another set of shelves. Tall displays held stout shelves laden with small hand tools and bright-yellow boxes of nuts and bolts. Everywhere she looked she saw something unique; it was almost too much to assimilate all at once.

An older man's crusty voice sounded from within the maze of displays. "Carrie, come on out here! It's Wendell's grandson, young Connor! Carrie, come on out!"

A short balding man wearing a shopkeeper's canvas apron appeared before them. Ellen hadn't even noticed what aisle he had come from; he was just *there.*

He grabbed Hawk's hand and shook it enthusiastically. "It's good to see you, young Connor, good to see you!"

"It's good to see you, too, Mister Horace," said Hawk good-naturedly as he tried to extract his hand. "May I introduce you to Miss Ellen Doyle, Maude Delafaire's niece?"

Horace took Ellen's outstretched hand and shook it nearly as vigorously as he had Hawk's. "Dee-lighted, Missy, delighted! So sorry for your loss, your *grande tante's* passing. A good woman she was—a good woman!" He leaned conspiratorially closer and added in a stage whisper, "Knew the benefits of a fine cigar, she did—she did!"

"Horace, turn that young lady's hand loose before you give her a bruise! This instant, Horace!"

"Ah, here's Miss Carrie," Hawk announced, grinning.

Ellen found her hand suddenly released. She looked over Horace's shoulder to see a grey-haired woman, no taller than her shopkeeper husband, bearing down on him like a thundercloud from the back of the store.

Hawk stepped deftly in her path and swept her up in a big hug, spinning her in a gentle circle. He set her down and gave her a quick peck on the cheek before releasing her.

Her husband chuckled as she blushed, patted Hawk's arm, and admonished him in a mock-stern tone. "Now you behave yourself, young Connor! And tell me why we haven't seen you lately—and introduce me to your young lady. Where are your manners, young man?"

"Miss Carrie, this is Miss Ellen Doyle—"

"Maude's niece! Maude's niece!" interrupted Horace, pointing at Ellen.

Carrie's hand moved like lightning, grabbing Horace's finger.

"Don't interrupt, dear! And don't point—it's impolite!" She gave him a baleful look, and released the offending finger.

"Ellen is living at Delafaire Farm," Hawk explained. "We're headed there now. But, you see, I promised her lunch. I've convinced her that the finest boudin in the parish is to be found right here, not fifteen minutes from her door. So, if it's not too much trouble, I'd like to get some to go. Would that be all right?"

Carrie smiled. "You're in luck! Just happen to have a fresh batch, made over the weekend—but you knew that, didn't you, *cher?*"

"Hmm, and maybe that Monday is your *red beans and rice* cooking day?" Hawk glanced aside and grinned like a mischievous little kid. "Well, maybe, a little. Could we get a couple orders of red beans and rice to go, too?"

Ellen smiled; she couldn't help but think he looked *so cute* when he did that.

"Horace, would you please fetch up some boudin and to-go lunch orders for young Connor, while we visit some? He still has to tell me where he's been, 'cause he ain't been 'round *here*."

As her husband hustled off on his errand, Carrie crossed her arms and waited for Hawk's explanation; obviously she wasn't going to let him off easily.

"Well, the simple truth is," he began, "that we've been very busy lately. And work took me out of the parish for a little while—"

"*Mon Dieu!*" Carrie blanched, her hands to her cheeks. "You weren't involved in that tragedy near Lafayette, where those officers were killed? Were you hurt?"

Pain washed across his face, but he quickly regained his composure. "I'm sorry, Miss Carrie, but I can't really talk about it. I wasn't hurt; I'm fine."

"I'm so sorry—I didn't mean to pry. Please, forgive an old busybody."

"It's fine. There's nothing to forgive." He hugged her with one arm and kissed the top of her head.

"So," Carrie looked up at him, "I see you're home now, and we're going to see more of you, right? Especially if you're going to be keeping this pretty young lady company, right? She's living at Delafaire Farm—why, that makes us neighbors!"

Turning to Ellen, she reached for her hand. "Ellen, please feel free to drop in and visit—we do a lot of *visiting* in this old place. Your *Tante Maude* and I, why we were a couple of regular old gossips, us. Sorry we had to miss the memorial. So, when you can find the time, you come see us."

Ellen smiled and gave the woman's weathered hands a gentle squeeze. "I think I'd really like that. Just give me a bit of time to get settled."

"I understand, dear, don't worry about a thing. Oh look, here comes Horace. Took his sweet time, he did, I swear!" The smile belied her brusque tone.

Ellen was drawn to a dried-flower display as Hawk paid Horace and accepted the warm bag.

Not quite out of Ellen's hearing, Carrie reached up and tugged Hawk's ear down to her level and whispered hoarsely, "That's Maude's niece there, Connor. You look out for her now; hear me, *cher?*"

Hawk winked at Carrie. "Yes, ma'am, I hear, and I will. She's special to me. You just try to keep Mister Horace on the straight and narrow."

With a twinkle in her eye, Carrie said, "Isn't he just my mission in life, my special burden? You be careful now, Connor."

They bid the Tippets good-bye, nodded to the whittlers on the porch, and departed.

WHEN THEY ARRIVED AT the house, the dogs were obviously glad to see them; and paid particular attention to the warm paper sack Hawk carried. One sniff set their tails wagging. Even Smokey deigned to notice the aroma-laden bag and promptly trotted toward the kitchen.

The pets hovered near Hawk as he opened the bag and began laying out the sausages. When he picked up the pets' food bowls, the tail wagging ratcheted up a notch.

Peering into her open refrigerator, Ellen remarked over her shoulder, "I've got some leftover French bread I can warm up. There's sweet tea, too—how's that sound?"

"Great!" He began slicing the sausages.

"No beans for the pets, okay? You're sure it's all right to give them some of that boudin? I don't want them to get sick," she cautioned.

"No beans—oh, I get it. The boudin shouldn't be a problem. It's just rice, pork, a little venison, and some spices. It won't hurt them at all. And just look at them; they can smell it. They know what it is—and they want it."

She relented. "Well, okay, but just a little."

As it turned out, "just a little" wouldn't do it.

The dogs scarfed it down with relish; even Smokey made quick work of his portion. Hawk and Ellen ate their fill and doled out just a little more to the eager pets. Within a few minutes the dogs found comfortable spots on the cool kitchen floor and began snoring softly. Smokey found a sun-warmed window ledge and settled in for a nap.

"So, have you heard from your mom and Stacy?" Hawk scooted his chair back a few inches from the table.

"Oh yeah, they're fine. They've each called a couple of times since they got home. Actually, Stacy has called a lot. I think she was really calling so often to talk to Mark. Now that he's gone back to New York, maybe I'll have more time to catch up on the journal and read the rest of the research materials."

"Research materials?"

"Yeah, the stuff from Madeline. Oh yeah, you weren't here. Hawk, we have some catching up to do. We couldn't discuss it on the phone or in public; and so much has happened. So, bear with me, please?"

Hawk grinned and nodded, as Ellen sat up straighter in her chair.

She spent the next few minutes explaining what he had missed, to include how Millie had confided in Madeline, and that eventually, with Ellen's approval, Madeline had subsequently shared that information with her husband, Armand.

Hawk was understandably surprised that so much had happened during his brief absence. He found it further unsettling to learn that so many people now knew so much about the existence of other realms. This just seemed to accentuate his dilemma. He was torn—just what was the right thing to do? He had knowledge relating to crimes committed in this world—within his own jurisdiction—that he could not ethically withhold. But, who would believe him?

He knew one person who would. And so, he decided to confide in Ellen.

She proved to be an excellent listener, a very sympathetic ear.

As he finished speaking, she placed her hand on his arm and gently squeezed.

"I see your problem, well, actually several with this Fenton Brewster situation. Just how would you bring a *vampire*, or even *Salidar*—whatever *he* actually *is*—to our form of justice? And that's if you can get a court to even *believe* you! But if I understand you correctly, you feel compelled to share the truth with your partner, Trey, *and* your chain of command. Well, that would effectively pass on any critical decisions to be made up the line, so to speak.

"But, at some point don't you also lose control of what might happen? If the knowledge doesn't *stop* somewhere and remain contained—and I mean very limited access—can't you see where this could lead? I can't begin to imagine the potential devastation and heartache. And you don't want that on your conscience."

"No, I don't," he agreed, "and I have a very strong conscience."

"I know," she said softly, "that's one of the things I like about you."

He leaned forward and drew her into a kiss. As he embraced her, her arms encircled his neck. They savored the moment in the stillness of the sun-dappled kitchen.

She broke the kiss, but still held her arms about his neck. Leaning back a bit, she whispered softly as she stared into his eyes. "I worry about you; I care about you."

He smiled. "No more than I worry about you; I care about you, too. Are you going to be all right, here, alone?"

"Well, I've got the pets—they're more than pets, really; they're family, you know? Of course, you *could* come and visit, you know. I believe I could tolerate your company." She smiled impishly and pushed away from his embrace.

"I think I could find some time," he allowed. "If you're not going to be too busy with all your *research.* But now, I really have to get back to the office. Can I call you later?"

"Sure, I'll be here. By the way, speaking of research; remember that story you told about the tragic lovers when we were in the Forest of the Damned, you know in—"

"Uh, yeah—I remember," he interrupted, feeling mildly uncomfortable at the memory of the bizarre events of that night.

"Well, I read something very similar in the research Madeline and Armand gave us, a handwritten transcribed tale attributed to your people—your ancestors, I guess—and the forest here on Delafaire Farm. Did you know whether or not the tale you told was supposed to be about this forest? Were your people really afraid of these woods?"

"What? No, at least I don't think so. Although I can remember my grandfather cautioning us kids to always be respectful and not intrude on these old woods. But come to think of it, I guess it's possible. None of us ever played here; but I don't remember any outright taboo about it. Why? Does it really matter?"

She shrugged. "Probably not—who knows? I just thought it was an interesting coincidence."

"Hah, lately I'm starting to believe less and less in mere coincidence. Maybe there is something to the concept of inescapable destiny—like I'm destined to be late if I don't get going."

"Oh, sorry, I didn't mean to keep you—"

"Ah-ha, a likely story," he teased as he stood.

"Maybe," she retorted. "Seriously, thanks for meeting me and seeing Mark off." She made a sweeping gesture to include the dozing pets. "Of course, we *all* thank you for the wonderful lunch."

"My pleasure," he said grinning, and executed a slight bow.

On the front porch, they bid farewell, and kissed once more.

Hawk's burden seemed somehow lighter and his heart buoyant as he drove away.

He unknowingly wore a silly grin all the way back to his office.

ELLEN'S EMOTIONS FELT equally buoyant as she returned to her kitchen; but physically, she was tired. The pets hadn't moved; they were sound asleep. She felt a twinge of envy. The notion of a nap had a strong appeal to her; the ample lunch she had just enjoyed was slowing her down. She puttered about, cleaning up after the meal, and fought the occasional yawn.

Oh yes, a nap is in my immediate future. Maybe I could try to read a little? Ha! Who am I fooling? Five minutes of staring at a printed page would be as effective as a lullaby.

Making her way to her bedroom, she was only slightly surprised to hear the clicking of dog claws upon the stairs. Despite appearances, Max and Sophie were rather light sleepers and tended to follow her from room to room, only to plop down in the new location and be snoring away within minutes. It didn't bother Ellen in the least; in fact, she found it comforting. Their presence was always reassuring.

She pulled the shades to darken the room, lay upon her bed, and stared at the shadowed ceiling. Unable to keep her eyes open, she fully relaxed as the events of the day unwound in sequence; captured moments were savored once more in the ethereal theater of her mind. Her smile betrayed the sensual replay of the kiss. *I think I really like Hawk . . . more than a little, to be honest.*

It amused her that the pets took to him so well. Of course, sharing his boudin with them today didn't exactly diminish his esteem in their eyes, either. It was almost as if they had established a special bond.

Yeah, over boudin, henceforth to be forever revered as the ceremonial sausage!

She was so glad that the pets seemed to really like him. She believed they were excellent judges of character.

As she drifted off, her thoughts were becoming hazy. *I wonder what Maude would think of him? She was a pretty good judge of character, too.*

. . . Oh, I like him, too. Don't let him get away! He's a keeper!

. . . What? Maude, is that you? Am I dreaming?

. . . Yes, it's me—and if we're having a conversation, you must be dreaming.

. . . Ah, and we're doing the telepathy thing again. Why can't I see you—oops—I can see you. Oh, I remember—I had to will it, right?

. . . Well, it is your dream, but you're right. You have to maintain control.

. . . Yeah, I know. And by the way, I kinda like this telepathy trick. Anyway, I've been reading like you suggested. But how do you even know about Hawk? Wait—you can observe me?

. . . Well, sort of . . . I can only know what you consciously, or subconsciously, want me to know. It's entirely at your discretion. Don't forget that if you ask me

something, I can only confirm what you figure out on your own. So, think things through and you'll arrive at the right conclusions.

. . . So, if I might have, even subconsciously, wanted you to know stuff, that means you pretty much already know a lot of what I've seen and done. I'm not sure how I feel about that—it's kind of creepy, almost like possession.

. . . Don't be silly—you're not possessed; and I'm no voyeur. You know perfectly well that I'm discreet and would never pry. Remember, I can only know what you want me to know. You really are in control.

. . . I understand, I think . . . Of course, someone might argue that this is all in my head.

. . . Perhaps—if you were to tell someone; but, you know where that might lead, don't you?

. . . Yeah, no thanks—I've seen enough of hospitals lately, thank you very much.

. . . Well, it seems you initiated this dream; so, wasn't there something you wanted to discuss?

. . . Yeah, there is. I'm sure you know we found the coins and the still. You stashed the coins there, and you let the Dwarves run the still—and bootlegging?

. . . Yes, well, as you know, economic depressions are tough times for folks.

. . . You also had some arrangement with the Light Elves. They did your gardening and you allowed them access to your forestland. Something about that lingers, I think, because there aren't any weeds in the gardens. I'd like to restore such beneficial arrangements.

. . . You would not regret it; the Dwarves and Light Elves would be excellent friends.

. . . And you know that Stacy and I visited the Guildmaster in Storm Haven; that's how I came to know some things. He was your friend, wasn't he? You worked with him on many things. He still misses you.

. . . Yes, we were good friends; we accomplished much. I miss him, as well.

. . . He told me that I must appear before the Council at the next meeting and announce that I am the Steward. He emphasized that it was important. And I must stop Papa George from ascending to the Chair of Man.

. . . Yes, that is all true, and important.

. . . And finally, you know I have met and dealt with Lady Leanan—a vampire! I'm still trying to wrap my brain around that! I don't know what to make of her. She tried to hurt me once, but insists she was duped by the Dark Elf, Lady Diere. Leanan now says I am in no danger from her. She said she was your friend. Somehow, I don't think she's lying; I guess I believe her.

. . . We were friends, for a very long time; and yes, Leanan is an elder vampire. More importantly, you are right; she does not lie—she has no need to do so. But as for Lady Diere, you are wise not to trust her—I never should have.

. . . I always have so many questions for you, but I can never seem to think of them all when we do have the opportunity to communicate. It's so frustrating.

. . . Don't fret, dear, we will have other opportunities. Remember, you only need control your dreams. But you should wake up soon. You're going to need to be aware and alert; things are about to get, um, interesting.

. . . Wait! What do you mean? Maude? . . . Maude?

EVEN IN THE DARK ROOM, Ellen realized she was now more awake than asleep. A cold nose nuzzled her hand and she absently scratched Sophie's head. Max *huffed* from across the room. He was either making sure she was awake, or he was hungry again. How long had she been asleep? The sun had set and dusk was fading to true dark.

. . . aware and alert . . .

Ellen made her way downstairs to the kitchen with the dogs in her wake. Smokey was typically nowhere to be seen. Max and Sophie were hungry; it had been almost seven hours since lunch. She prepared one of their favorite suppers; dry dog food, chunks of leftover chicken, and warm gravy.

But to her surprise, both dogs suddenly ignored their food, went into an alert stance, and stalked toward the front of the house.

Smokey was already there, crouched in the center of the front hall, facing the front door. His tail twitched in measured agitation, in a sort of cadence with his low pulsing growl. He glanced to either side as Max and Sophie came up to flank him; all three stared at the door in a tense silence.

The abrupt knocking startled Ellen; but, the pets never flinched. She stepped to the door, and flipped the wall switch that activated the front porch lights. She hesitated a moment, then pulled the stout door open, careful to keep the outer screen door closed and locked.

Near the base of the front porch steps, just beyond the pool of illumination offered by the decorative carriage lamps, a cloaked figure stood washed in the eerie light of the waning crescent moon. The figure tore its gaze from the gardens, slowly turned to face her, and dropped its hood.

Lady Leanan—the vampire!

"Try not to look quite so surprised, Lady Ellen. After all, you did invite me."

Ellen's breath caught in her throat. She felt the dogs press against the sides of her legs, and could feel the vibrations of their nearly inaudible growling.

"Are you not going to invite me in?" the Sidhe asked.

Ellen's mind raced. She barely recalled making some passing reference regarding an *invitation to visit* to the kindly mage, Jalash-el, when she and her friends had departed from Leanan's castle. She had to pull herself together!

Ellen straightened and asked, "Why should I trust you?"

"Oh Ellen," the elder vampire sighed, abandoning any sense of the theatric. "We have no time for this. We *must* talk. I have already told you that you have nothing to fear from me."

"You haven't answered my question," Ellen reminded her firmly. "Why should I trust you?"

Leanan considered Ellen for a moment, and shrugged.

"Very well. You should trust me because I am trying to prevent something very bad from happening, something that may affect many realms, perhaps even your own. And, I need your help. If it will make you more comfortable, I will take a binding oath not to harm you. Is that acceptable?"

Ellen thought for a moment. "Include that those whom I hold dear shall come to no harm by you, and I will accept such an oath."

"To whom do you refer, specifically?"

"Well now, that could be quite a list. Let's make it simple; my family and friends."

Leanan's face clouded. "Do not toy with me, Ellen. This is a perilous time."

"I do not *toy* with you, Leanan! You want my trust and my help? You will *earn* both, very slowly, if you persist in petty games. Now, I have it on good authority that you do not lie; so, give me your oath and I will accept it. Then we'll see."

Somewhat mollified, Leanan sighed in acquiescence. "Very well. By the Powers of Air and Earth, Fire and Water, I, Leanan of the Sidhe, House of Lamia, do hereby swear to cause no harm to Lady Ellen Doyle, Steward of the Grand Portal of the Realm of Man, her family and friends. Are you satisfied now?"

"I am," Ellen responded. "Of course, I wouldn't want my pets to come to any harm either—they're family too, you know."

Leanan smiled and shook her head. "Ellen, it is clear to me that you do not fully appreciate the nature of your *pets*. It is very unlikely anyone could harm them, intentionally or otherwise. Nor, for that matter, could anyone enter your home *uninvited.*"

Ellen offered a smile of her own. "Oh, I am aware that this house is strongly warded. And furthermore, that as a *vampire*, you must be invited into any home. That raises a question; does each entry into a home require a separate invitation?"

"Not in most cases, provided of course, that the person who issued the invitation still resides there." Leanan arched a lone eyebrow. "However, in some cases—like this house, which *is* heavily warded—you must extend me an invitation each time. In fact, your initial invitation, conveyed by Magus Jalashel, only allowed me to mentally manipulate the iron knocker upon your door, and even that only from where I stand, before the steps of your porch. So, on this occasion, you must further invite me to enter."

Ellen unlocked and swung the screen door open.

"In that case, Leanan, I have accepted your binding oath. On this occasion, I invite you into my home."

As soon as the screen door was open, Smokey streaked outside and disappeared in the gloom.

The dogs eased back a few inches, but held their ground, still alert, but no longer growling.

Leanan ascended to the porch level and hesitated. "There is one more thing; I did not come alone. I ask that you extend an invitation to my companion as well—it is vitally important."

"Who are you talking about?" Ellen asked.

Leanan gestured and a large form came forth from the darkness and ascended the porch steps.

The Sidhe started to make an introduction as the big man stepped into the dim light. "Lady Ellen, this is—"

"Miska?" Ellen gasped. "Is that you?"

Stunned, Leanan looked from Ellen to Miska and back again.

Ellen had no doubt that this was Miska. He had Smokey in his arms and was happily scratching behind the contented cat's ears.

The dogs relaxed and sat down; obviously not perceiving him as a threat. After all, he seemed to have Smokey's approval.

"Lady Ellen," mumbled a surprised Miska, as he tried to bow without dropping the cat.

"Ah-ha, you two are acquainted, I see," observed Leanan dryly. "Oh yes, we most certainly need to talk."

CH 12

THE STREETS OF DERINSEUM were crowded with a colorful mélange of masked and costumed revelers, carousing about in loose-knit groups, laughing, and singing boisterously repeated choruses of bawdy sea shanties. Whatever they may have lacked in articulated lyrics, they more than compensated for with volume and enthusiasm.

The Fertility Festival of Mer had commenced in earnest. And if this first rowdy afternoon was any portent, the following days and nights would be a madcap celebration of uninhibited excess.

Salidar had spent his time in Derinseum carefully venturing about, making certain contacts among the local street people. They were typically an excellent source of information, if one had the coin, or something of equivalent value to barter. Should it be that something other than information was sought, someone could usually be found to provide that as well. The festival was traditionally a very profitable time, in one way or another, for all the residents of Derinseum.

Unfortunately, Salidar had not found Padraic the Rogue in the few days he'd been here, despite his best efforts. Of course, it was possible that Padraic had not yet arrived; but, Salidar didn't think so. He thought it far more likely that Padraic was here, keeping a low profile.

In the midst of this citywide exuberance, Salidar sat alone in his dingy room at the Inn of the Blue Crab and groused at the irony of his luck. Here he was, in the heart of one of the most eagerly anticipated events among the Council Realms, a fabulous bacchanal, in which he should be thoroughly enjoying himself. However, he was compelled to patiently bide his time, closeted in an overpriced and undersized chamber on the uppermost floor of a third-class establishment, waiting for a local street urchin to make contact.

Over the past few days Salidar had exhausted all his leads and hunches. Despite the apparent lack of progress, he had carefully cultivated a network of informants, laying tendrils at every lair and den of iniquity he thought Padraic might frequent. Now, he could do little more than wait, a spider patiently monitoring its web. For the moment, he couldn't even leave the inn; the boy was overdue.

Venturing to the window, Salidar looked down upon the throngs of garishly costumed festival participants dancing through the cobblestoned streets to a cacophony of pulsing music and throbbing drums, a kind of sloppily choreographed chaos.

The corners of his mouth turned down. *Where is that little guttersnipe?*

The long afternoon had dragged on interminably. Shadows stretched as the sun set. Encroaching pools of darkness bled from every nook and cranny.

Salidar watched as a lone lamplighter made his way slowly through the groups of frolicking celebrants and undulating dancers, stopping briefly to point a wand at the globe atop a tall post. A small glow formed at the tip of the wand and floated lazily upward. When it reached the globe, the orb flared with a soft golden light, spreading a gently diffused illumination over the milling crowd. The stoic lamplighter moved on, seemingly unaffected by the festive ambiance.

It had come as no surprise to Salidar when he made the rounds of the city's nether regions that many people knew of the bounty on the Rogue's head; Duke Briar was nothing if not persistent. Such notoriety could potentially be a problem; Salidar might not be the only person seeking Padraic. He would have to be careful; no doubt Padraic was being careful as well.

It was fairly common knowledge among the street people that Padraic the Rogue always attended the Fertility Festival, and habitually visited certain sites. In fact, one of those locations was within the same city block as the Inn of the Blue Crab, on the opposite side of the street, just a few doors down. This was the primary reason Salidar had agreed to the inflated price for accommodations at the dubiously maintained hostel.

Once more he peered carefully through a corner of the room's sole window; at least it offered an unobstructed view of the street below and most of the block. The building he watched was not far, only a stone's throw down the street. The carefully manicured façade appeared to be the unassuming home of a prosperous merchant. In reality, it was a rather discreet high-end brothel, whose clientele valued their anonymity, even during the Fertility Festival. Salidar had been assured by numerous sources that Padraic would visit this house sometime during the celebration.

The teenager, upon whom Salidar now waited, was a streetwise youth called *Slip* who occasionally ran errands for the proprietress of the brothel. At their first encounter, Slip had warned Salidar that Madam Iris was not to be trifled with; she could be quite stern and unforgiving in matters of commerce or in defense of her business.

Copper coins pressed into Slip's palm bought Salidar more information. Madam Iris was a *halfling*, born of a human mother and an unknown fairy father. She appeared to be of middle years, but Slip insisted that she'd been running the business for generations. Salidar chose to take that assertion with a grain of salt. Slip, apparently human, could not be older than sixteen or seventeen summers; therefore, he would likely only be repeating popular rumor or hearsay.

Despite his apparent youth, the wily rascal had firmly negotiated Salidar's initial offer of a few coppers into an agreed upon amount of silver for periodic reports of timely information. For the past few days, the boy had met with Salidar twice a day, just after sunrise and sometime before sunset, to pass on any information. For the most part, it was a recitation of the most recent patrons of Madam Iris' establishment; nonetheless, Salidar listened with interest. After all, one never knew when such information might be useful.

Now, Slip was more than an hour late. Salidar found that most irritating; but, he could do little about it. The boy could be caught up in the festivities, and probably wasn't coming.

Stretching out upon the narrow bed, Salidar squirmed around a bit to get reasonably comfortable on the old straw mattress. He might as well nap for a few hours, then venture into the streets to seek out some of his other contacts. Besides, it was never his habit to rely upon just one source of information.

SALIDAR DIDN'T KNOW how long he'd been asleep; but, a persistent whining kept drifting past his ear, pulling him into a reluctant state of semiconsciousness. He flailed his hand over his head, hopefully to discourage the pest, no doubt a hungry mosquito. He hated to lose blood—for *any* reason. The aggravating nuisance continued; Salidar became increasingly irritated.

The timbre of the whine altered; it was wavering slightly, almost in short measured waves. Was this damned mosquito *laughing at him?* He was almost fully awake now, and sorely annoyed.

He barely heard the weak knock upon the room's door. For a moment he froze—had he really heard something, or not? The knock came once more, feeble yet insistent.

Salidar was out of bed in an instant and fumbled to light a candle. In the glow of the solitary flame, he found his dagger and stepped to the door. However, he heard nothing more.

Standing off to one side, he opened the door and raised the candle to illuminate the darkened hall. At first he saw nothing; but there, on the shadowed floor, lay Slip, unmoving and breathing in shallow gasps.

Seeing no one else, Salidar sheathed his dagger, placed the candle on the floor, and carefully dragged Slip into the small room. The young man was conscious, but limp, and barely able to speak. He moaned and mumbled something as Salidar retrieved the candle and quickly shut the door.

In the taper's poor light, Salidar could see no wound or mark on the young man. Yet his eyes were barely half open and he seemed only somewhat aware.

Salidar shook the boy's thin shoulders. "Slip! You are late! Where have you been? What happened to you? Are you hurt? Are you *drunk*, lad?"

Slip wet his lips and managed to whisper, "N-nay, d-drugged methinks, the wine and ale—something in the drinks. The one y' seek was there; arrived alone just before sunset, he did. Many patrons be in the house then, an' among `em, a group of seafaring men. Water? Have y' any water?"

Salidar quickly poured a measure of water from his traveling flask into a small cracked cup and held it to the boy's lips. The lad sipped greedily; but Salidar would not let him drink too much, or too quickly.

"Thankee, good sir," Slip said, a bit more comprehensively. "I feels better. I think m-maybe this drug, wearin' off it be."

Salidar poured more water and handed the cup to the boy, who had managed to sit up. "Here, sip this slowly, take your time, and tell me what happened."

Slip nodded as he took the cup. "Aye, twas late in the afternoon. About to leave the house, I was. Madam Iris stopped me and asked that I pass a round of drinks to the patrons in the front parlor—twas a good crowd. She pointed out two new casks for me to tap. This big sailor had come with these two casks, wine and ale, and offered `em up to the house. Of course, Madam accepted. So, like a good lad, I tapped, poured, and served. Aye, twas then I spied him arrive, that man, the one you set me to watch for. Alone, he be. Madam Iris greeted him all warm-like; took him up to her rooms, she did. Ah, more water, if'n you please, good sir?"

Salidar tamped down his impatience as he refilled the cup and prodded the boy to continue. "Sip slowly, now—there's a good lad. Then what happened—with the man, I mean?"

"Alas, see him again, I did not. But . . ."

"But what?"

"Ah well, y' see, had me a little sip of that wine when no one was looking, din't I? Twas good enough, methinks. The big sailor insisted all loud-like, w' jolly curses `n' all, that everyone keep drinking. Raised his mug in many a toast, he did. At first, methinks he just wants to get drunk along with everyone else. But then, spied I, him and his mates—his *crew*, he called them—raised their mugs to their lips, toast upon toast, they did, but drank nary a drop. Refilled many times the other patrons' cups, I did—but never theirs. Strange that, eh?"

"Indeed," agreed Salidar, his suspicions leaning toward confirmation. "Go on."

"Um, tis fuzzy, but the last thing I can remember was stumbling a bit as I made m' way back t' the kitchen. Then on the floor, I be, when I wakes up. Everyone else, all the patrons and the girls, all passed out in the parlor, they be. The big sailor and his crew be gone; at least I *think* they all be gone. Twas dark then, and late. To you here, I knew I had to come. Aye, in truth, made it, I did, but not sure quite how."

"You did well," Salidar assured him. "What about the man who went with Madam Iris?"

"I-I do not know," Slip stammered. "Into her rooms, forbidden to go, me."

"Can you walk now?"

Slip tried to rise, rocked to one side, almost losing his balance, and sat back down heavily. "Oof, y' pardon, good sir. The room, it swims."

"Never mind! Stay here until you feel better. I must go." Salidar pressed two silver coins into the boy's hand. "Speak of this to no one! Do you understand?"

Slip nodded slowly, his confusion evident; but, his attention was clearly focused upon the silver coins on his palm.

Salidar grabbed his pack and staff and reached for the door. Turning back, he made sure he had left nothing behind, and regarded Slip ominously.

"Remember—*no one!* Wait until first light. You will be safe; the room is paid for. Lock the door. You have not seen me."

Salidar slipped into the dark hallway, quietly closing the door. He waited a moment until he heard the soft *click* of the lock, then disappeared down the staircase.

As he passed through the common room, he saw that the fire had burned low and only a few revelers were left, hunched around the glowing hearth, still drinking and leaning upon one another for support. More costumed people lay about on benches or slumped over tables, snoring loudly.

As Salidar silently passed one drunken sleeper, he relieved him of a dark half-mask that resembled a cat, complete with feline ears and whiskers. If Salidar was going to venture out in the streets, it appealed to him to be masked. Most celebrants were incognito; so, it would be wiser to blend in, as anonymously as possible.

He draped his cloak over his pack, fitted the mask on his face, and flipped up his hood. He now resembled a bipedal hunchbacked cat. Leaning heavily upon his staff, he exaggerated a bogus limp as he lurched forth into the street.

THE CROWDS WERE NO longer as dense; but, there were far more people about than Salidar had expected. The mood was still festive; but, there was a drunken edge to the otherwise benign chaos, the sort of ominous air that warns of easily tapped belligerence and potential violence. Salidar tried to give the swaggering groups a wide berth. If someone came too close for comfort, he would start coughing and gagging as if very ill. That trick was fairly effective, and most avoided him—but not everyone.

"Hold there, good man—are you unwell?"

Salidar found himself confronted by two men of the Derinseum Watch; he had not seen them approach. In this crowd, it should not have been surprising; but, he cursed himself for not being more observant. He now had no choice but to play out his ruse.

“Ah, good sirs . . . I am fine—too much food, and perhaps the wine was a bit old. I am bound for a bed,” Salidar said earnestly and gestured down the street.

One of the watchmen chuckled and pointed in the same direction. “Well now, good man, the only beds available in that direction be those of Madam Iris and her ladies. Would that be your destination, now?”

Salidar paled under the mask, but he brazened it out. “Why, no, good sir, I did not know of this. But do you recommend *such beds?*”

The other watchman leaned forward and uttered conspiratorially, “Aye, good man, if you are of such a mind, you could do no better. Tis a fine establishment.”

“And, it would be wise to find your entertainments indoors this late,” offered the first man. “Between now and the dawn there is always the chance of problems with a few of these bolder groups. Anyone out alone might draw their attention—*if* you take my meaning, good man.”

“I do, good sir, I do indeed,” responded Salidar, coughing lightly and swiping his chin with the edge of his cloak. “Perhaps you can direct me?”

“Aye, that we can, good man. Tis that fine home, yonder. You have a fine night, now, good man.”

“I thankee, good sirs. And a fine night have you, as well,” said Salidar gratefully, and then feigned a mild coughing spell.

The watchmen hastily stepped back and then continued down the street. Salidar headed for the shadows. He encountered no one else, and was soon at the door of Madam Iris’ establishment.

THERE WAS NO RESPONSE to his knock, so Salidar pushed the unlocked door open and slipped inside. Not really knowing what to expect, and not wanting to be surprised from behind, he took a moment to turn the lock, securing the door behind him.

The light was dim; only a few low candles still burned and the hearth held only glowing embers. The scene was just as Slip had described. Bodies lay about, not in repose, but as if suddenly collapsed. Salidar felt for a pulse on one woman—nothing. Another was barely breathing. If this was the result of some drug, he assumed that sufficient quantities could poison. Some of the bodies in the parlor were already growing cold in death.

Padraic!

Salidar spun in a circle, spied the staircase, and sprinted to the upper floor. In the darkened hallway, he tugged his hood back and tore off his mask.

He tried every door on that floor. Some rooms were empty; but most were not. He did not recognize any of the unmoving bodies, nor did he stop to check for signs of life. He kept searching.

At the back of the hall he found another set of stairs, which he hastily ascended.

A solitary door stood closed at the top of a candlelit landing. He turned the knob, but the door wouldn't open more than a crack. He put his shoulder to it and carefully shoved. It moved a little more; clearly something was blocking it near its base.

He listened carefully, but heard nothing. Abandoning his usual caution, he grunted, giving the door a mighty shove. It swung wide, as a limp bloody body rolled away from the door.

This room was small, like a reception area, and opened to a much larger room, almost the size of the entire attic, but dimly lit. A lone candle guttered somewhere low in the big room, near the floor, in the vicinity of a set of open windows on the rear wall. Huge shadows cast by the furnishings pulsed around the room in the bleak flickering light.

Salidar returned to the landing and took the candle from its wall sconce. Holding the taper low, he allowed the paltry light to wash across the face of the dead man. It was not Padraic. No poisoning here; it was clear this unfortunate had succumbed to a gaping stab wound in the neck. Moving the weak light down the length of the prone body revealed coarse seaman's clothing and the calloused hands of a sailor.

So, not of the house staff. . . A customer? Or miscreant?

Carefully making his way deeper into the larger space, he realized the room was in shambles; someone had fought fiercely here. Blood spatter shone in the candlelight like wet ink spots; a smeared crimson trail led toward the open windows. He followed cautiously.

A soft moan froze him in his tracks—another drew his attention to an upended bed to his right. He approached, holding the candle high. Something moved beneath the disheveled bedclothes on the floor. Flicking the sheets aside with the end of his staff, he found a woman in a nightgown, bound and gagged.

As he bent to help her, he heard another sound—a scraping followed by a groan—somewhere behind him. The woman's eyes went wide with fear—then flared with rage. She started to shake; whether from fear or anger, Salidar knew not.

Placing his finger to his lips for silence, Salidar whispered, "We are *not* alone."

Her eyes narrowed in impatience as she nodded and tilted her head so he could more easily remove the gag. She then turned silently on her side, so his dagger could quickly sever the ropes that secured her hands behind her back. She carefully rubbed her tingling wrists, as his blade easily sliced through the ropes securing her feet.

The scraping sound came again, like boots trying in vain to find purchase on the smooth boards of the floor.

Salidar and the woman froze, looking into each other's eyes. In the candlelight, her long unbound hair cascaded over her shoulders and entangled in the lace of the gown's low neckline. With deft flicks of her freed wrists, she tossed her chestnut tresses over her shoulders with practiced ease. Her brows knit in concentration and her full lips narrowed to a determined line.

She pointed to his knife, and opened her palm; she wanted the weapon.

He hesitated only for an instant, then handed her the dagger, hilt first. He gripped his staff and slowly stood, looking in the direction of the last sound.

She arose as well, and he noticed she was almost his height. Her short nightgown hung only to mid-thigh and her arms were bare; she was lean and well muscled. Salidar would not have guessed her age beyond the mid-thirties; and yet he sensed that he would have been wrong by a considerable margin.

A finger to her lips, she pointed into the room's dark recesses, and without a sound, padded off into the shadows. Salidar hesitated, then followed, holding the candle before him and gripping his staff for reassurance.

He flinched at the sudden crash of toppled furniture and the sounds of an ensuing struggle, but quickly recovered and rushed forward. Rounding a tilted armoire, he found a man trying to choke the flailing woman and pry the knife from her hand. Without a second thought, Salidar set the candle aside and swung the butt of his staff in a wide arc, thumping the man just above his ear. The assailant collapsed like a sack of potatoes, nearly smothering the squirming woman.

"Get this *pig off me!*" she gasped.

Salidar grabbed the dazed man's collar and rolled him free of her.

She was on her feet in an instant, the blade vibrating in her fist, her fury unquenched. A bruise was beginning to rise along the side of her throat. With visible effort, she fought to calm herself, and regarded Salidar critically. "Now, just who are you? Why are you here?" She watched him carefully, never relinquishing the dagger.

"I am Salidar—I have nothing to do with any of this! I simply came here to deliver a message to Padraic the Rogue. However, it appears that I am too late. Neither this man, nor the one by the door is he. And who might you be?"

"I am the proprietress here, Madam Iris," she said with more than a trace of pride, and raised the point of the dagger a bit. "And why do you seek the Rogue—the bounty?"

"Ha! Were that the case, it would seem that someone has beaten me to it. But I have already told you that I am only here to deliver a message. Now I must search anew, for he is not here now."

"Aye," she admitted, "he was taken—*forcibly*—by these *louts.* And I have no doubt for the *damned bounty!*"

"Can you tell me what happened? It may aid me in my search."

"Aye, I owe you that much—my thanks for your assistance," she acknowledged and squared her shoulders. "I don't know how long it would have taken me to free myself. I didn't even know that *this bastard,*" she emphasized her disdain by delivering a swift kick to the ribs of the unconscious seaman, "was still here! The others—there must have been half a dozen of the blackguards—made off through the windows. And, aye, they took Padraic, all trussed up, with them."

Suddenly she looked at him wide-eyed. "You don't suppose there are any more of them about, do you?"

He shook his head. "Other than the dead sailor by the door, I think not, madam. I should tell you that many of your patrons, and staff as well, I found on the floors below. All are, at best, unconscious—but I fear that some are certainly dead. Drugged or poisoned, I know not for certain. The front door was closed but not locked. I secured it when I entered, after receiving no response to my knocking. Perhaps you should summon the city watch?"

Madam Iris had grown very still as she listened to his words. Only the whitening of her knuckles as she grasped the dagger's hilt betrayed her rising ire. She mumbled something that Salidar could barely hear, but her voice grew in strength and he easily understood her.

"Drugged? The bosun's casks! *Damn his eyes!*" she fumed, and then immediately fought to compose herself. "The watch will have to wait, Salidar. I have an *arrangement* with the watch, and the Merchants Association. No word of this event will be upon public tongues—*bad for business, tourism might suffer.* It will be as though it never happened. But I *will* know who is responsible for this! Help me get this one into a chair, and then fetch those ropes."

Salidar did as she asked and they soon had the groggy sailor well secured in the wooden chair.

Salidar pointed to his knife, which Madam Iris still held deftly in her left hand, like one skilled in its use. "Madam Iris, do you intend some sort of torture to get the information you seek?"

"Nothing so crude, I assure you, Salidar. I will resort to a *truth spell* of sorts, nothing as sophisticated as that used by elves, but nonetheless as effective. A little *blood magic* will serve."

That caught Salidar's attention. *Blood magic* was a remnant of very old sorcery usually attributed to the Old Ones; and, as its name implied, it required fresh blood to work effectively. It was not exactly *black magic* or even especially dark-natured sorcery; but, it certainly was *grey*—and dangerous. For it was thought that if certain doors, better left alone, might be opened, even if only a crack, it just might be enough for something unsavory to slip through. Then the subject of the spell, or even the spell caster if the slightest bit careless or inept, could be exposed to grievous harm, demonic possession, or much, much worse.

As Salidar watched, Madam Iris made her preparations, and kept up a rambling account of what had transpired earlier that evening.

"It was a good crowd for the start of the festival, and my staff was kept busy. A visiting ship's crew arrived and offered casks of wine and ale for the house; rounds were poured and served. I took Padraic to my rooms upon his arrival, so neither of us sampled the gifted drinks. I thought all was well."

Madam Iris chalked a large double circle on the planks of the wooden floor, completely enclosing the seated, semiconscious man.

"But within the hour, six burly salts burst into my chambers and tried to seize the Rogue. Aye, he fought like a whirlwind, laying two of them out in no time at all. He would have likely rendered them all bloody senseless had not the bosun and another man seized me, and held sharp steel to my throat. Aye, twas the only way the blackguards secured Padraic's surrender."

Her captive was now fully aware, and graced them with a surly sneer.

She ignored his insolence and set about carefully chalking a succession of runes and symbols within the twin lines of the large circle.

"Padraic then warned them that he would curse them and any ship they might sail upon were they to harm me in any way. Y' should've seen their faces pale at that! Sailors tend to be a superstitious lot, and such a threat from a rogue fey tis not taken lightly. So, they bound and gagged us both. Me, they left unharmed and bundled in the bedclothes; him they took. But I saw it all; they made their escape through the rear windows, down a rope ladder. Twas much later that you came. Y've my thanks, Salidar. Now, let me be about this business."

Her preparations finished, she slapped chalk dust off her hands, and stood before her prisoner.

"Never let it be said that Madam Iris did not give a man the chance to square away. Now tis your chance, me bucko. Tell me your *true name,* and we'll have a comfortable conversation. Do not, and we will still have the conversation; but you'll be findin' it a mite uncomfortable. Now, what'll it be?"

The hard man simply scowled at her and spat on the floor.

"So, that's how it's to be. Very well—remember, you were given the fair chance." Stepping carefully into the circle, without disturbing the chalked lines, she leaned into his face. "But your spittle won't do—I need your blood!"

With a flash of her wrist, she sliced his cheek with the knife; a line of blood welled forth as he grimaced and cursed at her.

She held a small cloth to his bleeding face; but, it was no act of compassion. She let the cloth become soaked, dripping in his blood. Carefully stepping out of the circle, she placed the bloody wad in a shallow bowl and recited a brief incantation over it. She then took the dagger and dipped its point into the blood. She started a soft chant and began to sway to its cadence. Then keeping with the slow rhythm of her chant, she paced sinuously around the circle, allowing a drop of the man's blood to fall from the blade's point upon each symbol and rune.

When each mark had been thus baptized, she set the bowl to the side of the circle and went to a small cupboard. Taking an unmarked bottle from within, she returned to the bloody bowl. Pouring from the bottle, down the dagger's blade, she filled the bowl to its brim.

Salidar caught the scent of liquor as she poured. He thought it especially strong, and dared to ask, "Rum?"

She smiled. "Aye, the finest, not some watered grog as this poor fool is used to."

The restrained man sneered and tried to staunch his bleeding cheek by pressing his jaw against his shoulder.

Madam Iris considered the bottle for a moment, then brought it to her lips, upending it in a long draught. Handing the bottle to Salidar, she smacked her lips. "Tis a shame to waste such good rum on the likes of this scum. Have a taste if you like. Don't interrupt me now; this spell can be a bit dicey."

Salidar eschewed tasting the rum, putting it aside. He watched Madam Iris in fascination as she recited another incantation over the brimming bowl. Then taking a candle, she dipped its flame toward the side of the bowl until the alcohol fumes ignited. A blue flame leapt up, dancing above the rim, and small greenish sparks began to flare within the flickering azure shape.

The more Salidar stared at the flame, the more he thought he could make out a small purple form within—tiny head and shoulders, arms and hands—grabbing and consuming the verdant sparks. He watched in awe, not quite believing what he thought he saw, until the flame winked out. He leaned forward and lifted the candle high. The bowl was now completely empty, no trace of rum, blood, or cloth remained—not even any ash residue.

The chalk circle began to glow with a soft purple light, and the characters within its band began to pulse with a sickly green flare. Salidar realized, with a bit of a shock, that the meter of the flaring pulses matched the heartbeat of the restrained man.

Madam Iris placed the knife on the floor, stood before the prisoner and held her empty hands, palms down, before her. She whispered something under her breath and allowed her voice to rise in volume, until her final comment was heard as a command.

". . . and now, by such powers, you will, this moment, tell me your true name!"

The man's face was deathly pale. It was evident that he resisted with every fiber of his being, all to no avail.

"T-Thomas Cutfin Cambridge . . ."

Her eyes narrowed and she smiled. Salidar sensed that she had the sailor now; he could withhold nothing from her.

"How are you called by your shipmates?" she asked.

"Dogshark of the Seadogs . . ." he replied, his voice taking on a toneless drone that seemed to wind down as he answered.

"Seadogs?" she repeated, alarmed. "Bloody pirates! Who is your captain?"

"M'lord Captain Bloody Bane."

"Bane, eh? Does he still captain the *Doom Wind*?"

"Aye, he does."

"Where is she berthed?"

"She is anchored offshore, outside the harbor, in sight of the East Inlet."

"How came you ashore—her boats?"

"Nay, a junk sailed with us. We boarded her to enter the harbor and come ashore."

"What name does the junk bear?"

"She bears no name. Her crew refers to her as the *Xanthippe.*"

Iris balked in momentary surprise, her lips thinning in a grim line. "A crew of eight, who hardly ever speak?"

"Aye."

"Is Padraic the Rogue bound for the *Doom Wind* by passage aboard the junk?"

"Aye."

"Is the *Xanthippe* still in the harbor?"

"I know not."

"Very well. I command you to sleep."

The sailor slumped forward, unconscious.

"What now?" asked Salidar, impressed with the simple effectiveness of the ensorcelled interrogation.

"I must deal with this mess within my establishment, and soon. I cannot hold off the watch for too long." She picked up the dagger and sighed, looking around at the destruction of her room. "You need not be here when they arrive—I have enough to explain. Besides, you now know where Padraic is bound, and how."

He merely nodded as he tried to digest what he had just learned.

Facing him, she cautioned, "Be warned, Salidar. These vermin are undoubtedly *pirates;* Captain Bane has long been suspected of piracy. And since Thomas, here, has confirmed that the crew of the *Doom Wind* is actually the pirate band known as the *Seadogs*, we have proof enough for even the timid Merchants Association to take some sort of action."

"What would this Merchants Association do? Rescue Padraic, or at least attempt to do so?" He considered the complications this might present.

"No, I think not, at least not a rescue, per se. Remember, there is a bounty on his head; so, that may appeal to some. However, these pirates—*the bastards*—harmed innocents during the Fertility Festival in seizing him; that will be deemed a serious offense."

"So, they'll hunt the pirates?"

She shrugged and admitted, "To be honest, I doubt it. Perhaps a search could be organized, but not likely in time. It would be a challenge in the midst of the festival. The watch is already committed and spread thin; it would take too long to muster volunteers. They'll no doubt formally declare Captain Bane a *pirate* and put a price on his head; beyond that, I would not expect too much. Of course, once this episode of the Rogue's tale circulates, more bounty hunters may take up the chase."

"Damn the luck," cursed Salidar. "I still have to find Padraic and deliver the message. I have no choice."

He pointed to his dagger in the hope it was no longer required by her.

Madam Iris shrugged and returned the knife. She stared at the slumped man tied to the chair.

"Salidar, listen to me. My guess is that Bane and his scoundrels are just after the bounty, or perhaps a ransom; but they will have to get away from Derinseum and Essa first. They will soon be wanted men for what they have done here. That means they have to get to the *Doom Wind* at the soonest opportunity. She's known to be a fast ship; I doubt anything the Merchants Association could press into service could catch her."

He sighed in frustration. “Bloody hell!”

Iris shrugged in sympathy and continued.

“You will have to find this junk, the *Xanthippe.* But beware; I have heard of this vessel. Its master is a woman said to be a sea witch; its crew rumored to be ensorcelled.” She then surprised him by making a very old defensive gesture with thumb and forefinger traditionally used by peasants to ward off the *evil eye* before she continued. “But I think you may have time enough to find it. The harbor is very crowded during the festival; however, they are not likely to attempt to depart in darkness, nor without a favorable tide.”

“Is there not a lighthouse?”

“Aye, there is,” she acknowledged, “but it does not provide enough light by itself to avoid the reefs and shoals. The channel markers can barely be seen at all in the dark.”

“And what is to become of him?” He gestured to the sleeping captive.

Madam Iris sighed. “I, too, have no choice. He will be turned over to the watch. He has broken the laws of hospitality during the festival; he and his brethren employed force and did harm. I did not understate that this is a serious offense; his life is now forfeit. Actually, I knew that he was lost the instant he yielded his true name.”

“I see. It appears that there is little more I can do here. But I am reluctant to leave you alone. You will be all right?”

She smiled and assured him, “I appreciate your concern, but I will be fine. You really should hurry. The tide will turn shortly after sunrise. You can be assured the *Xanthippe* will put to sea at the earliest opportunity.”

“Then I shall bid you farewell, Madam Iris,” he said bowing, “and you have my thanks.”

“You have *my* thanks, as well, Salidar. Perhaps we shall meet again. Fair winds and following seas.”

He nodded. *Yes, I do believe I would like to see you again. You are an impressive woman.*

Salidar made his way through the dimly illuminated house and paused at the front door. The macabre scene in the front room had softened by degrees now that the few remaining candles burned lower, but the morbid pall lingered. He would not soon forget this needless tragedy. He felt an unaccountable measure of sympathy for the woman who would have to deal with it. This surprised him; he shook off this unbidden, and unexpected, flare of empathy and left the house.

It was still several hours until dawn; the dark held sway over all but for the sparse glow of staggered lampposts. A few revelers were still roaming the streets. He put the cat mask on and pulled his hood up, thinking it better, under the circumstances, to be incognito once more. He made directly for the harbor, moving as quickly as he dared, for he wanted to attract no undue attention.

A BLOCK AWAY, WITHIN the deepest shadows of an alley, a short wiry figure, no more than two hand spans high, looked up to another, somewhat taller and far shapelier figure in the night, whose voice was wetly musical.

"Twit, you are certain he goes to the harbor? Do you not have your lads watching, even now?"

"Aye, Selene," he twittered. "They be on him like green on the grass. He goes, all determined like, toward the harbor." The dour minor fairy pointed to the south and then wiped his sharp-featured nose along his narrow sleeve.

"And you found the junk? The Rogue is aboard?" she pressed.

"Aye, we found the *Xan*—"

"Hush! Speak not that name! You should know better!"

"Forgive this old spriggan," Twit bemoaned. "I forgets m'self sometimes. Ye'll not be tellin' Tullos, now, would ye?"

"He would not be amused with you, now would he?" she scolded. "Keep your wits about you!"

"I thankee, missy—I'll be sharp, I will! Twas no trouble; we found the boat. The Rogue was taken aboard; all trussed up, he was. But, the likes of us canna go aboard—there be some strong wards on that vessel, and a taint of some darker magic."

"Have you got someone watching it now, Twit?"

"What do ye take me for, Selene, an addle-headed sprite? Of course, m' lads watch, even now. We'll know when Salidar finds it, too."

"Then under the circumstances, well done, Twit," she conceded. "Please maintain your vigilance. I have to see Tullos now and keep him informed."

"Give `im my regards. Ah, not be mentioning, um, my little slip, will ye?"

"Not *this* time, but be careful, Twit. Remember, we are only to observe; we are not to interfere. I *know* that you took certain liberties when Salidar needed to be awakened in his room at the inn. Do not let that happen again! There may be unpredictable forces involved that can be quite dangerous, as you well know."

"Aye, missy, that I do, that I do. Now, away with ye—I gots me work to do." With a wink and a nod, Twit's small grotesque form faded into invisibility.

Selene heard a trace of his high-pitched twittering laugh as she turned toward her own path. She couldn't suppress a small smile.

DOWN AT THE HARBOR, Salidar found the *Xanthippe* easily enough; it was the only vessel at the docks with any activity upon her decks. Lanterns hung from her mast cast an eerie glow amidships as a number of stevedores carried sacks, boxes, and barrels aboard and stowed the provisions in her hold.

Near the junk, two team-less wagons laden with goods stood unattended on the dark dock.

Salidar crept forward for a better look, but kept hidden in the shadows. He could see that the stevedores were almost through with a shrinking stack of crates to his left. They'd start unloading these two wagons soon enough. He was about to move off lest he be discovered, when he heard a voice rising in anger.

". . . and I'm bloody telling ye that we have to shove off *now!* Y' can come back for the rest of the bloody cargo!"

"Like hell! I have my orders, mate! And my mistress has not yet returned. Besides, most of these provisions are for *your* bloody ship! We will follow *her* orders; finish loading the cargo, and await my mistress. The soonest we sail will be with the morning tide. Now, you and your men can either help with the loading, or stay out of the way! It was hard enough to find dockhands willing to work during the festival, much less *at night!* I need no more problems. So, you can either help or move aside. Or would you prefer to incur *her* wrath?"

Salidar heard no more conversation between the two, only the angry crunch of boots as one man stormed away.

"Right . . . Well done, lads! Those two wagons next; that'll be the last of `em. Look lively, now!"

Peeking through the spokes of the wagon wheels, Salidar saw half a dozen silhouettes start toward him. Slipping further back into the shadows, he stuffed his cloak and mask into his pack and threaded his staff through its straps. He hovered soundlessly and waited. He dared not make his move until the junk's bosun was preoccupied and the wagons were nearly empty.

Salidar's chance came. He slipped from the shadows and hefted a sack of grain over his shoulders. He managed to hide his pack and staff under the bulk of the sack. Following the last man up the gangplank, he successfully came aboard the junk. But just as he stepped upon the deck, he felt a mild tingling twinge and almost stumbled. He quickly recovered and kept moving, following the man ahead of him down the hold's ladder, desperately hoping no one noticed an extra dockhand. He dropped his burden atop a pile of similar sacks and slipped unseen behind a row of stacked barrels.

He knew he had crossed a *warding* of some type; that twinge he'd felt when he came aboard was an unmistakable clue. He relaxed and allowed his eyes to lose focus. The old trick worked after a moment. Where bulkhead met deck and overhead, he could barely discern a sickly purple glow with sable figures floating within, arcane runes he could not read. This vessel was assuredly warded in some fashion; but just how, he knew not. That was enough to cause his stomach to clench.

What if this warding is akin to that which prevents any transit spells? Perhaps I should wait until I am off this vessel before I should try to transit—I would not want to become incapacitated on board. I can only hope I haven't triggered some sort of alarm. At least no one has reacted—not yet.

Apparently, there was no way out of the cargo hold other than the way in, or at least none that he could find in a very brief scan of his surroundings. As more cargo was brought aboard, the less space there was in the hold.

It is starting to get cramped in here; I'll need to move soon. Getting aboard was fairly easy. So, I'll just follow the last man up the ladder when they return, and then lose myself in the shadows on the deck. It shouldn't be too difficult to stay unnoticed in the darkness. Of course, I still have to find Padraic and deliver the message.

Hmm, it's been a while since that last bit of cargo was brought down here. What could be keeping them?

Oh no! Could they be finished loading the cargo?

That sobering thought spurred him to action. He snatched at the straps of his pack as he scrambled from his hiding place and moved toward the ladder. Suddenly his pack snagged on something unseen among the piled cargo and he rocked to one side, nearly losing his balance. He tugged firmly on the straps, and the pack pulled free. His staff came loose, promptly entangling his ankles and tripping him. He pitched forth, face first, into the base of the ladder. His jaw connected with a lower step with a resounding *crump;* his eyes rolled up in his head.

In his dwindling consciousness, the last thing he saw was the overhead hatch slamming shut, and merciful darkness.

SALIDAR FINALLY CAME to with the gentle rocking of the vessel's rolling motion. He was at sea!

He heard voices from somewhere above him—*the main deck?* He managed to sit up, and was rewarded with a flare of pain in his tender jaw and a throbbing headache. A sudden wave of nausea washed over him, but he managed to calm his roiling stomach.

This is not good—I must remain calm. I must think! How long have I been unconscious? How far out to sea am I?

Footsteps overhead interrupted his thoughts. With the creak of old wood, the hatch opened a few inches allowing bright sunlight to stream into the dark hold.

Salidar frantically crabbed backwards out of the light; he must not be discovered! Still, he could taste the tang of salt air as he scrambled to hide amidst the cargo.

The hatch now fully open, the cargo hold was awash with daylight.

The bosun's voice boomed from above. "Get to it, lads! Bring up the *Wind's* cargo and secure it on deck. We'll offload to her boats within the hour. Redistribute and secure our own provisions. I'll not have her prone to list—not with a storm comin' on in two days time."

"The mistress foresaw a storm?" asked another voice.

"Aye, she did; it'll be a bad one. We'll do our best to outrun it. Now get below, me buckoes! We're in sight of the *Doom Wind* already!"

Two men scrambled down the ladder and arranged an open cargo net. They repeatedly placed stacks of assorted cargo in the net's center; sacks of grain and milled flour, barrels of salt pork, fresh water and rum, and various crates and boxes. They then stood back as successive netted loads were hoisted by means of an overhead block and tackle.

As they bent to the task of refilling the cargo net, Salidar spied a cleverly camouflaged hatch at the base of the aft bulkhead, something he hadn't seen before—a good thing, too. He was running out of cargo to hide behind and would soon be discovered.

At one point, a crate shifted as the cargo net rose; a pair of long boxes slipped loose and crashed back down to the hold's deck. Both boxes broke open; the contents, assorted edged weapons, cutlasses and boarding axes, clattered forth in disarray.

"Avast, y' bumblin' fools! Get that cargo gathered! Carry it up here, you louts; and bring the broken containers! Ship's carpenter to the main deck; mend them boxes!"

While the two sailors were distracted, Salidar stealthily made his way to the concealed hatch and found it secured with a hidden but simple locking latch. That was hardly a challenge to one such as him. He defeated the lock in a matter of seconds. He crawled through the small opening and pulled his staff and pack in after him.

The hatch secured once more, he found himself crouched in a narrow space between bulkheads, its overhead about shoulder high—no doubt a smuggler's cache. Thin cracks between the broad boards allowed just enough light to filter through for him to see almost to arm's length. Maintaining a stooped crouch, he found he could maneuver fairly unhindered through the shoulder-width space.

The level of this deck was a bit lower than the hold; he surmised it must be just above the bilge. There was a bit of debris, making his footing somewhat unsure. He heard some scratching and scurrying in the darker recesses. Something bold and furry ran across his foot. A rat, he guessed, only a rat—or so he hoped. He pressed on, feeling his way for the most part.

He stubbed his toe on something solid in the gloom. *What—a wooden box?*

Reaching out, he realized it was a stack of small crates. In the dimness, he counted ten. His curiosity was instantly aroused. *Now what kind of contraband would be hidden in a smuggler's cache on a vessel such as this, I wonder?*

He was sorely tempted to pry one open—just for a small peek—and even drew his dagger for the job; but, he hesitated. On a hunch, he stared at the stack in the near dark, and let his focus relax. Sure enough, he soon saw that the entire pile pulsed with the same sickly purple glow he'd seen in the hold. But something was different; the ominous blackened runes that seemed to waver in the glow were repeated, in a larger font, fire-branded upon each box.

Some of these runes he thought he recognized, *wards* of a very dark origin. He had seen them recently, on a page in an open book of great age, in the Baron Von Kestel's library, a tome scrutinized by Magus Jalash-el in preparation for a *rite of execution*.

No, he would not tempt fate by tampering with any of these curious crates.

Sheathing his dagger, he moved carefully past the hidden cargo, and soon found a small hatch at about elbow height. Crouching to one side of the hatch, he pressed his ear to the wood of the aft bulkhead. Muffled gruff voices were easily heard in this compartment. He moved on.

Within a few paces, he came to another hatch at the same height. He could hear a thumping, not truly rhythmic, but oddly repetitive. This one, he would investigate.

Carefully feeling around the hatch frame, his fingers found and released the inner latch. Gently pushing the hatch open, he saw that the access was at the lower deck level. He peered up into a dim compartment with spare furnishings. A dirty porthole was the sole source of light.

Salidar pulled himself through the hatch, and closed it behind him. The hatch seemed to disappear and become part of the woodwork of the bulkhead. If one did not know it was there, one would never notice it.

He looked about the simple compartment. It was bare but for a narrow bunk, which was tucked into the starboard bulkhead. Something was bundled on the bunk, something that moved, and *thumped* against the bulkhead.

He cautiously approached. The supine figure was man-shaped, wrapped in a bedsheet, and bound in ropes; a black hood covered its head. A seaman's knot secured the hood at the neck. Salidar carefully untied the knot, and slowly pulled off the hood.

Padraic!

The gagged captive's eyes blinked, then bored into Salidar's own. Defiance and confidence flared in the depths of Padraic's intense stare—as did an unspoken question—*who are you?*

Salidar cast his eyes about and explained in a pinched whisper as he untied the ropes.

"M'lord Padraic, please make no sound, lest we be discovered. I am Salidar, sent by the Lady Diere, to deliver a message, an invitation to visit with her, and, if necessary, to assist in an escape from your present circumstances."

His hands free, Padraic tugged the gag loose, licked his parched lips, and wheezed, "So *you* say! How do I know this is true—and you seek not the *bounty* on my head?"

"Ah! One moment, m'lord."

Fishing in the depths of his pouch, he produced the topaz ring and presented it to Padraic.

"M'lord, Lady Diere instructed me to give you this ring. It confirms my *bona fides,* and is your means of transit, if you accept her invitation. It may presently serve as your means of escape. You need only twist the stone in its setting for the spell to work."

Padraic took the ring and examined it closely. "This is strong elfin magic. Very well, I accept that you speak the truth. But, if I am to escape—I can see that the spell will only transport one—what is to become of you, Salidar?"

Salidar's face fell. "M'lord, I was supposed to find you in Derinseum. Then I was to stay for the festival. But now, we are at sea. I have a modest ability with transit spells, but I fear this vessel is *warded.* Somehow, I must get off this ship, or at least to the uppermost deck, undetected. Perhaps a transit spell would work from there . . . Oh, m'lord, I just thought, will these wards impact the ring's spell?"

Padraic paused in thought. "Not likely; these wards are not of elfin origin. I sensed them when I was brought aboard. They are of insufficient strength to impact the ring; but as for your innate transit ability, I have doubts. However, you may be right, if you could get to the uppermost deck, or perhaps the rigging. Of course, you must remain undetected, an unlikely event under the circumstances. These pirates will kill you out of hand upon discovery, unless . . ."

"M'lord?"

"Salidar, I have an idea."

THE TWO VESSELS FLOATED a short distance apart, riding at anchor in sight of the East Inlet. Boats from the *Doom Wind* had made half a dozen trips to the *Xanthippe* to transfer cargo; and now, the two ships' business was nearly complete.

The final boat came over, bearing Captain Bloody Bane. A tall and robust man in the prime of life, wide of shoulder and stout of limb, he wore his black hair wild and free. He had woven his coarse black beard into half a dozen thick braids with small animal skulls affixed to the tips. His blood-red tricorn hat with the broken black ostrich feather had seen better days. However, he considered it *lucky;* so, he always donned the worn chapeau when conducting business.

He was quite conscious of the importance of maintaining the proper image as the master of the *Doom Wind,* one of the fastest sailing ships afloat. So, he wore a brace of muzzle-loaded percussion-cap pistols in his wide leather belt and his favorite cutlass sheathed at his hip. He fancied a scarlet sash draped over one shoulder and across the front of his black frock coat, once a commodore's proud surcoat, now sun-faded and spotted with old bloodstains. Unlike most of his barefoot crew, he wore soft leather boots that folded over just below his knees and revealed the hilts of hidden dirks.

He was just as ruthless as he appeared—and he relished in it.

As he stepped upon the deck of the *Xanthippe,* he acknowledged the junk's mistress. "My compliments, Lady Circe. I understand we have been successful, although at a cost."

An unnaturally thin woman with sharp patrician features stepped forth. She was clad in a high-collared narrow gown of blues and greens woven in a flowing seaweed pattern; a dark skullcap hood with a severe widow's peak accentuated her aquiline features. Her eyes were recessed well into her skull, and seemed to change color in varying waves of sea green. One bony hand, its long thin fingers tipped with black lacquered nails, gripped a twisted staff encrusted with dark gems and topped by a small stylized amethyst octopus. The other hand absently stroked an amphibious lizard that leered over her thin shoulder.

"Welcome aboard, Captain Bane. As to success, we shall see. I am told your men grew quite impatient and demanded an early departure—notwithstanding my previous orders to the contrary. I had my own business to conduct in Derinseum; otherwise, I would not have consented to make this voyage. I alone determine where and when this vessel sails. It appears your crew lacks discipline."

Captain Bane bristled. "My dear Lady Circe, *I* will be the judge of discipline when it comes to *my* crew! Now, if you do not mind . . . Bosun! Bring our guest forth!"

At the direction of the *Doom Wind's* bosun, two stocky sailors carried a bound and hooded form across the junk's main deck and dropped the sheet-wrapped bundle at their captain's feet. At a gesture from the *Doom Wind's* master, they snatched the captive up and jerked off the hood.

The gagged man blinked and squinted in the harsh sunlight.

Captain Bane leaned forward and examined the man's face closely. The pirate's expression darkened ominously. "Is this your idea of a joke, Circe?"

"What do you mean, Bane?" she responded coldly.

"I mean that *this*," he growled, spinning the captive around, "is *not* the Rogue! What game are you playing at here?"

"Look not to me for answers, Bane," she spat, then pointed at his bosun. "It was your men who snatched him and brought him aboard the *Xanthippe*—already trussed and hooded! *I* was not even aboard at the time. *Your* fumbling fools obviously grabbed the wrong man!"

"Bosun!" boomed Captain Bane. "What happened? Is this the man I sent you for? Answer me!"

"Aye-aye, Cap'n. He came in, hooded and all quick like, and went upstairs with the madam. We bust in on `em and he puts up a helluva fight—lays out two good men—but we take `im. Bag his head and truss `im up, and we makes for the docks. We put `im aboard this junk and locked `im in—never even untied `im. We put out with the morning tide, and here we are, uh, sir."

"Captain, if I may?" broached Circe.

Bane nodded in frustration, his mood no better.

"Bosun, have you ever seen Padraic the Rogue?" she asked.

"No, m'lady."

"Or any representation—or likeness?"

"No, m'lady."

"So, you had only a description of him, and a location where he would be?"

"Aye, m'lady, twas all we had."

Turning to Captain Bane, Circe said, "It appears that it may have been no more than a simple mistake, perhaps based on faulty information. How did you learn of the Rogue's supposed movements?"

Bane still scowled; he could see the possibility that the sea witch had it right. But she didn't need to know any more.

"I have my sources. But, more to the point, who is *this?*" He pointed to the bound and gagged man.

"Let us find out, shall we?" She smiled and tapped her staff twice upon the deck.

The gag was removed, none too gently, and the man gasped.

"Ah . . . w-water, please, water?"

Circe gestured and a pewter cup of water was held to the captive's lips.

"Now then," she cooed, "tell us who you are, and how you came to be here."

"I-I am Salidar . . . I was on the trail of Padraic the Rogue—the bounty, you know. I learned that he liked to frequent Madam Iris' establishment. I went there to question her, and perhaps sample the wares. But things did not go as planned; and well, you know the rest. More water, please?"

"He's another *bounty hunter?*" Captain Bane fumed and turned on his bosun. "You bagged a bloody bounty hunter by mistake? *Our bloody competition?*"

The bosun remained quiet, a wise strategy, as the captain started mumbling to himself and audibly grinding his teeth.

But one of the sailors came to the bosun's aid and murmured, "Well, it *was* bloody dark, and—"

Instantly, the pirate captain spun around, his cutlass flashing in a sweeping arc. The sailor's severed head thumped to the deck and rolled haphazardly, its eyes frantically shifting about, then listlessly staring into unfocused oblivion, like the final roll of *snake eyes* in a crapshoot.

The teetering body collapsed in stages; first, dropping to its knees, then slowly slumping forward, and finally flattening its chest and limp arms upon the deck with a soft *whump.* Bright arterial blood spurted briefly in diminishing arcs and began to drain slowly to and fro across the deck in patient cadence with the rolling pitch of the vessel.

Wiping his sword on the dead man's clothes, the captain stood, sheathed the blade with a flourish, and faced Circe. "How's *that* for discipline?"

The sea witch raised one eyebrow in mild annoyance.

Leaning into her face, Bane grinned evilly and hissed, "I have no need of your *special water* to keep a crew in line—*fear* does quite well. Oh yes, sorry about the mess."

The crewmen of both vessels kept wide-eyed silence.

Pointing to Salidar, Captain Bane decreed, "Take this one aboard the *Doom Wind* and hang him from the yard. I don't need, or *want*, the competition!"

"Hold a moment, if you please, Captain," Circe cautioned, in a voice dripping with condescension and irony. "I would not act too rashly."

She extended her arm diagonally; her lizard crawled down and dropped to the deck. Cautiously approaching the sailor's headless body, the reptile began to lap up the spilt blood. As it consumed more of the cooling sanguine spatter, its scaly skin began to take on hints of a ruddy crimson hue.

The sorceress smiled benevolently at her pet and commented absently. "It *is* possible that we may yet see some profit from this mess."

The mention of *profit* snagged Bane's attention. With some reluctance, he tore his eyes from the macabre scene. "Profit? Indeed? How so?"

She held up a finger for his patience. "Everyone *serves* someone, in some manner. Observe."

Turning to Salidar she spoke an incantation under her breath, and pressed her thumb to his lips.

Bane recognized it immediately; a very simple truth spell of short duration. But how this would turn a profit, he had yet to see.

"Tell me, Salidar, whom do you serve?" Circe asked.

Bane knew this was a direct question the damned bounty hunter could not avoid answering, no matter how fleeting the spell.

"I serve the Lady Diere of the Dark Elves."

Circe smiled at Bane. "This may yet work to our advantage. I have heard of this Dark Elf. To harm one who serves her would not be wise in the least. On the other hand, she may have no problem *ransoming* a loyal servant. Elves understand such things—especially Dark Elves. Join me in my cabin for a few moments and let us discuss this."

"Very well," Bane reluctantly agreed. "Bosun, keep him here—unharmed for now."

HELD ON THE DECK OF the junk, Salidar's mind was racing as witch and pirate discussed his fate.

Ransom? Padraic predicted this would occur to them—in fact he counted on it. But would Lady Diere actually even consider paying a ransom for me? Ye gods! Who am I kidding? Somehow, I'll have to get out of this one on my own.

The plan had been to transit out of this predicament at his earliest opportunity—that is, as soon as he had passed on the *disinformation* as to what had happened at Madam Iris' establishment. In fact, he rather enjoyed the Rogue's proposed ruse because it not only covered Padraic's escape, but it made unwitting fools of these captors.

Unfortunately, neither Padraic nor Salidar had adequately considered what role the sea witch, Circe, might play.

Special water?

Salidar sensed that there was something in the water he was given that further inhibited his transiting ability. Was this water ensorcelled or drugged, and thus kept her crew compliant and loyal? Was giving it to him intentional, or merely coincidental?

In a sudden flash of insight, he remembered Slip's tale about the drugged casks of wine and ale provided by certain seafaring customers—likely this very group from the *Doom Wind's* crew. No doubt the sea witch had a hand in the preparation of those casks as well.

A drug or a spell? Perhaps both? Were the subsequent deaths at Madam Iris' brothel intentional or merely the result of the general propensity during the festival for overindulgence?

Whatever the case, this truth spell was clearly deliberate. But wait, that enchantment is wearing off; I can feel its grip waning.

Circe and Bane returned. The pirate scowled and shrugged as the sorceress smiled and gestured with an open hand. Salidar sensed that they had agreed upon something.

The sea witch turned to him once more. "Salidar, would your mistress ransom you, given the opportunity?"

He took a deep breath, and in his most earnest voice responded, "Absolutely, I have no doubt."

Casting her gaze back to the pirate captain, Circe tilted her head and smiled. "You see, Bane, there is still some profit here. You will have to take him aboard the *Doom Wind* until ransomed."

"*What?* I'll not—" he began in protest.

"There is no other choice!" she spat. "He cannot stay aboard the *Xanthippe*—not where I am bound! No, do not even ask! You do *not* want to know!"

The buccaneer's expression soured into a sneering pout. He leaned into her and hissed, "You think I don't know your course will be set for the Southern Ocean, the Keys of Osiris, perhaps? Do you think I am without mine own resources? You know what is said, *that there are no secrets upon the seas—only thereunder.*"

She blanched. "What? How? Never mind—it matters not. The point is he will not be going with me—it is impossible."

Bane shrugged dismissively. "My sole concern is the possibility of profit—and profit alone!"

"I realize taking him aboard the *Doom Wind* is a bit of an imposition," she soothed, "so I will even forgo half of my usual percentage—*this* time."

Somewhat mollified, he folded his arms. "Agreed! So, you can send the ransom demand to this Dark Elf without further compromise to our arrangement?"

"*That* is not a matter for your concern. Leave it to me."

"And what am I to do with him in the meantime? He has to be kept fed and healthy if we are to see any ransom. He is not a tourist passenger and this is not a pleasure cruise!"

"Why, Captain," Circe cooed sweetly, "By my count you are down two—oh, excuse me—*three* crewmen, are you not?"

Bane bristled as she languidly gestured at Salidar.

"Your new *guest* still has his head upon his shoulders, no? Were I you, I would put him to work."

The captain's brows knit for a moment; then his face broke into a broad and somewhat unnerving grin.

And so began Salidar's career as a *pirate*.

Coming Soon

The tale continues in ALAS, THE BEST LAID PLANS, Vol. III of THE STEWARD.

The conspiracy is fraying. Lady Diere's carefully hidden agenda is in jeopardy.

Padraic is far more than he appears.

Atrellan and Daegon clash, opening doors better left closed.

The cartel moves tactically against Papa George.

Millie and Stacy gone missing?

Despite all this, Ellen must deal with the Council, its inherent political intrigue, and Lady Diere, whose seething animosity and dark ambition fester unabated.

About the Author

M.D. Ironz is the pseudonym of a former government official, based in an undisclosed location in North America, and now serving as a confidential consultant on matters of intelligence, security, and investigations.

www.ingramcontent.com/pod-product-compliance
Lightning Source LLC
Chambersburg PA
CBHW030536310726
48979CB00010B/1931/J

* 9 7 8 1 7 3 3 7 5 9 4 3 4 *